Son of Ballymead

E. Elizabeth Watson

A *Prince of Lions* novel

Candlelight Treasury

ISBN 0-9986751-0-5
ISBN 978-0-9986751-0-7
Second Edition

To my children, for inspiring me to write.
To my husband, for inspiring me to branch out.
To my family, for always championing my writing.

E. Elizabeth Watson Books:

Fantasy Fiction:

Prince of Lions Series:

> *Prince of Lions – 2016*
> *Son of Ballymead – 2017*
> *Brother of Honor – coming soon*

Historical Romance:

Ladies of Scotland Series:

> *An Earl for the Archeress*
> *The Maiden's Defender*

Perthshire Series Novellas:

> *One Scottish Knight*
> *Christmas Wore Plaid*

Standalone romances:

> *Two Brides for Ewan de Buchan*

Prologue

The Great War

Sebastien looked down at his father, King Fernando I, lying twisted upon the earth. King Bain's sword protruded through his back. The air surrounding them was thick with the tang of blood, pungent excrement, and the buzzing of a million flies festering within the fresh field of corpses. Sebastien, covered in his own blood, turned and surveyed the carnage as far as the eye could see with stoicism belying his fear. He had grown up in the Lispagnioc capital of De Luc, groomed to be king. Now, he needed to act as one.

King Bain's sword extended upward like a sailing mast through his back with a Bainick banner tied upon the point – a final insult. A trickle of blood rolled down the corpse's contorted face, creating a grotesque smile. This kingdom, this pile of shite his father had left behind, was now Sebastien's to rule. Every last hungry man and woman. Every last frightened noble. Every last ailing farm, dried crop, every cow with so little fat it was as if someone had stretched leather over skeletons.

His father's empire was well and truly toppled. The thousands of slaves so instrumental in holding up the legs of the monarchy had fled. They had clambered into balingers destined for the coasts of the Kingdom of Bain, the Hadstadt Kingdom, the Land of Spices—Freedom.

He stared at King Fernando's lifeless body and the insult left behind by the Bainick king and his First Knight, Sir William the Brave. One of his father's henchmen lay beside him. Alonso, was it? The man, his throat slashed, moaned a long, unbroken moan, gurgling as he tried to speak. The slice had not reached the rich blood vessels traveling up either side of his neck. With some healing, the man might have a chance, and Sebastien flicked a finger at a soldier in waiting to fetch a litter and collect him.

As far as the eye could see, the Lispagnioc army had been wiped out. The field shimmered with dark blue and silver bodies strewn across the hills surrounding Du Luc. Their livery colors created a mirage, an illusion of the sea, as if he stood surrounded by sun-soaked ripples.

The ones who were not quite dead were moving, slow contortions as they twisted in pain, awaiting death. Their undulations created the blue ocean waves, the silver threading glinting in the blazing sun like frothy crests. In the midst of such carnage, it was serene. Peaceful.

Lord, what a mess. What an absolute disaster. And all of this was his to put back together. Sebastien hated King Bain and his first knight for it.

"Take up the crown, Your Highness," crooned his father's advisor, interrupting Sebastien's thoughts.

Sebastien turned, noticing the diminutive man with rat-like features, hair long and grey, and a dowager's hump slumping his back. Such was an ugliness that had always irritated Sebastien as a child. Of course Mateo had missed the fighting. He had probably prophesied the loss while hiding in his tower, mixing raven feathers and oxen blood, or some such divining potion he claimed allowed him to see the future.

"Your father's crown. Take it," Mateo continued, his fingers drumming together in the quirky habit of a man who spent too much time in the dankness of his lair. "You are the heir. You must succeed your father, not Christophoro. Your father groomed you for the job, not Christophoro. It must-not-be Christophoro. It *must* be you!"

As Mateo leaned closer, Sebastien's eyes never wavered from the old man's stare. He felt compelled to pick up the crown. Mateo watched him, never breaking his gaze. Sebastien slid the crown off the dead king's head, which thumped back to the earth as if only a rock.

Sebastien shook his head with disgust. His father had lost. His father had been too weak to win. His father hadn't enslaved enough people. His father had attracted the ire of the Bainick lions who descended upon De Luc on their holier-than-thou quest to be the world's shining example of valor.

Well, spit on them. Where his father had been weak, he would be strong. Where his father had misjudged, he would be cunning.

Where his father had been felled by the gleaming sword of Bain, he would make Bain fall on *his* sword.

Eventually, Lispagne would flourish again. Eventually slaves would burgeon the masses again, women would bolster his harem, and the crown would be supported once more on the stilts of the people beneath him.

But right now, his kingdom was weak. He had much to do.

He turned around and began striding back to the castle, leaving Mateo in his wake, leaving the dead and dying, leaving the surviving soldiers to sift through the carnage and return the body of the late King for burial. He placed the bloodied crown, sparkling with sapphire and silver splendor, upon his head. Right now, he needed to build an empire.

An empire would require labor. An empire would require heirs and plenty of spares. And only women could give him such. 'Twas best now if he took to the drawing board in the council chamber. Mateo might divine the future in his spider-infested hidey-hole, but even that little man couldn't divine the seeds of a plan as cunning as that taking shape in Sebastien's mind.

Your mind is weak, his inner voice lamented. *Mateo only preys on the easily controlled, and you're merely his puppet, as was your father...*

"No," he argued aloud, shaking his conscience away.

Mateo had nothing to do with this. *He*, Sebastien, King Fernando *II*, was the architect of the thoughts forming in his head, not the frail Mateo. King Bain and his black lions might think Lispagne was bested. But Bain had yet to understand the power of true determination.

Chapter 1

Seven years later, Bainick Highlands

Lady Amber's heart soared.

William of Ballymead was visiting today. True, his brother Gavin also arrived, for Gavin was to marry her older sister and they would all have a double wedding in three months. But all that mattered was that William would be here today. Nothing could make her happier.

She fingered the wooden figurine she kept in her skirt pocket. Ever since the age of twelve, when her breasts began to bud and her shape began to transform into that of a woman, William had given her a carved dove at Christmastide, and she had long since developed the habit of keeping the latest dove in her pockets as a good luck charm.

It had been two months since they had last seen each other. Their previous meeting had been in the capital of Bain, celebrating the marriage of William's widowed sister, Gwenyth, to the Prince of Bain. Amber remembered William's hand sneaking into hers as they sat side by side, listening to the ruckus of dancers, laughter, stomping, and music that filled the towering ceilings of the king's great hall. Will's fingertips had drawn circles upon her skin. She held her hand now as the memory caused tingling to surge anew.

He had leaned into her ear, their hand-holding hidden in the volume of her skirts, and jested about the fanfare, making her giggle. She giggled now. Will had become a reclusive man these past two and a half years, after suffering the enemy attack that had taken his eyesight and his left foot. But she had heard through Sarah's gossip – and her sister was excellent at gossiping – that William had told his sister *"knowing I'll marry Amber makes me smile again."* Such words filled Amber's heart with joy.

She spun around, her basket of berries swinging on her arm, so happy she could not contain herself. *Does Will have any idea what a smile he brings to my face?* Probably not, but once he arrived today, he would know. She would tell him. The youngest son of Ballymead might not be in line to inherit his familial highland fief, famous for its mead. He might not be perfect in the physical sense. But he was perfect for her.

Young, devoted, and loyal. That he had strong muscles from racking cask upon cask of mead, and warm, soft kisses, was an added boon. She had fancied him all of her youth, and blessed be, but God finally saw fit to give her to him. Soon. Very soon. They would be married. She would be his wife. He would be her husband.

"What will I wear when he arrives?" she thought aloud, halting in her tracks.

It wasn't as if it mattered, for neither of them could see her gown. She was blind too, due to a fever in her youth, which of course was why their fathers thought to pair them together. But still. *A pretty dress would make me* feel *pretty.* Much like the lavish textures of her brocade gown made her feel decadent, a gown that Sarah described as a fine compliment to her complexion.

"What am I doing out here, collecting berries?" she gasped. "He'll be here any moment!"

Sakes, but she daydreamed too much. She knew she looked like a mess. She wore an old gown, one of Sarah's cast-offs. Her hair was tied back in a bun against her head, lacking any semblance of styling. There was no point in wearing fine fabrics and doting upon her appearance when she spent her days climbing through shrubs, foraging for the berries and blossoms she used to make her soaps. Such a chore would ruin her skirts, and though her father was a vassal of the king and Lord of Dunstonwoodshire, he would grouse about the expense of replacing a fine gown ruined for such a silly reason.

She adjusted her basket and made her way out of the glen, heading back to the Dunstonwoodshire castle proper, the home of her birth. She knew it by heart, even if she could no longer see it. She knew the path, how many steps it took to reach the end of the berry patches, and had long since stopped relying on the rope fencing her brothers had strung along the path so that she could visit the glen on her own. She knew each dip, each rut, and could find the little bridge made out of rough planks that carried her over the stream, running through their fief, and out beneath the wooden brattices delineating their property.

She had yet to arrive at the side entrance when a commotion erupted in the bailey. Voices, the clinking of weapons, and sounds of excited serving staff filled the yard. Horse hooves plodded to a halt. She heard the voice of her father – and Lord Loddin of Ballymead!

"Good day to you, Loddin man!" boomed Edward of Dunstonwoodshire.

"And to you!" Lord Loddin boomed in reply.

"He's here," Amber whispered, her stomach flipping with anticipation.

The deep voices of Ballymead's men, her father, and her two brothers, Angus and Morgan, filled the background with their greetings. She could hear giggling coming toward her as Sarah and their maid descended the path.

"They're here, sister," Sarah breathed, grasping her hand, excitement giving her voice a nervous wobble.

Amber lurched as Sarah wrenched her forward. Their maid and Sarah put their heads to hers and giggled some more.

"William of Ballymead is still quite handsome, milady," Gretchen, the maid, teased. "What with his finely pressed tunic. He appears as though he pained himself to look impeccable for you."

"And I am wearing this raggedy mess," Amber muttered, pulling her hands free.

"Indeed you are. Look at you," Sarah tsked, taking her hands once again to guide her. "I know it matters not to you, considering neither of you can see. But everyone else can."

Amber frowned. Sarah must have seen it, for she stopped now.

"Here, sister. Let me help."

Amber withdrew her hands again, feeling Sarah's expert fingers push loose curls over her ears and tug stoutly at the wrinkles in her bodice. Sarah sighed. "It's the best I can do. Come along."

Her sister grabbed her hands again but Amber withdrew once more. She didn't need Sarah guiding her. Her family's remarks about her blindness had long since ceased to hurt. At least they no longer hurt like the gouge they once were. Her sister stated a fact. William was blind, as was she. The two would make a fine match because of it.

True, Will had doted upon her while she grew up. Amber was friends with his sister, and he had delighted in teasing her. Then, as she approached womanhood, he had started carving those little doves for her. Their families were long-standing friends, remote in the highlands of Bain. Will's father was a childhood friend of the king, which made the House of Loddin an attractive alliance.

And with Will's sister, Gwenyth, married into the Bainick house, the Loddin family held much clout with the capital so far away to the south.

"He might not see my gown with his eyes, Sarah, but he might feel it," Amber reminded.

Sarah inhaled. "Goodness! But you're always so quiet and polite! What a scandalous thing to say!"

Amber smiled, resisting a shake of the head. Normally she wouldn't say any number of things rolling through her mind, but that didn't mean she wasn't thinking them. "He's blind, as you so aptly pointed out. If he wants to see me at all, he must do so with his hands. There's nothing vulgar about that, considering we are to be married."

She certainly hoped he would touch her cheek, give her a gentle kiss when he was certain they were alone, and oh, now the memories assaulted her, her and Will alone, in the meadery at Ballymead after their betrothal was sealed. *How he kissed me...*

"I would come to the end of the earth to see your honor vindicated," he'd said.

Such sweet words he had murmured. Such a sweet kiss he had offered. Nay, not sweet. Sinful. Divine. A secret joining of lips that Amber had kept to herself. Amber, the quiet, well-behaved daughter who made her soaps and handed everything over to her father, adored William's attentions. It was her secret to feel so wanton for him.

"Come. They await," Sarah tittered, oblivious to Amber's tumbling thoughts. "Oh goodness, sister, will we really be married in three more months? I can hardly believe it!" Sarah exclaimed, taking her hand yet again and pulling her onward.

Amber gave up. Sarah was determined to lead her and Amber acquiesced. She knew Sarah was decked in a beautiful gown, as she always was. She knew Sarah had probably required the maids to fret over her hair all the morn. And here she was in an old cast off with dirt on her hands and her long curling hair falling loose from a utilitarian bun. And William had pained himself to look fine? Lord, already she demonstrated the kind of wife she'd make. Distracted, drifting, daydreaming... *Ah, Will's kiss—*

"Goodness, Amber, you daydream constantly. Come along!" Sarah dragged her onward again.

"She's daydreaming about William of Ballymead," teased Gretchen.

Amber ignored the teasing and disentangled herself from Sarah's grip once more.

Despite her state of dress, her pulse jumped. She was about to see, nay, *experience* Will again, for the first time since attending Gwenyth's wedding. The trepidation over her appearance gave way to excitement. Mayhap they would have a moment to sneak away and walk together. Mayhap they would get a moment when no one was watching, when it was just the two of them, like they'd had at Ballymead when they visited the meadery upon the signing of their betrothal contract. She would show him Dunstonwoodshire and her work chamber, much like he had shown her Ballymead and, again, the meadery, just the two of them, alone among the casks as he placed a sample of the famous drink on her lips.

Goodness, but that memory of the meadery was determined to remain at the center of her thoughts.

She shivered a pleasant shiver. It was a warm memory, their first kiss, the sweet mead on their lips, the muffled quietude of stacks of casks, the feel of his tall body pressed to hers, the feel of *that* part of him pressed against her stomach as he leaned over her, his lips brushing hers... Ah but just thinking on it was beautiful. Just thinking on it made her stomach flutter and her lips tingle.

"Come along!" hissed Sarah, renewing her grip on Amber.

"There they are," announced Lord Edward as his daughters came around the castle wall to the bailey, Gretchen fluttering behind them in a futile attempt to set Amber's skirts to rights. "My daughters. Sarah! Amber! Come present yourselves!"

They hurried to the front.

"My, my," said Lord Loddin, the creak of the saddle followed by a thud of boots telling Amber he had just dismounted. "What is a man to do in the face of such beauty?" A rustling of fabric indicated that the highland lord was kissing Sarah's hands first, then Amber felt him take up her hands, doing the same. "I shall be pleased indeed to know my sons awaken to such fairness each morn."

Amber blushed, then promptly placed her hand upon her burning cheek. Lord Loddin chuckled as he withdrew.

"Come, men, come inside," Edward offered. "Supper will be in a couple of hours and undoubtedly you all need refreshments."

"Aye, and of course we should discuss Prince William's concerns about Lispagne and King Fernando II. If problems should increase, there is a possibility our sons will be called into military service," Loddin added.

There was a general murmuring of less formal greetings as her brothers, Morgan and Angus, engaged with two of William's older brothers, Hershel and Gavin, and a thudding of many feet as the men dismounted. Still, Will hadn't made his presence known.

"Lady Sarah," she heard Gavin's deep voice beside her.

Her sister sighed demurely. The sound of a hand being kissed followed.

"Lord Gavin. I'm so pleased to see you again so soon," Sarah replied.

Amber could only assume they still held hands, for she could feel Gavin close beside her, could hear their murmuring, feel the nearness of his body and the scent of his riding leathers.

"Nay as pleased as I, lass," Gavin flirted, an appraising exhale escaping him. He was no doubt looking Sarah over and appreciating everything he saw, for Sarah had always been stylish. "A fetching sight, aye. Aren't I a lucky man? And what perfume is this? Smells of elderberry."

More giggling. More murmuring, as if they'd put their heads together to whisper to each other.

"'Tis the soap we make at Dunstonwoodshire," Sarah replied. "Amber's forever lost in her work chamber, lost in thought, or out in the glen collecting the ingredients for it."

Amber tensed at the careless remark. She wasn't lost, but of course Sarah had never understood Amber's need for introspection.

"Hmm, sounds just like William, always lost in thought out in the meadery. Anyway, the scent succeeds in making you lovelier still," Gavin continued, then kissed her again, most certainly not on the fingers this time.

Their fathers must have already gone inside, Amber deduced, for Gavin only sneaked kisses when their lords' backs were turned.

Amber remained all but forgotten as Gavin led her sister indoors, the bailey quieting. Her excitement ebbed away. After a few more uncertain moments, she finally turned to enter the hall alone. A horrible thought entered her mind. What if one of them had whispered to William how atrocious she looked?

It's nay as if William can see you anyway, she reasoned, trying to assuage the emptiness she felt, for Gavin had come to greet Sarah enthusiastically. *How would William have known I remained here to greet him?*

"Let me help you dismount, Will," Amber heard Hershel, their third brother, say from behind.

She paused, her heartbeat speeding up again.

"I'm fine, man," Will grumbled, leather creaking as he dismounted. "Will you guide me to her?"

"Aye," Hershel replied. "Eh, Lady Amber?"

"Aye, Lord Hershel?" she replied, the skip back in her pulse.

She heard them come closer, felt Hershel's hand take her fingers up, felt him place a perfunctory kiss upon the knuckles—Hershel never was a flowery sort, what with his pending vows to take up the cloth.

But then she felt Hershel join her hand with a broad, callused one. A hand she would know anywhere, even though it had only touched her intimately a few times. The hand that had drawn circles on hers in the Bainick capital while the revelers danced and danced in celebration of Prince William and Gwenyth's nuptials.

Will's fingers encased hers. Warmth spread over her, and she heard Hershel's footsteps recede up the stairs into the keep, the door open, and close. William brought her hand to his mouth, though unlike Hershel's formal peck, this kiss was slow, soft. His lips lingered on her skin. He inhaled deeply, and Amber felt the warmth of his exhale across her knuckles. She remembered what his lips felt like pressed to hers as he offered her her first kiss in the meadery.

"I would go to the end of the earth to see your honor vindicated..."

If what had happened to Will's sister ever happened to her—such a horrid memory for them all—he would come to rescue her or die trying. That was what he'd meant when he'd whispered those words to her in the meadery. Such a romantic thought sent Amber's heart fluttering. Will was quiet. Pensive. Most certainly not a fighter though he had a sculpted physique and had been trained like the others. He was, however, determined, and she had no doubt he would follow through on such words, even though he had been teasing her when he spoke them.

Her other palm covered her heart as the memories continued to tumble through her mind. She held her breath. Her hand was still at his mouth.

"Aye, Elderberries," came Will's deep voice. "But also honey, and a hint of lavender."

She smiled at his assessment of her soap. "Aye, my lord."

She felt his body heat enfold her, felt his arms slide around her waist. His next words were spoken close to her ear.

"You must always call me Will." His lips dropped to her cheek, offering a chaste peck. "For I'm nay really a lord since I own no land."

Except it wasn't a chaste peck, even if it was simple and sweet. There was desire simmering in that kiss. She knew Will wanted more than a peck upon her cheek, but neither of them could be certain eyes didn't spy on them. Her hands migrated to his forearms, firm from hoisting up casks of great mead and encased in a fine tunic. Her exploration traveled up to his broad shoulders, firm with lean muscle. She could feel the edges of his leather coat, the sleeves removed, could smell that he had washed with a simple soap, plain but clean, could feel the ends of his hair skimming her hands.

He indeed had dressed well to meet her, and he had been traveling overland no less. What was her excuse for looking so shabby? His fingers trailed up her back to her neck until he felt her hair wrapped in its knot. She shivered.

"I'm sorry, my lord," she muttered, "for not having more care to be presentable. I was out collecting berries from a thicket and wasn't sure when you would arrive and then all of a sudden my sister was running for me and—"

"Shh." He chuckled. "You also smell of fresh air and sunshine, two of my favorite things. Where did you get the scent you wear?"

"I, eh, I made it," she breathed, embarrassed and excited by his assessment.

"You make your own perfumes?" he asked, surprise in his voice.

Heat raged across her cheeks as she felt Will's hand slide down her arm, take her hand, and turn toward the castle to go inside. Amber took the first step, leading the way.

"Indeed," she replied. "Father has his wool trade and my brothers assist him. Sarah embroiders kerchiefs and ribbons. It all brings in a fair price, but as you know, such moneys aren't frivolously spent on luxuries like soaps and scents."

"'Tis hard work," he replied.

She shrugged, feeling the weight of his hand in hers as they arrived at the steps. No one paid her soaps much attention, even if they were a substantial portion of Dunstonwoodshire's profits.

Will's peg leg thumped onto the steps, alternating with a footfall. She listened to the cadence. Everything about him was still so new, even though she had known him her whole life. His presence, his touch. His affection. So very new.

"'Tis easy enough," she replied. "I enjoy my work."

"'Tis easy to find work pleasant when you find satisfaction in the task," he concurred. "'Tis how I feel about making mead."

They reached the doors, hearing the voices within. Will dipped his head to hers, feeling her nose with his to guide himself to her lips. He landed a secret kiss, then felt his way through the doorway, pulling her with him.

Her other hand flew to her mouth. Surely her blush revealed to anyone looking at them what had just passed. *So Will really did want to kiss me.* Her cheeks raged red. She dropped her hand from her mouth to encase their joined fingers.

He squeezed her hand, a reassuring gesture.

Lord Edward was proposing a toast as they entered, his voice booming through the din. Though she could no longer see her father's rich heraldry, she knew the great hall was resplendent in red and gold standards of a horse. At one point in history, Dunstonwoodshire had been known for its horses, legend stating that the proud fief of Dunstonwoodshire had once outfitted the king's cavalry with a thousand steeds. The king had bestowed the standard of the horse rampant upon them. To this day, Amber still felt the pride evoked by the blazon.

Salutations spilled from the men's lips as they lifted goblets and tankards. Drinks found their way into William and Amber's hands. She led her betrothed along the wall to where a bench was situated in a shadow. They sat, listening to the commotion of serving staff and family chatter. It was summer, but a fire was crackling heartily in the hearth, a stone structure so huge that Amber remembered standing within it as a child when it was cold. The smell of the fire now was pungent, yet entrancing. Or mayhap the man beside her was causing the entrancement, for her heart hadn't slowed since his arrival.

"To Gavin and Sarah's marriage! And to William and Amber!" announced Angus, Amber's second brother.

The men clanked tankards. Hearty exclamations were made. Liquid sloshed and drinks were imbibed. Amber caught threads of gossip, talk of Prince William in the capital, talk of Lispagne and the cryptic missives sent to all of the king's vassals.

She felt Will's tankard tap hers.

"I know nay what our future will hold, Amber, but I can't wait to start the journey," came a quiet declaration near her ear.

She blushed anew. Giddy. Girlishly giddy was the only way to describe her emotions.

Will is shy? Nay. Everyone, including me, is wrong on this account. Will's quietness should never be confused with sheepishness.

More likely he was direct only when he wanted to be.

She couldn't find words to respond, but squeezed his hand and took a sip of the ale, as did Will.

"The ale is good, man," Lord Loddin stated. "You've added elderberry to your recipe."

"Coming from the Master of Ballymead's meadery, I'll take your opinion as a high compliment," Edward replied, and ordered another round of toasts.

"In truth, I have my son William to thank for that, for in recent years, he has worked overmuch to run the operation," Loddin said. "You would never know the lad was blind when you taste our great mead, and that is a fact."

Amber could sense the attention shift to the man beside her. She felt him stiffen.

"Well done, William," Lord Edward stated. "I indeed haven't tasted a difference in years. It must be a challenge for you, considering."

Amber felt more tension emanating from Will even though he hadn't yet spoken.

"My thanks," he pushed out. "In sooth, I don't need eyes to do something I've done all my life."

"Even still," Lord Loddin directed at his son, ignoring his deflection. "With your lame leg and without the use of your eyes, you've worked hard to uphold Ballymead excellence. I'm indebted to you."

"Here, here," muttered the brothers, Gavin and Hershel, Morgan and Angus, and another, more subdued, toast was drunk, for no one liked to recall the reason why William was so deficient.

Will sighed. Amber sensed why he was irritated. She had felt the same way. Because of his injuries, Will was treated differently now than he had been before. Likely, he went unnoticed on most days, or he was the object of marvel when he managed to do something well, but there was nothing in between. It must be insulting. Apparently, his rigidity now indicated it was exactly that.

Chattering, jesting, and conversations resumed, and slowly William relaxed beside her.

"What is the nature of your visit, my lord—*Will?*" she asked.

"To post the banns," he replied. "And to discuss your dowry. Did you nay know?"

She dropped her head, the din loud. The two blind ones were forgotten again.

"Aye, of course. I suppose I become so focused on my craft, sir, I tend to drift. My father probably made mention of it, but I forgot. I, eh, I haven't started embroidering my wedding linens yet," she confessed, her voice shrinking. "The task, well, it doesn't come naturally to me, considering I can't see the designs. Sarah was supposed to help me but she too has been overly busy with hers for Gavin, and Gretchen says she'll help me and I suppose I..."

His callused fingers weaved into hers, hidden in the folds of her skirts. She lost her string of thought.

"Shh," he whispered, leaning down to her ear. "What would I do with such items besides lay my head upon them to sleep or use them for washing?"

His words were simple, and yet the implication was clear. He would only benefit from their utility, he would never see their beauty. *He wishes to ease my mind.* It saddened her. She had long since come to terms with her blindness, but right now, she wanted to see so badly. She wanted to make him beautiful things and be the perfect wife. She used to pray for a miracle, that God restore her eyesight. But the visiting priest had long ago insisted she cease doing so. It was God's plan to make her blind, whatever such a plan may be. For how could someone ever regain their sight after it was lost?

Chapter 2

William of Ballymead was sitting shoulder to shoulder with Amber of Dunstonwoodshire, and all he could think about was the smell of her scent and how he wished he could see her messy hair. That, and how no one at Dunstonwoodshire seemed to notice her. He cared not about dowry linens and hated that she felt so guilty about it.

"And I do nay mind what you look like, either," he added. "I know you're overly conscious right now about your lack of formal dress."

Amber's hand stiffed in his.

"I grew up with a different sort of father," he continued, "one who encouraged my sister to be every bit as active as a lad. A knotted bun and old gown worn for berry picking only shows me you're much more my type of woman. It's something I've always liked about you."

She didn't say anything, but he could feel she was nervous.

Lord Loddin and Lord Edward erupted in laughter at some jest, husky chuckles that surely shook Lord Edward's rounding belly. No one had spoken to them for some time. The others spoke of exploits that only people with the power of vision could appreciate, and William leaned back down to her ear.

"What say you that we depart and find a quieter venue?"

"Aye. And I know just the place to escape," she replied.

Even though they had known each other since Amber was born, even though Will—a lad at the time—remembered holding her as a babe, he realized, he still had much to learn about her.

What were her favorite meals?

Her favorite melodies?

Her favorite bards' tales?

Did she enjoy staying up late? Or rising early?

He remembered her light brown curls swinging in the wind as she played girlish games on the hillside with Sarah and his wee sister Gwenyth. He knew he felt something special for her, even if he didn't fully understand what it was that made him feel so. It was a feeling a man had when he was with a woman who made him happy, and the emptiness he felt when they were apart.

He felt her stand and pull his hand with hers. They walked out of the hall. With his fingers in Amber's confident grip, he remembered the countless times he had teased her as a lass. She had indeed blossomed into a lovely young woman, and he had done well to wait, even if he could no longer see her. Their fathers and brothers didn't see them go, or so it seemed, for no one questioned them. He didn't know Dunstonwoodshire like he knew Ballymead, and he followed along trustingly. It made him smile.

The corridor they entered was quiet, the stone absorbing the sound of their footfalls.

"To where are you luring me?" he teased.

An anxious giggle escaped her.

Dammit, but he had made her nervous.

"My work chamber," she admitted. "I thought to show you what I do...of course if you wouldn't be interested in such, I understand—"

"I'd like to see it," he replied.

He swallowed the bitter aftertaste of his words. He couldn't see anything, least of all her work chamber. She made her own scent, but surely such a simple task didn't require an entire work space.

"What else do you do?" *Sewing? Nay*, he thought. She had already said she struggled to embroider her dowry linens.

What other task could a blind lass do?

"I make the soaps we sell at market," she replied.

"Ah, you assist your father and sister?" he clarified. He felt her bristle as she turned a corner, leading him through a doorway. She didn't answer, but the cloying smell of herbs, spices, and beef tallow assaulted his nose. "Did I say something?" he asked.

This was one of their few precious moments alone and he didn't like the tension emanating from her.

She squeezed his hand, halting. "Don't apologize, my lord—"

"*Will*," he corrected.

"My father told me I should always address you respectfully."

"Your father doesn't know what I prefer, lass. I'll be your

husband, nay him, and expect you to listen to *me*, nay him. It pleases me to hear my name on your lips," he added. "So how do you help him with such a craft?"

She fell silent. Her hand dropped and he sensed her shift away.

"I do the task myself."

He stayed his initial surprise and sought better words, sensing such a reaction might compound his offense. "You must be skilled. Does your father require this of you?"

"Nay. I always enjoyed helping here in my youth. When I went blind, I continued my work, for it is solitary. Gradually, as our servants aged, I took over the task completely."

"Dunstonwoodshire is known far and wide for two things: Woolen goods and soap. Clearly you excel at the craft. I only assumed... I'm sorry."

"Most people assume as you do, that I only assist others, if they know I help at all, though 'tis rare my father bestows credit upon me. Please don't apologize." She shrugged. "I suppose I'm overly sensitive. My father is usually credited with the praise for our soaps since he's the one who sells them each month at market. I don't mind overmuch—"

"Aye you do," he replied, finding her nearby and touching her arm, trailing his fingers down to her hand again. "I should have known better. People assume the same of me, that because I'm blind and crippled I can't do for myself. I was surprised to hear my father credit me tonight. He still works with me from time to time, for he's stubborn and doesn't want to admit his health declines, but he ages. His limp has worsened and he grows overly tired. I love the Highlands. I wish Ballymead would eventually be mine but with four brothers in front of me, it's unlikely. Still. It's the only life I've known. I just wish everyone would stop treating me as if I'm incapable and I fear I treated you exactly like that just now."

"None of your brothers help you?"

He shrugged. Her voice, always gentle, softened further. He sensed her pity. "They've other things in life. My oldest brother, Loddin—*Lod*—is a Bainick Captain for Prince William and lives much of the time at Fort Michaelmas on the Northwestern Coast, across the strait from Île-de-Neige. Gavin aspires to be a captain in the army, too, and lends his sword to Prince William's regular army."

"And Hershel has decided to join the monastery, no?"

"Aye," Will replied. "He leaves his young namesake in the care of Lod's wife at Ballymead and will probably take vows soon. Father wishes him to remarry, but he'll nay consider it, for he remains devoted to his late wife."

"But that leaves George. Doesn't he work in the meadery?"

William shook his head, an old habit, and clarified. "He helps when Father requests it. All of us have been trained in the craft since we could walk. But he's nay interested overmuch. And now that he seeks a wife, he spends most of his time traveling to different vassals to inquire about their daughters. Right now he's in Soughgate."

"Is that far from here?"

"Aye, far south of the capital. It takes nearly three sennights to travel there." They fell silent. "Show me what you do, Amber," he changed the subject.

She hesitated.

"I'd like to know firsthand just how skilled my wife-to-be is," he added, and she shifted to a table beside them, what turned out to be a long board against a wall.

She put a cut wedge of soap into his palm.

"This is my newest," she said. "Elderberry. It smells wonderful, do you nay think? I expect it to be popular among the ladies."

He smelled it and contemplated. "Aye, like the scent upon your hands, nay?"

"You have a good nose," she replied, then giggled. "What a thing to say..."

He chuckled too. "What else do you have?"

She handed him another and he lifted it to his nose. "Ah, no mistaking. 'Tis cinnamon. In a soap?"

"Aye. 'Tis an established Dunstonwoodshire seller, in high demand. And then there's this one made with thyme."

He heard her clinking a knife, shifting a block of soap in front of her to cut a wedge off for him to smell.

"Ouch!" she exclaimed, the knife clattering to the surface.

"What happened?" William worried, grabbing at her, catching her arm and once more sliding his hand down to hers.

She was clenching her left hand.

"Nothing. Just nicked myself, 'tis all."

He pried her grip away from the injured hand, his fingers feeling over hers. Moisture coated the crux of her thumb and finger where the two made a joint. He felt a drip thud upon his boot.

"Nay just a cut, lass," he argued, grabbing the end of his tunic and wrapping it around her hand, squeezing. "Let me stanch it for a moment and then we ought find your sister to stitch it."

"'Tis unnecessary," she said. "Sarah isn't one to deal well with blood, or anything that requires dirtying her hands. I can stitch it, even if it's crude, granted it needs it. 'Tis nay my first cut or bruise. I'm sorry to be so clumsy. I think my hands shook for I'm..."

"You're nervous," he finished for her, reaching up to brush her cheek. "But you needn't be."

She said nothing. He felt blush heat her cheek. But now her palm was pressed to his bare stomach with her hand wrapped within a turban of fabric. He felt a shiver, the sensation of her hand upon such an intimate place making his own nerves jump in his gut. And then, like so many times before as he thought of her, his desire stirred. Before, he had been imagining her touch, but now, her palm was branding itself upon his navel. Her fingers were warm, tickling the trail of hair that led beneath his trousers.

William wasn't inexperienced with women, but he wasn't experienced either. His few exploits had been in his youth, long before his eye sight was stolen and his foot was lacerated and his hope for a future of his own making had vanished. The memory caused him to shiver, but Amber's innocent touch now assuaged it, softening the blow of such poisonous recollections.

"Are you all right, eh, *Will?*" she said, honoring his request to call him by name. "You shake."

Her hand still sat encased in his tunic, but he brought his other hand over it to press her palm more firmly against his flesh.

"Your touch upon my stomach is an unexpected sweetness," he murmured.

"Goodness, I didn't mean—"

She tried to yank her hand away but he held it fast.

"Your cut," he reminded, hoping no one searching for them had overheard this part of his conversation, for they would surely get the wrong idea.

But her touch felt good, like a balm upon the memories tainting his thoughts. His nightmares... *Christ, but when we marry, Amber will share my bed.* What if he continued to awaken on a scream, shaking, sweating, reliving the horror of that brutal surgery? He woke with screams of agony on his lips still, and oft was unable to fall asleep afterward. He would depart his bed and settle in the chair before his hearth after loading the grate with wood and stoking a roaring fire.

When he closed his eyes, he relived the torture. He relived begging his sister's release from her first husband who'd beat her. He remembered protesting at the gates of Dwyre, though the soldiers had never let them in. They'd never allowed a missive to reach her. And on that fateful occasion, the Ballymead contingent had been chased away. The Dwyre soldiers had thrown quicklime in his face, blinding him. And then the swords had lacerated him, cutting him, thrusting him from his horse with such pain burning his eyes, his leg, his arms and sides...

He'd never stood a chance.

He'd landed on the ground, the back of his head smacking the earth so hard he was too stunned to feel it. He remembered confusion, hands upon him, grabbing, fighting to subdue him. Thinking them Dwyre hands, he had flailed until he realized the hands belonged to his father and Ballymead's soldiers withdrawing him from the fight.

The Dwyre soldiers had singled him out, the youngest, spryest man with the most potential to do them harm. They'd known that Lord Loddin would back off if his son's life was put in peril. It had worked. His father had been devastated. Devastated for Gwenyth and devastated for Will, too. His father had pitied him. Lord Loddin had never forgiven himself, and William lived since that day with his father's guilt shrouding him in a protective mantle. Lord Loddin was too afraid to let his youngest son, William, ever truly live again.

Someone was always ensuring an ill-placed chair was moved from his path before he walked, nay, *thumped* near it, so that he didn't trip. Someone was always trying to help him cut his meat, as if he were a damned babe unable to use a knife. The draft blowing into the meadery through a hole near the roof joists was going to ruin the batch on the top rack if it didn't get patched soon. And it nagged at William every day that his father didn't let him climb a ladder to fix it.

"It's too risky, lad," his father had said when Will argued with him about it. *"You can't see, and your foot is missing. How will you manage on a ladder? I cannot bear for you to put yourself in such danger, for you could fall..."*

Lord Loddin, however, couldn't climb the ladder either, due to his age and his own worsening limp.

"Give me back my sister! You bastards! Burn in hell, you bastards!"

The memory of those words ripping from his throat as he realized his wee sister was lost to him echoed in his mind. Gwenyth was safe now. She had been widowed, *blessedly*, when her bastard of a first husband met an early demise, and was now married happily to the Prince of Bain. But the memory was always there as a tolling prelude to the agony that followed, the searing pain of his amputation, the realization that his world had gone black forever, and the reality that now, despite being his own man, he would forever be dependent on Ballymead for his survival.

It was a horrible tonic to swallow.

He had already been a man when the attack occurred. He had already earned his spurs. He had already earned his beautiful sword. He understood his father's concerns. But he hated living beneath the weight of them.

What if I wake up screaming and frighten Amber? She would have every right to fear him. What if he woke up thrashing, flailing, not only frightening his bride but harming her too? *I could never live with myself.*

"Will? Whatever is the matter?" Amber said, interrupting his reverie.

"Nothing. Your touch," he muttered hoarsely. "It pleases me. 'Tis all."

After some moments of silence, Will released the pressure on her injury, removing her palm from his stomach muscles. It felt as if a print had been left upon his skin, for just like his missing foot often felt as if it were still attached, he could still feel her hand upon him.

He lifted up her hand, feeling over it, noting that the bleeding had ceased, and kissed it. For some foolish reason, her wound had triggered such dark memories of his own. But he couldn't have such tarnished thoughts stewing in his mind and be a mindful husband at the same time.

"I had no idea you were so industrious, Amber," he said, clearing his throat. "Do you remember when I showed you the meadery at Ballymead?"

She nodded, and William could feel her begin to relax.

"Aye, 'tis such a sweet memory," she whispered.

"I meant every word of what I said to you then," he replied. "I hope to teach you how to work the meadery with me. I had thought, admittedly," he added with an air of guilt, "that you would be good at sewing the netting needed for straining the drink when I rerack it. But I had no idea you were doing all of *this* by yourself. I wonder... the elderberry added to your ale...was that your father's idea? Or perchance was it yours?"

"I added it," she replied. "It tasted good, and my father enjoyed it."

He nodded, kissing her injury again. "Now that I've learned what you do, I know you can offer so much more."

"I wish my father saw that," she breathed. "He often dismisses me when I seek him, as if a blind lass has no need of him, or he calls upon my sister to mind me as if I'm a wayward child—" She shut her mouth. "I'm so sorry to speak poorly of him. Of course I love him dearly. Goodness my tongue is loosened overmuch."

He chuckled. "Aye, and I wouldn't mind knowing such a loosened tongue again."

Heat ravaged her face beneath his fingers. "My lord—"

"*Will*, Amber. You must only call me such."

"Okay, *Will*. I'm embarrassed by such a memory betwixt us spoken aloud," she replied, though he could hear a smile on her words.

He bent his head, his finger tilting up her chin.

"*My lady*," he gushed, imitating a lowland courtier. "I simply bring up a memory I quite enjoyed and wish to relive."

She shivered, her injured hand now clenching his. His teasing ebbed. He leaned further down, his lips brushing over hers. Beauty. Pure, soft beauty. He pulled away, his blood rushing.

"Ah Amber," he sighed, his voice a deep rumble. "I can't wait to marry you."

"Why me, Will?"

Amber might be demure, he thought, but she certainly wasn't shy. He toyed with her curls falling beside her face. "I've known you your whole life. Watched you grow up. Watched you become beautiful in the way men appreciate."

"Sarah is the beautiful one," she muttered, still pressed close to him.

"Sarah is fetching, aye. But you? Nay, she's not beautiful like you are. Your hair is rarely coiffed properly," he teased, fiddling with the massive knob on the back of her head.

Her hand shot to the bun, colliding with his as she self-consciously inspected the wad of locks. "Goodness, it's certainly nay a reason to like a lady—"

"It's as soft as a dove's feathers," he muttered. He ran his fingers across her cheek, feeling her reddened skin. "And your gowns are never perfect," he added, grinning.

"You give me reasons for which a man might reject a suit," she scoffed.

"Ah, there, you see? You come across as demure and quiet, but in fact, your tongue is spirited."

"Why do you tease me so?" she begged, and he could hear the sound of her smoothing her cast-off skirts. "Even now, after all this time. You teased me mercilessly when I was young, and you tease me now—"

"Amber," he chuckled, taking her arms and wrapping them around his waist, draping his own arms upon her shoulders. "I nay tease, at least, not now. Don't you see? A woman who loves to roam the hills? Nay worry herself overmuch about her perfect appearance or embroidery? This suits me well, no matter what you've been told about men's preferences. And you're the only lass I know like that."

"Besides Gwenyth," Amber said.

William screwed his mouth sideways, snorting with disgust. "Aye, my *sister*. Make no mistake, I adore her, but I was referencing lasses other than kinswomen."

She giggled too at how ridiculous the comparison was.

"And you create with these hands," he added, signaling her grip upon him. "You can make something out of nothing. That's the kind of lass for me."

"You didn't know about my soaps until just now," she argued.

"True. I didn't. But I knew my impression of you before visiting your work chamber."

"And you think I would make a dutiful wife when I cannot even be bothered to fix my hair according to my station?"

He tsked. "Lord, woman, are you trying to turn me cold toward you—"

"Nay!" she hastened, then composed herself. "I mean, nay. I just don't understand. Is it, that I, too, am blind? You can be honest."

His jesting chilled and he tried his best not to stiffen. She wasn't trying to be hurtful, but it stung. For she was suggesting what their fathers hinted at but would never explicitly say: that their blindness made them a detriment and limited their options, and that mayhap he would be more interested in someone else if he could see.

"You insult me," he muttered. "And yourself."

He felt her tense and withdraw, but he held her fast.

"Do you think I've lied in expressing my happiness for our marriage?" he pressed.

"I would never dream of calling you a liar," she whispered, again attempting to withdraw.

"Don't shy from me. Talk to me. I can't describe how I feel toward you, for I still have much to learn about you. I've wanted to know you as more than just my sister's friend ever since you started becoming a woman. I wasn't blind then. And I could see that you were becoming lovely. Every family gathering, every Christmastide our families spent together. I could see you, even if you couldn't see me." His intensity gentled. "Do you remember at Christmastide, when you were only twelve years and your family had come to visit Ballymead, and your sister started screaming because a spider was crawling on her skirts?"

Amber tried not to smile, caught off guard by the memory. But Sarah really was a babe when it came to such things. "How on earth do you remember that when I can hardly remember it myself?"

William's chuckle returned. "You scolded Sarah under your breath and shooed the critter away, blind and all. That was when I realized, seeing your careless hair..." His hand fondled her mess of tresses once again. "You had fearlessness in you. I knew your prospects for marriage would be limited due to your eyes, and you know what I thought about it?"

"What, sir?" she whispered.

"I thought that less competition for your hand was fine by me." She stilled. "I knew you were too young back then." He squeezed her, pressing his front to her. "But it didn't stop me from pondering what you might be like as a woman. And I vowed to myself to wait and see if my suspicions would come to fruition, instead of taking interest in another and starting a family. And you turned into this beautiful woman before me now who cares not a whit about some windblown locks or a spider on her skirts."

She giggled.

"I was right to wait," he finished, chuckling with her. "You know that feeling you have when you're with someone who makes you smile so, and the empty feeling you have—"

"When they're gone?" she finished for him. "Aye."

"There's no word in our language to explain it," he added.

"But it's love," she replied.

They both stilled. He nodded.

"Aye. It's love. You're young still. Mayhap you aren't old enough to know how you feel about me but..."

"That first year you gave me a dove?" she prompted.

He remembered. He loved woodworking. He had found himself carving the dove on a lark and knew when it was finished that it was meant for her. And he had kept his gift-giving secret from his family.

"Aye, you were twelve," he replied. "And a dove every year thereafter."

She peeled away, tugging on his hand to follow. The smell of beef tallow intensified as they neared the hearth where she simmered the oil and ash together. She stopped walking, lifted his hand, and guided his fingers to the mantle. His fingers met with a wooden bird, a small trinket. Then another, and another...

She had placed each bird he had ever carved her in a row. Then she guided his hand to her skirt pocket. His pulse jumped at the intimacy of touching her thigh, except he felt something hard, round, with a point. She withdrew it from her pocket and placed the dove he had sent along with a missive this past Christmastide in his hand.

"You've saved every one of them," he said with wonder.

"Of course. They're special to me," she replied. "I might be young, as you say, but nay too young to know how I feel about you, sir—"

"*Will*," he insisted. "Say it."

"W—Will."

"Again," he whispered. His name upon her lips made something in his heart swell. It made his heart feel young again when his injuries had aged him.

"Will," she obeyed.

"Again." His lips descended upon hers once more, for he sensed no one was nearby. No footsteps sounded in the corridor, and the din from the great hall was muffled by distance, stone, and rushes.

Her lips were so soft, so sweet, and he sensed her nervousness had dissipated. Good. He wasn't a formal man, and hoped that with time she would grow to trust his easy manner. He took her hands and slid them back onto his stomach, pulling his tunic out of the way so her fingers met with his skin again.

The heat of her palms touching him made his skin tingle pleasantly. He wrapped his arms back around her, pulling her close, and rejoiced the moment he felt her hands slide around to his lower back of their own accord, resting on the rise of his buttocks.

Ah, but he wished he could feel every inch of her. He refrained with his remaining thread of restraint. Still, he ran one hand up her back, securing her waist to his with his other, feeling his manhood pulse in steady surges to remind him he was ready to mate. He needed no reminders. *Get yourself under control, man,* he scolded himself.

Except she sighed, returning his affection, brushing her tongue across his as he plundered her mouth with no shame.

"Amber," he croaked, his voice thick. "How am I supposed to wait three more bloody months?"

He walked her backward, hoping they would stumble against a wall for support. He nipped at her lips, her ears, her jaw, feeling a frenzy surge through his blood. She released his back and grabbed his cheeks, her fingers splaying into his hair over his ears, allowing him to back her up until she was braced against the window shutters.

Will slid his hands down her sides, up her sides, over her breasts, into her hair, cupping her cheeks, unable to pick a place to rest his touch. It all felt so good, especially as his injuries had made him feel like less of a man for so long. She was so warm, soft mews of excitement escaping her, and he pushed his hips against her, a soft nudge, hoping such a motion would ease his lust. Ah, but it made it so much worse.

"Three months will be misery," she concurred, catching her breath between his smothering kisses.

He nodded, occupying her lips again, remembering how sweetly he had held her against him in the Ballymead meadery. He was acting beastly now in comparison. But his desire was wound so tight, ready to spring forth and force him to abandon his good sense. He reached down to her thighs and pulled her upward, splaying her legs around his hips so he could cradle himself betwixt them.

"Amber, Amber, sweeting," her murmured, nudging against her in spite of their layers of clothing, enjoying how her legs clenched around him to keep from falling.

He kissed her wildly. He had never abandoned his reserve with a woman – until now. She clung to his neck, her fingers digging into his hair, meeting his kisses with a frenzy of her own, her gentle mews of pleasure escaping in pulses that matched his nudges against her.

"My God, William," she breathed. "What's happening?"

"Be damned, lass," he growled, pinching her lower lip in his teeth. He resumed their kissing. They weren't married yet. He needed to stop. He couldn't.

She reached out to brace the wall, knocking a ladle off a hook with a piercing clatter.

"Dammit!" she exclaimed.

Her hands slapped over her mouth.

William stilled, listening, but after a moment, no one called to them. No footsteps entered the corridor. They both burst into laughter, as if of one mind. Her hands covered her face to muffle the outburst, pushing his out of the way in the process, making him laugh harder. He rested his forehead to hers.

"I shall shun all crockery now, for it clearly conspired against us," William jested. Amber buried her face in his shoulder, unable to stop laughing. "And it would seem, *my lady*, you have an uncivil tongue."

"I'm *so* sorry, William," she said against him. "I'm horrified!"

He couldn't stop grinning. "I like it."

"Goodness," she whispered, "but we'll rouse suspicion if we don't return to the hall."

"Aye, we might," he grinned, letting go of her rear to slide his hands onto her cheeks, keeping her pinned with his groin. He placed a slow kiss to her lips. "And I nay want your father to have reason to see me castrated before we say our vows."

"Wouldn't that be a shame for our wedding night," she jested.

He embraced her, his laughter rumbling in his chest, and held her close as he stepped back so her legs could descend and stand on their own. "Ah, lass, but indeed you speak your mind. Aye, I want you, but I happen to love my bollocks, too."

She giggled, then she threw her arms around him. "Will," she said on a sigh. "Will, Will, Will."

His laughter dissipated and a warm smile captured his lips. He had smiled more since his betrothal than in the last two years combined. The last two years had been dark, and this was his reward for enduring such hell. "And don't ever call me differently, or I'll have a mind to kiss you senseless again."

"*My lord*," she taunted.

He pinched her rear. "Cheeky wench, eh?"

She squealed, attempting to twist free, though Will subdued her in his arms. He kissed her again, as promised, swallowing her playful laugh, rubbing his hands down her arms to grip her fingers. In their frenzy, it seemed, her dove had somehow transferred back to her hands. His hand encased it.

He pulled apart, leaving her lips well-softened, knowing that the tiny prickles on his cheeks and chin from his morning shave had likely reddened her skin. Mercy, but could they be any more obvious? *Lord Edward and Father would have to be blind themselves not to see that I've just dragged my betrothed down the path of debauchery.*

"Your punishment has been dispensed," he teased, then grew serious. "Don't ever change, Love."

She sank into his hold, her arms encircling his waist again, albeit, outside of his clothing. Her reaction told him that he might be the first person who'd ever told her that. She was probably used to keeping her thoughts to herself and sitting out of the way with her hands folded in her lap.

"I used to imagine that you fancied me and that was why you

teased me, but I never could believe it, for you're older and I knew a blind lass would never gain a man's interest."

He petted back her stray curls, cupping her head so her cheek was pressed to his chest. "I'm glad to know it was meant to be."

She was blushing again. He smiled. He loved it. In this moment, his heart didn't ache that he couldn't see her beauty, because he could feel it.

"You should help me make mead recipes," he said, his hand still playing with the loose curls around her face. "It's nay often I venture to produce a new flavor. But you, Amber, I wager would be excellent in that regard with your skill in pairing scents, and as you did with the elderberry in your ale."

He felt her smiling. He had pleased her by complimenting her craft and clearly, as she said, no one else had paid it attention overmuch.

"Come," he said. "Lead the way back to the hall, before someone notices we've dallied off. You're soon to be mine, but you're nay mine yet, and I'd hate to draw your father's ire."

"Certainly no, for he can be a hard man when he wishes it."

"With a daughter as lovely as you, I blame him not."

He counted the steps back to the hall, as was his habit. The noise increased. Their fathers' and brothers' laughter grew louder, goblets clanked, servants chattered, and the fire popped and crackled.

Then Lord Loddin's voice grew more serious. "Ah, but Prince William has issued a warning to all the vassals to remain vigilant."

"Aye, though I pity any man who attempts subterfuge on my lands," Lord Edward said darkly, and his sons gave a round of affirmatives oaths. "Did the prince state his reasons why?"

What discussions have I missed? Will pondered their conversation. He wouldn't trade his time alone with Amber, but the prince, Gwenyth's husband, didn't issue missives unless he had a serious reason.

"Nay," replied Lord Loddin. "A missive arrived not long ago stating if we note anything unusual, we ought alert the crown. His missive didn't sound too alarming."

"Aye, it only stated we should account for all our villagers and serfs each sennight's end," Hershel remarked.

"But you know he has his reasons," Gavin said. "Prince William doesn't do anything without calculation. Why would he issue such a warning if he wasn't concerned about the peasantry?"

"Aye, he must have some concern," Morgan agreed as Lord

Edward's pageboy made rounds, requesting to top off drinks.

The conversation turned to wool prices. Just as Will could sense that they were about to enter the great hall, he pulled Amber back into the corridor. She fell against his chest and he kissed her once more. He teased her lips until she opened for him, an earnest joining as he cradled her cheeks.

"Do nay knock anymore crockery to the floor, woman," he whispered, both of them stifling their laughter so as not to tip off their fathers that they stood just around the corner with their tongues tied together. "Or else your father might hear."

Amber batted his arm.

"Shame upon you, Will," she admonished. "He'll hear us now. Act normal or you'll give us away."

"You're stuck with me, Love, my teasing and all."

"Goodness, how will I ever endure?" she played.

He grinned at her scolding. He already loved her so much. He already knew his marriage to Amber was going to be a loving one. God, but now that he knew he had her, what would he ever do without her?

Chapter 3

Amber stood outside in the yard beside her sister, her hands folded at her waist, this time bidding the Ballymead party farewell as they rode out of Dunstonwoodshire's gates. She felt hollowness within her chest at the rumble of receding hooves. Aye, that emptiness she and Will had spoken of had no word to describe it, but it was there, threatening to make her cry.

Three days hadn't nearly been enough time together. They'd walked in the glen. They'd dined aside one another. He'd assisted her in her work chamber, learning her craft, surprising her with his deft fingers as he helped her weave withies into mesh for filtering the ash water into the cauldron.

Men normally couldn't weave a single line, let alone withies.

"I used to mend my sister's clothing," he had told her. *"I sew my own hair-strainers for filtering mead, too, though my brothers tell me I create a dreadful stitch. Mayhap we can ruin embroidery together, lass."*

Despite her heartache, she almost laughed now. A nobleman who could stitch? Incredible!

Ah, but she had giggled and chatted more when William was around than she ever had before. A strong foundation was established for a solid marriage, she could feel it. A marriage based on mutual respect and shared understanding. Love wasn't simply attraction. Love was... *this*. A foundation. Trust. Companionship. *My, but Will was right. There really is no word for the feeling.* Love was the clenching of the heart and the tears one tried desperately to withhold as their other half rode out of the bailey, to be apart again for three months until the day they walked to the altar to submit their commitment to God.

She put her hand over her mouth now to stave off those tears.

Finally, they were gone. The gates had been closed. She took a deep breath and dusted her hands together. There was no point standing around pining when she had plenty of work to do. Pining wouldn't make three months go by any faster.

The Ballymead men had accomplished what they came to do: the banns were posted on the chapel door. Sarah and Amber's dowries were settled – silver on reserve, linens, household goods, and the future profits from Sarah's embroidery and Amber's soaps would be divided in half, Dunstonwoodshire keeping part of the profit and Ballymead gaining the remainder. Her father had fought hard on that account, saying that with the departure of so much silver in one giant swoop, he would need the livelihood from his daughters' crafts to rebuild his coffers.

Her soaps might not be her own, she sighed, returning to her work chamber, tying an apron around her waist and pulling down a canister of thyme to crush in her mortar. But the meadery would be *Will and I...only us.*

Three months was so long to wait to finally marry, yet she had no choice but to endure. Instead, she bore down on the mortar with her pestle, taking out her frustration on the innocent thyme. Minutes passed by until the entire canister was ground, and she realized it was still only midday. *Lord,* she huffed. Pray she had enough herbs to keep her hands busy until her wedding day finally came.

***

The Prince of Bain was usually a serious man. It was only when he gazed at Gwenyth, his wife, that his face softened and his green eyes twinkled, sometimes with mischief, always with affection. And right now, while he and King Bain sat in the corner of the empty council chamber, a cavernous room with banners hanging in succession across the ceiling, Gwenyth's skirts caught his eye. The arched windows flooded the commons with natural light, setting Gwenyth's pale hair aglow. His stern eyes, contemplating the missive in front of him, warmed.

"May I order some new gowns made for the weddings?" Gwenyth whispered in his ear, referencing her brothers' double wedding in three months to her childhood girlfriends.

The missive they had been poring over moments ago was now folded upon the table beside a map and other documents, the words obstructed. He hated keeping secrets from her. Thankfully she understood that his duty as Prince and First Knight sometimes required it.

Prince William had three separate lives: his courtly life as his father's heir, his life as the Bainick kingdom's First Knight commanding the army, and his life as a husband. The three did not always intersect.

He felt Gwenyth's hand slide upon his velvet surcoat and rest upon his shoulders. Her nails wove through his sable hair protruding from beneath his crown of lions rampant. Her affectionate touch always distracted him, for she did the same thing when they made love. Their marriage was still young. It had been difficult for her to trust him. Her first marriage had soured her toward men and Lord knew he had made his share of mistakes courting her. But they made progress. Not a day went by that he wasn't thankful.

"Of course," William replied. "I'm certain my father would allow you to deplete the royal stores of fabric if it so pleased you." He brought her knuckles to his lips and kissed them.

King Bain chuckled, nodding. "Take what fabric you desire, my princess."

She smiled, her permission granted. God, but her smile could light up a cave.

"My thanks, Father."

"Father" was the expected informal title, instead of "king," for she was now King Bain's daughter through marriage.

"I'll be pleased to also take some samples to Mary, Sarah, and Amber. They'll be thrilled at such a treat. I'll leave you be," she said.

Mary, Gwenyth's oldest brother's wife, would adore the fabric, for she was ever addicted to needlework. And of course, Sarah would put it to good use with the embroidery she made for Dunstonwoodshire's market. Amber might not enjoy sewing overmuch do to her blindness, but what woman wouldn't appreciate the royal pleasure?

"I see you only butter us up with your beauty in order to abuse my generosity," King Bain teased, shaking his head.

She grinned, dipping into an exaggerated curtsey. "But my king, you already granted me permission to take what I desire," she teased back. "And what I desire is to give my dearest friends a treat."

Bain rolled his eyes and Prince William chuckled, knowing she only jested. The king waved a dismissive hand. It had taken some sennights for Gwenyth to blossom from the shell she had been when she first arrived at court. But in time, she had come to trust King Bain's easy manner and fondness for her.

"See you at supper?" she asked her warrior husband, still

smiling from King Bain's teasing. "I have a matter to discuss."

"If it's important, tell me now," Prince William replied.

She simply shook her head. "It can wait."

He brushed his thumb across her knuckles, as if rubbing in his kiss. If it could wait, it meant she wished their conversation to be private. "I might be late, Gwen. Father has ordered a table laid here this eve. My commanders arrive soon for an afternoon of discussions and tomorrow, we meet with dignitaries from the Hadstadt Kingdom, the Land of Spices, and hopefully the Neigian duke. I'll be tied up for days to come. I won't be joining the great hall for the meal."

She frowned her displeasure but nodded and whispered in his ear. "Then I'll tell you when your head meets the pillow tonight, my dearest."

She walked away, leaving a smile on William's lips. He did his best to return his thoughts to the missive on the table, ignoring his father's grin.

"'Twould seem you might get lucky tonight, son," the king teased. "Mayhap after two months of wedded bliss I'll finally hear you announce the coming of my first grandchild."

William ignored the jest. He got lucky nearly every night and wasn't he the grateful bastard for it? But King Bain needn't be privy to such happenings. The castle maids who attended Gwenyth gossiped enough as it was about what they overheard on the other side of the keyhole.

He slid the missive back in front of him and unfolded it, scrutinizing the handwriting. It was the same every time, identical penmanship, which meant the informant was the same. And he suspected he knew who the informant was.

After seven long years, Lispagne was becoming a problem again. William thought that he and King Bain had quashed Lispagne for good when King Fernando I was left impaled upon King Bain's sword. He had been a fledgling knight before the Great War that had freed hundreds of enslaved men, women, and children, forced to labor for King Fernando I. The maidens of Bain had sung songs about him.

"Sir William the Brave, to knighthood from knave, champion of kings and savior of slaves...but ne'er a husband will he be to you..."

Even Gwenyth had grown up singing such a song.

The battle had secured Prince William's place in the kingdom's lore and earned him the title of Bain's most eligible bachelor, until the day he finally took Gwenyth to wife.

Bainick forces had wiped out King Fernando I's standing army.

At the time, Prince William had thought such a display of military might would be enough to devastate the Lispagnioc monarchy or at least, make them think twice before abusing their people again. But the young Lispagnioc King Sebastien Fernando II, was proving resilient.

"They need new leadership," Prince William began. "New leadership in the form of a royal bastard. We know King Fernando I sired two sons. Sebastien with his queen, and a street rat whose mother was a brothel whore."

"We ought to determine what has become of the bastard son," King Bain replied. "Christophoro, is it? Our spies tell us that he was abducted by the Lispagnioc crown right off the streets when he was a child—so Sebastien could keep an eye on him."

"And no doubt control him, so that no one would obstruct Sebastien's ownership of that crown," Prince William agreed.

He could relate to growing up a bastard and scratching out a rough existence, as King Fernando II's young half-brother had. Such plights often shaped a good leader. Through adversity, one developed compassion, fortitude, resilience. By removing the Lispagnioc bastard from the streets and raising him in the palace, King Sebastien had been able to keep a watchful eye over the boy who could very well challenge him for ascension to the throne.

He contemplated King Bain. *Even my father doesn't know the complete story.* And that was how Prince William wanted to keep it for now.

There was more to Christophoro Maria de Fernando. Prince William hoped his own investigations were accurate. King Bain needn't know everything that William did, until William was certain of it himself. His sources told him the Lispagnioc royal bastard was a scrapper, was savvy, was growing up, and had disappeared a couple months ago—oddly, around the same time the first secret missive like this one had arrived. That first missive hinted at information about King Fernando II as if testing whether or not it was safe to divulge more.

But there was no further indication as to where Christophoro had holed up after fleeing the Lispagnioc court. The last Bainick spies to report to Prince William had noted Christophoro boarding a balinger in the dead of night, disguised as a Lispagnioc sailor. Unfortunately, King Bain's spies had lost track of the balinger at sea.

William narrowed his eyes, thinking. King Bain's spies might have lost him, but William's personal spy had picked up some promising clues. If he could confirm his personal suspicions about the lad, learn Christophoro's allegiances, and mayhap see to the lad's protection, Christophoro might be exactly what Bain needed to destroy the threat posed by the ever growing Lispagnioc realm under King Fernando II.

King Bain motioned to the missive on the table. "What of this purported news? King Sebastien has sired a number of heirs and spares."

"They're still young," the prince replied, rubbing his chin. "But yes. Sebastien, it appears, is rebuilding his empire after we left it devastated. On the backs of more slaves. And with many a woman on their back beneath him. It sounds as if he has built a harem over the years and acts diligently as a breeding stallion."

"The lad must be exhausted," King Bain chuckled. "Tending such vast flocks all by himself."

William cracked a smile at the jest. "What baffles me though, is to have sired so many children, he must have many women. And unless we underestimated Lispagne during the Great War, I didn't think there were many women left other than the ones in the Lispagnioc court, most of whom are his relations." William sighed contemplatively. "I didn't think enough people remained in Lispagne after the liberation to rebuild much of anything, let alone birth a royal nursery."

But again, King Sebastien was proving to be a resourceful man. Pray these bits of information from his spy would prove useful. A knock upon the council chamber door echoed across the tiles.

"Enter!" called King Bain.

The door pushed open. Sir Cavanaugh, Sir Thomas, and Sir MacTierny strode across the tiles to present themselves in their decorative surcoats as a guard secured the door closed behind them.

William slid the missive off the table and tucked it into his surcoat, gesturing to a sideboard. "Help yourselves to some refreshments, men."

The men did so, Sir Cavanaugh coming first to the table to sit beside the prince. Not only was he a strong first in command, he was also William's closest friend.

"How's your wife, man?" Prince William asked.

"Heavy with child. Cranky, *demanding*, if truth be told," Cavanaugh chuckled, raking his hand through his blond hair worn in the mullet of a champion knight. "But very well."

William chuckled too. Frances' wife, a sweet woman, was preparing to birth Cavanaugh yet another child.

"You'll pass her our regards," William replied. "And praise her for doing a fine job keeping you ill-slept and poorly shaved. It offers the rest of us good entertainment."

"Bollocks to you, *my liege*," jested Cavanaugh in return. "One of these days Lady Gwenyth will bestow 'miraculous' tidings upon you and soon you'll be the frightened water fowl chased by the ravenous jaws of a mongrel."

The men rumbled with laughter, including Prince William, except for Eoin, who merely lifted the corner of his mouth. It was, in truth, a major reaction to a jest, coming from him.

Sir Eoin scooted out a chair, flipping it around and straddling it with a heavy clop of his boot. He rested his arms across the back. In his paws, he cupped a tankard of ale. He was a quiet man, bearded with a fringe of unruly red whiskers around his jaw, observant, and valiant to a fault, even if his burly breadth made him intimidating, even if he came from the highlands of Dwyre.

"And how fares your wife, Eoin?" Prince William continued, knowing he would get a typical one or two word response.

"Well," Eoin replied gruffly with an abrupt nod. "Happy."

The man was a private sort. William could respect that. He too, rarely opened up to anyone. Lady Gwenyth was the only one who knew the real him, knew his demons. He even kept Sir Cavanaugh at an arm's length, and as much as he loved his father and king, it was a process learning to act freely with the man who had only revealed months ago that William was his illegitimate son.

"Good," Prince William nodded.

"She thrives in these times of peace," Eoin added, taking the men aback, for he rarely strung so many words together outside of tactical discussions.

All knew Eoin had taken a peasant who had escaped Lispagne to wife when King Bain slayed King Fernando I. She had fled to Dwyre with her two children who were left fatherless during the war. Eoin took her and her fledglings into his estate. Intimacy blossomed betwixt them. He sired three more children on her, finally tying the knot, then added one more child after their marriage.

But he never spoke of her time as a slave. All understood that what she had been through was too hard to put into words, too personal to share.

"Why do I get the sense from your dark looks, Your Highnesses, that the times of peace Eoin just spoke of are fragile?" Sir Edmund Thomas smirked as he brought his goblet of wine to the table and sat.

William looked at the map rolled out on the board. Everyone knew that a map meant discussions of a deployment, or a problem that needed pinpointing. He and King Bain exchanged a glance. King Bain nodded for William to speak.

"True. Bain is relatively secure," the prince remarked. "It's Lispagne that's becoming a thorn in the side."

"Again?" Cavanaugh sighed with the air of a lad asked to repeat a boring chore when a sibling was supposed to have the next turn.

"And yet it's a map of Bain that we look upon right now," Eoin noted. "Nay Lispagne."

Edmund Thomas had been too young to fight in the Great War. However, Frances and Eoin had fought there, Frances a freshly-dubbed knight, at the time and Eoin already a hardened warrior of three and twenty. Eoin bristled as if the mere mention of Lispagne was an affront.

"I've received correspondence from what I believe is a trustworthy source, indicating we have a problem brewing," William added.

"What's the concern?" Thomas asked.

"An incident was reported to me a couple months ago," King Bain began, leaning back in his chair so that his robes draped open. "The entire village of Soughgate on the southern coast was in the midst of searching for a boy of one and ten years, and his older sister, seven and ten. The two went missing whilst tending the washing at the river. Indeed the only reason we heard of it was due to one of my royal contingents traveling overland to Fort Beasley on the southern sea. They reported that the entire village was up in arms searching."

Prince William spoke now. "George of Ballymead, one of my wife's brothers who is visiting the Lord of Soughgate, headed a search of the area, though the girl and her brother were never found. The villagers swore that the pair had been busy all the day, laundering their clothing in a shallow of the River Fey. Their mother reports that they never returned as the sun set. Their washing was discovered upset upon the ground, their baskets left overturned."

"Mayhap an animal got to them?" Thomas suggested. "Wolves perchance?"

Frances leaned back and waited to hear more. Eoin hadn't moved, but his eyes were furrowed in concentration.

"No blood, no bodies to be found for miles in every direction," Prince William replied. "None of the signs of an animal attack."

"Could the sister have taken the boy elsewhere?" Frances

offered. "Mayhap the daughter decided to run away with a man and raise her brother? Mayhap the old woman is a shrew and the pair escaped?"

"The girl carried on with a local lad and the two were planning to marry. No one indicated that the widow was overbearing," Prince William said.

"Surely people run off from time to time. I don't know that it matters overmuch the choices a peasant makes," Thomas remarked, propping his ankle on his knee and his arm over the back of his chair. "Though I suppose it's significant if you hold a council just to tell us about it," he added.

"Tracks?" Eoin grunted, trying to get to the point, whatever it may be.

"Aha." William pointed a knowing finger at him. Eoin was an expert tracker and his fief had made a livelihood as trappers and pelt traders. Tracking, to him, was in his blood, a habit that offered clues to solve a puzzle. "There were tracks upon the riverside for about a half mile, at which point, at a bend in the river, the tracks entered the water and disappeared."

"The River Fey is deep and wide south of Soughgate," Cavanaugh pointed out. "The current could take a deadly twist. Why would they try to cross it?"

"How many sets of tracks were there?" Eoin asked. "Just the two?"

William looked at him, then at them all. "Four." The men sat quietly and listened. "And there were signs of a struggle early on."

"They were nabbed..." Cavanaugh remarked.

"Seems that way," the prince replied, throwing his arm over the back of his chair and drawing a swallow off his goblet. "And even though they be only peasants, I grew curious about something, so I sent out riders to several other villages, some remote, some closer to the capital, to see if this has happened elsewhere."

"Let me guess. It has," said Thomas. All three of William's commanding men furrowed their eyebrows. "There have been no reports," he thought aloud. "Is it the same persons, do you suspect? Or many actors working together?"

"Or mayhap a series of coincidences? How many kidnappings total?" Cavanaugh inquired.

William finished swallowing and looked down at his map upon the board. "One-hundred and forty-two, only people young enough to lose in a struggle yet old enough to be useful. As you know, the kingdom is vast and many of these villages were well over a sennight away with steady riding. The poorer folk have no means and no mounts to send a message to the capital. Each village considered the loss of their loved one a tragedy and considered them dead, or reports to their vassal lords went unheard."

"One would think a recent spate of over one-hundred disappearances would garner some sort of broader reaction," Thomas remarked as he took another drink. "Surely you would have heard *something.*"

"I have t'agree," Eoin muttered. "A hundred and forty-two recent kidnappings, and one would expect gossip to travel about."

King Bain leaned forward, pulling the map closer. "No one said 'recent.'"

They now looked perplexed. "William, did I mishear?" Cavanaugh asked, leaning forward. "I thought this last one just happened a few months ago."

"It did," Prince William remarked. "But these nabbings have happened slowly, over the course of about six years. Oddly, 'twas seven years past that King Fernando II ascended the throne in wake of his father's passing and his slaves liberated."

"I like blaming anything atrocious on Lispagne," Thomas quipped, "but only if the clues point in that direction. How do you draw the connection between missing Bainick peasants and a Lispagnioc monarch?" Thomas asked, also leaning forward, now giving the map a closer inspection.

"I cannot share the details yet, but I recently discovered an 'informant' if you will. I trust the source if they are who I believe them to be. A few missives have come, each after a supposed nabbing, but they came from the north country, the region of the Cambrian Forest near the Abbey of St. Mathilda's, not anywhere near Soughgate."

"St. Mathilda's," Eoin muttered cryptically, Edmund and Frances giving him a curious look.

"St. Mathilda's is indeed remote. There's nothing nearby for leagues," Cavanaugh said. "Is it a monk acting as your informant then?"

"No," William replied as Eoin's comprehension dawned. "The priest of the monastery is relaying the messages. As you know, the supplies for the religious holdings go out every fortnight. On one of these trips, as my contingent arrived there, the priest brought my captain a missive and asked it be delivered to me."

"Not King Bain?" Thomas asked.

"They specified 'The Prince' as the recipient," King Bain

remarked.

"The captain brought it to me, sealed still. Now, each fortnight when Sir Eoin goes home to visit his wife, he makes a special trek to St. Mathilda's to determine if another missive has been delivered to them and relays the correspondence, if any, to me."

Frances and Edmund looked at Eoin again, then at William.

"I do nay know the content of any messages," Eoin defended. "Only that my prince asked me to make the voyage."

William noted the offence on Sir Thomas' brow. "No disrespect, William," Edmund began. "But I would have gladly completed the task for you."

In truth, Edmund Thomas had been a loyal commanding knight for longer than Eoin had been part of Prince William's inner circle.

"Before anyone considers that I pick favorites," William cautioned, his friendly tone transforming into an authoritative one, "know that each choice I make is based on strategy. Edmund, you and Frances are southern men, from this area. Eoin is a highlander. Mayhap from Dwyre to the east, but his castle tower is northward, in the same sorts of remote territory as St. Mathilda's.

"Indeed neither of you questioned his absence, for you're used to him departing for home, and I need someone who no one would suspect of transporting secret missives. It made more sense to request his service for the task than yours. I don't consider grown men to harbor hurt feelings. Respect that now."

William sensed the king watching him interact with his men. He had a way of leading them, even those that would be considered friends, and had always been proud that his father took notice. His father had told him he would make a fine king because of it, so long as he always remained fair in circumstances such as these when others might grant favors to placate wounded prides.

"Does your informant know they correspond with *you*?" Edmund asked, his tone polite again. "After all, they requested the missive be delivered to you."

"No, though if they are half as astute as I think them to be, then they would be a fool not to suspect they have my direct ear. They did, as you say, request the missive be sent to me. However, I intend to remain vague. If they know for certain it is me responding to them, and in truth, have mal intent, they could use that to manipulate us," William replied. "Tomorrow, and for many more days, I entertain diplomats from the other kingdoms to conduct regular talks, but I also wish to know if this has been happening in their countries too.

"After that, we travel northwesterly to Fort Michaelmas on the coast to bring them a supply of helmets. We'll be stopping by St. Mathilda's along the way, and I expect Eoin to inquire for more missives, as if I'm not privy to them at all."

"What of this map then?" Frances asked, sliding it closer to himself to inspect a series of numbers written upon tiny squares of parchment and pinned across the expansive kingdom. "These numbers on the map...what do they mean?"

"They represent the number of people taken from each village, usually only one, sometimes two though never any more than that at the same time. And the date, as close as can be estimated based on a peasant's time keeping skills," King Bain said. "William put it together to study for patterns. As the reports came back, he found some. Look here."

William placed his finger upon the map and trailed down the rivers. "First, note how villages along river routes are targeted. And those that are taken overland rather than from river villages are almost always taken from remote areas with little habitation—"

"And little chance of being spied," Frances thought aloud. "So rivers supply a quick means using a boat or raft, and overland has few people to witness the raid, so that they remain unnoticed."

"And secondly," William added, "Those taken are always young women and younger lads, the women all of fresh womanhood years, and the boys typically between the ages of eight or nine and fourteen years."

"A design, you suspect?" Thomas asked.

William nodded. "Most definitely. Their age and sex matters, for it's consistent throughout. *Why* they are being nabbed is not entirely clear, and the routes used by the smugglers are also hard to determine. But they want women of prime childbearing years, and clearly want lads of prime labor years who are too young to fight back. Those are facts that continue to snag my attention."

Their conversations shifted to studies of the map and discussions of the helmets, a newly-invented piece of armor that was bound to give Bain an advantage in the short term until other countries developed the same. As the knights departed in the early evening, it was time for William and the king to prepare their welcome for the royal ambassadors arriving in the morn from the other kingdoms.

The hour was late—or early in the morn—when William finally departed for bed. In the back of his mind all day had been

Gwenyth's need to discuss something with him. He nodded to the castle guards outside Gwenyth's chambers and entered. The guard bowed his head, closing the door for him.

The hearth was cold. Summertime this far south made a fire unnecessary. Moonlight shone through the arched windows along the walls overlooking the inner courtyard. They bathed the chamber in pale blue. And upon her four-posted bed draped in canopies, Gwenyth lay still, sleeping, her linens held at her chest, exposing her back and rear. Even in the dark his sharp eye could see the contour of her hip sloping into her waist, then up to her bare arms. Her hair, braided simply for sleep over her shoulder, draped across her breasts.

He stood and admired the view, finally removing his own clothing. Normally a page would help him disrobe, but he never could get used to such pampering. He draped each garment, his surcoat, his belt, his tunic, and his trousers over the arm of a cushioned chair, leaving his boots and stockings on the floor. Then he propped his sword aside the arm and laid each dagger, each pocket-sized weapon, and each heraldic ring adorning his fingers on the seat. Once he was down to his braies, soft linen that laced between his thighs over his bulge, he climbed into bed. The creaking of the bed ropes caused Gwenyth to stir.

"You're here..." she murmured dreamily without opening her eyes as he snaked his arm beneath her head so that she rolled to him.

Her head was now propped between the wedge created by his shoulder and his heart.

"I'm sorry to be so late," he whispered, planting a kiss against her brow as she settled a hand upon his stomach. Such a touch made his lust stir. But as much as he wanted to roll on top of her and ease inside of her, he sensed her news should take precedence. His fingers grazed up and down her arm, hugging her to him. "What matters did you have to discuss?" he added, before planting another kiss to her brow.

Except her breathing had already evened out, soft breaths tickling his chest hair in steady pulses, and he realized she was deep asleep. He wouldn't rouse her. But dammit if he didn't have to rise in the early morn to prepare for the important dignitaries. He wouldn't have another chance to talk to her until tomorrow night at the soonest.

Still, one corner of his mouth quirked up in a lazy smile. He wouldn't get lucky tonight, as his father had predicted, and give the castle maids more fodder for their gossips. But he was indeed a lucky bastard, and not a moment slipped by that he wasn't humbled by the simple fact that this woman knew everything about him, and him her, and yet she loved him all the more for it.

Chapter 4

Amber lingered beneath her covers, sunken in the soft mattress, daydreaming away the morn. She had already missed the morning meal and did not care. A sennight out, and she pined for William still. She rolled over, burying her cheek against her pillows, reliving their stolen moments together. Her skin heated, remembering his body against hers, his smell, his taste, his warmth as he enveloped her.

She knew what a man did when he hoisted a woman's legs around his waist, even if she had never experienced it, for any lass that had grown up on a fief that kept livestock knew what husbandry was. That was the part of a man that seeded a woman. That was the part that maids in the scullery tittered about, made vulgar jests about. Perhaps it was scandalous, but she longed to feel William doing...ah, doing what a man would do. She couldn't shake the longing.

She held her face in the pillows to blot out the thoughts of William all together. The morn was already late. She had mountains of work to do, having wiled away the hours abed imagining her wedding night instead.

The chamber was cool and she could feel a draft blowing through the shutters onto her cheek. *Ah, but enough time wasting!* She threw back her cocoon of blankets, standing, her night shift falling around her ankles in a billow of plain linen that cinched over her breasts. She moved the eight paces it took her to reach the window and thrust the shutters open, a habit she'd had since childhood. The sounds of the fief's offices were already loud, smithies hammering, carts wheeling hay from the bales stacked against the far wall to replace the rushes in the great hall, the typical jingling of soldiers' chain mail.

Voices rose and fell. Soldiers discussed training or mentioned exploits from the night before. "...the man's a cheat at backgammon. Never wager him to a match..." a voice muttered, followed by a round of chucking as the group walked beneath her window.

The air was damp and dense. Amber could sense that it was foggy, though it mattered not to her whether there was fog or not, for she knew the path to the glen in the outer pasture by heart—it was where the hedges of plants grew that she liked to forage from. Her stomach growled. Judging from the inner yard's activity, it would soon be time for the nooning meal. She knew she had slept away the morn, but sakes, it was later than she had suspected. She would do well to wait rather than bother the kitchen staff for some morsels.

She was about to turn away to get dressed when she heard a flutter of wings and the tell-tale cooing of a mourning dove as it landed upon her window. A smile lifted the corner of her lips.

"A dove. Like my trinkets. Did you send a dove to say good morn, Will?"

She giggled and shook her head, retreating from the window. *Hopelessly smitten, I am.* Missing the morning meal had been well worth the stolen moments in bed, pondering William. Would her wedding chamber be strewn in rose petals? Would her father see fit to drape the bed in silks and velvets? How would *it* feel? The scullery maids made it sound most pleasant. Lord, she blushed, and her hands flew to her cheeks to cover the stains of redness.

As if the dove on the windowsill cared one whit about the tumult in her mind, she giggled.

Finding her cast-off gown, she rummaged through a trunk for a clean chemise and fresh stockings. She stripped off her nightshift and fished her arms and head into her chemise, letting it tumble to her feet and cinching the ribbon to tighten the neck hole. Then plopped into her chair to worm her feet through her stockings. She stood again and slid them up her legs, stretching them over the gentle curve of her hip bones. Due to her frequent excursions to collect plants, she was more slender than the average noblewoman, though after Will's visit, she knew he liked her shape.

She dropped her kirtle over her head, fastening the waist and shaking out the wrinkles. Then she donned her sleeves and secured her bodice lacing, tying the brown panels of fabric up the front. The old fabric probably made her look like a peasant, but she didn't care.

After her hair was wrapped into its utilitarian bun, she collected her cloak and exited into the corridor to the spiraling stairs that led down to the great hall. She had learned long ago never to dash. Once, she had tripped upon furniture that had been moved for cleaning. Their father had chastened Sarah for not minding her wee sister and preventing the accident, as if Amber's tripping was somehow Sarah's fault.

She crossed the hall and arrived at her work chamber where she collected a basket used for gathering calendula. The golden-orange flowers were starting to bloom and she was low on medicinal soaps used for washing burns and skin lesions. She only had one more block, which wouldn't be nearly enough for the next market in a fortnight.

"Good morn, milady," Gretchen greeted as they passed each other.

"Good morn, Gretchen."

She hurried along the corridor, maneuvering through the cooks scuttling about the kitchen to prepare the nooning meal on time. The savory smells of bread baking and meat roasting filled her nostrils and made her mouth water. She grabbed an apple from the barrel by the kitchen exit and crunched into the sweet fruit as she made her way out into the yard. Her foot sloshed in a puddle and she muttered an impolite phrase.

"My lady, you have an uncivil tongue," she scolded herself aloud, giggling. Goodness she missed Will's teasing!

"Good day, milady," a guard said as he strode past her, dragging a cart.

"Good day, Anwall," she greeted. "Am I correct to assume it is foggy this morn?"

"Aye, milady. And it grows thicker, shrouding the glen. Best be careful if you're returning that way today."

"I will, sir, though it matters not to me if I can see my footing," she jested.

"Be careful all the same, milady," he replied on a chuckle and continued on his way, his cart wheels creaking behind him.

She continued onward. Clanking of weapons reverberated through the yard, sword meeting sword, as Dunstonwoodshire's soldiers and her brothers kept their training sharpened. Morgan called out commands. Muted by his orders, she heard the far-off bleating of sheep in the eastern pastures.

She arrived at the side gate, passed beneath the archway, and exited into the outer expanse of property behind the fief. The incessant sounds of the castle yards died away as she wound her way down the path. The fog dampened her skin and weighed down her bun. She pulled her cloak around her more tightly and crossed the little bridge, knowing it was only about fifty more paces until she reached the stone walls where the calendula plants grew in haphazard clumps.

Forty-eight, forty-nine, fifty... she thought, and stepped off course into the grasses, reaching out to touch a wall, a crumbling enclosure around a fallow pasture that had once been dotted with mutton.

The livestock had been moved to different fields so nature could replenish the grasses. It was quiet. A bird warbled and called out, seeking its mate, fell silent, then warbled again. Other birds farther away chirped and chatted, and the scuttling at her feet as she settled on her knees to begin picking told her field mice scurried away.

"I hear titmice and magpies. But where's your dove?" she asked William, as silly as it was to converse with a person who wasn't there. All knew magpies to be harbingers of bad luck and doves good. "Silly," she remarked. "William's dove already bid you good morn. The day's luck is yours."

Unable to stop smiling, she bloomed her skirts over her knees and fluffed them out to set to work. A twig cracked, as if trod upon. She stilled. Deer loved to come out of the nearby copse and lip at the fresh growths. There were no predators here that would dare come so close to the castle.

No sound followed.

"Hello?" she called out.

Silence

"Don't be ridiculous," she muttered again.

But the birds, chattering just moments before, were quiet now. The hair on her arms stood up. A deer would flee at the first sign of danger, but there was no sound of deer bounding through the underbrush. She shook her head as if to shake away the jump in her pulse. Why was she worried? The outer pastures and woods were surrounded by Dunstonwoodshire fences. Her father would never permit the blind daughter to venture out alone if he suspected her safety was in peril. Dunstonwoodshire was well-insulated by mountains to the south, the infamous Northeast Pass leading to Dwyre in the east, and a few friendly fiefdoms.

She shook her head again and settled back into her task. Her fingers would be yellow and sticky from the flowers, and she would do well to remember to wash before the nooning meal which, gauging by her stomach rumbling, would be ready soon. Even out where she sat, she could hear the clanking of bells outside the kitchens to call the servants, soldiers, and household members indoors to partake of food.

She began humming a tune, crunched off another bite of apple, replacing it to her basket. She had heard a lutenist play the melody at the Bainick Capital when they celebrated Gwenyth's wedding. A bard had sung romantic words to it, though she could only remember a verse or two, but the song was satisfying to hum—

A hand slipped over Amber's mouth.

Her eyes widened.

A scream welled in her throat. Foul fabric was wadded in her mouth. A band was tied around her head to secure it. She coughed violently on her apple bite, flailed, tried to rip out the gag, but the hands now gripping her upper arms dragged her away.

She grunted, forced out a muffled scream. Her feet flailed, kicking the basket and upsetting the contents. She floundered, terror seizing her lungs. Her assailant's arms, strong with male bulk, encircled her waist and encased her chest. She tried to scream again. Hardly a sound escaped.

His arm squeezed her ribs, her breasts. Tears leaked from her eyes at the pain. Still writhing, the man tossed her belly down before the saddle. She coughed, her lungs winded, and froze, equally terrified of the fall from such height. The man joined her in the saddle, turning the horse, and kicking it into a canter. Disoriented, Amber grappled for the pommel, the man's leg, anything, bouncing as the jostling threatened to toss her.

He caught her arm and wrenched her up as she began to slip, bracing her down so hard she knew she was bruising. He smelled. He hadn't bathed in some time, and as her breathing returned to normal and her mind began to clear, she realized he had taken her into the woods surrounding their pastures. They moved deeper into the trees, toward the outer wall, the sound of leaves and trunks insulating them.

God in Heaven...he's taking me away from home!

Of course he was, she thought. No man from her home would treat her in such a way.

She screamed into the gag again and resumed thrashing, no longer caring if she fell from the saddle. She might never see her family again. She might be raped, tortured, sold into slavery.

She twisted around and clawed at him.

"Be damned!" growled the man, his voice gravelly as if pebbles resonated in his throat. And his accent... where was he from? He wasn't from the highlands.

He subdued her easily, dropping the reins to wrangle down her hands. Her torso torqued, trying to free herself, thrashing for what must have been an hour? A quarter of one? She couldn't determine the length of time, but eventually she grew too tired to continue fighting.

The man mistook her relaxation for submission and removed the gag around her mouth. Her tongue felt fat, like a piece of wool. The corners of her mouth were split from the tightness of the restraint.

"Help!" Amber shrieked, her words hoarse, her throat raw, praying that if someone were nearby, they would intervene. "Help! Please!"

"Enough from you!" her assailant barked, his grating voice shooting chills up her spine. He clasped a dirt-stained hand over her mouth, urging the horse into a gallop.

"Nay!" she screamed, fighting free of his hand. "Let me go! Oh God, let me go!"

"No one can hear you out here, woman," he grumbled, though she continued to scream. "Can't you see that we're in the countryside?"

"My father is going to kill you! He is a vassal directly to the King of Bain!" Amber cried. "He and my brothers will come for you!" she persisted, realizing as the words were pouring out, that although her father was strict and oft dismissive of her, he would be enraged if he discovered that someone had stolen her away... *If.*

The word hung in her mind. What if her father never attributed her disappearance with a kidnapping? What if her family discovered her gone or decided an animal predator really had ventured into their pastures and killed her? Would they still come searching for her?

I would come to the end of the earth to see your honor vindicated...

Will's words echoed in her frantic mind. The memory of that moment alone in the meadery swirled to life, grounding her. If Will discovered her missing, would he come for her? How could he when he was just as blind as she was? And for the first time, a horrible thought entered her mind.

She was glad he was blind, too. Despite his kind words and gentle banter, if he could see, he would have a wealth of prospects apart from her. He wouldn't be dependent upon their marriage like he was now.

He might have said kind things about wanting only her, but without the power of vision, he didn't know if he was missing out on another prospect. If he could see, he might not care as much about her industrious fingers. He wouldn't need to be saddled with a blind woman. Should she ever disentangle herself from this mess, she was glad to know he would be at Ballymead waiting for her.

She trembled, shaking, praying a miracle would deliver her home. She would take her sister's child-minding and her father's dismissal any day of the sennight over whatever fate—one she couldn't fathom—lay ahead of her.

Sakes, she needed to calm down. *Pay attention!* She needed to escape. There would still be time for flailing if things became dire and it was her only recourse, but if she didn't regain her wits, she might miss opportunities. Mayhap Will had been right. Mayhap she did have a spirited tongue, for all she wanted to do was harangue her assailant and barrage him with insults.

Nay. You need to bide your time and get away, she thought. Unless he raped or murdered her first. But it hadn't come to that yet. She would do well not to dwell on such horrid things, lest she go mad with fear.

***

Shite, but Sergio was going to be angered by this mishap.

The man stuffed the gag back in the noblewoman's mouth. *A noblewoman?* Christ, he had thought her a peasant in her old brown dress and her hair tied up in an unassuming knot, foraging through the glen. He had watched her for a sennight, noting she came out of the keep to forage alone. He had thought her most likely a kitchen maid collecting plants to use in the cooking. The fog today had been the perfect cover for him. The horse, already galloping, surged at his command, panting.

She kept struggling, managing to free a hand from his vice grip to rip away the gag he had just replaced.

"What do you want from me? I beg you tell me!" she cried. "We can ask my father! Money? He has coin!" He'll gladly—"

"Shut it, woman!" he cursed, trying hard to mask his Lispagnioc accent.

He needed to think and couldn't do so with her screeching.

She succeeded in wiggling loose again and nearly slipped from the running horse. The man caught her and wrenched her up again. *Damn, but a lord from Bain will skewer me from one end to the other and take great pleasure in it, if such a man should pursue.* He had to put distance between the fief of Dunstonwoodshire and himself.

Fast.

If he let the woman go now, she would run back home and tell all about him, what he looked like, sounded like, everything. He couldn't risk that. Yet he was under strict instructions to take only peasant maids and in these remote parts of Bain, a highland lord would surely give chase with his flail mace swinging, ready to crush his daughter's assailant.

The woman had the good sense to finally settle down. At least without her crying and thrashing, he could begin to think of his explanation for such a blunder. But if the one in charge should find out, there might be no escaping this mishap.

Yet as the days began to pass, as he traveled with this noblewoman who kept her gaze downward and her demeanor cold, he was at a loss. No explanation seemed convincing when he mulled it through his mind. He was in trouble.

***

Amber stood in Lord Loddin's solar, hand in hand with William, their fathers having just signed their signatures to parchment making the betrothal official.

"Welcome to the Ballymead family, Lady Amber," Lord Loddin stated, and a round of affirmatives resonated off the walls as Will's siblings, her father, and brothers, offered congratulations.

She was floating. She was going to marry him. *She was going to live* here. *The sons of Ballymead had been sought after, admired for their loyalty, their health, their success, and their attractiveness. And she and Sarah had been two of the lucky women to marry into the venerated family.*

After the ceremony, Will had guided her around Ballymead, passing the offices, the smithies, the soldiers striking the quintains in the practice yard, explaining to her every sound of her soon-to-be home. Then they visited to the meadery.

He excelled as a brewer, the profession for which Ballymead was famous.

"Come inside the meadery, Amber," he guided, placing his hand at her back to usher her into the insulated protection of the ancient outbuilding. "I spend much time here, blending, racking..."

"The famous Ballymead meadery?" she asked, her mouth dropping, the sweet smell filling her nostrils.

"The one and only," he replied with a smile that she could hear, even if she couldn't see. "Come this autumn, Ballymead will be your home. My father's pride and joy, as it was my grandfather's and the father before him and so on."

"It smells so sweet," Amber said, inhaling a deep, satisfying breath.

"Aye. I harvest the honey myself most summers, and we've

recipes for the best blends of berries and fruits. I know them all by heart." William said, his fingers squeezing hers.

She smiled. He clearly took pride in his craft.

"Loddin, my oldest brother, is due to inherit it all, but no doubt he'd allow me to continue managing it, for Lod doesn't care overmuch about the work himself."

William took her hand, leading her between two dense rows of racks. Holding her hand, the sound within was muted from hay insulating the racks as well as the walls and floor. Being alone, here, with him, feeling her hand within his broad, protective one, made her nervous. Excited. What if he...kissed her? She should be terrified at the idea of such liberties, but in truth, the idea thrilled her, made happy skips bounce through her belly.

"Do you wish to taste it?" he asked, his voice soft. "It's a special boon only for those who work here," he said playfully, "for most men would pay a pretty coin for such a wee taste."

"I shouldn't." she said. The thought of drinking an ounce of the precious liquid that had made Ballymead one of the richest fiefs in Bain's outland regions seemed wrong, considering she hadn't paid for it.

"With me as your husband, you'll be entitled when you wish it," he replied, his voice softening further.

The newness of such words, husband and wife, were awkward on the tongue. She blushed as he dragged his finger down her cheek then withdrew his touch. The stillness around them roared in her ears. Or mayhap it was her blood doing so. Or mayhap the butterflies within her stomach were now bumblebees. Or mayhap, it was the noise of hammering beside her as William tapped a cask that filled the cavernous outbuilding with a steady rhythm. Or mayhap—

A small cup, sanded and smelling of oak, was placed against her lips.

"This has been racked for three years, Lady. The batch is ready for its purchasers to come collect it. It was sold the year it was made, and it's our best stock."

He tipped the cup and the honeyed warmth breached her lips. It rolled over her tongue, pure and clean, and trickled down her throat. It was so smooth and sweet, she could swallow without wincing at the potency. The different fruits played upon her taste buds. She warmed just feeling it in her belly. Lord, but drinking mead at his hand, alone as they were, feeling his thigh touching her lightly as she leaned upon the rack behind her, was the most intimate sensation of her life thus far.

"What do you think?" he murmured, close enough to her she

could feel the heat of his breath upon her cheek, and she realized he sounded different. More gruff than usual.

The potion hit her stomach, making her heady.

"Warm...sweet...delicious...smooth..." she began, her voice feeling rough. Or perhaps it wasn't so, but just sounded so because she was self-conscious. "Perfect."

She felt his finger upon her cheek again, drifting downward, over her jaw, down her neck, onto a swell of her breast.... Her chest rose and fell. It was so blasted warm in the meadery. One would think in February there would be a horrible chill.

"Like you," he whispered.

She blushed so intensely she thought she might cry. Goodness, wait until she gossiped about this to Sarah! Nay. Her older sister and she might gossip about much, but this... This would be a special moment for only Will and her to share.

"May I kiss you?" he asked, still a whisper. "A proper kiss, whilst we're alone?"

She nodded, and he seemed to understand from her body's gentle wiggle that she had nodded, because the next thing she knew, he tossed back the remainder of the cup's contents, the cup tapped as he set it upon the rack behind her, and his callused hands slid over her cheeks pushing into her hair. His body came flush with hers, tall, lean, muscled planes beneath his tunic touching her stomach and chest, and the warmth of his breath breezed over her brow as he dusted his soft lips upon her forehead.

Fire.

She was on fire.

The heat of his face close to hers warmed her cheeks further.

She felt his lips lift from her forehead and press to her mouth. She held her breath and felt his tongue brush across her lips. He withdrew, licking his lips clean of the mead that had clung to hers.

"Warm... sweet... delicious... smooth..." he whispered, a finger playing with a lock of her hair, his nose brushing hers, then he kissed her again.

It was so heart-meltingly gentle, the way he held her cheeks and savored her lips. And then his tongue prodded entry to her mouth. This wasn't how she thought kissing was done, but she opened her lips as if the most natural thing to do.

Warmth flooded her, the desire to put her hands upon him too strong to resist. She reached tentatively under his arms and up onto his shoulder blades. He inhaled. Somehow she knew the sharp intake was a good sign. Somehow, on some primal level, she knew it meant he appreciated her touch. He drew apart again, his forehead resting to hers as they remained pressed together.

"Perfect."

"The mead upon my lips?" she breathed, her fingers pressing harder into him to keep herself from shaking. "Or me?"

"You, love," he replied.

The endearment made her want to cry. How long had she wondered what it would be like if William held her? Too long. But those two perfect words made the wait worth it. Yet he had waited even longer. William was eight years her senior. He must have flirted and courted others. But she knew he wasn't the trysting type. Will was a quiet and honorable man. Broken leg or no, broken eyes or no, William was the man she had always fancied.

"Will you be happy married to me?" he asked, still holding her, the silence so strong that she heard a distant mouse rustling in the hay. "Because now that I know I have your favor, I would go to the end of the earth for you if it meant making you happy."

She smiled and placed her cheek to his chest, feeling his arms encircle her and his palm cup her crown to hold her close. His heartbeat was new, and it made her whole body tremble. She squeezed him. "And I would go to the moon and back if it would please you," she replied.

He chuckled, dusting her head with a kiss. "The moon, eh? What of the stars?"

A gentle laugh escaped her. "If it pleased you, it would please me to go to the stars as well. And you?"

He chuckled more. "Do you flirt with me, Lady Amber?" His arms tightened on her as she began to withdraw, embarrassed. "Nay, don't pull away. I haven't yet outdone your declaration." Another kiss landed upon her forehead. "I would brave the depths of the ocean if it meant making you smile."

"Hmm, the ocean...but not as grand as the stars," she teased, giggling still.

Laughter reverberate in his chest against her ear. He rested his chin upon the top of her head.

"Ah, you like to tease. Well you already took the stars and moon," he jested. "I would seem unoriginal if I simply followed in your steps." She laughed harder, holding him harder, feeling his grip tighten further in return. "I suppose, lass, I could attempt heaven though, and bring a piece back for you to show my devotion."

"Heaven is indeed more impressive," she grinned. "But would you *fight for my honor?"*

"I would lay down my life." His answer was immediate. Resolute. "I'm nay a fighter at heart, lass. A simple life in the country with you is a life that would please me. But if you were ever in peril, I would protect you to the bitter end, eyes or nay. I would offer up the rest of my leg, my whole body, if needs be to see you protected," he added, and she could feel him lean to gesture at his amputated foot. "I would travel to the end of the earth to see your honor vindicated."

He pressed his lips to hers again, and knowing what to expect this time, she responded more gracefully. His lower body pressed to her and she sensed he would make a passionate lover from the evidence he exhibited in his trousers. The idea thrilled her. Scandalized her. Made her stomach jump leaps.

"I've wanted you for a long time," he continued as he pulled apart, their lips warm and wet. She sensed a smile in his voice. "And now I've debauched you," he teased. "No going back now, for you're stuck with me..."

Stuck with him.

She jolted awake. The ground, upon which she had slept for several nights, was hard. She was cold. Her skirts were damp and skin clammy with morning dew. What she wouldn't give to be pressed between Will and the protective racks of mead again.

Nay. She was leagues and leagues, no, *days* from home at the mercy of her assailant, sleeping on the cold, hard ground. And William hadn't even a clue that she had been nabbed. Considering the days that had passed, mayhap still no one knew.

Her captor jostled her, as he did each morn. She kept her face downward, silently rejecting his control upon her.

"Get up."

He took her arm. She tried to twist free, tears for the sweet memory of her dream streaking down her cheeks. The man, unsympathetic, forced her onto the saddle again. At least, now that she had calmed down, he allowed her to sit upright.

They traveled hard for hours. Her assailant finally slowed his mount and walked the panting beast, stopped to let it drink in a stream, then pushed onward again. Amber's stomach ached with forgotten hunger. She had only taken two bites of apple before being dragged away and after that, her captor had graced her with a few crusts of stale, hard bread each day and no broth in which to dunk it.

As the day turned to night again, her abductor was forced to stop so his horse could rest, lest he risk injuring the animal. She listened. There was a river nearby. A lone hawk screeched high in the sky, floating over the land like a king looking down on his dominion. The wind blew in gusts.

If only I could fly like the bird and soar away...

Despair set in. *How can I ever be free of him?* What could she do to deter him? Never before had she felt so helpless, for at Dunstonwoodshire, despite her sister's childminding, she could take care of herself.

The man dismounted and took her about the waist, pulling her down.

"Go and sit over there," he demanded.

She had no idea to where he was directing. Normally he marched her to where he wanted her to sit. In their days of forced company, this was the first time he had directed her to move alone. She took a step, then another, patting the ground with her feet.

"What are you doing?" he barked. "I told you 'over there'."

"I'm blind," she retorted. "I can't see where you wish me to go."

"Blind?" the man scoffed.

"Aye, 'tis what I said," she snapped, her lips pursing as she felt her temper brewing.

A pause ensued. The man released a slow, resigning exhale.

"Shite..." he muttered. "You're blind?"

"Aye. And mayhap you're deaf," she quipped.

"Easy woman. Watch your mouth as you would watch your step," he rumbled. "How is it you go out every day alone if you're so blind? Why were you picking herbs like a kitchen maid?"

She bristled. The man had been watching her? She shivered, but schooled her expression, straightening her back and taking on her strictest tone.

"I was born and raised at Dunstonwoodshire, and I haven't always been blind, only since the age of eleven years. I've memorized my home. I go where I please in my own home and 'tis I who makes our soaps to be sold at market. I've been doing so for years, and for that, I need to harvest plants."

She felt the man step close and reach around her. She shoved him, jumping backward, but he gripped her arms and shook her.

"Cease your defiance, woman!" he barked. "I'll not keep saying it without consequences. If you continue to fight me, I'll strike you. And it won't be pleasant, for when I aim to strike, I subdue my quarry. You'll be healed and pretty again by the time we arrive at our destination."

Amber froze. Swallowed. Panic burgeoned anew in her throat. Her hands trembled. Knees trembled.

He eased his crushing grip. She was too afraid to fall to her knees in supplication for mercy, too afraid to cry. She felt him take the strings of her hair, pulling them loose so the tresses fell from the remains of her messy bun. Her curtain of unwashed curls tumbled down to her rear.

She sucked in, held her breath.

"Please don't hurt me... I'm innocent still," she beseeched, fighting back tears. "I've remained pure for my betrothed... please spare me..." But if he chose to overpower her, she knew he could.

"Shite," he cursed again, but he also stepped back from her. "You *are* a noblewoman."

She held her breath, unsure of what was happening, and could only deduce that he really had thought her a peasant. Her long hair clearly convinced him otherwise. She dared to release a sigh of relief. Why was his concern over her lineage important? Whatever the reason, the fact she was a lady was enough to cause him to retreat.

"Do not flee. I'll chase you down, woman. You have to stay with me now," he stated flatly, having come to a distasteful conclusion.

"As I said, I'm blind. I cannot see. I know not where I am. But my family must be worried," she added, a final plea. "Please see fit to return me. Drop me in the glen at home. You would be free to leave unimpeded and I could return to my family and—" She choked on the word. Sweet Will. Oh, how she needed his unfailing, steady presence and gentle manner to give her confidence now. "My betrothed."

He didn't say anything, didn't even acknowledge that she had spoken, simply moved away from her. Her chest rose and fell, faster and faster. A fury of sobs threatened to launch from her throat. Panic. She took one careful step. Then another. Then one more. Her captor snagged her arm again.

"You step much farther and you'll step to your death."

She sucked in. He would kill her? Except the breeze whistling over her face told her that...*Oh Lord in heaven*... "A cliff?"

She stood precariously close to a cliff. She knew nothing of what lay beyond Dunstonwoodshire, apart from Ballymead and a few other places she had traveled. But she remembered seeing a map in her father's solar as a child, and she remembered how vast the landmass beyond their corner of the highlands was.

She could be anywhere.

"It isn't high, but enough of a drop you would break your legs at least," he replied.

He took her arm and led her in the opposite direction, up a gentle incline, where he pushed her to sitting. The ground, littered with scraggly plants and patches of grass, scratched at her hands. She had a wall of rock to her back. Gratefully, she leaned upon it.

The man shuffled away, the creaking of leather telling Amber that he was rummaging through his packs. Moments later, he returned and dropped something onto her skirts. She touched it.

More stale bread.

Distaste roiled her stomach as she brought it to her lips. She nibbled it, fighting against the dryness in her throat to swallow. As if the man knew what she needed, she felt a skin of water touch her hand. She clasped it and gulped it down.

"We stay here tonight," the man grumbled as she consumed her last bite. He was squatting in front of her. "Put out your hands."

"Why?" she asked.

He wrenched her hands forward. "Because I said so."

He was binding her wrists together. She tried to drag her hands free.

"Stop it!" she squirmed fruitlessly. "It's been four days and just now you try to bind me?"

He fell against her, his knees splaying over her lap, and wrestled her against the rock wall. Pain swelled as her head thumped against it. She dragged her hands free again and shoved him. He fell off balance, scrambled back. His hand lashed her cheek.

Hard.

Her head whipped sideways. Her skin stung. She gave up struggling against his muscle and felt him cinch the rope around her wrists. If she resisted, there was no telling how much more she would anger him. There was no telling what atrocity he would commit. *Rape, torture, murder...* Yet with her hands now bound, he backed away. Nothing in his demeanor indicated he wanted liberties from her.

"Why? Why must you do this?" she pleaded.

"If you're blind, as you say, you'll roll off this edge in your sleep," he stated, unbothered by the exertion it had taken to subdue her. "And if you lie about your blindness, you're trying to fool me into letting down my guard so you can flee."

"Why do you need me? What can I possibly do for you?"

"It's not what you can do for me," he grumbled. "Soon, you'll be far away from here and out of my hands."

What sort of answer was that? Amber's mind was exhausted.

Begging him for explanations was futile. And her stomach still rumbled, yearning for sustenance, fraying her nerves further. *I have to get away!* But with her wrists bound at the edge of a cliff, escaping seemed impossible. She lifted her hands, smashed together, and tried to push away an errant lock clinging to her lip.

The rope connected to her wrists grew taut.

So he tethered me, too.

There would be no getting away tonight, just as there had been no escaping the past several days. She settled back against the stone, curling closer to what she discovered was a tree trunk jutting out of the rock behind her. The rope was tied to it in a tight knot. She was cold and her cloak was trapped beneath her rear, constricting her throat like a noose.

Suffocating. She couldn't breathe and grabbed at the clasp at her throat, desperate to loosen the buckle and give her windpipe some slack. It did little good.

The man had settled down. The sound of fabric whipping in the air suggested he had laid out a blanket. After some time, all remained silent, except for the occasional shifting of the horse and the whistling of wind. She began to pick at the little bunches of weeds and grass, nervous. If she fell asleep, let her guard down, to what might she awaken? The man didn't seem interested in bedding her. *Thank Father in heaven,* she sighed. But she wouldn't put it past him.

Out of habit, her fingers felt mindlessly over the tree trunk. The soil, loose and pebbly at its root where it grew from the split in the rock, was easy to sift. An idea struck her.

She felt along the hem of her bunched skirts, running her fingers over the old trim concealing the stitch, and began picking at the threading. It loosened. She picked some more, willing her fingers to work slowly and silently. She dare not wake the man who was breathing in the heavy, even rhythm of sleep.

Finally, after several minutes, a piece of the trim separated from the hem. She pulled on it, loosening the embroidery threading. The trim, with frayed endings, sat in her fingers at long last. She placed it in the cavity of pebbles between the tree trunk and rock wall, wedging it into place. She could feel that it protruded from the soil. If her father led a search party, he might see it. She prayed it was inconspicuous enough that her captor didn't.

If this horrible man was bent on dragging her away from her life, her family, and her beloved betrothed, she would leave a path for her father's search party to follow.

She stifled a sigh. How silly to think her family wouldn't deduce that she had been nabbed. Certainly, her father would come in search. He was a smart man and would find the signs of a struggle in the glen. He would reason that she had been taken against her will. He would eventually find her captor's trail and launch a search party. Mayhap he already had. And anything she could do to help, she would, no matter how slim the chances of success. She would leave a trail as best as she could in spite of her deficiency.

Alone with her thoughts, she missed William so much it ached. Her chest felt hollow and her heart hurt more than anything should be allowed to hurt. What if she never returned home again? Never married? It wasn't the first time the thoughts had tainted her mind. But right now, alone and bound to a tree, she knew she might be gone forever, and William would never know what befell her.

Chapter 5

William balanced upon the ladder in the meadery in spite of his father's protests that he might fall. He was weary of acquiescing to the old argument. Someone needed to repair the hole in the upper wall. A meadery as famed as theirs could ill-afford a draft near the upper racks. It would ruin last year's batch and everyone who awaited orders would want a return of their payment.

His father's limp was worsening. The old man thudded incongruently about the keep, dragging his lame foot, and couldn't do as much as he used to. Which meant more duties for William in the meadery. Will shook his head wryly, swung his mallet, and pounded the fastener between his fingers into place, withdrawing another one from his teeth to do the same. An old crippled man and a young blind one. What a pair they made.

He pulled more nails from the smithy apron he wore, sticking them between his teeth, and hammered another nail through the board over his head. Though the hole in the timber siding was now covered, he added more nails for good measure. The meadery timbers were ancient, dating back to well before the time of his great grandfathers who had turned the Ballymead fief into what it was today. It was a wonder the building hadn't crumbled at Will's pounding.

Thoughts of Amber crossed his mind. He smiled, a secret smile only the hole he was patching could see. It had only been a fortnight since he had departed Dunstonwoodshire, and yet, he could still feel her contours and smell her wholesome scent. Aye, thoughts of Amber were a welcome distraction to thoughts of his father grumbling at him. *"Will, Will, Will..."* Who knew she had such a playful side? Who knew she was excited for not just their wedding, but their wedding night as well?

They had been inseparable the whole of his visit. It seemed that while everyone had been watching Gavin like a hawk to ensure his propriety, Will and Amber had been fairly well ignored. Normally being ignored or dismissed chafed, but not this time. No, Will had relished their days of uninterrupted time together.

His smile turned into a grin, the corner of his mouth lifting as he removed another nail from his teeth and pounded it into place. *Aye, she makes me smile.* Amber and the curse she'd uttered at almost getting caught fooling around. Amber and her little doves. Now *that* pleased him. She had kept each carving he had made her over the years.

And she wouldn't shy away from hard work. He might find himself attracted to her body, but he appreciated the kind of person she was just as much. Amber would only contribute more to the rich tradition Ballymead's forefathers had already created. She was willing to push up her sleeves and get her hands dirty. She would need a work space for her soap-making when she moved to Ballymead.

Aye, 'tis the perfect wedding gift for her, a new work chamber, outfitted with tools and crockery, a rich starting stock of tallow and a large hearth.

He began to plan, hammering another fastener with steady thwacks. The old steward's house beside the meadery had been unused for years and had become piled with odds and ends that needed clearing out. However, the cottage was made of sturdy stone, contained a broad hearth with ready hooks for cauldrons, and he could enlist a few guardsmen to help him replace the old roof thatching with some of their surplus of rushes in the storage barn.

It's perfect, he thought, imagining the pleased smile she would give him when he presented it to her. He would show her the glens, the herb gardens, the rolling hills. He would show her all the places to forage for ingredients for her trade and no doubt, she would discover new ingredients. And mayhap, just mayhap, they could elude his watchful family who was always afraid for him, as if he were a child still needing minding, as if being blind and crippled made him less of a man. Mayhap, they would find stolen moments alone, by the pond, in the outer pastures, and he could lay his woman down among the grasses and wildflowers...

The stable doors banged. A tremor vibrated from the adjoining wall. William heard talking and the creaking of hinges as the doors now swayed on the breeze.

"Your horse, sir," the boy said, the sound muffled through the meadery doors.

"My thanks," replied Hershel.

So Hershel was departing to St. Augustine's now, much to their father's disapproval.

"I want grandchildren," Lord Loddin could be heard grumbling. "And be damned, son, but I want you to take another wife. You age to your prime and should have sired a gaggle of babes by now. Please reconsider."

"Father, allow me to depart in peace, I beg you," came Hershel's tired reply. "Nothing official has been decided. But 'tis my right to decide for myself, and it's high time you learned to respect the decision. I plan to take my initial vows and enter the monastery."

"I'll summon Sir William to say his farewells," the groom said when the sudden rush of men and clanking of arms, muffled by the stone foundation of the meadery, met Will's ears.

He adjusted his stance on the ladder and listened.

"What is this?" Lord Loddin demanded.

"Take the reins back, lad," Hershel added. "It appears to be a messenger from Dunstonwoodshire."

Will hammered in another nail, then paused again, listening. Dunstonwoodshire? Hopefully the messenger carried with him a word from Lady Amber. His heart skipped a beat. God, but he adored the lass. Smitten, aye, he was, for the prospect of a word from her made him smile once more, a welcome change from the past couple years when he wasn't sure he would ever smile again.

He plucked the remaining nails from his mouth and dropped them back into his apron, thinking on his stolen kisses with Amber, her sweet taste, her scent. He could smell elderberries, lavender, and spices just reminiscing about it. He wasn't completely naïve when it came to the fairer sex. He shouldn't be so excited. But the messenger from Dunstonwoodshire thudding to the ground in the bailey made excitement surge through him, as if he was a lad receiving a gift around the Yule log, as if he hadn't just passed three days with the lady a fortnight ago.

He jammed the hammer back in his apron and began to descend the ladder when Hershel barged through the meadery doors.

"Will, come quickly! Urgent news!" he shouted.

Will started. His peg leg faltered. His weight thrown off balance. He scrambled for footing. The ladder tipped backward,

backward... He arced through the air, falling toward the floor between the rows of racks.

"Hershel!" he bellowed, letting go of the ladder in a futile attempt to brace his fall.

He crashed to the floor.

The back of his head slammed hard against a cask, cracking through the endcap. The wood splintered. Prematurely-aged mead gushed over his face, neck, and chest, mixing with blood from the gashes to his scalp. It pooled beneath him, soaking the rushes.

"Will!" Hershel shouted, dodging through the aisles to the back to find his brother unconscious, his head stuck in the breakage of the barrel. "*Iesus*, brother!" he exclaimed, falling to his knees. "Father!" he hollered, fighting to extract the wood fragments from around William. "Father! Bring men! Quickly!"

Carefully, Hershel extracted Will's head from the cask and cradled his neck. Will's dark blond hair rested in the puddle of mead and blood, the rushes absorbing the disaster. Hershel's boots, knees, and hands sloshed through the soggy straw, feeling Will's arms, his legs, his chest rising and falling, checking him for breakages. He placed his fingers to William's throat. His heart beat steadily.

"Father!" Hershel hollered again as the old man hobbled through the doors with several guardsman.

"Hershel? William?" Lord Loddin called.

"Back here, Father!"

The old man maneuvered through the maze of racks to the back, finding his youngest son lying on the ground, blood seeping from punctures around his neck, the ladder broken and cast aside. The hole he had been meaning to cover for sennights now was patched.

"What the hell happened?" Lord Loddin thundered, dropping onto his good knee to feel William's breathing.

"He fell, sir. I came to tell him the grave news brought just now from Lord Edward's messenger... Mayhap I startled him, for he crashed down."

Lord Loddin rolled up his tunic sleeves and unbuttoned his vest, taking a dagger from his boot to slice the smithy apron from his youngest son and examine him for injuries.

Will groaned, his head lolling to the side. "Bloody hell..." he croaked, reaching up to rub his head.

The last time he had struck the back of his head this hard, he had been fighting against the men of Dwyre who had thrown quicklime in his face. "Where am I?" he asked, his voice dazed, and blinked his blind eyes open...

Light stabbed his eyes. Agonizing, blurring light. Light more intense than heaven's pearly gates shot through his mind. He slammed his eyes closed, sucked in a lungful, and rubbed them with his thumb and forefinger. He blinked again, moisture brimming his eyelids.

"God, the pain..." His head lolled and he pinched shut his eyes again, feeling them water more freely.

"Easy, son," Lord Loddin muttered.

William braced both heels of his palms against his eyes, rubbed them further, and tried to sit up as tears spilled onto his cheeks.

Lord Loddin and Hershel eased him back down.

"What has passed?" exclaimed Gavin, barging into the meadery.

"In the back!" called their father.

Gavin dashed to the huddle of guardsmen, pushing through the chain mail and green surcoats.

"Bloody hell, Will. What did you do to yourself?" Gavin exclaimed, dropping down.

"Fell," William groaned.

"You don't say," Gavin retorted, eyeing the broken ladder and the ruined cask of mead now empty except for dregs floating in the bottom.

William attempted to open his eyes again. "Damnation..." He hissed, sucking in.

More pain.

"Let's get him to his chamber, lads," their father directed.

"I'll fetch a litter," Mathew Whitcroft, a trusted Ballymead guardsman, said, dashing away.

Water continued to leak out of the corners of Will's eyes. Soon, Mathew, along with more men, pushed back through the meadery doors with the litter, knocking against the work table and jostling Will's hair-strainers and wood-working tools with a rattle. They wove it through the racks and laid it beside Will.

Will tried to sit up again. "I'm fine, really," he grumbled.

"Nay. Lie down," Lord Loddin ordered.

William scoffed but withheld his remarks. Even now, when he could feel every bone in his body in working order, his father wouldn't trust him to make his own decisions.

Hoisted onto the litter, he was carried out into the daylight.

"*Iesus*," Will gasped, but the overcast sky was brighter than sunshine. He rolled onto his side, shielding his face

"I told you it was too dangerous for you to be on the ladder,"

Loddin scolded him.

"If Hersh hadn't slammed through the door like hell was lapping at his heels, mayhap I wouldn't have fallen – Ah..." Will groaned, pain shooting through his mind and reverberating off his skull.

Tears saturate his hair and ears further. The jostling of the litter only rattled the pain. He clamped his hands over his eyes to shield them. Be damned, but what was causing such agony? It was as if he had stepped out on a sunny morn after being confined to a dim chamber, but so much worse.

They carried him up the steps to the main keep, Lord Loddin followed by Gavin and Hershel as the other guardsmen dispersed to inform the servants and spread news of the accident.

"Beatrice!" their father called as they entered the main hall.

A faithful maid, her hands working the drop spindle, sprang from a cluster of other maids in the corner, dropping her yarn and swiping the wrinkles from her skirts.

"Aye, my lord?"

"Hot water, clean linens, soaps for washing, salves for a poultice, to William's chambers now. He's suffered an accident," the Lord replied, limping as fast as he could to follow his son above stairs. "I knew something like this would happen," he grumbled to William. "You can't do the things you used to, climb ladders and such. You must have someone help you. I told you to wait to patch that hole, that I would do it—"

"When, Father?" Will snapped, eyes still pinched closed as he jolted upon the litter. "Your leg isn't getting any better either and we risked ruining a good batch of drink by ignoring that repair."

"At least I have the power of sight and two actual feet, no matter how unsure my lame one becomes," Lord Loddin admonished.

Will pursed his lips, keeping his disrespectful utterance at bay.

He opened his eyes again, protected by the dimness of the stone corridor. Blurring. More pain. In spite of the water blurring his eyes, colors began to emerge. He closed his eyes for the remainder of the journey to his chamber. Skirts swished and boots thudded as servants threw back his door, stripped back his bedding, and raced in with supplies. He felt the maids' hands unlacing his soiled tunic, trousers, and boot in quick succession. His peg was unstrapped from his stump, and soon, he rested bare.

"Enough!" Will ground out, bolting up and cupping his hands over his cock, doing his best to shield himself from any curious eyes no matter how urgent the moment. He had always retained his modesty. The only maids that had seen him naked had been the ones who minded him when he was a babe. "I can undress myself. Bring a bath—"

"You shouldn't be moving," Lord Loddin chided, pushing him back down. "If you've injured your back, you must lie still—"

"Do you nay think I'd know if my back was broken?" Will fumed. "I can feel it, Father. Nothing feels out of place except for the pounding in my head. I have a bloody awful headache and am covered in filth and blood. A bath would do me well."

"The maids will clean you," Lord Loddin replied, his tone cooling at Will's defiance. "And you'll damn well lie still for it."

Will's jaw pumped, his teeth clenched shut as his brothers lifted him to the bed, the maids having laid out clean linen sheets beneath him to absorb his grime. He held himself rigid as he felt the washrags roving over his body, tensing uncomfortably, still cupping himself in a futile attempt to hide his virtues.

"Father, 'tis unnecessary, such precautions," Hershel muttered. "Will seems unbroken. You're embarrassing him."

"He's obviously never fought in a real war, for such things as modesty matter not when you're lying gutted in a surgery," Loddin dismissed.

"We're nay at war, Father," Gavin said, lending his support. "And Will is fine. Leave the man be."

A pause in their conversation ensued. Will lay as stiff as a fence post. The maids began to clean away the mead and blood from his wounds.

"All right," Lord Loddin conceded. "Bring a bath for Will. Allow him to wash on his own."

The hands disappeared. Will shivered and bolted back up. His head swam and he braced himself until the throbbing had passed. He patted the foot of his bed and yanked a blanket up to conceal his body from the waist down.

Gavin leaned close to Will's ear and muttered, "Though I will add that Lady Amber is going to be quite a lucky woman, if you know what I mean. And every maid here has seen that. *Iesus*, wee brother, but you're hung like a bull—"

William shoved Gavin's shoulder. "Fok off," he grumbled, causing his brother to laugh.

Eyes still watering, he dared to open them again. The colors were bright, blurred, and taking on forms. Finally, eyes squinted, his vision clearing enough to determine shapes. He looked to his father, the colors around him vibrant and painful, the shapes distorted but recognizable. Everything looked warped, colors trailing from object to object as his eyes roved over his chamber faster than he could comprehend.

It took a moment too, to recognize that the colors he was seeing, were the colors he remembered, as well as the shapes of things. More than two years was enough to forget what they actually looked like. But slowly, the scowl induced by his father's chastisement moments before dissipated and Will sucked in.

"*Iesus*," he breathed, rubbing his eyes again, spots blurring his vision.

He blinked back open, pushing the moisture away. Their father was much greyer now than the last time Will had looked upon him. Much had happened in that time to age the old man. Hershel looked older too, with crows' feet at the corners of his eyes despite still being in his prime.

Gavin, having the same dusty dark blond hair and brown eyes that all the Ballymead son's shared, was thicker with neck muscle from his continued training for the Bainick army. William dropped the linen, reaching out to snag each of his brothers' tunics.

"I can see..." he whispered, his eyes focusing on their faces and blotting out the distorted shapes wavering in his periphery.

He bolted to his foot so swiftly his head spun in agony. He clung to their tunics for support. He could see. *I can bloody see!*

"Father, you...your tunic is tan...Hershel, you're wearing your Ballymead surcoat and the belt your wife made you during your courtship...Oh God above..."

A laugh work its way out of his throat. He took in his family's dumbfounded expressions.

"You can see?" his father expelled on a breath.

Hershel crossed himself in the name of the Father, his eyes wide.

"We're witnessing a miracle," Hershel whispered.

"How many fingers do I hold up, son?" Lord Loddin urged, his lower lip quivering, a wobble on his voice.

"Three. Your middle, ring and end finger!" William exclaimed. "God be damned!"

Normally Hershel would have paid him choice words for cursing with the Lord's name, but he didn't now.

"God be damned indeed!" Gavin exclaimed, shouting a whoop.

William dropped his grip. Leaning an arm on his bedpost, he turned around as if he had never set eyes on his bedchamber before, unaware of the blood still oozing down his neck. He rubbed the back of his head, feeling the skin split open over the bone.

Loddin threw his arms around his son, paying no heed to his nudity. The old man shook with puffs of husky air. Will swallowed the lump in his throat. His father cried.

"God has indeed blessed you, lad," Lord Loddin muttered thickly. "He has blessed you! And not a moment too soon!"

Before William could ask what he meant, Hershel's and Gavin's arms enveloped them both. They remained standing in such an embrace until the clearing of a throat told them the serving staff wished to reenter with the tub for bathing.

"God, but this must look suspect," Will muttered, the men all laughing but drawing apart.

Loddin clasped Will's face in his hands to stare at his reddened eyes, still honing their focus.

"Do you think it only temporary?" Will thought aloud.

"There's no way of knowing. I thought after over two years, if the effects of the quicklime never wore off, it meant the condition was permanent. But now, I have to wonder," their father replied.

"I've only read that quicklime blindness is either short and temporary or permanent," Hershel remarked, of course resorting to scholarly discourse to try to comprehend. "No physician's texts have been written to say otherwise. To gain sight back after so much time lapsing from the poisoning makes no sense."

"Unless it wasn't quicklime," Gavin shrugged. "Mayhap we thought it was, but it was something else instead."

"It's possible," William said. He continued rubbing the split skin bleeding down his back onto his buttocks and winced. "Father," he paused. "When we rode against Dwyre's guards and they attacked me—" Just hearing William reference the assault that he had rarely spoken of caused Lord Loddin, Hershel, and Gavin to still. "They threw quicklime – or *something* – in my eyes, aye, and injured my leg beyond help. But I fell off my horse and knocked my head...right here," he added, still feeling his open wound.

"What if it wasn't their poison that blinded you?" Gavin thought aloud, rubbing the stubble growing into a beard upon his chin.

"Aye..." Hershel thought. "Indeed, it's been noted that a blow to the back of the head can damage eyesight. What if falling off your horse is what blinded you, nay the poison?" He shook his finger as if having a premonition. "What if another blow to the head set your vision to rights again?"

"It could happen...couldn't it?" A grin split William's face. "I can't wait to tell Lady Amber—"

He cut himself off. He was always the quiet one, reserved, the one who stayed home to do the work the others wouldn't do. 'Giddy' wasn't a flattering color to wear for the stoic, steady son. Yet there was no stifling his excitement at 'seeing' Amber again.

"Dunstonwoodshire," Hershel stated flatly, his smile dropping. "'Tis why I came to find you in the first place. Lord Edward's messenger brings alarm. Take your bath and dress."

"He needs to rest," Lord Loddin grumbled to Hershel as if Will wasn't standing right before him.

"You look distressed. What has passed?" Will asked, ignoring his father.

"Your betrothed might be in peril," Gavin stated.

"What?"

"In the hall. A messenger arrived from Dunstonwoodshire bearing a missive," Gavin added.

Disoriented by his new eyesight, Will maneuvered across the chamber to his chests to withdraw a clean set of clothing, hopping on his good foot and bracing the furniture as he went. The colors were growing more vibrant, as were the nuances of the wood grain, the greys of the stone, the textures of the tapestries, the knots in the flooring, the Ballymead crest bearing the sun upon his wall in green and gold splendor.

Each shadow was vibrant, assaulting his vision. Every crease of fabric in the blankets seemed pronounced. Yet his perception was distorted still. He reached for the chest, slamming his hand against it. He closed his eyes to conduct the remainder of the task as if blind.

Wrenching open the lid and dragging out a new set of undergarments, trousers, another tunic, another belt, another stocking for his foot, he set to dressing. Once clothed with his peg strapped to this leg, he thumped around the bathing tub being filled with buckets of boiling water. He burst through his bedchamber door, overwhelmed at the assault of imagery on his fresh vision. God he had missed this. If he had thought a strong whack to the back of the head might cure him, he would have thrown himself off a ladder long ago.

He stopped dead in his tracks, creating congestion in the corridor, and looked down. In the wavering torchlight, he could see it. For the very first time.

There was no foot on his mutilated left leg, halfway up his calf.

He had blindly secured his peg back on with no thought. But now, the sight froze him. The lower part of his leg was simply gone. The peg his father had fashioned for him was strapped to the nub wrapped within a trouser leg. *Be damned*, he thought, but seeing the injury brought back the memory of it in full force. He had felt it, aye, but he hadn't had to look at it. The vivid nightmare that plagued him when he slept tore through his mind now, dashing the excitement he had felt moments before. His eyesight might have returned, but he would forever be lame.

Enough self-pity, he scolded himself and began jogging again, the peg stabbing the flooring with each footfall, causing pain to jar his nub. But concern for Amber overrode his good sense. He descended the steps two at a time to the great hall. Jumping off the last step, he saw the vibrant red horse upon the yellow background, denoting the Dunstonwoodshire standard, draped upon a messenger by the hearth.

"Good day. You bring news from Lord Edward?" he began, and his sister-of-marriage, Mary, now sitting with the maids in the corner, ran to his side.

The messenger bowed his head and handed the missive to William's outstretched hand, casting a quizzical look to Lord Loddin and his other sons coming off the stairs behind him.

"William, you look an honest mess," Mary began, inching toward him. She placed a hand on his arm, gaping at the sticky mead and blood drying in his hair. "And your eyes... tell me, do *my* eyes lie? Pray tell, brother of marriage, is what they say true? Has your sight returned after all this time?"

William smiled, his cheek dimpling boyishly despite the fact he had almost five and twenty years.

"'Tis a miracle, Mary," he replied, looking back at the parchment. The letter had been sent to Lord Loddin since all knew Will was blind. His eyes focused on the lettering, struggling to make sense of the script he hadn't read in over two years. His thoughts trailed away.

"What is this?" he looked up, his grin falling, letting Gavin withdraw it from his hands to read it for himself. "Amber is missing? Since when?"

"A sennight ago, sir," the messenger replied. Will took in the man's road-weary appearance, details one forgot how to recognize without working eyes. "I ran five horses near to the ground to tell you. Lord Edward has launched a search," the messenger continued. "I pray you and any able men return with me to Dunstonwoodshire."

Will took back the missive from Gavin and scanned the script again, willing his eyes to work more clearly.

"Has the king been informed?" Lord Loddin asked.

"Aye, when I was dispatched, Lord Edward sent a messenger to Bain as well, though even with hard riding our missive won't reach the gates for another sennight. Lady Amber went out to forage for plants and never returned for the nooning meal. At first, Lord Edward thought nothing of it, for she oft skips meals when she is engrossed in her work. But when she didn't arrive back for supper, Lord Edward sent Sarah and their maid to fetch her back for the eve. They returned to sound the alarm. She wasn't in the glen. We searched throughout the evening and night, though our efforts yielded no sign of her."

"She's missing?" William repeated, his family casting silent glances at him. "What is being done to recover her? Where was she last seen?"

Lord Loddin nodded, glancing at his son. "Were there any tracks to follow? Anything that would warrant the suspicion?"

"She's blind. Mayhap she simply became turned around whilst walking and got lost," William argued, his pulse jumping as he fought to maintain his composure.

"Lord Edward has no evidence that his daughter's disappearance is related to the prince's warnings," the messenger clarified, "but you can imagine the man is jumping to all sorts of conclusions. And it does seem unlikely she got lost," replied the messenger. "She knows Dunstonwoodshire through and through. She could very well be found safe and in good health by the time I return, of course."

"You know the glen is nay in sight of the main house," William remarked. "Could it be she was nabbed?" He hated the suggestion, but it was possible. "No one would have seen it." He turned to his family. "Hershel, Gavin, Father, you'll come, aye?"

All three nodded readily.

"St. Augustine's can wait. Your betrothed cannot. Let's ensure your lass' safety," Hershel stated.

"And my betrothed's sister," Gavin added.

Lord Loddin turned to Lod's wife.

"Mary, see to it four traveling packs of food are prepared. You there," he called to Mathew Whitcroft. "See to it our horses are saddled. William, go gather your packs..."

But William was already bounding up the spiral staircase to his chamber, biting back his winces with each jar to his amputation. He pushed back through the heavy door of his chamber with such force, it banged the wall. The servants filling his tub jumped. There was no time for his bath now. He would wash in a river as they traveled.

He threw open a trunk in the corner that hadn't been opened in some time, removing the rug cast over it in decoration, and pulled out the green surcoat bearing the sun crest, the standard of Ballymead in golden stitching. Beneath it was his hauberk, a pristine coat of mail he had only worn a few times. Tossing them onto his four-posted bed, he withdrew his equally clean gambeson and began the laborious task of dressing. He knew not if his eyesight was permanently regained. Best to make the most of each moment.

The mail was heavy on his frame, sagging his shoulders. He would no doubt be exhausted after a hard afternoon of riding. His muscles were toned from lifting casks, not from bearing the weight of chain mail whilst swinging a weapon. He had never cared for fighting, even if he had earned his spurs and been knighted like his brothers. War, fighting, killing...they held little appeal. Creating something simply with his hands completed him. Making mead, making woodcarvings. He loved prosperity, simplicity, Amber.

With his surcoat secured by his sword belt over his accoutrements, he moved to an upright case, opening the latch, a hook made of a single piece of wood that he had carved as a child with a sun in the center. It was shiny and smooth from constant wear. He had crafted the entire case, but it was the detailing of the Ballymead sun on the latch that gave him pride. It was his first effort at make something simply for the sake of its visual appearance. He had missed seeing such details more than he realized.

Shaking himself from the reverie, he pulled back the lid. Within sat his broadsword, a massive piece of metal with an emerald stone embedded in the hilt, an expensive gift from his father for earning his spurs. He had barely been eight and ten, and had only carried the massive weapon a handful of times. The last time had been on that fateful night of his injury, when his life had changed forever.

Checking to make sure everything was to rights, William began to stride out of his chamber, when his reflection in a copper mirror stayed him. He slowed, then picked up the frame, looking at his deep brown eyes for the first time in so long. His hair poked out of his chain mail coif and padded yoke. He regarded his features. He had changed, his face having hardened, his jawline had become chiseled, and he needed a shave.

His eyes, no doubt bright moments ago, looked lifeless now. And for the first time, he feared meeting Amber. He knew she was beautiful, sweet, her features timeless, gentle, and kind. He had felt her face, memorized each dip, each curve. But she wouldn't be able to look back at him. He would regard her, and she wouldn't be able to do the same. It caused his heart to squeeze, and he set down the polished plate and walked out the door.

Sweet Amber, the girl whose braid he used to tug... His heart was restless. Pray she was safe, unmolested, and unharmed, that all this precaution was for naught. He had never been a killer, but he could easily find the strength to slap a man's filthy mast and jewels upon the chopping block and see them amputated should he find out Amber had been violated. The idea held grisly appeal. Aye, he would do it and more. What better punishment for a whoreson rapist than to rid him of his very tools of terror.

Chapter 6

Resisting the creature who had stolen her away was a fool's errand.

Amber was bound at night, forced to eat her meager meals with her wrists bound, and lifted onto the saddle each morn for more weary riding. She had never been one to favor sleeping on the ground, and by now, her rear was numb and bruised from being wedged so in the saddle.

And she was cold.

Her cloak did little to warm her against what had to be a northern highland chill. The sun on her face yesterday told her they traveled west, though unfortunately today, it felt bleak and overcast and there was no telling the direction in which they moved.

But her kirtle trimming was mostly gone. She had left her trail as best as she could manage. *So long as a horrible storm doesn't upset the landscape, someone will track me,* she reassured herself.

But the prospect of that happening was diminishing each day.

It had been days upon days and still her father hadn't come raging after them to administer highland justice, swooping down upon her assailant for the transgression of stealing a Dunstonwoodshire daughter. The air was frigid at night and she slept poorly, shivering, before passing out in the wee hours of the morn. The man with the gravelly voice hadn't said much else to her, but she sensed he wasn't acting alone. Someone else was involved. This had to be a route he traveled frequently, based on his hasty retreat. He knew the path well, never stopping to negotiate a better path.

There was no point in struggling anymore. No opportunity to flee had presented itself. The horse finally slowed into a lope at the end of yet another day, then a trot, until the beast eventually halted.

Her limbs ached, as did her stomach from contorting herself to ride so crookedly against her captor. Wind rustled through leaves. Branches creaked. The sound around her was dense, hushed, aside from the unmistakable chatting of squirrels scolding them for disrupting their quietude as they rustled the undergrowth.

The horse emerged from a forest path and plodded into an open space with a breeze blowing errant curls from her face. A small hut or outbuilding might be nearby, she realized, as she smelled a fire and the hammering of metal evoked the sounds of a blacksmith. She bristled with renewed guard. There were no other sounds. Why on earth would her assailant bring her to a blacksmith shop in the middle of a vast wood?

***

Alonso dismounted and left the lady he'd kidnapped aloft in the saddle, sensing she would no longer give him trouble. The woman had fought like a hellion on and off for the first few days but wisely had resigned herself to his charge. Good. The voyage across the western sea would be a choppy one, and only those with strength would survive the trip, not to mention what lay in wait beyond the boat ride, the endless hiking, and the voyage to Lispagne. She would need her hellion strength.

Sergio, a man with blond hair and soft blue eyes, stepped away from the hut where he was hammering a horseshoe and lifted his hand in greeting "Ah, there you are, Alonso—"

"Shh." Alonso cut him off with a slice of his hand.

Sergio quieted. He glanced back, noticed the woman with tangled brown curls sitting in the saddle clenching the pommel, and gestured with a nod toward the hut, thrusting the horseshoe into a pan of water with a hiss. Both men retreated indoors, the hut a tiny frame of uneven planks, and left the door cracked.

"Yes?" Alonso replied. Like Sergio, he was also blond, his eyes also blue. He ran his fingers through his hair and glanced at his twin.

"How many does this make?"

Alonso tallied up the total count again. "Fifteen from these highland parts. If King Fernando's other mercenaries can capture at least the same amount from the Hadstadt Kingdom, and the Land of Spices, then it will be quite the harem, no? Only trouble is, this one is blind."

"Blind? King Fernando won't be pleased with her," Sergio countered. "He needs women of strong blood. Hers might be weak or tainted from the blindness."

"I know, but I can't release her now, can I? Blind doesn't necessarily mean daft."

"Then why did you take her?" Sergio peered back through the ajar door, perusing her shape. "Fetching though. Good breasts, fine hips, small waist. Young. King Fernando will like her otherwise. 'Twould be a fine one to plunder." He rounded back to Alonso. "But King Fernando was specific. 'They must not be flawed'."

"It's not as if I did it on purpose, Sergio. She walked quite knowingly along a path each day and gathered plants as if she could see them. There was no way to see this flaw, for everything else looked fine, exactly what the king specified."

He couldn't bring himself to admit yet that she was a noble.

Sergio shook his head, resting his hands upon his hips, and sighed. "You're right, Alonso, we can't let her go. But it's our tails that King Fernando is going to skewer if he doesn't have another need for her. How did she go blind? Was she born that way?"

Alonso shook his head. "I've no idea." He walked to a basin in the corner filled with water and scrubbed the grime from his hands. These covert hideouts in enemy territory made living as filthy as a mole's burrow and equally depressing. Thank goodness for the washbasin, even if it *was* only a hollowed-out piece of wood filled with rain water. "But between the two of us, I'm certain we can sell King Fernando on a use for her, if only to save our hides. Mayhap being blind will serve as a bonus. 'Tis harder for a woman to run away when she can't see."

"At least she's a peasant," grumbled Sergio. "And at least King Bain and that guard dog of a prince have no idea we operate here still."

"He might soon," Alonso replied, rubbing the ragged scar along his throat, hating that he felt so indebted to his king for saving his life so long ago. He would always be in service to him now because of it.

"What in the hell does that mean?" Sergio scowled, wiping his sooty hands on his tunic.

Alonso didn't meet his brother's piercing glare.

"I'm waiting."

"As it turns out, the woman's father is liege to King Bain," Alonso admitted. "And she is betrothed to the son of one of the king's favored men in the Highlands, Lord Loddin of Ballymead, or so the wench says."

Sergio took a deep breath, as if trying to convince himself he had misheard. Everyone knew of Ballymead. And both citizens of Bain as well as enemies had heard of Ballymead's men who had tirelessly searched for Princess Gwenyth. Such a story had already become Bainick lore. "Explain yourself."

"She looks like a peasant in her simple gown, doesn't she?" he defended, "And she was doing servant's work, picking flowers and foraging for plants."

"Did you overlook her hair hanging past her arse?" Sergio quipped.

"It was tied up, hardly ladylike. But, ah...she gave me a tongue lashing about how her father is Bain's man and how he is going to carve my heart out after he sends his swords after us."

Stunned, Sergio let the truth set in. He lunged at his brother and slammed him to the planks with a thunderous rattle.

"You were only supposed to take peasants! How in the hell did it take you so long to figure out she was a noblewoman? How long did you conduct your watch before deciding to move in on the mark? One bloody minute?"

"A sennight!" Alonso hissed back, landing a kick to his brother's midsection to fight him off. He rubbed his throat, watching Sergio catch his balance.

Sergio jabbed the air in front of him, pointing. "The girl's father need not send swords, because I'm going to carve your heart out myself."

The lady in the saddle jumped as he slammed his brother against the wall once more for good measure, her gaze jerking toward them at the sound. Both brothers looked out through the crack in the door. Alonso shoved his brother back with another boot to his stomach and threw a finger across his lips.

"Shut the hell up, Serge!" he whispered.

"*Mierda.*" Sergio balled his fists to punch his halfwit of a twin. "You're an idiot! They'll send more than swords after us if she's a nobleman's spawn. They could very well beg their king for soldiers! We need to clear out of Bain. Now. King Fernando needs to know what's happened. His operation here might be blown to hell because of you. If we can get her to Lispagne, the only hope we have is that King Fernando will see the merit in foking a noblewoman, or perhaps he'll be able to ransom her."

"I was thinking as much," Alonso agreed. He brushed out the wrinkles Sergio had just put in his tunic.

"Oh yes, Alonso the great thinker," Sergio retorted. "My thanks for your well-thought insight. Do you think he'll see the merit in it before or after he disembowels us?"

"He'll be displeased, yes, but she wouldn't be able to escape him," Alonso defended. "The kingdom continues to ail after all these years. Our king is still rebuilding after what the Bainick king and his bastard son did to our country. 'Tis impossible to grow a kingdom without womenfolk and laborers."

Sergio shook his head, unable to look at his brother. "Nay, he had womenfolk. But they were Lispagne peasants and whores and he needs women from other countries. Women whose babes he could align in low-level marriage suits."

"Then see? I know he thinks peasant women are safer to steal. But a noblewoman would be an even better prospect," Alonso replied, almost pleading against the murder he saw in Sergio's eyes.

"That may be true, but it's riskier," Sergio replied. "Peasants are low risk. Dispensable. And that doesn't change the fact that none of this is for us to decide! King Fernando knows what he wants and why he wants it. We're neither his advisors nor kin. We have no right to go against his dictates. We're dispensable too. Look at you," Sergio frowned, motioning to him with a petulant nod of his chin. "He saved your damned life. He knew you served his father and saw a use for you. And this is how you repay him?" Sergio peeked out the door again at the woman upon the horse, taking a breath to continue.

His face went ashen.

"Alonso, she's gone..."

Alonso's head whipped to the door. He pushed it open. The saddle was empty.

They bolted through the door, glancing around the clearing. Empty. The men fanned out, circling the camp, looking for a swish of a skirt, a flash of brown. But the sky was already darkening toward nighttime and there was no sign of a blind woman bumbling through an unfamiliar wood.

"This cannot be happening," Alonso whispered, fear sinking into his gut.

Sergio rounded back to him, a scowl so piercing, Alonso wasn't sure blood ties would keep him from feeling his twin's wrath. "You so sure she's blind?" he whispered.

Alonso looked away. His face reddened. The young lady might have played him for an enormous fool, pretending to be so injured. Still, finding her now was crucial.

"If she finds help," Sergio growled, "all she needs to do is point the finger, describe us, and that will be it for King Fernando's operation in Bain. Prince William will sic his lions on us, on our kingdom. If he figures out what we've been doing—" He shut his mouth.

Lispagne could ill-afford such a blow when it barely stood on wobbly legs after seven long years. Alonso glanced at his brother's angry brow. He might have just signed the executioner's warrant to put both their necks on the chopping block.

He motioned in one direction. Sergio nodded, motioning in another. They took opposite sides of the clearing. Moving in slow sweeps, they crept in and out of the trees. Carefully, Alonso pulled free the lacing of his gauntlets, setting them down gently in case she was listening nearby. But after an hour of searching, the forest now black with night, their search proved fruitless.

"I can't believe it...I just can't..." Offering no warning, Sergio strode across the clearing and pummeled Alonso's jaw.

Alonso fell beneath the blow. Sergio pounced, wrestling his twin into the pine needles, landing a hard jab to his gut, another, then another. Alonso curled sideways as Sergio spit on him, leaning close to his face, and clenching his tunic in a choking grip. Alonso wheezed.

"That was *my* death warrant you signed too, you foking bastard," Sergio growled. He rose, his initial burst of energy spent, and walked away with a disgusted scoff. "What kind of idiot loses a god-damned woman?"

Alonso fell into a fit of coughing, gasping for air as he gripped his middle. By the time he staggered to his feet, Sergio was nearly finished securing his saddle packs.

"You would have been deceived too, brother," Alonso retorted, moving to gather up their few traveling possessions.

"I find that unlikely," muttered Sergio. "I've had conquests put up a fight. Some were downright wily. But I've never lost my quarry."

"You lost a boy once, an urchin who sliced your saddle cinch and sent you careening toward the ground."

"He was recaptured, Alonso. And it just so happens that he was the bastard half-brother of Fernando II himself, a gutter rat named Christophoro who has more street savvy than you or I ever will," Sergio slighted.

"You never told me," Alonso replied, trying to swallow his offense.

"Such never mattered. You weren't part of this particular raid. You know Christophoro's mother was one of the late king's favored whores."

"Yes, the whoremonger kicked the lad to the gutters when he had only nine years on him, saying Christophoro was old enough to fend for himself. Which means you were bested by a *child*," Alonso scoffed with satisfaction.

"But the boy's escape never threatened to reveal Lispagne's plots. And as I said, he was recaptured. But you've been bested by a woman, a young one at that, and she has gotten away. Such a blunder is ridiculous."

"Just because she's a woman doesn't mean she's a dimwit," bit back Alonso as he marched to his horse and threw his bedroll upon the back of the saddle, strapping it down. "I'm ready. Let's get out of here."

Sergio shook his head. "The king will be pissed that you misjudged your quarry. He won't be merciful."

"We don't have to tell him," Alonso replied. "There's always a chance he'll never find out."

"Don't be daft. He has a way of knowing things. He probably has spies spying on his spies, spying on us," Sergio replied. "He'll find out, and if we try to lie about it or simply omit the truth, then there's no negotiating that our heads will be lopped off and send rolling to the sea."

Chapter 7

Amber's heart raced as she braced the wall of shite and soil surrounding her. Wrists still bound, her arms shook from the exertion. She could feel the slimy excrement and God-knew-what-else soaking through the stitching of her boots, through the fabric of her stockings, her skirt hems bathing in the viscous waste and piss-soaked feces and foodstuffs of these men and whoever else had been at this encampment. The stench threatened her stomach. Uncontrollable heaving churned her gut. She swallow desperately to remain silent.

But they were gone. Thank the Lord, she had heard their altercation and felt the ground as the horses trotted away. She stood, her body trembling, and pulled herself up onto the grass, dragging her sopping skirts behind her. And as she thought of the vileness soaking between her toes, her stomach finally evacuated.

Vomit rolled up violently.

"No, no..." she muttered, sweat soaking her brow and upper lip. What if the men, Alonso and Sergio, were still close by? What if they could hear her?

She had no idea where to go, where to hide, or where to turn. But there were no sounds of horses either. After some moments, she dried her mouth upon her sleeve. She was good and truly alone.

Thank God for the cesspit, she thought, despite her vomit and the shivers of disgust racking her body at the repellent substances coating her legs and feet. *Thank the Lord in Heaven, he has delivered me. At least, from the fate they prescribed for me.*

The men could have filled in the cesspit as most men did when they departed a campsite, thus finding her, but blessedly, their fear over losing her had prompted a hasty departure. Praise God. She had thought all hope lost, that no escape would be possible. Praise God she decided to take the only chance to present itself.

"And yet, how humiliating," she whispered, trying to conjure to mind what a stinking disaster she must look like.

Still. Despite the odor of waste clinging to her skin, the stickiness invading her toenails, she was free of them. And she was utterly lost.

She felt tears wet her eyes. "What on God's green earth am I to do?" she whispered, lifting her bound hands to swipe at her cheeks, remembering at the last moment that they were also filthy.

Revolting. The odor upon her hands made her heave again. Doubling over, more vomit rolled up. Pain tingled her chest as if her rib cage was ripping open. The uncontrolled heaving continued, until her stomach was empty of all its bile.

The retching finally waned, her stomach muscles spent from so much clenching. She had no choice but to use the back of her hand to wipe at the sweat that clung to her lips. A sob worked its way up in quickening breaths. She doubled over again, pressing her forehead into the ground, and pushed her cries out into the pine needles.

Now what? She asked herself, over and over. "Now what?"

She sat up, staving off more cries, and took a deep breath. She stilled, listened, and blinked the tears from her eyes so they slid down her cheeks.

I cannot wander in hopes of finding a path, she reasoned. Nay. She would most definitely get more lost. However, if men from Lispagne were sneaking about these remote parts of Bain without being caught, then there was little chance a passerby would happen upon her. It might be days still before her father found her, if he was even searching upon the proper trail.

The parchment.

In her disgust and fear, she had already forgotten about the roll of parchment she discovered protruding from the saddle pack as she attempted to dismount. It had been poking the back of her leg for the better part of their journey, though she hadn't known what it was. While her assailants had argued, she had withdrawn the roll and though her hands were bound, they weren't immobile. She managed to twist her skirts to wedge it into her pocket. Alonso, was it? He had no possessions other than what he carried. If such a parchment was one of his few precious items, it had to be important.

And if they had recaptured her, what was the worst they could do? She shuddered. They could do much, much worse.

She might be distressed, but she wasn't daft enough to think it couldn't get worse. They could force her to their will in a fit of rage, both of them. They could tear her apart, murder her, toss her body over a cliff, torture her, rip away her fingernails and—

"You must cease this!" she hissed. *Maddening myself over the endless ways in which my situation could deteriorate further isn't going to help my predicament now.*

Alonso she'd heard him called, her capturer, had made it clear he would take no liberty with her. He'd practically ignored her. Now that she was quiet and calming her frantic mind, she felt her pocket, the corners of the folded parchment poking her finger through the fabric and pondering what it could be. She was thirsty, desperately so. Retching just now had only made it worse. They had been in the saddle for so many numbing hours and not once had she been offered a drink.

She could hear nighttime insects buzzing and chirping around her loudly. There were no other people or animals to scare them silent. *I have to find shelter,* she finally deduced on an exhale. "Quit your ridiculous crying," she scolded herself. "'Twill help you none." There was no telling what sort of wild predators lurked in this upland forested nightmare.

If her father was indeed looking for her, it would suit her well to be exactly where the trail she had designed with her skirt fragments led. Alonso hadn't taken precautions meant to throw off trackers. He had charged right through streams and overland.

"He isn't daft, so he must have done such intentionally, thinking he would get away long before anyone comes searching," she thought aloud. "Or if he thought me a peasant, he might nay have been overly worried about search parties to begin with."

She rose to her feet, wiped her tangled tresses out of her face, and took tentative steps back in the direction she had come from. The first order of business was finding a way to cut apart the rope cinching her hands together. The rope was thin, but strong, and no amount of tugging or twisting had undermined it.

Smithy sounds.

"That's right," Amber exhaled. "The man, Sergio, was working at some sort of metal craft when we arrived."

She could still, amazingly, smell the metallic odor in spite of the stench of cesspit upon her. Sitting atop the horse, she had known the hut or shelter was to her right. There must be tools lying about, something upon which she could saw the rope.

Dear Lord, but she could no more fend for herself than could a tiny chick. "Nonsense," she stated, tamping down the panic that threatened to consume her again. "You will either manage or you will nay, and there are no other ways about it. Think."

Maneuvering back from whence she had come, or so she thought, her toes finally kicked something hard. Reaching out, she felt heat radiate onto her skin. "The blacksmith fire."

Hot coals could burn apart a rope. They could also burn right through her skin. She patted around the rim of the fire ring. Her arm bumped a tool handle. It clanked, and water sloshed in a basin. She lifted the tongs out, setting them down, and felt the wet horseshoe in its grasp, still warm to the touch. But as she patted around the ring, she felt no knives or sharp edges.

She extracted the horseshoe clumsily and used the tongs to shuffle around the coals, sensing from the popping sound that she roused a flame. Did she dare lean her hands into it and willingly burn herself? She shuddered, swallowed. Panic once again threatened to ruin her steady breathing and obstruct her throat with an immovable lump.

"I have no choice," she whispered, unable to speak louder for the tremble in her voice.

She needed full use of her hands, and the coals would eventually cool. She had to remove the bindings while she had a flame. She felt for the basin of water again so that she knew where to soak her burning skin. Taking a deep breath, she closed her eyes and plunged her hands forward.

"Ah, God!" she cried. Searing heat bit into the balls of her fists and the tender skin of her forearms. "Mercy please!" she begged, biting her lips to keep from shrieking.

The rope sizzled. She whipped her hands back. Yanked them apart. Felt the rope snap. Plunged her hands into the water. The relief was short lived. Her skin bit with pain so intense, tears pooled on her lids. She would have scabs, to be certain.

But her hands were free. Aside from her inability to see, the rest of her functioned as normal once again. Stinging plagued her skin. She withdrew her hands from the basin, bracelets of rope still knotted around each wrist irritating the wounds. For a moment, she simply clenched her hands against her stomach, squeezing, as if the pressure would alleviate the pain.

She remembered William pressing her hand against his stomach as he wrapped his tunic around her cut. Such a memory seemed so distant now, and it had only been a fortnight since his visit.

Shaking herself from her reverie before her heart began to ache for him, she began to take furtive steps. She needed to get inside the hut and out of the open for the night. Pray it wasn't piled full of corpses or more rubbish.

"Mercy, but this is more than a nightmare," she whispered, crossing herself in the name of the Father.

Aye. This was a living hell. Her hands, still smelling of the nauseating cesspit, slid over her mouth. Tears bubbled freely again. She no longer tried to dam them. *Corpses?* This situation could still become ten times worse before it ever improved. What if she had managed to escape the gravelly-voiced Alonso only to fall prey to a highway man come the morrow who might kill her, or worse, rape her?

What on earth had her father and Lord Loddin been thinking when they betrothed her to William? She could barely fend for herself. How on earth would she manage her wifely duties with no eyesight? How on earth would she manage children if she couldn't see them to keep track of them when her husband couldn't either? Of course they would have servants, but it chafed that they would *require* them.

"Why has God made me blind when I desperately need to see?"

This last thought, a plea of sorts, shook her shoulders. She had long ago grown accustomed to being blind. But this was unfair.

Alone, cold, she took a shaky breath and worked her sobs out of her throat. She tried to calm her racing pulse. She envisioned the camp the way it had sounded and retraced her steps to where the horse had stood. Her foot landed in a pile of horse manure.

"God be damned!" she exploded, before throwing her tainted hands over her mouth.

But this was the final stick to break the woodsman's back. Still, it didn't excuse cursing. Lord Edward had never been a violent father—neglectful, aye, for he knew not the first thing to do with her. But such unladylike blasphemy might earn any woman a slap across the mouth from a father bent on maintaining control of his household. Still, the urge to vomit roiled once more in her stomach as she withdrew her ruined slipper from the manure, shaking off the chunks. Turning to her right, she took furtive steps, careful to pat the ground before placing her weight upon each foot. She arrived at the fire once again, maneuvered around it, and continued onward.

A chill shook her shoulders just thinking about the darkness now enveloping her. Whether she could see the darkness or not, bad things happened at night. Beasts that otherwise stayed distant grew bold and hungry. And the crickets filling the nighttime with their trilling chorus told her it was indeed past sundown.

She shivered again. Stepping around the coals and patting her feet, she felt her way forward, at long last, she ran into a wall. Patting the siding as she walked the perimeter, she felt her way around the hut until she came to the door. She pushed. It creaked open.

"He...hello?" she asked.

Heart racing, she stepped over the threshold onto the compacted dirt floor. She knew the camp was abandoned, but what if by some chance she was accosted by a hidden bandit? The door creaked again behind her. She jumped and whirled around, but it creaked back the way it had come. A breeze moved across her face, rustling her unkempt hair. She exhaled a shaking breath, her hand clenching her throat where her cloak was clasped.

What had the King of Lispagne wanted with her? Why had her assailant possessed such a gravelly voice? It was almost as if he had been injured at one point and his throat had never healed. Were they truly taking her to the hated King Fernando II? She had heard her father and the men of Ballymead talk about Lispagne, talk of the Great War that had ended King Fernando I's life. She had only heard dark things about the country. But they had mentioned other women too, other women who had been nabbed.

Finally convinced that the hut was empty of corpses and hidden bandits, she tapped her toes, walked carefully, and ran into a washbasin for freshening. Beside it, she discovered a cake of soap.

"Blessed *Iesus*," she sighed, offering up thanks for the small token of kindness.

She scrubbed her hands, kicked loose her slippers, ripped down her nasty stockings, tossing them in the corner. She lifted her leg, ignoring how grotesque such a stance was, and plunged her foul toes into the water. She scoured each foot, balancing on the other, scrubbed each toenail, convinced they would never feel clean again, and ignored the breeze to her exposed femininity. Once finished, she dropped each slipper into the putrid water and did the same until they were as clean as the situation allowed.

She still smelled of cesspit, the smell laced into the very fabric of her skirts and skin, but there was nothing else to be done about it.

Feeling beside the basin in hopes of finding a drying cloth, instead her fingers met with...

"Oh blessed be!" she exclaimed.

There was a jug. Twisting free the cork, she smelled watered wine, and took hearty gulps to quench her thirst. Next to it sat a clay jar containing almonds and sweet dried apples, and some sort of soft, chewy fruit, also sweet, dry but sticky...she'd never eaten the likes before, but her hunger overpowered her and she latched the door, curled in a corner, and placed unladylike handfuls in her mouth until every ounce of the container's contents was in her stomach and she was picking her teeth.

It wasn't enough to sate the hunger pangs, but it was much more than the stale crusts of bread she had been given. Now if she could sleep, she might wake up to realize all of this was a terrifying dream. *Indeed that's it. I'll wake on the morrow and discover myself abed, maids hustling about the corridors on errands.* She would arrive on time to break her fast so as to never miss a meal again.

Oh, but just the thought of softly boiled eggs, seeded bread, and watered wine sounded delightful. Her father might often consider her an afterthought due to her quiet nature, but no more. She would eat when she wanted, speak when she was concerned, and command herself with strength. Strength was the only way in which to survive this ordeal. Her father would come. William, blind as he was, would come too. They might even arrive on the morrow and rouse her with a joyous reunion. She rubbed her eyes as exhaustion claimed her, her burns still stinging, and felt the edge of the parchment she had pilfered.

Sleep captured her. Thoughts of William teased her subconscious, his easy manner, his kisses, his doves... his hand upon her breast as she lay plastered between him and her workroom shutters while his mouth made love to hers and his more personal parts pushed against her. His confession that he wanted her, his request that she never change, swirled in her mind. He had seen the real her, not just the quiet her, with no working eyes at all.

Chapter 8

Captain Loddin, the oldest son and heir to Lord Loddin of Ballymead, stood above the wind-worn cliff. He had traded in his black and wine Bainick surcoat for a plain grey one, and had been careful not to wear his mail should the sun decide to shine glints upon him. The strait separating Bain's rocky northwest coast from the sheer cliff on the Île de Neige extended in each direction as far as the eye could see.

And his eye could see a balinger. Did anyone have permission to sail today? No one had sailed from Fort Michaelmas in a couple months and this vessel was struggling to stay a course. Prince William, his brother-of-marriage, would have briefed him of any sailings.

"Odd," he muttered to Michael, his young squire, a red-haired lad of three and ten years.

"How so?" Michael inquired.

"We're far up the coast, and there's no port up here, lad. That balinger shouldn't be here." Aye, the sail was unmarked and the vessel was a drab beige that could easily rest unseen when docked against a rocky shore. "There's no port on the island across from us for miles, nor are there any guard outposts."

"And I suppose no settlers or crofters out this far who might spy them, either," Michael deduced.

Lod looked down at him and nodded with approval. Michael would make a fine knight someday. His parentage hadn't afforded him any advantages, but he was strong, quick-witted, and observant.

"With the soil in these parts stone-ridden, there are no arable farms, and only one vassal to King Bain who lives more than two days' ride from here. No one is watching a balinger sail across a strait to an uninhabited shore, and no one ought be sailing from here, either," Lod explained to the boy.

"Is there any reason of import to sail to Île de Neige?" quipped the lad. "It has naught to offer."

Île de Neige was a small duchy, formerly under Lispagne's control, though it cut free its ties during the Great War. The castle of the Duke of Dubois sat on its northerly coast, far from them, in a snowy region even colder than northwestern Bain. The duke presided over much of his elderly father's kingly duties, for the old man was no longer able to travel and therefore left matters of diplomacy to his son.

"No reason for a Bainick man to travel there, and if they did, they would have left from Fort Michaelmas," Lod clarified, still squinting at the balinger struggling against the winds. "And I would have known about it, seeing as I command the post. But Jean Louis, the young Neigian duke, is worth keeping an eye on. Prince William has told all his captains and commanders that the Duke of Dubois is increasingly open to negotiations and discussions with King Sebastien of Lispagne."

Michael bristled. "That can't be good."

Lod shook his head. "It's not, even if we don't think Lispagne poses a significant threat." But Prince William and King Bain were suspicious.

"Did you notice, farther up the coast, a fisherman there has two new horses? Fine animals. What would be his reason for needing them?" Michael questioned.

Captain Loddin patted the lad's shoulder approvingly. He had noticed too.

"Whilst I have no evidence, the likely conclusion is that he bought the beasts."

"How so, when there isn't a trading post for miles?" Michael continued.

"Someone probably needed to unload the horses," Lod replied, his eyes resting upon the balinger again, "and there weren't any folk to buy them except for the fisherman."

"How would a fisherman afford the upkeep of such stout beasts?"

Loddin chuckled, even if Michael asked disconcerting questions. The lad was inquisitive. "He probably can't, but he can take them to King Bain's northern vassal and sell them there for a better price than he paid. Still. You're correct that it's suspicious. Come, Michael, let us steal a closer look. Put up your hood, lad and cover up that bright hair of yours."

He descended the shore, his squire following him. Rocks and boulders provided good camouflage for their plain surcoats. The balinger wasn't far out onto the water yet, and the oarsmen made slow progress cutting across the current. Its lone sail struggled to find congruency with the wind. Which meant if Lod could get closer, he might catch a better glimpse of the men aboard the vessel clad in plain browns and blacks, before they got away entirely.

He was rewarded. As he moved down to the shoreline, he noted the two men. Their hair was blond, one with a ponytail, one with hair cropped close to the neck. They were so close in height and build there wasn't much more to distinguish them. He couldn't determine anything else. They were too far away to hear, though they didn't appear inclined to talk either, focused as they were on trying to stay a course, *any* course.

The balinger was small. Mayhap five oarsmen on each side. And up close Loddin still saw no markings.

"Aye, suspicious," he reiterated, Michael glancing up at him.

Likely it meant nothing, but should it mean *something* and he didn't act, he might regret it. Best to pen a missive to Prince William and King Bain right away.

***

Amber woke, her neck sore, her brown hair stringy about her face. She could hear Sarah in her mind, clicking her tongue at the disgraceful image she must make. She shook her head, laughing sardonically. Why on earth did she care a whit what she looked like at a time like this?

Her muscles ached. Her clothing stank. She hadn't woken in her own, warm bed, realizing that all of this was a nightmare. She was curled in the corner of an abandoned hut, the chill of the morning seeping through the cracks and awakening the perpetual shivering that had accompanied her on her entire voyage so far. Who knew if the sun was even up yet?

"I cannot stay," she finally concluded. She might have thought to remain yesterday in the event her father tracked her, but she hadn't been thinking clearly. "I could wait days, even sennights for Father to figure out the way, and I have no food or water."

She had to try and find her way to other people, people who could help her send a message home. Of course she ran the risk of encountering people of a seedy sort who might take advantage of her, but she couldn't let her fear of the gravelly-voiced man sour her to all strangers.

Most country folk, like her, were kind, and she needed to remember that more often she had experienced goodwill than bad.

She stood, numb to the pungent odor of the human waste embedded in her skirts. If she stumbled through a creek, she could rinse her skirts there. The fabric was ruined anyway, she sighed, if not from the excrement, from the tearing and wearing of a sennight of hard travel.

She brushed back her curls behind her ears and began feeling the walls, moving furtively to the door. The latch was still set. Good. No one had visited.

Patting her pockets to ensure she still retained her stolen parchment, she exited. She could tell the dawn had broken. Birds chirped in their morning conversations, and though she could never describe it, she could always sense when it was daylight, even if her eyes couldn't see it. It smelled of rain, though bending to feel the earth told her it hadn't rained yet. A shower might be moving in. Her stomach rumbled, but there was nothing to be done about it.

Walking onward, she toed the ground carefully as she placed each step. If God were to add insult to injury, he might place another cesspit in her path and she didn't think her resolve could handle much more. *Such blasphemy!* She shook her head at her horrible thoughts. Of course God didn't like to see his flock struggle. She would endure this trial, and she would manage to find safety, one way or another.

She lifted her skirts and ripped free a remaining section of trimming. When she ran into a pine branch, she felt her way through the soft needles, touching the trunk, and patted around it until, low on the tree, she discovered a knot hole. "Perfect," she said, and stuffed the trim inside it.

As the day wore on, as she wove through suffocating trees and underbrush, she tripped constantly. Her slipper ripped off, leaving her barefoot, for she had discarded her stockings in the hut. She squatted, patting the ground, searching fruitlessly for the slipper that was likely caught in a mesh of brambles. Her breathing wobbled. She inhaled hard to regain her resolve.

"Fine. This shall all go from bad to worse," she muttered, pursing her lips. "Who needs slippers?"

She ripped off her other slipper and angrily lobbed it into the woods, resuming her walking. She hadn't gone barefoot since she was a girl, and her soles were tender. Still, as she progressed to God-knew-where, she was thankful that the ground hadn't pitched steeply in any direction.

She heard babbling water, a brook or a narrow creak.

"Pray I can manage to cross it without falling in or twisting my ankle," she muttered cynically as the rains finally began to fall, pattering the leaves and pine needles above until they managed to breach the canopy. "Though it *would* be keeping with my luck."

She shook her head. Self-pity was an ugly shade to wear, no matter if someone was too blind to see it. So far God had delivered her. She should be grateful.

She approached the water, patting each toe before planting her weight upon it, and tip-toed into the stream.

Shock blasted up her legs. The water was icy. She had to be lost in the northern parts of Bain where streams descended down into the cutting River Fetch from the frozen mountain peaks. She gave her feet a moment to adjust.

The forest around her was deafeningly quiet, empty, even if she could hear the creaking of branches high above and the occasional cry of a bird. Kneeling down, she allowed the water to flow around her skirts, taking care to scrub them underwater. The smell wasn't completely gone, but blessedly it was much reduced, even if the fabric, now sodden with water, weighed down her frame.

She splashed water on her face, the chill refreshing her, and cupped her hands to bring a drink to her mouth. It was crisp and pure, heavenly, and she drank until her thirsty throat was sated.

Ascending the opposite bank, the forest floor rose steeply. Branches and thorns snagged at her skirts, causing runs to further mar the fabric. She grabbed hold of saplings to keep her balance. Her back ached from the exertion until she finally crested the slope. The forest floor was spongy with blankets of pine needles, causing her to slip.

"Who goes there?" demanded a male voice.

Amber froze. She had been concentrating so much on not falling down an incline or tripping on a rut that she'd lost track of the passing hours.

"Lady Amber of Dunstonwoodshire," she replied, lifting her chin for confidence.

"Dunstonwoodshire?" the man questioned. She could hear his confusion and imagined him furrowing his brow. "If that's true, then you're a long way from home, woman."

"Indeed, I'm lost," she replied, praying the man was trustworthy, but the stress of not knowing threatened to snap her last nerve. She almost spoke a curse. This ordeal was loosening a tongue she had kept hidden in the recesses of her mind. Her last fragment of self-control stayed her. "I was kidnapped and escaped my assailant. Might I ask where I am? A village perhaps?"

She continued to feel outward, trying to walk toward the voice, bumping a tree in her haste.

"No place significant. The Cambrian Forest, at a mountain man's bothy," he replied. "Do your eyes nay work?"

She felt her lips wobble and a child-like sob nearly burst from her tongue. "Nay, my eyes don't work!" she exclaimed, dropping down to her knees in resignation. "I'm blind! And I want to go home!" That ugly sob rolled out of her throat, sounding louder in her ears than it actually was. "I just want to be home... I want to be with my sister, and I want to marry William..."

Silence followed her initial outburst as her cries softened. Aye, she wanted William and his gentle hands holding hers. He understood her struggle and still cared for her in spite of it. At least they were in the same predicament together.

Rustling perked her ears. The man was walking toward her. She cowered back. He could be a butcher, a madman, for all she knew. This might very well be her demise. Except a broad hand found her dainty one and lifted it, coaxing her to her feet.

"Rise up, my lady," came the next words, much more refined in tone than before. His voice was unmistakably young. And did she detect a hint of an accent? He was trying hard to cover it up if she had heard him correctly in the first place.

His hands were well-worn, callused. But he wore a ring, an extravagance that would do nothing but hinder a woodsman who worked with his hands.

"Come inside and let me offer you something to eat."

She swiped a hand across her eyes and took a deep breath, gathering her wits. "I apologize, sir. I am so very overwrought and lost my composure just now." Even now her words sounded feeble in her own ears. "I'm tired, sore, filthy, and miles from home. And I'm so very afraid," she admitted on an exhale.

"No need to fear me," he reassured. "Come. You may trust me."

Nodding, she let the man guide her to his door. He opened the port and ushered her in. Cozy heat enveloped her in the stone shell. As did the promise of cooked food – soft bread, a hint of spices and herbs that warmed the senses. The fire smoke was cloying but not overpowering, as if the cottage lacked good ventilation. And sakes, but it was a welcome smell.

He saw her seated in a sturdy chair lined with cushions. She felt the chair arm, realizing a table sat beside her. The creaking sound nearby told her the man was swinging a bar out of the hearth and dropping a ladle full of food into a bowl, probably stew judging from the savory smell of meat. Then a sawing sound, faint, told her he was slicing bread. He brought her a bowl of fresh water, guiding her fingers to it so she might thoroughly rinse them, and handed her a napkin.

A napkin? In a remote woodsman's cottage?

"You live well for a woodsman, sir," she finally spoke. "I thank thee for your generosity and apologize for my crying fit outside your door. 'Twas most ugly, I know."

"It matters not," he replied, ignoring her first comment. "Eat heartily and rest your bare feet. I wager it has been a while since you last supped and I have plenty."

Supped? Had she been walking all the day long and it was now supper time? She could tell he hadn't moved away. Was he watching her? *Oh God,* she thought, the fear of uncertainty gripping her once again. Had he laced her meal with a poison of sorts?

"Is there something wrong?" he finally asked. "I assure you the fare is safe."

Her fears were preposterous, she reminded herself again. "In sooth, sir, I'm confused. May I ask your name?"

"You may," he sighed, and she could hear him walk away. "Though I would be disinclined to answer. I apologize if I seem rude, but it's for the best."

She absorbed his reply. Another mystery man and aye, he had an accent. He might be falsifying a fine Bainick country accent, but his word choices were wrong for a woodsman in the wilds, that and if her blindness had ever blessed her, it was because her broken eyes had caused her other senses to sharpen in compensation. She could hear nuances that many with a full repertoire of working senses didn't notice: this man was from Lispagne, just like the man who had assaulted her, and he was no peasant at all. He was noble, in spite of the coarseness of his hands.

Unease prickled her skin. Why on earth would a young noble from an enemy land be hiding in the middle of a forested nowhere? Serving her a meal, no less? What if the men from yesterday had intended to bring her here, and Lord above, she had walked right into the Lispagnioc bull's lair? What mess was she wrapped within, caught in this snag of secrecy? Her wooden spoon clattered back to her bowl. She set it aside on the table. Only, she misjudged the edge and the bowl plummeted to the floor.

The dishes clattered. Warm stew splattered upon her bare foot. She stood, feeling her chest heave up and down.

"Lady Amber. What ails you?"

"Sergio and Alonso..." she whispered. "They work for you? Are you the one I was being brought to? Why? Why kidnap me of all people? Who are you—" His hands grabbed her upper arms. She flailed. "Let go of me! I have to leave! I have to find my way home!"

"Hush, lady! Hush..." he replied, trying to calm her, gripping her arms until she settled enough to hear him. "I want nothing more than to help you. Calm yourself," he continued, his voice gentling. "Please, worry not... worry not..."

She was crying again, shaking her head, and threw her face into her palms. "Why are you here? You're from Lispagne, no? I can hear it in your words and Lispagne is our enemy."

"Yes, Lispagne is. But I am not," he replied. "Please sit back down. No harm will come to you here. I beg you eat, relax, and perchance sleep, and then we'll talk and get to the bottom of your conundrum."

She nodded, shaking, trying to find the ability to simply trust. She had nowhere to go, and clearly, this man was in hiding. But she sensed honor in him—she *needed* him to be honorable—and though his finger was ringed, his abode comfortable, and his words educated, there was a ruggedness about him. He clearly lived alone, which meant he knew how to cook, clean, hunt, and sustain himself. And when she had felt his hands gripping her arms, he was indeed strong.

She ate, nodded off to sleep, curled against a soft pillow, and didn't realize when the man lifted her in his arms and carried her to his bed. She rested dead still, her chest rising and falling, not once feeling the knife he withdrew and pressed against her skin...

Chapter 9

He inserted his blade beneath the vestiges of bondage encircling Amber's burnt wrists and sliced away the rope. He looked down at the maiden. She was bedraggled, damp, and her clothing was disgusting, though once finely tailored even if simple in style. The only thing that made him believe she was a lady was her long hair, stringy as it was, and the fine material out of which her brown skirts were made. That, and not a single wrinkle marred her young face. Her skin was milky smooth, unblemished, and my, she was fair. Her cheeks were a naturally rosy pink and her eyes were a lovely shade of brown, like the wide eyes of an innocent doe.

Her language was cultivated too, another indicator that she spoke the truth. He couldn't be too careful, hiding here as he was. Any trespasser was cause for alarm. He wouldn't put it past the corrupt Lispagnioc king, Sebastien Fernando II, to send a spy in the form of a pretty, "blind" skirt meant to soften his meager five and ten years of defenses. For that very reason, he couldn't let the young woman go just yet. He had to examine her further.

But her remarks about Sergio and Alonso worried him. He had been watching the twin men, keeping notes on their activities in these remote northwesterly parts of Bain that were so sparsely populated they were forgotten. The Bainick crown only marched through here on occasion and those contingents never traveled the forgotten deer paths. But he had the ear of a correspondent in Bain, a man he suspected to be the prince, and he would do everything in his power to keep the line of communication open.

"Mayhap I ought to take you to the Abbey of St. Matilda," he whispered to her, but more to himself, watching the rising and falling of her breasts.

The abbey was in actuality a pile of stones so bare of riches, the chapel and monastery seemed more like a byre, long and plain with thatched roofing. It was there that he conveyed messages to his Bainick correspondent and collected his replies. Only Father Crispen, the priest, for the abbot lived some days away, received his messages before offering him a meal to which he always declined, and then closed the oaken doors behind him as he trotted away in the veil of night.

He had seen the pair of men Lady Amber had just mentioned, riding down the forest path toward the coast empty-handed only the night before. The twins had kidnapped a few young peasant women and a peasant child that he had seen, though their operation was hardly new. He chuckled. How marvelous that the one to escape and elude them should be a blind woman who had run into a tree just moments ago. Served them right.

He would ask her more questions and if all seemed in order, he would deposit her with Father Crispen at St. Matilda's. The holy man was kindly and would pen a letter to Dunstonwoodshire, and her ordeal would be over. He backed away from her, brushing his dark hair behind his ears, and gathered a rag to begin cleaning what she had spilled. He might be the royal seed of King Fernando I, but no amount of tutoring in his half-brother's palace walls could educate away the meager birth that had taught him to dirty his hands.

Sebastien, his kingly half-brother, was as much a scoundrel as their father. One day, would he, *Christophoro Maria de Fernando*, be able to right the wrongs of the Lispagne bulls and return honor to the monarchy he was part of by the very accident of birth, he would live for that day. He would continue to endure his isolation and solitude. He was damned lucky to have escaped his brother's house arrest, an incarceration veiled as a royal education, to sail to this land. And it had been thanks to his anonymous Bainick confidant that he had even established himself here.

There was no love lost between him and Sebastien. Fernando II was as much his brother as was a pig or a rock. Fernando II was a madman, much like their father, what with the way he bended his ear to his crazed advisor, Mateo. Mateo was brewing trouble, and Sebastien had turned into his puppet.

Have care, dear brother, that you don't release the black lions from their Bainick cage again, Christophoro thought, gazing at the young noblewoman asleep on his pillows, her chest lifting with peaceful breaths.

Lispagne could ill-afford another massacre at the hands of the Bainick king and Prince William.

He pulled up a blanket and fur, draping them over her. A rushing sound outside told him that the rains had unleashed into a downpour. He walked to the window and wedged open a shutter, looking out into the greyness of the forest, droplets pummeling puddles.

Thank God, he thought, crossing himself in the name of the Father.

If the rain kept up, it would ruin the woman's trail and wash away her scent, which would cause any search parties tracking her to lose her trail. His hand migrated to where his heavy sword sat perched by the window, a paranoid habit he had come to live by. No one aside from his confidant in Bain knew he was here, and even that person didn't know his exact location, only his general whereabouts. It needed to remain that way, no matter how much the young Lady Amber might wish for someone to find her. He'd best extinguish his hearth fire, lest he send a smoke signal to anyone who might be searching.

***

"Is that Lord Edward?" asked Will, pointing across the River Fetch.

The highland river, known for its deep ravine and deadly rapids that cut through the northwestern forests, settled into a wide, meandering river this far south. Beyond Will's finger was a trail of red surcoats trickling down a rocky path from the opposite mountain with a swarm of dogs trotting around the horses' hooves.

"Aye, I believe it is, son," said Lord Loddin. "I can hardly see him myself."

It was inexplicable, Will thought, such return of vision. Perhaps it really was a miracle, as Hershel had stated.

The Lord of Ballymead and his sons maneuvered their horses through a pass framed by steep slopes burgeoning into peaks. The river cut a lazy path into the sandstone basin. Lush grass filled the valley. Turning the reins, they began a winding descent down the rocky path, and finally came out of the trail mouth.

Cattle grazed on the hillsides, contained within stone walls crisscrossing through the pastoral grasses. They lifted their heads to gaze at the newcomers, chewing, their shaggy fur hanging into their eyes. Storm clouds carrying the smell of rain rolled overhead from the northwest, ruffling their surcoats and their horses' manes, threatening the valley's tranquility.

Hershel pulled up beside his youngest brother and placed a fraternal grip on Will's shoulder. "We were speaking yester eve, Father, Gavin and I. We're pleased for you," he said. "The return of your sight is a gift. Mayhap Lord Edward has found Amber and brings with him more good tidings."

William nodded. "Pray that it's so."

He tapped his heels into his mount, urging the beast into a canter, then a gallop, trying to ignore the irritation conjured by the thought of his father and brothers holding a council to discuss him as if he were a novelty. But as he neared Lord Edward's party, his irritation ebbed. A sense of foreboding replaced it, the sensation upsetting his stomach as he rose and fell in the stirrups with each leap. Edward seemed to have spotted them too and began galloping to meet them.

William's horse sloshed through the lazy river. The other horses did the same behind him. Emerging on the other side, Amber's father and brothers converged with them in the valley. The Dunstonwoodshire lord dragged back the reins and his horse tossed his head at the inconvenience, halting, Amber's brothers doing the same. Their mongrels trotted into the river, tongues lolling, to drink.

Edward's face was haggard, his brow heavy with lack of sleep, and his eyes dull.

"You haven't found her," Will stated. "It's written all over your face, my lord."

"Wait one bloody minute..." Morgan maneuvered his horse through the other men and came alongside William, filthy in his road-worn surcoat. William's gaze shifted to Amber's brother. "Your eyes...they're focusing. You can see me..."

"Aye. I fell hard and slammed my head through a cask of mead. It seems to have put my eyesight to rights—"

"You can see?" Angus interrupted, his deep voice rising and his eyes brightening. "Praise be. 'Tis a miracle!"

Edward spared a weary smile for the young man betrothed to his daughter. "A miracle indeed..." And then his eyes rimmed with redness he tried to blink away. "Pray we find Amber, so that we can all share in your joy, William. I'm sorry I cannot be happier right now. She's so helpless."

William shook his head, his face long. "There's nothing happy about this moment. I'm sick with worry, sir. It's been four days since your missive arrived, over a fortnight since she went missing. Pray tell what you've discovered."

"Nay much," Angus said, wiping sweat and grime from his heavy beard. "The dogs found a trail passing through a weakness in our fief's walls. It took us northwest into the Cambrian Forest as if headed for the northwest coast. We arrived some days ago at an abandoned hut, a ramshackle pile of planks which showed promise. The dogs went mad, hot on both the hut and the clearing. There's nary a doubt Amber was there."

They all fell silent, a look of illness upon the men of Dunstonwoodshire's faces.

"How could you tell?" Will asked, examining their expressions. "There's more than just the dogs catching her scent, isn't there?"

Edward struggled to form words as a dangerous scowl clouded his brow. "Her stockings... They were ripped and—" Rage made his voice tremble.

Will's stomach dropped and his lungs seized up. The color drained from his face and he felt...rage? Helplessness? Confusion? He had no word to describe the mental paralysis.

"We found them tossed in the corner of the hut," Morgan finished for his father, his voice steady and brow stoic. It needed no elaboration as to why such an intimate garment might be torn and discarded. "We were certain she was nearby, but the summer rains moved in and washed her scent away, and though we searched high and low all around the clearing, she's gone."

"We suspect she's been taken toward the coast," Angus added, shaking his head and readjusting his reins. "But we can't be sure of any direction in which to go. We doubled back this way in hopes of intercepting more men who might join in the search."

"And the king has been written?" Will questioned.

"I sent a missive to King Bain at the same time as I sent one to your father," Edward ground out. "I'm sorry, William lad. I know I promised her to you. I'll compensate you should our search be unsuccessful—"

"Speak nay of such things," Will growled.

The thought of what a man might do to Amber—might have already done, given the evidence—made his stomach brew. What in God's name had she endured? His heart hammered his ribs. He wanted to punch something, anything.

"Lod was recently promoted and stationed on the west coast." William turned to his father. "Do you think this is why Prince William ordered him away so soon after Gwenyth's wedding? Do you think he suspects something happening of which we might nay be aware?"

"Aye," Lord Loddin nodded, thinking. "Considering his request for all vassals to remain vigilant of their people, that might very well be the case."

"We should go northwestward," Hershel added. "'Twill be several days of riding for you, sir," he addressed Lord Edward and his men, "but I think we all agree that she might have been taken in that direction. The clues indicate such."

Edward's voice was gruff. "No luxury of rest for me. I'll ride to the edge of Bain and back again, as many times as I must, until I find her... alive or nay."

"It won't come to that," muttered William, his jawline hardening, shaking his head with disgust at their despondency. "She's alive." He turned to his brothers and his father. "We must all believe her to still be alive. Amber is clever. Being blind gives her a different way of seeing the world which I must believe gives her an advantage, not a hindrance." He willed the words out, hoping to make them true with his conviction, but his words were empty in his heart. For Amber was lost in a world she couldn't see to navigate, with a captor she couldn't see to undermine. "Come. I cannot sleep until my betrothed is safe."

"So in spite of your eye sight returning, and her probable..." Edward couldn't say "rape." "You would still marry the lass with her deficiency and all?"

Will scowled. As a man, he didn't need to marry a blind woman. He could back out of the betrothal and it would be within his rights. The law was grossly unfair in his favor. It angered him. He had always pledged to be a fair-minded husband to Amber.

"Be damned, man, but I would hope you consider me much more honorable. How can you suggest such?" Will countered. "You, my father..." He looked back and forth between the two men. "You pushed for a betrothal because you thought the only prospect for a blind daughter would be a blind son from a favored fief."

Edward's eyes hardened at Will's insult. "How dare you claim to know—"

"Do nay act as if you had any other motive, sir," William seethed. "Our families are longstanding friends, but you know King Bain and my father are friends, and my sister marrying the prince doesn't tarnish our family any. However, you never asked *me* if I wanted to marry her. You assumed, as fathers do, that you could decide our fate. Which gives truth to your motive: to marry her to a blind man in a favored family.

"Still, I was well-pleased by the betrothal, even if I felt as if she deserved a whole man, nay a maimed one like me. I could care less about her eyes, Lord Edward. I know what she goes through far better than any of you ever will, which makes her far fairer to my eyes than simply her bonny face." William scoffed. "I'm insulted you would even suggest such dishonor from me. Amber is my betrothed and unless she dismisses me, then this contract is binding. Are we to sit in the saddle all day, wasting hours over talks of honor and contracts? Or are we going to move forward with a plan?"

Lord Loddin sat dumbfounded at his son's audacity, but Hershel and Gavin sat up straighter, nodding approvingly. Edward's piercing glare settled on Will, but he finally nodded with something akin to approval too. He turned his horse, offering no directions to the others, and began trotting in the direction they had come from, his sons following suit, as well as their soldiers.

Will tapped his horse to follow, but his father pulled up beside him and stayed his reins. He rested anxiously, waiting for the old man to speak.

"It's hard for me, William, to see you as a man," Lord Loddin finally began. "I forget often. You'll always be my youngest lad who befriended his wee sister before tragedy befell you. But you indeed have developed the honor and conviction of a man who has earned his spurs."

Will frowned. His father meant well right now, but mayhap his father was the blind one, because all those years of his "youth," it had taken a man devoted to family to learn to braid his sister's hair, take her riding, help see to her tutelage. It had taken a man who could juggle the demands of the meadery, fill the gap left by his brothers whose lives pulled them away from Ballymead. It had taken a man to continue the work whilst his father's leg grew lamer and lamer, while the old man grieved endlessly upon the death of their mother.

Right now, his father acknowledged that he was a man. But what no one seemed to realize, Will thought with dismay, was that he had been a man for a long, long time, when he should have been a lad. The quiet, gentle, dreamer Will, the steady and dependable son, had always been taken for granted.

"I've been a man since Mother fell ill," Will stated flatly. Loddin regarded him. "I took care of Gwenyth because mother couldn't and everyone else wouldn't."

The words streamed faster and faster, now that they were flowing.

"And you know what? It wasn't so bad. Because I learned a few things about devotion over the years. Gwen's my wee sister, aye, but she became more of a daughter, thrown upon me as she was. I took responsibility for her. And while all of my brothers were busy with their lives, she became my friend. Do you know that despite the 'tragedy' that befell me, I manage almost everything in the meadery and have done so for years? And the business has only become more successful. I wonder when you will start nay just seeing me as your wee lad with an injured body, but might accept that your wee lad was a man long ago?"

Loddin rubbed his chin, thinking. And Will sensed a rift growing between them.

"I don't say these things to garner sympathy," Will said, watching Edward's men and his brothers grow smaller on the path ahead of them. "I know I've had a good life by any man's standards. But I'm nay a lad anymore and haven't been one since I was young. I'm nay incapable. And I did earn my spurs, over *six years* ago. Hell, I can even make babes if I wanted to, even if I've rarely wandered down an immoral path."

Loddin scrutinized him, his brow crinkling.

"Aye, you didn't know that?" Will continued. "That I'm nay a green lad anymore? You've always seen me as a naïve boy with no experience beneath my belt? I have practically five and twenty years, Father, what did you think? I'm your youngest son, but I'm fully a man of my own who knows what he wants, even if I'll never be able to claim the meadery as my own, even if I stand to inherit nothing as your fifth son, little better than a serf who tills the land solely due to rich parentage. I know my life is good and am grateful for it, even if I have no future of my own to offer Amber. I just hope that it wouldn't have taken my betrothed to go missing and probably—" he couldn't say the word "rape" either, "for you to finally see that I have a man's honor, and a strong streak of it at that."

Lord Loddin didn't have any ready reply. Will turned the reins and tapped his horse into a canter to close the gap between himself and the rest of the search party. Amber's stockings had been found in a hut cast in the corner. But nothing else had. She could have been violated. But there could be other reasons too. Mayhap she cast them off. Aye, he had to consider that. He couldn't think of the alternative, for the thought squeezed his heart, and if the squeeze grew any stronger, his heart might start bleeding.

He envisioned the wee lass he had watched grow up,

remembered tugging her braid, remembered watching her play with Gwenyth. He remembered giving her each carved dove. He remembered watching her body take on the shape of a woman's. He imagined her soft hair, *like doves' feathers...* sliding through his fingers as her body wrapped around his, envisioning another man rutting upon her now. He felt a stubborn tear for her pool in the corner of his eye as he watched their future together drain away. Pray they didn't find her body mutilated and used. Pray...

***

"Tell me, Lady Amber, about these men who nabbed you."

Amber, groggy, finally remembered that she was snug in the cozy bed of a forest bothy. The heat from a fresh fire was comforting. Rain pelted down around them, landing heavily upon the thatching. If only she wasn't so filthy, she might have found it relaxing.

She took his offered hand and joined him by the hearth to eat her fill, and set aside her bowl.

"I believe Alonso is the one who nabbed me. His voice was hoarse, raspy. We were alone for the journey, and it wasn't until reaching an old hut that I heard Sergio's presence."

"Of what did they speak?"

"At first, nothing to give themselves away." She wiped her mouth on a napkin. "But they argued about me. It seems I might have been stolen by accident. The one who took me was surprised to learn I was a noblewoman, nay a peasant, and that I was blind. It wasn't until I managed to lose them that they spoke freely, thinking me gone."

He handed her a warm mug and she soon realized it contained mulled red wine, not watered. A delicacy, even for the daughter of a lord. She sipped it. Heavenly.

"Pray tell how you managed to elude them, my lady."

Amber was careful. "You seem concerned, sir. Is there a reason why?"

"There's always a reason for wanting information. I wish to know what dangers might pass by my abode if you're followed," he replied.

He sounded so youthful, so fresh, she thought. His voice had depth, but lacked the richness of a mature man.

"You seem so young," Amber remarked, more to herself.

"And you can see this without your eyes?" he asked.

"It's the sound of your voice."

He sighed, weighing what he should and shouldn't say. "You're correct. I have five and ten years."

"And yet you live a rich life," she continued, sipping the spiced wine from what she could tell was a wooden goblet carved in detailed relief. Were they bulls? Her fingers traced over the design. "Whilst living so sparsely in the forest... Are you hiding from someone?"

The man, nay, *lad*, said nothing. When he shifted to his feet and spoke next, she realized her folly.

"Have you been sent to spy on me?" His words were cold.

She swallowed, shaking her head of stringy hair. "I was lost," she whispered, slowly setting aside the goblet. "I only wish to go home, I swear it, but can you nay see why, blinded as I am and quite alone, how I might wish to know more about the man who helps me?"

He neither spoke, nor moved.

"Why would anyone spy on you, sir?" she pressed, hoping to soothe him with the title even if he was younger than her. "It's an easy conclusion that you're someone important to Lispagne. I've heard your accent before at court. You try to cover it up now, and quite well you do, but I hear the hint of your true tongue behind your efforts."

She ducked her head to her lap, a demure habit, but she pressed on. "I've clearly stumbled upon someone in hiding, and wouldn't that just be my luck?" she laughed wryly. "I have no desire to interfere with your predicament, whatever it may be. I'm sorry it's you I encountered, for I fear I've put you ill at ease. I just want to go home and marry my betrothed..." Her palms covered her face.

She could tell he moved now by the rustling of his clothes, and then she felt the stem of her goblet placed back against her fingers. She peeled a hand from her face and took it. Pray the man hadn't poisoned it, for it would be rude to refuse the hospitality. She brought it to her lips, sniffing, rather than drinking, and pretended to swallow.

"You're an astute lady," the young man finally said, then exhaled like one did when they waved a dismissive hand. "It's not poisoned, by the way. I hide, but I pose no threat to your king or country. I hide because *my* king and *my* country pose a threat to me. Trust that I don't share the same intentions as the men who stole you away. You're not the first woman they've nabbed, but you're the first noblewoman to be taken and they know they shouldn't have."

Amber's breath hitched and her hand came to her chest. "Why do they take us? What do the poor peasant women of Bain have to offer them? For it shouldn't matter if I am noble or serf."

"I wish I could tell you, but—"

She sensed the lad's hesitation.

"But what? Pray tell, sir, if you know. Their plots must be

foiled. What did they want with me?" When he didn't speak, Amber sighed. He was choosing not to answer her question. And it angered her. She shook her head. "You offer me no answer when I sense you know one. Have I no right to know why your countrymen prey on women from mine? I cannot bear to think of my family's grief right now. Yet you might know why these men nabbed me and choose to remain silent?"

"It's complicated, my lady," he replied. "And I haven't remained silent. I remain careful. These men...they're part of a bigger scheme. I am merely one man and cannot stop this scheme by myself."

"Then why not tell King Bain?"

"I'm doing what I can," was all he offered. "I'll help you return to your family. The Abbey of St. Mathilda's, a small monastery, is a couple hours easy riding from here by horse. I'll take you there. Father Crispen, the priest, will send word to your loved ones."

"I would be most grateful." She withheld a sigh of relief. Mayhap they would offer her a bath too. Pray they would, for she must look worse than a drowned cat. "My father, Lord Edward of Dunstonwoodshire, no doubt will wish to compensate you upon my safe return home. I wish I knew where to direct a reward."

"No—" He regaining a thoughtful tone. "No payment. I know what it's like to be kidnapped and held against my will." She heard despondency in his voice and wished to know more of his story, though she minded her tongue. She had already tested him. "I do this as a favor, nothing more. You'll be quite safe at the monastery. We'll leave in the early morn on the morrow. I cannot risk being out much later in the day, even if these forests and mountains are sparse of life."

"My thanks to you, sir."

"You never told me how you managed to escape your captors," he diverted.

"'Tis an embarrassing, and somewhat disgusting story," she shuddered, "and a story I'm nay certain I wish to share."

"I was raised in the gutters on the streets, the son of a whore. Trust I have seen, smelled, touched, and indeed tasted things far worse than a gently bred maiden such as yourself. If you managed to get away, you managed to succeed. There's no shame in it."

***

Christophoro watched Amber's expressions. If she playacted, she was a phenomenal actress.

"When the men convened in the hut," she began, drawing in a deep breath, "I was left alone on horseback with my hands bound together. In a strange place so far from home and blind at that, I don't think they considered I would dare go anywhere, let alone escape."

He sat back, thinking of Alonso and Sergio. She was beautiful in spite of her disastrous state. If the twin henchmen had succeeded in whisking her away, there wasn't a doubt in his mind that King Fernando would appreciate adding her to his harem, even if Alonso had royally erred in nabbing her. She would probably be one of his favorites.

"When I heard them argue inside, I dismounted. Though I'm nay proficient with reins, I *have* been riding before, and so I felt I could drop to the ground. I thought for certain they would spy me, for I had no idea if they could see me and hadn't a clue the right way to move or what I might stumble upon. I figured that I had already endured so much and the worst they could do was capture me again."

"A bold but wise idea," he nodded.

"The ground turned out to be flat and I managed to find a pit. 'Twas their cesspit," she muttered, her face burning brightly. "I was so utterly lost, so I climbed down in it, for I didn't know if I would find another place to hide from them.

"They discovered me missing and both men departed to search for me. So I stayed hidden, though I know not how long the time was. They finally returned, certain I had escaped, and argued. They were certain that I'd signed their death warrants by escaping."

Her voice trailed away. He noted she still hadn't attempted another sip, despite his reassurances that it wasn't tainted. *Smart lady,* he thought. The wine was good, but she was wise to remain so wary in the company of a stranger she couldn't see.

"Where did they intend to take me?" Amber whispered. "If you know, I pray you tell me. My father and my betrothed both have a right to know, as do I."

Christophoro reached out to take her hand. King Fernando II was a whoreson, a lowly snake like their shared sire, but with even less scruples. Sebastien managed the Lispagnioc Monarchy by wielding fear and with a wealthy royal purse that made others in his command give him deference—for no one else in all of Lispagne possessed such a purse—when in truth he was the most dangerous kind of madman: a madman with the ability to decide all his subjects' fates.

All the king needed now was his army and his succession. And if he could betroth a few of his bastards to neighboring kingdoms, he would be well on his way to regaining alliances that might split up the maritime forces keeping Lispagne under their heels.

The young man felt Amber's icy fingers upon his. His touch had made her stiffen. "I cannot tell you more than what I am about to say, lady. You would have been a mistress to King Fernando II... He needs a web of heirs and has no marriage suits, for no kingdom will agree to sentence their daughters to such a fate. So he swipes peasants who won't be missed, but whose nationality will matter more when he needs to marry his children off. Bain won't promise *him* a princess. But they might be willing to promise one to a child born to a Bainick mother, no matter how lowly her station."

"Monarchs rarely worry themselves with the fates of a few peasants," Amber said, a sad truth.

"Nay Bain's Prince William," the young man countered. "Prince William grew up lowly and beaten by his father before he learned of his bastard royal heritage, and has a stake in what happens to the poorer folk. If the man's not careful, 'twill be his weakness for King Fernando II to exploit. I know this, because I know the Lispagnioc king. You have escaped a dire fate, and if hiding in a cesspit was the way to escape it, you were right to be so desperate."

Her fingers squeezed his. Strength. She had quite a grip for so small a maiden. In fact, they clenched his hands so hard he shifted his fingers to alleviate the discomfort.

***

Amber shuddered. Thank God she had escaped. *But someone must help the others. Someone must tell the king and Prince William about King Fernando's plot,* she thought to herself, knowing that that someone should be her.

Chapter 10

Prince William surveyed the high council chamber filled with men from across the world. Serving staff lined the polished walls and made rounds refilling goblets. Prince Heinrich from the Hadstadt was muttering something to his younger brother and two cousins. The emir of the Land of Spices stood in flowing robes of white trimmed in indigo, his beard meticulously manicured, speaking to two of his commanders.

No one sat in the space designated for Île de Neige. No messages had arrived either to indicate whether or not the Duke of Dubois would attend. Prince William sighed and took a pull off his wine goblet as if it were a tankard of ale at a tavern.

"How on earth do you conduct such meetings year after endless year?" he finally remarked, leaning into King Bain beside him. "I'd rather a flail mace bludgeon me."

"Get used to it, son," chuckled King Bain. "'Tis your lot when I'm sent to sea on a funeral pyre."

"There's naught to be accomplished here," Prince William remarked, reaching up to scratch where his crown rested. The gold, rimmed with lions clasping each other's tails, always itched.

He addressed the chamber. "So no one else has noticed a problem with your kingdom's daughters going missing?"

The room hushed a degree.

The emir shook his head. "Such occurrences have never been reported to me, though I will designate an investigator upon my return home."

"Nothing we're aware of either," called Prince Heinrich over the mutterings of the other dignitaries. "We've never looked into the matter."

William sighed. He had made headway on other important issues of trade during this summit, but none would be made on this issue. "I urge you all to look into the matter—send out riders to check on your villagers in your far-lung territories. I've noticed a pattern. Peasant women of prime young years and older lads still in their youth appear to be those targeted."

"How did you know to look into this matter? Did your people bring you a complaint?" the emir asked.

Prince Heinrich also raised a curious eyebrow.

"Our soldiers happened upon a crisis to the south of here in Soughgate. A maid and her younger brother had gone missing and the village was conducting a search," Prince William explained. "Neither were found and there were signs of a struggle. I looked into the matter further, sent out men across the countryside to gather information, and discovered that this has been ongoing for the last six years."

"They could be accidents," Prince Heinrich suggested. "A peasant's plight rarely reaches a royal ear. People die. They move. They're attacked by animals. Such is the nature of the world."

"I see your line of reasoning and originally thought each explanation probable," Prince William conceded. "Until I learned that all of those who have disappeared are nearly the same ages and their routes of disappearance all bear similarities."

"Why do you suspect it is happening in Bain?" the emir questioned.

Prince William glanced sidelong at King Bain, leaning into his ear once again. "I'm not ready to divulge my suspicions just yet."

King Bain nodded once.

"I suspect they have been nabbed, but in truth, have little evidence. 'Tis merely a hunch right now," Prince William announced.

"Who do you suspect of the nabbing?" the emir pressed.

The chamber now rested silent.

"I'm still trying to figure that out," William replied. His green eyes darted from the emir to the prince of the Hadstadt. Both leaders watched him, as if trying to decipher his impassive expression. Whether they believed him or not, William didn't care. "Today marks the last day of our discussions, and we've indeed made progress on some important issues of trade. I would request upon your leave, that you evaluate your kingdoms for such missing persons. I would be interested to know if this is happening elsewhere too."

"And what then?" Prince Heinrich spoke up. "We inform you?"

"I would appreciate the knowledge, yes," Prince William replied.

Prince Heinrich offered a polite nod, continuing. "If you don't know who is responsible for this—"

"He knows," the emir interrupted. "Or at least, *suspects.*"

William took a deep breath. Bain's relationship with the Land of Spices had always been a good one, but warmth ebbed and flowed with whoever currently held power. The emir had only stepped in to assume power after his brother, the previous ruler, died. Though his brother had selected an heir to succeed him to the throne, the boy was still too young, and therefore, the regency had landed upon Emir Mura el Salim standing before him now.

Prince William leveled a look at the dignitary. "I have a suspicion forming in my mind, but you will understand that I need more evidence to determine if it's even a viable suspicion."

"So you can control the investigation, if it turns out to be a crisis of worldly proportions?" Salim questioned.

"No," Prince Heinrich stepped in, directing his remarks at the emir. "He makes a wise decision now. If his suspicions leak out and are false, he risks damaging relationships with the accused. And if his suspicions leak out and are true, then he risks tipping off the perpetrators, which ruins his chances of capturing them, or risks war."

Prince William nodded and stood so that his ceremonial surcoat draped around his boots. "Please, men. Enjoy more refreshments and a nooning meal in the great hall," he gestured. "Prince Heinrich is correct in his assumptions. I've discovered a potential problem and wish to know if such a thing plagues you, too. 'Tis a matter of goodwill, Mura," he addressed him as a friend, hoping to thaw the emir's expression. "I bid you keep your investigations silent for now, until we can meet again to discuss the matter."

"I would be pleased to host the summit," the emir offered. "All will be welcome at my palace in Ba A Gavra."

"We would be pleased to accept the invitation," King Bain replied.

"Come. Food will do us all good, for it's not my intention to introduce controversy, but instead to work together on a matter that has potential to harm us all," William concluded.

The servants by the double doors drew back the handles at King Bain's gesture. Prince William and the king stepped down from their thrones to walk upon the carpet rolled out toward the exit, when a road-weary messenger hastened through the doorway.

"Permission to interrupt your proceedings, Your Majesty!" A Bainick guardsman exclaimed on behalf of the messenger, bowing.

King Bain stepped forward. "Granted. Indeed do tell, for it seems important."

William regarded the filthy rider, draped in chain mail and a red surcoat with the red and gold horse of Dunstonwoodshire upon the breast. The man's clothing was laden with traveling grime and his eyes were both tired and intense.

The rider bowed, withdrawing a crumpled missive. He handed it to King Bain. "Lord Edward of Dunstonwoodshire's younger daughter has been nabbed. They searched high and low, and discovered signs of a struggle leading out of the fief's woods."

Bain took the parchment and ripped the seal as a Bainick guardsmen explained further.

"Dunstonwoodshire's messenger was tasked with seeing this missive into yours and Prince William's hands."

Bain nodded, skimming over the words.

"Lady Amber, no?" William furrowed his brow as King Bain held the missive between them so they both could read. "She is the youngest child of Edward, and slated to marry my wife's brother. I met her at my wedding. A sweet maid."

The messenger nodded. "Aye, Lady Amber. She went out to collect plants and berries for her trade and never returned. Lord Edward and his sons discovered her basket upset in the glen, the contents scattered. Footprints suggest a man captured her."

"She's blind, is she not?" King Bain asked the messenger. "I recall her and William of Ballymead sitting together during the wedding festivities."

Both William and the messenger nodded, when William noticed a shadow in the corridor, a dark green gown. Gwenyth. She stood away from the men against a buttress, her hands working a kerchief at her waist, clearly trying to be unobtrusive so close to his court. He turned his attention back to the rider, the image of her distraught behavior worrying him. He hadn't seen her the whole of the sennight as he and his dignitaries held discussions. The one time she had tried to intercept him as he rose from bed to slip out before the sunrise, he had dismissed her. With so much on his mind, he had been anxious to get on with his meetings. Upon the fourth night, he had come to bed in the wee hours of the morn, only to find her doors barred, which forced him to retreat to his own bed that he never used.

"She is indeed blind. Such is more cause for worry," the rider verified. "Lord Edward was forming a search party upon my departure. He worries himself over the warnings you delivered to your lords, and wonders if Amber's disappearance is due to your—"

"She could have been found by now," Prince William said, cutting the man short and glancing back at Gwenyth who was watching him. She looked away, her face upset, and her dark eyes unusually stressed.

"Indeed, such is probably the case," King Bain agreed, clapping William confidently on the shoulder. "But it still warrants an inquiry. A missing noblewoman should raise an eyebrow, hmm? We'll look into the matter."

"Lady Amber is missing?" came Gwenyth's uninvited voice.

The mood of the council chamber shifted. The visiting diplomats were unprepared for an encounter with the princess whom they had only met upon their formal arrival. When at first no one spoke, she continued.

"I saw the messenger's Dunstonwoodshire blazon," she clarified, seeming to realize her rude entry. She clasped her hands in front of her, holding her stomach, as if holding in the need to retch. "I apologize for intruding upon you, my lord."

She said nothing else, and waited for her husband to acknowledge her. Prince William held a hand out to her, beckoning her to his side. He hated the formality of "my lord," even if was necessary right now, and the worry on her brow distressed him.

And he missed her.

"See here, wife," he stated, transferring the missive to her hands, noting the dignitaries appraising her. He placed his hand protectively at her back. They were good men, but his wife's blonde hair and ethereal beauty had become renowned. He hated seeing the lust that sparked in most men's eyes even if he should appreciate it.

She began reading. Her grip tightened upon the parchment.

"Is there nothing else to report?" William demanded.

"We must do something, husband," Gwenyth interrupted, shaking her head. She sent the parchment back into King Bain's hand and grabbed William's arm. "We must try to find her. We must send men. I must go to Dunstonwoodshire, for surely my brother Will is sick with worry for his betrothed, assuming he knows already. He won't be able to go after her, what with his injuries. Pray I can plan a party to travel immediately. Pray you will send a search party, or better yet, go yourself—"

Prince William rested a finger over her lips. *No more formalities, it seems,* he thought, his lips curling up. He loved her conviction, even if her timing right now was ill-placed. He sent a glance around to the visiting men and noticed their polite but uncomfortable expressions.

"I apologize for my wife's conduct," he told them, receiving nods of understanding, then steered Gwenyth back into the corridor.

They traveled some paces down the hall so that they stood concealed behind another buttress.

Gwenyth's brow furrowed. "Lady Amber is my dear friend, indeed she, Sarah, and I are very close."

"You cannot simply interrupt the king's council at will, Gwen," he admonished. "I plan to look into Edward's missive, but Bain has other pressing issues as well."

Hurt captured her eyes. "You *know* Amber. You've met her. Edward is one of your important highland liege lords, and yet, you would relegate her disappearance to the bottom of your priorities? Beneath such items as, as, the taxes levied upon the fullers? Really? It is less important than that?"

"Of course not, and don't misunderstand me. I said we have other pressing issues too, not that this matter is less important than them."

William pinched his eyes with his thumb and finger. God, but he wished he could confide everything in his wife. She would know that Amber's disappearance alarmed him deeply. He noted her eyes begin to glisten, though she did her best to blink away the moisture. She swallowed, tempering her tone, and dropped her gaze to the floor.

"I am frightened for her. God alone knows what has happened to her. What if, what if she has been—"

Gwenyth gripped her stomach, and William sensed she was about to vomit. He hollered to the nearest guardsman.

"Go and fetch her handmaidens. Immediately. Gwen, are you well?" He eased her onto a bench. Sweat was collecting along her brow. She gulped, gripping her middle, and dabbed her face with her kerchief.

"Well enough," she whispered. "I... I cannot say the words, what might be happening to her. My lord—"

"You know I wish you never to call me thus in private," he scolded, lifting her chin. "I'm only your lord in formal settings."

And there, as his eyes met hers, he saw the memories of her ordeal, the rape, the beatings, and the unabashed fear that Amber might be suffering the same fate. In that moment, he realized his honor as a husband was at stake, that to Gwenyth, Amber's abduction carried an urgency that really was more important than the fullers' taxes.

Gwenyth brought her kerchief to her mouth. She wasn't often a crier, something else that alarmed him. She had emerged from such a horrible past with her head high, lifted by strength and grace. Which made her pending tears now all the more perplexing. "What if she has been—"

"She hasn't," William interrupted, laying his finger across her lips again, his hand beginning to shake with anger at the memories of how Gwenyth had been so wronged. *Will of Ballymead's mind must be in tumult now*, he thought, and he understood such tumult firsthand. "Tell yourself that all is well."

"I cannot bear to think on how she is suffering," Gwenyth muttered, as if not hearing him. "And I would care not if you're in the midst of the king's council or a coronation, if my—"

"My Princess," he cut her off as he sensed King Bain approaching. His father adored Gwenyth, but even *he* might not appreciate the direction of her current statement, even if William knew she spoke out of frustration.

"Prince William," the king said. "I bid you send your wife to her chamber and rejoin with the party."

Just then, they noticed Lady Caris and Lady Eunice, Gwenyth's closest ladies-in-waiting, as well as two servant women, billowing down the hallway. They were followed by the guardsman who had run for them.

"I've summoned her ladies to accompany her," William replied to his father, standing. "She might be ill and is in need of rest."

King Bain glanced down at her as Caris and Eunice each took her hand, helping her rise. Caris, the daughter of a Bainick enemy who had been rescued months before, didn't look at him, but simply helped Gwenyth steady herself. Eunice, however, sent him a discreet glance, her lips pursed.

"Please return to your chamber, wife. I'll come to visit you in due course when the time allows," William said. "This matter is distressing and I've only learned of it myself. Pray you calm down whilst I hear what else Edward's man has to tell. Guard, accompany her to ensure her safe arrival."

Playing the role of a husband in charge of his wife wasn't a sport he liked, and it left a bitter taste in his mouth, especially when she seemed so unwell. She studied him, knowing him too well, and her eyes glittered with something more than tears of worry. With a reproving frown, she managed to nod her head in concession and whispered, "As you wish it, *Your Highness.*"

William remained silent. He felt his father place a hand on his arm to urge him back to their visiting company. He pinched the bridge of his nose again, but turned back to the chamber where Prince Heinrich and the emir still waited with their men.

"Excuse me for such an intrusion, good men," he offered, plastering a fake smile on his mouth. "My wife is dear friends with the missing woman in question, and as you can imagine, such news has shaken her."

"Allow my guards to lead the way to the great hall," King Bain gestured with a sweep of his arm. "I shall be along in a moment. Do begin your *repas* and enjoy heartily. Eh, man of Dunstonwoodshire," he addressed Lord Edward's messenger. "Please remain a moment longer."

The Bainick guard led the dignitaries down the corridor buttressed to the vaulted ceiling in a succession of supports.

"Pray tell, messenger, anything else you know," King Bain stated, pushing closed the door to seal them in.

"That is all, My King," the man bowed his head. "Lord Edward begs men, search parties. He fears for his daughter, for she is not strong, and her lack of eyesight makes her quite helpless. Any man who has taken her could be doing vile things to her."

Prince William's pulse jumped. Anyone who knew him also knew of his disdain for rapists, and Gwenyth's supplication to him moments ago had only made his anger surge. It made him ache to seek Gwenyth, and caused guilt to wash over him for his dismissal of her. She didn't look well.

"I'll go to investigate," Prince William declared, his jaw tight.

"You can send Sir Thomas on such an errand," King Bain dismissed, returning his attention to the rider. "Does the lord remain at Dunstonwoodshire?"

"Nay," the messenger replied. "He found a trail leading northwesterly, returned to his manor to pen the missive to you and one to Ballymead, and ordered me on my way. He and his sons were preparing to track the trail when I departed, Your Highness."

"He could be anywhere right now," King Bain remarked.

The prince cleared his throat. "Indeed, but I must go to Fort Michaelmas anyway with our first batch of helmets. And Sir Thomas has other engagements at the moment. Our summit ends tonight. I had planned to take a contingent to Fort Michaelmas after a couple days of rest, but will command a score of men to be ready at first light on the morrow. We have to traverse the northwestern territory and cut through the Cambrian Forest to reach the coast anyway. I'll locate the lord as we travel."

King Bain nodded, turning to the messenger. "Go, man, and find a warm meal in the lower hall with the other soldiers. Help yourself to the barracks to rest for the night."

"My soldiers would be happy to have you," William added. "I'm afraid there's not much more I can do at the moment."

The messenger bowed. "Lord Edward and his sons will be most grateful to you."

"I can only imagine his grief," William replied, clasping his shoulder. "Take your leave, man."

The messenger departed, opening the door.

King Bain closed it again, sealing them in privacy. "And the plot thickens," he remarked, reaching up to stroke his chin.

William ripped off the ceremonial crown and raked his fingers through his raven locks. He settled his other hand at his hip, gazing toward the windows as if looking at nothing.

"Lady Amber isn't a peasant woman," Bain continued.

"It doesn't fit the pattern," William remarked. He shook his head. "Unless this is something different, an abduction unrelated to the others." His jaw muscles pumped. "I've grown to know Gwenyth's brother well. Will loves Lady Amber. This must gouge him deeply."

He turned around and faced his father. "I won't know anything more until I can speak to Edward. And I won't know anything further about the nabbings until the other kingdoms investigate which could take months, if not a year or more. I have a hunch..." He shook a suspecting finger. "A *strong* hunch that they're going to uncover a similar scheme. Pray the emir decides to cooperate, and damn it all to hell if all of this isn't frustrating me right now." He sighed again, slouching his hand upon his belt. "At the earliest, I will cross Lord Edward's path in a sennight. But that's if providence is in my favor. Likely I'll have to scour the Cambrian Forest and mountains, not to mention the cliffs leading to St. Mathilda's. 'Twill be arduous."

"Go to Gwenyth," King Bain said, placing a hand upon his shoulder. "I see that you're frustrated. You've neglected her these past days and she is still unaccustomed to the demands of court. If she is unwell, she could use her husband. I'll entertain our visitors until you join us."

William nodded, relieved, and departed the chamber. He glided past statues of former kings, torches ensconced in crenelated brackets, and ancient royal standards hanging in succession. He ducked into a narrow servants' passageway, passing maids hustling to the laundries, kitchens, and embroidery rooms, passing page boys and men carrying burdens to various offices.

He acknowledged their bows and curtsies with a curt nod, but proceeded without stopping to converse as he normally did. Climbing a set of spiraling stairs, he finally arrived in the upper corridor that led to the women's chambers. The Queen's Quarters were at the far end. King Bain had gifted them to Gwenyth upon her marriage to William, after making it clear that he didn't intend to marry again.

Prince William nodded to the guard outside her door and lifted the latch without knocking. The antechamber was empty, save for a maid pacing before the windows, bouncing the babe Louisa in her arms. He spared a smile for his niece, a child that Gwenyth had agreed to raise.

The sound of retching traveled through the open door to Gwenyth's bed chamber, causing alarm to surge in his blood. He bolted through the door, arriving in time to see Gwenyth huddled before a chamber pot, her maids holding back her hair while Lady Caris dashed for a clean kerchief and a wine decanter.

"What's wrong?" he demanded, pushing through the servants.

The maids jumped at his presence and dropped into bows.

"Gwen," he murmured, squatting beside her.

He grabbed her face, tilting it to him so he could look. Her skin was pale, her brow sweaty, and she gripped her stomach.

"I'm fine," she said, her voice gentle in spite of her obvious upset.

Caris returned with a goblet of wine, and Gwenyth swished a swill around her mouth to freshen, then spit. A maid held forth water, and Gwenyth drank heartily, then took a pinch of mint from the metal box held open for her. She chewed the leaves, spitting them into the pot as well.

"Are you refreshed, my lady?" the servant asked.

William scooped her into a cradle and carried her to the bed as her maids fretted.

"I am. My thanks. You may leave," she added, gesturing to her maids.

"My lady, shall I run for the physician?" begged Eunice.

"Nay," Gwenyth smiled, placing a hand on the woman's arm.

"All is well. I'd like a few moments alone."

"Aye, run for the physician." William undermined her. Gwenyth's smile dropped and she shook her head but William silenced her. "I won't argue it, wife."

"Nor will I," she challenged.

Lady Caris came to her side, reaching behind her to fluff up her pillows. "Have you told him yet, Princess Gwenyth?" she whispered.

William furrowed his brow. "Told me what?"

Gwenyth flashed her eyes at him again, but she directed her comment to Caris. "Nay. He's been most preoccupied all sennight."

"Eh, should I, or shouldn't I fetch the physician?" Eunice fretted.

William looked to the lady, then to Gwenyth, who was smiling again to put Eunice at ease.

"I've seen my symptoms time and again at Ballymead," Gwenyth replied. "And I have already seen the physician."

"Why haven't you told me such?" William questioned. "If your health is in peril, I need to know. Father needs to know. You'll need—"

Gwenyth took a deep breath. "I had hoped to tell you about it. Please, husband. I wish for the others to leave and I would be grateful if you would spare just one moment of your busy time for a word in private."

William nodded. "All right."

The others filed into the antechamber and Lady Caris closed the door. Gwenyth stood.

"Nay, woman, lie down," William ordered.

"I'm fine, I really am."

She walked to her table draped in cloth, seemingly recovered, and took up her goblet of sweet wine to drink.

"Gwen, you were vomiting into your chamber pot," Will scoffed. "I insist you return to bed."

She turned to face him, the light from her arching windows casting her in a silhouette, and set aside the wine. For a moment, neither of them spoke. He started.

"Gwen, I'm sorry I had to dismiss you downstairs. Rest assured the men understand you're upset—"

"I'm with child," she whispered.

William sputtered to a halt. "You... you're what?"

"I've waited up for you night after night—"

"Did you say, 'with child'?"

"After the diplomats arrived and your father relegated me to another table and you said nothing to intervene, I was angered. I know your meetings are important. I know that as Prince, you have much responsibility. But am I not worth just a moment of your time? Is this how it is to be? I had hoped to tell you a sennight ago. I had just come from the midwife, who had confirmed the good news."

He strode to her and took both her arms. His voice softened.

"Did I hear you correctly, love?"

She looked up at him, her despairing words vanishing at the lopsided smile he knew claimed his face. "I had hoped to make the telling special," she muttered. "But it seems there would never be a good time, for you've paid me no mind all sennight. And now the sickness sets in. I assure you, I am quite well, and quite pregnant."

He slid his hands down to hers and lifted her fingers, holding them both to his mouth. He pressed his lips to them in a long kiss, inhaled, exhaled, then threw his arms around her and lifted her off her feet.

He dropped her back to the floor and released her. "Christ, Gwen, I didn't hurt you just now, did I? I shouldn't squeeze you so, I might, I might..." His voice trembled.

She reached up, taking each of his cheeks in her palms. "Hush, William. You can squeeze me all you like. It won't hurt the babe."

He pulled her back to him, carefully this time, and clenched her hair and gown. "Placing you at a different table was never meant to degrade you, only to make it easier to continue diplomatic discussions. Otherwise I would be tied up for another day of negotiations, if not longer. Forgive my father and forgive me?" he whispered.

He tipped his head and looked into her face. She threw her gaze askance from his. "I didn't feel degraded. I just wished to tell you that the future Prince or Princess of Bain was rooted in my belly. I was selfish, for I couldn't wait to see the pride on your face. I'm sorry. I shouldn't have been offended."

"Woman, you are forever on my mind, even when I cannot be with you," he scolded. "Have you any idea how much I love you? I'll be pulled away from you during our lives. Sometimes on voyages, other times like these. But if you have need of me, I'll make certain to listen to you. You must simply say the word and I'll make the time. Going forward, I promise this."

She nodded and he kissed her. He slid his hands up to her cheeks, imagining what she would look like with her belly rounded. With child. *My child.* Surreal.

He drew apart and dropped down to a knee, sliding his hands

down her arms and spanned her narrow waist with his palms. He remembered the first time she had delivered a child, the seed of her first husband, a stillborn babe. A tremor of fear snaked through his body, followed by a fierce need to protect this babe from any harm. He ran a hand over her stomach and placed his lips to it, inhaling her rosewater scent. He would miss her come the morrow, but tonight, he wouldn't be late to bed, and he wouldn't sleep alone.

"I will love this babe," he affirmed to himself, kissing her navel again, for all knew he had grown up roughly. "I will protect it always. As I do its mother. My seed."

Gwenyth ran her fingers through his hair, holding him to her womb, and he finally looked up at her. "Remember, husband, that Lady Amber's father wishes to do the same. We have to help her. I'm sick over this news."

He gazed up into her dark eyes and remained kneeling. "I leave in the morn, Gwen. At first light. Our summit is at its end. I had hoped to spend a couple days with you making amends for this difficult sennight, but as you said, we must act. I promise to do what I can for your brother's betrothed."

She nodded and he saw relief fill her eyes.

"I know you will. And I leave in the morn as well. I shall travel to Dunstonwoodshire and remain in residence there until Amber is found. I know with you helping my brother, you'll prevail."

He rose and took her hands. Of course she was glowing. He had heard men say that their wives carried with them an aura of beauty when carrying a child, an essence that hadn't been there before.

"Gwen. I will do my best, but don't underestimate your brother," he cautioned. "Will has honor and I have deep respect for him. Blindness and lameness won't stand in his way if he's determined, because when I watched him with Lady Amber at our wedding, I saw a man who looked at her exactly the same way that I look at you. And what I feel when I look at you cannot be put into words, but at its core, it's love."

"You know he cannot look at her," Gwenyth countered sadly. "I know you try to be sweet."

William took her hand. "Close your eyes."

She crinkled her brow.

"Go on, close them," he pressed.

She did. He ran his hand over hers, wove his fingers in and out of hers, watched as the furrow on her brow smoothed, and finally leaned down to her ear. "What do you feel?"

She smiled, allowing his hand to continue. "I know what you're saying," she replied.

Prince William grinned. "Which is?"

"Love. I feel the way my brother looks at her."

He pulled her into his arms.

"Your family is one of the strongest I know. Your father means well in everything he does, and all of Lord Loddin's children mean well, too. You worry for each other, and fight for each other. Just now, you tell me you carry my seed, and yet will still leave in the morn to go to Amber's family. Already you've accepted Edward's daughter as your sister. And I know if I told you that you had no permission to leave because of your condition, you would saddle up Luna and defy me anyway. Don't take that from Will by assuming he cannot act on his honor and do what he must for the lady he loves, for I know if he looks upon her as I do you, blindness won't hinder him. I would die trying to find you, even if I were blind. Give him the respect due a man, not the sympathy due a cripple."

She nodded and squeezed his waist, burying her hands in the fabric of his ceremonial cape thrown over one shoulder. "You're wise, husband."

He separated from her and smiled. "Come. Eat beside me tonight. And when I announce your tidings to the great hall, I suspect you'll weary of Father's doting, for he's most excited to be a grandfather."

"He wants to make things right with you," Gwenyth remarked, taking the arm he offered. "He missed your youth and regrets it. He will forever try to make amends for the ways in which you suffered. Our child will be a second chance for him to devote himself to you. 'Tis much more than being excited for a grandchild."

William, in mid-step to the door, paused and looked down at her. He dipped his head and dusted a peck upon her lips. "You, my dear wife, are fairly wise yourself."

***

"You can see!" Captain Loddin exclaimed as his youngest brother dismounted inside the gates of Fort Michaelmas. He tackled Will into a bear hug, slapping his back. "'Tis such a miracle, my God, Will. What a blessing upon you!"

Will couldn't conjure a smile, despite his efforts. His face was furry with blond stubble and his eyes, weary from over a fortnight of fresh use.

"I wish I could celebrate it, Lod, but I can't think of celebration with Amber missing."

The summer rains fell relentlessly, the party's sodden clothing was heavy and their chainmail cold. Angry waves thrashed the rocky coast beneath them, and through the fog and hovering clouds, the distant cliffs of Île de Neige's eastern shore was barely visible.

"What has happened to your betrothed, man?" Young Loddin asked, taking stock of the somber eyes and haggard faces of the party. "Why have you all traveled so far? When my outer guardsman relayed to me the standards he saw traveling our way, I've never been more surprised."

"She was nabbed, Lod," William uttered, swallowing the distaste of the words. Swallowing the memory of the abandoned hut.

Amber's stockings had been left where they lay. He had seen them for himself, smelled the foulness upon them. Illness had roiled in his gut. The hut had been dilapidated, filthy, and stank of excrement. The water in the basin had been fouled. She had been forced to endure squalor. God help the man who had brutalized her. The memory of the hut caused his hands to tremble with rage now.

Lod stood dumbfounded. "What? By whom?"

"We don't know who is responsible," replied Lord Edward, his voice hoarse. "We tracked the men until the rains moved in and we lost our trail. This seemed like their logical course and so we continued."

"No women, no parties at all have ventured to the fort," Lod replied. "We'd have seen a woman, and I would have recognized if it was wee Amber."

"There was a path that split from the main road going farther north, but it led to the coast and no one was traveling it," Gavin added. "It ended at the shore, near a fisherman's hut with two head of expensive horseflesh. The rains made it impossible to determine if anyone had traversed the area."

"Might we spend the night here, son?" the Lord of Ballymead asked his namesake. "I think we concur it's time to regroup and discuss our next course of action."

Lod nodded. He too, like his brothers, had inherited the Ballymead complexion: blond hair and dark brown eyes.

"Indeed you may," he replied as they began walking to the alehouse. "But I wonder..."

"Wonder what? Have you seen anything suspicious?" William asked his oldest brother. "We know nay who we track, but they were clearly headed westerly."

Lod stopped, his brow crinkling. "Four days ago I spied an

unmarked balinger crossing the strait over to Île de Neige," he remarked. The other men also stopped to listen. Lod let his gaze drift, thinking. "Two men were on deck, looked to be tall, about the same height, fair-haired. They were near to the termination of the path you spoke of. Hardly anyone inhabits this outland region. The soil is rocky and makes for poor farming, and the summer isn't warm enough or long enough to cultivate large crops. So it was strange indeed to see people on the water so far north. One would freeze to death in these waters, even in summer, which makes these men's endeavor that much more foolhardy."

"What became of them?" Will and Edward pressed in unison.

"I watched them for as long as I could see them. If they made land, it was after dusk. The sun must be its brightest to notice any movement on the opposite shore. Prince William instructed me to report on anything out of the ordinary some time ago," Lod relayed to the party. "He didn't state why, only suggested I keep the matter under coifs. I've sent men regularly to inspect the coast, though it's a vast stretch of land and we can only observe so much. Several days pass between sweeps. So mayhap these men have crossed before, but we failed to be there at the same time to see it."

"Did you tell the crown about this?" Hershel interjected.

"Aye. I penned a missive to Prince William the moment I returned," Lod replied.

The men, sodden and hungry, eyed the lights and noises seeping from the alehouse. With a flick of his finger, Lod caught the attention of his second in command and ordered the portcullis dropped.

"This was out of the ordinary," Lod continued, gesturing toward the alehouse again, "because the balinger denoted no colors, no standard, a beige vessel hoping to become invisible. I sent my report to Prince William, though it takes a fortnight of diligent riding to reach the capital. No sign of a balinger in the waters since."

The din within the fortified tavern hall was loud. Off duty soldiers thudded across the planking, taking seats upon old barrels and roughly-hewn benches. Will shoved off his chainmail coif and pushed back the padded hood now soaked with rainwater.

A couple of wenches pulled pints from the casks stacked along a wall, their bodices worn and their breasts jiggling from the low hems of their chemises. "They must be the only women around here for miles," remarked one of Amber's brothers.

"There are only six women here, bar wenches," Captain Loddin confirmed. "They take turns working, for we use the tavern at all hours of the sundial. I've put in a request for more, for they keep the men entertained as well, and as you can imagine, with only six of them, they have an exhausting job."

Lord Loddin seemed to notice Gavin's eyes straying to them in the way his second son's eyes always did before he sneaked away to tryst. A soldier teased the brunette, pinching her rear as she shimmied by. Lord Loddin gave his betrothed son a discreet kick to his shin beneath the table.

"Hey now..." Gavin began, looking around to see which man had injured him, only to see the sharp eye of his father upon him. He crinkled his brow.

Lord Loddin scowled at him and leaned close to his ear to keep his words private. "You're spoken for, son," Lord Loddin grumbled. "No wayward eyes and no wayward cock either. You bring your 'purity' to Sarah."

Gavin noted his father's sarcasm and rolled his eyes, whispering back.

"That 'balinger' sailed long ago, Father."

It was the wrong thing to say. Lord Loddin's scowl turned into a punishing frown and his whispering continued. "Are you a frenzied lad? Or are you a strong man? Because it's a strong man that can put his maypole in his breeches and control when he takes it out."

Gavin, as always, rolled his eyes at his father's puritanical demands, but returned his attention to the seriousness of their visit. "Indeed," he whispered nonchalantly as one of the women brought them a fist-full of tankards, froth spilling down the sides of the wooden vessels. "Looking at a woman is like breathing to me. It doesn't mean I'm thinking about plowing the fields."

But Lod also watched the women as he took a seat on Gavin's other side next to William, women he was responsible for, and sent Gavin a warning look much like their father had just done. Glancing back to Will, Lod sighed.

"Your eyesight returning has been so fortuitous, wee brother. The timing is a blessing."

"God knew he would need his eyes to find Amber," Hershel nodded.

***

Lod continued to regard Will as the others swigged from their tankards. It would be his job as the heir to execute their father's will upon the lord's passing, a topic that had never been discussed with his younger siblings. Therefore, Lord Loddin had included Lod in his privy decisions. The name "Loddin" and the Ballymead fief went to the oldest, as tradition dictated. The other brothers were awarded parcels of land and funds to build a home. Hershel had already been given his, though after his wife's death, he refused to set foot in his home further and had allowed nature to reclaim it.

A shame indeed that William would inherit nothing but an allotment of coin as the youngest son. Will, the one who ran the meadery, maintained the apiary, and was blinded in recent years, had been allotted no land. Their father had assumed Will would stay at Ballymead to be looked after, and had amended his will to reflect it.

Lod had always thought it unfair, even if it was the way of things. Now, as he regarded his youngest brother whose sight was fully restored and whose heart was breaking, it seemed more than unfair. It was insulting.

***

"It's been nearly a fortnight since Edward's missive arrived," Will told Lod. "Aside from a hut deep in the woods, we've no more clues." Will couldn't stomach the ale and took to swirling it. "Was there any indication at all as to what was aboard that balinger?" he finally continued.

"None," Lod shook his head. "None at all, but I've sent a party northward up the coast to watch for their return. If they don't come back, I'm nay sure what to do. I sense from their lack of heraldry that they're smugglers. Of what, I cannot say. But if they are, they might very well come back, for it means they have a trade route through here. 'Twould make sense they're using the more divergent trail as opposed to this main road, since no one ever patrols the outland regions."

"Does Fort Michaelmas have hunting hounds?" William asked.

"I have a pair, aye," Lod nodded.

"We should take them up the coast," Will continued. "Lord Edward's hounds are exhausted and one has injured its paw. He favors it. They could use a rest."

"It's raining here harder than it did farther east," Angus replied, folding his arms and leaning back on a wall support. "They'll nay find a scent. I worry my wee sister is truly gone."

"I won't accept it," Will replied, his brow tightening.

Hershel frowned. "The coast is rock-strewn, with many a dip and rut. Perchance there's a spot retaining their scent protected from the waters. There's always a chance, no matter how small, that the dogs will sniff out something."

"It can't hurt," shrugged Lod. "You may use the curs. Worst that will happen is they find nothing."

"Aye and that's the problem," muttered Edward. All eyes looked to him. His voice was despondent, his eyes sagged with wrinkles that hadn't been there before. He shook his head. "Loddin, friend... How did you manage when Gwenyth was unaccounted for?"

"Come, man. Let's go out for a walk," Lord Loddin replied, hoisting himself to his feet and swiping up his tankard. It was clear to all that Edward was going to fall to tears, and no man, especially the Lord of Dunstonwoodshire, would want to be remembered for such lack of fortitude.

Will watched both men leave, feeling the same churning in his stomach he had felt since Edward's missive arrived. Such churning had prevented him from keeping food down. His eyes, perpetually heavy, felt leaden now. His chest, perpetually constricted, ached.

He thought back to the days of Amber's infancy, the pride her family boasted as they held their new daughter and passed her around to family and friends. He remembered the sweet girl playing on the hillsides, smiling freely without a care in the world. He recalled when his interest in her began, and the excitement he felt just knowing he might get to see her, the pleasure he felt as he carved her each dove. And he remembered when he realized she was the one. The memories seemed like wisps on the wind.

Intangible.

Elusive.

Several days of growth had turned his face into the dirty scrub of a vagabond. His stump ached to put weight on it. He knew his cheeks grew gaunt. His cheeks... Sweet Amber, she had touched his cheeks as she explored his features and developed an intimate knowledge of his face, held his cheeks as they exchanges kisses...

"Are you all right, wee brother?" Hershel finally spoke, nudging him in the arm with a fist.

Will hardly registered the intrusion to his reverie. He remembered sitting with Amber before the hearth at Ballymead, on the eve that they were betrothed, speaking in hushed tones so that his family nearby wouldn't overhear.

"We'll become more and more acquainted, Amber, as time wears on. I nay know if you'll continue to tolerate me, but know that I'll always do my best to take care of you. And I hope I can be worthy of earning your love and admiration," he had told her, holding one of her hands in

his.

Amber lifted her unoccupied hand and caressed the chiseled hollows of his cheeks down to his jaw. "How could I nay love you already, my lord?" she had stated, her words tender. "I'm so excited to be your wife. I can only hope that in time I prove to be pleasing to you."

"You already are, sweet Amber. God, lass, it's been so long since I looked forward to the future," he'd interrupted, unable to keep from smiling at her words and tender fingertips caressing his cheeks. "But I look forward to it now..."

The memories wouldn't stop plaguing him. They haunted him when he pined for her, and they taunted him now that he searched for her. God, but to be able to sleep, to cease feeling! To cease imagining what she felt like braced to her window shutters in her work chamber, their lips devouring each other's, the heat of Amber's core against his groin, the heat of her palm upon the planes of his stomach, and the desire in her legs gripping his waist. He had wanted to make love to her right then. He had wanted to find her worktable, sweep the contents from the surface, and lay her down beneath him. How was it possible for someone to be there one moment, and be gone the next?

"What's on your mind, Will?" Lod asked, eyeing Hershel and Gavin. "You're brooding. We all see it." Will cupped his tankard through the handle, swirling it. His broad shoulders were hunched. He stared into his drink. Stared at nothing. "I can tell you're nay really looking at the ale, wee brother."

William looked up and stared emptily at his oldest brother. "Wee brother." They still, to this day, called him "wee," as if a helpless child.

He had started out his journey in haste, with certainty that he would find Amber and they would be joyously reunited. But the days progressed, their prospects thinned, and the realization of success was waning. Nay. He couldn't give into the despair. There was still a chance to find her. He had to cling to it.

His eyes drifted to Hershel, then Gavin, then Lord Edward's sons. "What's the point of having eyes if one does nay have their lass to look upon?" he murmured to Lod, though Lod knew his question begged no answer.

Hershel leaned close to him.

"I don't think your eyesight is a curse, man." Will shot his brother a sidelong glare. "Think on it, brother mine. God grants you back your eyes just in time to learn of Amber's disappearance. Can you nay see what lies right in front of you with your wonderful new eyesight? *He* wanted you to be able search for her. When I think of it in that light, I come to realize we will find her; it's only a matter of time."

"I agree," Gavin added. "We all might know Hershel to be the stodgy churchman he is," he jabbed, "but he's right on this account."

"I don't feel sorry for myself, mind you," William defended, sitting up. "And because I lost myself in memories a moment ago, doesn't mean I've lost my focus. If anything, I've reaffirmed it."

"You show much honor, man, devoting yourself to my sister's search," Angus said. "But my father and your father know well that the time might be nigh for breaking the betrothal. If we haven't found Amber by now, it's unlikely we'll find her. I hate to think she's perished," he shook his head, "but there's no sign of her."

"I'm certain she'd be pleased to know you gave up so quickly," quipped Will, his eyes narrowing.

"Be realistic, Will," Morgan scoffed. "We won't give up looking for her, but the reality is that she's gone, and if we should be so fortunate to get her back, there's no telling what she's endured. She might nay be the same lass anymore. We've ventured all the way to the coast, for God's sake. There's *nothing* here. There's nary a soul except for the Bainick army at this fort."

Will shoved to standing. Damn, but now that he had rested his peg leg, it burned to put weight upon it again. If he were honest, he would admit it had been paining him for days. "There's the whole of the bloody country, man. Have we looked there yet? Nay. We've looked on one route—*one*," he held up a finger, "from Dunstonwoodshire to Fort Michaelmas."

"The trail led us here," Angus argued.

"And the trail is lost. This isn't the only road in Bain. Until I see her dead body at my feet, I'll nay concede that she's gone," Will replied.

Lod placed a hand on his brother's shoulder, urging him to sit back down. "Calm yourself, man. No one is giving up the search."

"Then I'd appreciate if everyone quit trying to let me free of my betrothal, as if I've been condemned to chains against my will and finally have a path to freedom," Will retorted. "I didn't consider my courtship to be a funeral march as some husbands do."

"But what man would want to waste his days betrothed to a lost woman?" Angus tried to reason. "You'll need offspring, heirs—"

"Heirs for what?" Will exploded, drawing attention. "For my *vast* inheritance? For my estates and coffers and tracts of land? What the *fok* do I need heirs for, man?"

Will's brothers all gauged him, uncertain what to do with his anger.

Angus took a calming breath and continued. "With your newfound eyes, you can build more of a future now. My whole point was to state that none of us would disparage you if you chose freedom from this contract. That's all."

Will shook his head, ready to argue further. He swallowed his anger. He was always the quiet one, the contemplative one. It would do him no good to have another outburst. The others got up to find a pallet in the barracks, leaving him alone with Lod. It had been a long journey and sleep beckoned. Except Will couldn't find the strength to relent and rest.

He took a deep breath and turned his scowl to Lod. "We have no other leads. The dogs are the only chance we have left." He began swirling his ale again, gazing at it as if it held answers in the amber liquid. *Amber. Be damned.* "They're right, you know."

Lod leaned back against a wooden support and folding his arms. "About what?"

"She's probably lost. But I just can't—" He swallowed, his eyes still fixed on his tankard, and whispered. "I can't relent. Lod. Brother..." he shook his head, feeling unseemly tears threaten to fill his eyes. "Why is this happening?"

Lod smoothed his bearded chin. "I know you don't actually ask for answers."

Will shook his head. He found his brother's steady presence calming. Loddin was a good, solid man, even if he had a habit with ale. His flaw of drinking was that of many men. He wasn't violent to his wife, and had grown to love her in the way that their father had loved their mother. Lod was confident. He was strong. And his strength and experience had given him wisdom. Will needed his strength now.

Loddin's stout hand came to rest upon Will's shoulder and clasped him.

"When Gwenyth was lost, it was you who told everyone we had to believe she was well and in one piece. It was you who lashed out at us when you thought us growing despaired like Amber's father and brothers despair now. It was you who was the strongest, who never gave up, until she was found."

"And Prince William," Will remarked. "But he had an entire army at his command."

"Aye, and him, because like you, he is honorable. And if needs be, you'll have the army too, for remember Prince William is our brother of marriage," he winked. "Even if Prince William didn't want to help, which would be unlike the man, Gwen would never let him rest peacefully until he had pledged a legion to your cause and repented to her upon the parapets of the capital."

Will huffed, his mouth curling upward at Loddin's jest. Prince William was already repenting for mistakes he had made courting their sister and made no effort to hide that he would do anything for her. But Will was just a simple man, not a prince. Still, he would do anything for Amber. He had pledged it once before and would die if needs be living up to his vow.

"I would come to the end of the earth to see your honor vindicated. I would offer up the rest of my leg, my whole body..." His leg was growing sorer each day. Pray that he didn't need to pay up on his declaration.

"You've never been a man of war, Will. Of all the men who deserve a corner of happiness in this world, 'tis you. You've endured so much. You've suffered greatly, and I know you anticipated your marriage in September. I wish I could fight this battle for you."

"Nay just anticipated, Lod. I've waited for *her*, nay just any lady."

Lod clasped his shoulder again. "Our brothers, Father, we all grieve for you and will carry arms in defense of you and Amber. Trust that."

William thought back to his father, his mother, when he was only a small lad. *"Will is the youngest... he is so quiet... such a dreamer... such a lad will need protection... never going to be a fighter..."* His jaw hardened.

He had thought he'd proven his worth to his father and brothers when he'd cared for Gwenyth all those years, when he'd taken on more and more duties in the meadery. And after his injury, he had been coddled, treated as incapable. He had hated it, but hadn't felt there was much he could do. He had stopped feeling worthy. He didn't want his family defending him because he was unable to do it.

"I can fight, Lod. I might not aspire to it, but I needn't sit idly by whilst my family takes the lead. Amber is supposed to be *my* wife."

"I know you can fight, Will. We've watched you fight these past years as you rebuilt your life without your eyes, without your foot."

"Nay, you've seen me struggle and wither," Will countered. "With the respect due you as my oldest brother, if those dogs bay at a single familiar smell, then we'll know this secret balinger belongs to the men who took her. And heaven help their souls, because I sure as hell won't need my brothers to give those bastards a fine send-off to hell for me," Will finished, finally taking a draw off his drink.

He swallowed slowly. Anything faster and he was certain the unease in his gut would cause him to wretch it up.

"You all think me weak, the wee one who does Father's bidding. But if those dogs catch a single odor, I'm going to scour the entire Île de Neige until I've found the thieving whoresons. And if they've whored Amber, or worse..." He took another swallow, grimacing at the taste, and shoved away from the table. "After growing up on Ballymead's fine drink, your army ale tastes like piss."

Lod cracked a smile and scrutinized William who threw back one more swallow before slapping the tankard down on the table.

"Aye. Some of my men jest that it actually *is* piss," Lod remarked, folding his arms and chuckling. "Do nay tell them I mistook the barrels in the buttery for a chamber pot last sennight."

Will grinned at the jest, his first smile in days, if only for a moment.

Chapter 11

Sebastien grabbed hold of the woman's thighs, thrusting hard against her. He tipped back his head, feeling the surge strengthen, and picked up his pace. His skin slapped hers and blast it, but the tavern wench seemed to like it. He didn't want her to like it. He didn't care much one way or another what she thought, but the last thing he wanted was a woman growing attached to him. He had work to do, her only being one of his many tasks.

"Your Majesty," she sighed, her words desperate. "Your Majesty..."

Be damned, but she didn't just like it, he was actually *pleasing* her. He could see it in the flush of her cheeks and hear it in the cries escaping her. She was pretty, he would admit it, which made the task easier, for some of the wretched peasants his men had brought him from the other kingdoms were as ugly as breeding bitches in the royal kennels.

"Your Majesty!" came a call outside his personal chamber door. He would recognize Mateo's mousy voice anywhere.

"I'm occupied!" he barked, straining to finish.

"Your Majesty, I must interrupt!"

Sebastien drove hard, taking no care if his thrusts hurt the woman, though by the sounds of her cries, he wasn't hurting her one bit. He blotted out Mateo's intrusive calls. If he tried to listen, he'd lose his stamina. Mateo wasn't who he wanted to think about when bedding a woman. His head still tipped back, he concentrated on the sensation of the wench wrapped around him, the bed ropes creaking, the heavy frame of the four-posted frame covered in blue velvet drapes jolting to the rhythm.

"Your Majesty! I've had a vision!"

"Fok off!" he barked back in the kingdom's ancient language, the wench beneath him bursting out into giggles. She might be from the Hadstadt Kingdom, but she was from the southern tip closest to Lispagne and most people, man and woman, understood many tongues.

"That's right, Your Majesty," she laughed. "Finish... I want it, you want it..."

Hell, but he didn't *want* her to want it, and yet her words drove him to the final thrust. There was something primal in knowing a man could leave a woman satisfied. He growled out a rough cry, releasing his seed, his legs shaking. How on earth had he lost his control? Why was she staring up at him as if he were God and she were about to become the next Virgin Mary? Lord, but that thought made him want to laugh, as sacrilegious as the thought was. Such terrain was probably more tilled than an ancient barley field.

Still, there was something about her gaze, her eyes, and the smile teasing her lips, that made him wish to keep her in his bed a while longer. She wasn't just pretty, she was beautiful. Rosy cheeks, soft, plump lips, luscious breasts that spilled over a man's hands, rounded hips, dark, curling hair splayed around her face.

The pounding on the door continued, a racket in his mind, followed by Mateo's frenetic calls. Anger was laced into his cries.

"My King! You must let me in to remedy your mistake!"

Pounding continued. Sebastien slumped his head down, anger welling inside him as the breeze from the arid land surrounding De Luc blew through the curtains hanging from the floor-to-ceiling windows leading out onto his veranda. The veranda overlooked the first green fields he had seen in Lispagne in years. The figures dotting them were older boys—slaves—and overseers managing them.

"My King, My King!"

"Enough!" King Fernando exploded, withdrawing from his union and bolting to his feet.

The prostitute gasped at the abruptness of the separation, left naked among his piles of linens. With the bed curtains drawn back, anyone who entered would have a full view of her. Sebastien ignored her and strode to the door, his trousers slouched below his rear and his chest bare, his softening manhood hanging free.

"Be damned you bastard, what?" he exclaimed, throwing the bar across his portal aside so that it clattered to the floor.

He wrenched back the door. Mateo shoved passed him, his eyes locked on the whore. He marched to her, reaching his gnarled hand out, grasping her throat. "She'll bear you a daughter, and that cannot happen—"

"That's exactly what I want to happen," King Fernando argued. "What are you doing?" he demanded when he realized the woman struggled for air.

He dashed after his advisor who was hunched and by all accounts a frail seer, and ripped the old man's death grip free of the woman. The woman coughed, gasping, curling on her side.

"She must not be allowed to birth your daughter!" Mateo exclaimed, his hair wild and his eyes gleaming, one dark brown, one pale green.

Sebastien shoved him back.

"You must listen to me," Mateo glowered, persisting. "This daughter, she will be tainted. She will bring your downfall."

But Sebastien shook his head. He had to admit he liked the wench, liked her on a primeval level of attraction, and come to think of it, he liked the idea of her bearing him a child. A daughter, Mateo seemed convinced.

"No, Mateo. You're my advisor, but you don't surpass me on authority. Ever."

If only you knew... came Mateo's voice snaking through the king's mind.

Sebastien shook his head, knowing the voice couldn't be real. It happened frequently, a thought, a word, as if imagining what the old seer would say in any given situation. Why, he could not explain.

"On this, I do not listen to you, you listen to me. Leave the woman alone."

"You must think on what I say," pleaded the old seer. For a moment, the king thought Mateo might fall to his knees to beg, but of course the advisor would never do that. He never even bowed. And try as King Fernando might, he couldn't see the old man terminated. His hands refused to touch quill to parchment to order his dismissal or execution, and his words would never come out of his mouth, as if his tongue was suddenly tied in knots, even though his mind pushed him to tell Mateo his services were no longer needed.

"The daughter will be tainted. She'll poison your line. She'll ruin you—"

Fernando's eyes locked with Mateo's as if he had no control over them. A feeling welled inside of him, Mateo's words again, not his own, as he stared into the old seer's face... *You know the woman should die.* It was such a strange phenomenon. *You want to strangle the woman. You should do it yourself, or allow me to finish the job. I am, after all, simply looking out for the well-being of your country,* Mateo tried to rationalize in Sebastien's mind.

"No!"

Sebastien wrenched his eyes away, feeling relief flow over him. His mind returned to his own. He liked the whore and didn't want Mateo killing her in order to kill off the child now taking root in her belly. And he certainly didn't want to kill her with his own hands either. He needed a lineage. He had several children already, and many who could be spares for his oldest son now about to turn six years, but he, King Sebastien Fernando II, would be the only man who decided which of his children lived or died, not Mateo.

Sebastien laughed, not looking back at the old advisor. "How on earth can a simple daughter be wicked enough to bring my centuries-old Lispagnioc monarchy to its knees?"

"She will. Mark my words. She'll give everything to Bain, as will Christophoro," the seer replied, standing still in the king's unrelenting grasp upon his arm. "If you haven't found your half-brother yet, you must. And the whore, she must die—"

"On this, you overstep your bounds. There's no way to determine anything about the babe you say is taking root in her womb. And if you've confirmed the whore will carry a daughter for me, 'tis only good news."

"If you believe me when I tell you it will be a daughter, then you ought believe my prediction, too," countered the old man. "For you have no way of knowing if either is true. I tried to intervene before your deed was done—"

"You expect a man to stop bedding a woman at such a moment?" Sebastien scoffed, glancing at him again. Their eyes locked once more. "Clearly you've never done it correctly if you think such is possible. I'm tired of you—"

Sebastien shook his head, fighting to push words over his lips. His tongue was knotted again. He tossed his head violently, but his choice words for Mateo wouldn't come out.

The whore was still catching her breath, holding her throat. Mateo turned his sights back on her. She shook her head, her nose running and tears leaking from her eyes. She fought to untangle her legs from the linens to crawl away from him when King Fernando reached out and clasped the old man by the back of his robe, drawing him back.

"Out." He severed eye contact again. "Or I'll be replacing you."

Mateo stood silently, staring at him, concentrating on his face, but Fernando gasped. His tongue, tied in knots moments ago, had finally said the words he'd been wanting to say. His mind reeled. He had never been able to get the words over his lips for seven whole years.

Eye contact...you always watch him, and he you. If you look away, you break the connection...he really is a magus. A seer. You must be rid of him... The words swirled in his mind and this time, they sounded like his own words, not Mateo's.

Disgust roiled through him. Remorse leached in. He could have taken control of the old man long ago had he realized his own strength. And in a blink, Mateo was gone, having disappeared into the corridor lined with silver-fringed flags and vaulted ceilings supported by buttresses. His whore was cowering in the corner with a linen dragged around her, a red hand print around her throat.

He looked at the prostitute. He liked pretty things. He'd keep her around, make her his consort, at least for the time being. It wasn't as if Bain, or the Hadstadt Kingdom, or even the Land of Spices would be offering him a bride anytime soon. Publicly, Lispagne was still shunned.

He gestured to the woman crouched in the corner, offering his hand. She took it and stood. The staff would need to rummage through his mother's old gowns to find her something acceptable. Trade was still weak. No one would do business with him, though it wasn't as if Lispagne had much to offer in the way of trade anyway. He would need to scrounge around the castle stores for what little silks and velvets he possessed so that a wardrobe could be made for her. He smiled. Maybe this daughter forming in the whore's belly would marry a Bainick son. Maybe, he thought, this would be his way to retaliate against Bain...

Another knock interrupted him. He turned to see his first in command to the Lispagnioc army, a broad man, his face bearded in a brown fringe around his jaw and trimmed into a point. Commander Marcus de Casteñeda cleared his throat and stepped out of King Fernando's line of sight, embarrassed. The woman gasped, clutching an arm around her breasts.

The king looked at the naked woman. "I've decided to make you my official mistress. For now," he muttered to her. "If you carry a daughter for me, as my advisor says, you may count on it that I'll see you taken care of, even when our liaison ends. Help me dress so I can meet with my man."

She nodded, hurrying to pull his undergarments up. She tucked his softened appendage within them and tied the laces, then drew up his trousers and did the same, tying the leather and hooking the clasps of his belt. He took up a lock of her hair, inspecting the curls between his fingertips, thinking. This woman had been abducted from the streets of Badderhaus, a port city on the southern tip of the Hadstadt. She had the air of mountain freshness about her, even though she had been nabbed by one of his men who had initiated a sard in a back alley in order to lure her away unseen.

"You swear that my henchman didn't bed you, woman?" he asked, still pondering her hair.

Disoriented by his question, she realized what he was asking and nodded. "Yes, Your Majesty. He only pretended to want me, but threw a bag over my head and dragged me away," she replied.

King Fernando II nodded, satisfied. "What are you called?"

"Gisela, Your Majesty."

He nodded again, then flicked his fingers to dismiss her. "I'll call for you again this eve. Be gone now. Casteñeda!" he called to his man as Gisela scurried for her chemise, skirt, and bodice. The hulking commander, clad in a blue surcoat bearing the silver bull and donning ceremonial jack chains down both arms, reemerged in the doorway. Unaffected by the prostitute's indisposed state, he sauntered into the chamber and appraised her backside.

"Come, to my offices, through here," King Fernando offered.

Casteñeda obliged, walking across the tile. He entered through the office door and waited with his hand upon the latch for King Fernando to pass through, then closed it. King Fernando dropped his tunic over his head.

"Why do you interrupt my afternoon, man?" the king asked, motioning for Casteñeda to help himself to a gilded tray of vinos. Considering the poor state of Lispagne's trade, the tray consisted of an extravagant selection.

There were always businessmen dispersed throughout the other kingdoms willing to sell under the table to Lispagnioc smugglers. The royal vineyards were new since his father's death, and what wine had been bottled still needed years to ferment.

Casteñeda frowned, raising a heavy brow while looking sidelong. "I assume you need a drink yourself to restore your energy after such bed sport?"

Sebastien chuckled, folded his arms, and moved to the door leading onto the veranda. From there, he could see outside and watch his commander's hands at the same time to ensure nothing other than vino was poured into both goblets. The breeze felt good.

"Indeed a whole bottle."

Casteñeda gave the rare harrumph. "That good, eh? From what I saw, such a mount looks as if she would ride well. A rare treat among the women brought here. Let me know when you're ready to discard her."

"I've just told her she is to be my mistress," Sebastien remarked, watching Casteñeda mull over his words.

Casteñeda turned around, his expression shuttered, and he paced to the king as if he hadn't said a word. He handed Sebastien the goblet. Sebastien smirked, taking it.

"Your henchmen, Sergio and Alonso, in Bain?" his commander began.

The king nodded. Wise of the man to get down to business instead, Sebastien thought, as his commander continued.

"They are attempting to return with no one. Our spies report that the pair captured you a girl who turned out to be a blind noblewoman, but that she escaped them."

Sebastien frowned, his dark hair ruffling on the balmy breeze. He took a drink before speaking, his demeanor cooling.

"How did this happen?"

Casteñeda shrugged. "Even your spy didn't see how the girl escaped, for he was too busy listening to the pair arguing. The brothers then fled westward, sailing over to Île de Neige, *sans* girl."

King Fernando tossed back the contents of his goblet and pushed away from the wall. He stalked to the sideboard and poured another goblet of the precious vino, throwing back those contents as well, as if it hadn't cost him three times as much as it should have.

"Has there been any word on my dear half-brother?"

"Christophoro?" questioned Casteñeda. "No. He seems to have disappeared. For all we know, he could have sailed to the Hadstadt. For search as your spies might, there seems to be no sign of him in Bain. He has vanished."

"Damnation," muttered Sebastien, pinching the bridge of his nose. "Boys don't just disappear."

Mateo wasn't going to be pleased, Sebastien thought. In fact, Mateo seemed more and more agitated as of late. He couldn't wait to be rid of the old man. As long as he didn't look into Mateo's eyes, he could terminate Mateo's position and blessedly be rid of the old man's voice inside his head.

He sighed, poured more wine, and gulped it down. Sweat broke out on his brow like it always did when he thought of his street urchin half-brother. Christophoro was the one favored with more attractive features and taller height. He was a natural swordsman. And damned good at hiding. Christophoro was well and truly lost. Mateo was going to hate this. Mateo might rail at him.

His sweat rolled down his temples. And then a distant thudding of boots, growing louder, sent a tremor through the flooring as a stampede neared his solar door. He and Casteñeda perked at the sound, their attention whipping toward the main doors. He marched across the chamber, wrenching open the iron hinges.

"Your advisor has fallen over!" a guardsman cried, his coat plated in squares of metal shimmering with his gait.

Sebastien furrowed his brow. "Then right him on his feet again. Idiot—"

"We cannot! He demands you come to him! He lies in the council hall. His eyes have rolled back and he shakes, he trembles!"

He's having a vision, Sebastien realized.

"Normally this happens in private," he grumbled, grabbing a coat hanging beside the door. "He rarely has visions," but they always meant something significant. "Get my accoutrements," he barked at his commander, who obliged and ran to his chests to withdraw the king's sword—no. *King Bain's* old sword, the one used to kill his father, and the one he now carried.

Fernando ran behind his guardsmen, sending a breeze upward to ruffle the flags overhead. Screaming snaked through the passageways, growing louder. They maneuvered down the hallway, down a set of winding stairs, through another corridor, and spilled through the double doors into the royal council chamber. The doors banged open. Screaming assaulted them.

Mateo lay shrieking on the floor.

"It's Christophoro!" he convulsed, writhing. "He's the blackness of death! He must be found! He must be stopped! He is in league with Prince William of Bain!"

King Fernando strode to the fallen magus and dropped down to one knee. He shook the man. Wrenched his hands away again. The old man was scalding. His palm burned to touch him.

"What do you see?"

"Christophoro! He lives! And he will kill *you*! He will kill *me*!"

Fernando listened to the nonsensical rubbish, shaking his head. "Christophoro is gone. We know not where to find him."

Mateo stilled. The shrieking stopped. His hair lay wildly across the tiles and his wrinkled face was spent. And then coolly, calmly, the old man sat up. He turned his brown eye and green eye toward the king. Fernando felt the pull and couldn't look away. Even though his body screamed at him to back up, to leave, and have the man stabbed through the heart right then and there, he couldn't utter a sound.

"He lives," Mateo said flatly. "And he will take your crown. And he will kill you. Unless you find him first."

Fernando's eyes narrowed as he tried to concentrate on the words spoken to him. Then the trance was broken. Mateo rose fluidly to his feet. Fernando also rose, then cast a look at Casteñeda. One nod was all he gave, and one nod was all that Casteñeda needed.

Find Christophoro.

Find Alonso and Sergio.

And find them fast.

Casteñeda swept from the hall, his metal flashing silver light, his cape thrown over his shoulder.

Chapter 12

The waters looked angry. Just imaging Amber on a boat, crossing the strait in weather like this, made Will's anger surge anew. He couldn't imagine the agony of drowning in such a watery hell should the boat leak or be pummeled by a massive wave and capsize. And he knew Lady Amber couldn't swim.

"I would brave the depths of the ocean if it meant making you smile..."

The rocky shore beneath them was a grey piles of stones tumbling down to the water. The dogs sniffed, tails straight, noses to the ground. And then, miraculously, one of them began circling a boulder and sniffing under a lip of stone. It sat back on its haunches, howling.

"They found something!" nearly every man exclaimed, maneuvering through the rocks.

"Christ's bones, I didn't think they would," uttered Gavin.

Conscious of his wooden stump, his shoulders aching from endless days in chain mail, William still hobbled into the lead, reaching the dogs now matted from the foul weather. There was nothing beside or around the boulder. They searched around its base, watching the dogs continue to sniff, always returning to that one spot.

"Either she was here or the men who took her were here," Lod deduced, shaking his head. "I'm afraid it might be true, that she was nabbed over to the Île de Neige. I'm sorry, Lord Edward, Will," he added, putting a hand on his youngest brother's shoulder.

William shrugged it off, turned around, and took a few slow steps, moving faster and faster, until he was striding back up the shore to the top of the slope.

This can't be real, he thought. It was unfair, unjust.

What sick-hearted man could steal a blind woman? He had plagued himself with the question as the days of searching accumulated. A blind lass couldn't escape. Was easy prey. By God, the notion made bile threaten to roll up his throat again. He swallowed it down. He had to remain composed. Rage rolled over him in red-hot waves. He wanted to hack her abductors to pieces. He was going to go on a rampage if he wasn't careful. And right now, he didn't feel like being careful. Didn't feel like being the composed, dutiful youngest son that everyone felt sorry for.

He sensed his brothers following him and turned to look. They were close at heel, pursuing him. Lord Edward remained by the boulder, gazing out at the grey waters and the sheer, impenetrable cliffs on the isle's barren shore while his sons stood beside him. Lord Loddin was following his sons, walking slowly back up to the crest, lost in thought.

"To where do you go, wee brother?" Gavin called to him as Will reached for his horse's reins.

Will stopped, holding the bridle. *Wee brother*. His brothers gathered with him, also stopping.

"Look at them. It's as if they've all given up." William spat with disgust, gesturing to Dunstonwoodshire's men. "I need a boat."

His brothers looked at him.

"'Tis too risky an endeavor, Will," Gavin replied. "They know it, and so do we."

"What would you have me do?" Will snapped. "Forget about her? Find another woman now that my eyes work and in doing so blind myself to what struggles she might be facing? Such apathy is an unbecoming shade on any man, let alone them," he gestured to Edward, Morgan, and Angus. "I won't wear it so plainly."

"What if she's been spoiled?" Gavin asked. "I mean not to diminish her person, but have you thought on that? Certainly we wish her found, but she could very well be ruined. I think we all know such is probably the case, even if she lives. Such topics are angering to discuss, wee brother. No one wants to think on it, but it's the reality."

William's eyes narrowed on Gavin, his fists balling.

"What the *bloody hell* do you think has been on my mind?" he boomed. "What *if* she has been spoiled? What of it? It might surprise you all to know your *wee* brother William has actually been betwixt a maid's legs before—" His older brothers started with surprise. "I'm not naïve. So what? If Amber's been spoiled, she hasn't been spoiled for me."

He kicked out his footless leg and slapped his thigh.

"And it's nay as if she gets a prize by any stretch. I might not aspire to be one of King Bain's favored knights like you and Lod, but I took vows upon earning my spurs and I stand by that honor. She's the one I want, and I do nay know how to make it any clearer! I doubt you know what that feels like, Gav, considering you're betrothed to a sweet lady and yet you can still be found in the villages getting a good lay when you want it."

"You bastard," Gavin retorted, stepping toe to toe with him. "How dare you claim to know how I feel about Sarah?"

"Enough, both of you," Lod intervened, shoving them apart as if they were two of his foot soldiers throwing down their gauntlets over a game of chess.

Will shoved Lod's hand off him, fuming, and jabbed a finger at Gavin. "I cannot just replace Amber with another skirt because she's been 'spoiled.'"

"And no one said you should," Hershel concurred as he raised both hands in peace. "You're right to want to do what you can to find her, and you prove to Sir Edward that he made a worthy match when he contracted his daughter to you."

Gavin, sullen, glared at William. "But we don't have a boat."

"But I do," Lod said, glancing at Will whose eyes shot to him. "I command Fort Michaelmas," he shrugged. "I have not one but four knarrs. But rest assured, Father won't like what you're scheming," Lod remarked.

"No. He'll nay like it at all," Hershel agreed. "He'll say it's too risky considering your lack of experience manning a vessel on your injured leg."

"Father can kindly stick his advice where Ballymead's sun doesn't shine," Will bit out. Lod chuckled, Hershel smiled, and Gavin, still angered, couldn't help but lift the corner of his mouth. "If this had been Mother missing, you can bet your arse he never would have quit. And in case none of you can count, I've five and twenty years on me. Hardly a 'wee lad' anymore. I make this decision of my own accord."

"So *wee William* has a dangerous side," Lod remarked as they watched their father coming closer, eyeing their obvious altercation. "You may use a boat, but I cannot leave my post to travel with you and keep your sorry arse from drowning. I need royal permission to leave. But my knarrs are marked, bearing the Bainick Lion, and I dare say they're notable. The cover of night is the only time to use them without being seen, though you'll never be able to handle the task by yourself."

"He'll have Gavin and me," Hershel stated, stepping beside Will and glaring at Gavin to do the same as he gave Will a nod of solidarity.

"Good," Lod agreed. "Mayhap the three of you could slip out soon, for indeed father will launch objections."

William nodded as their father approached.

"What are four of my five lads doing, standing about so?" Lord Loddin demanded, his eyes narrowed. "Conspiring?"

"Discussing," Will replied.

"Discussing what? More like scheming...and arguing."

All the Ballymead sons remained silent, as if lads lining up to hear their father's lecture. Lod shot quick glances at them to hurry up a confession so they could all move on, bowing out of the exchange.

"William and I had a misunderstanding, Father," Gavin finally offered, still glaring at William with his dark eyes. "But we've reconciled."

Lord Loddin looked at the black glares exchanged between William and Gavin, and shook his head. "Aye, most certainly," he grumbled. "Get ye back to the fort, lads. Edward and I agree we ought take a break from the search and discuss recourse to the crown instead."

"Why not borrow one of the boats from Fort Michaelmas?" Will asked, testing.

"Way too dangerous, those waters." Lord Loddin denied them with a slice of his hand. "Out of the question. What makes you think you could man a craft, William? You're young, lack experience, not to mention your leg is maimed." The brothers shared a look. Indeed their father had reacted exactly as Hershel had said he would. "And besides, Edward wishes to speak to you. He's coming to realize his lass might forever be gone and whether you like the idea or nay, he is going to sever your contract and free you to find another when you wish it."

"What?" William exclaimed. "You're jesting, correct?"

Lord Loddin tried to decipher his meaning. "Nay, I'm not. He realizes if he keeps you contracted, you might never have the chance to move forward and build a life. Now that your sight returns, you have other prospects. He's doing you a favor, even if you can't see it in your grief. You can still offer your aid to him to help find the lass, but if we're realistic about finding her whole and healthy—"

William was shaking his head, searching for something to say. "I have no words...I'm nay in the mood for this."

He turned to his saddle, readying to mount, but Lord Loddin stayed his son, taking his arm. "Think on it. It's wise to consider. We've searched for over a fortnight now. Of course he'll continue to look high and low, and the crown will have gotten his missive by now. But he's also realistic. Dear as she was to him, Edward knows at this point that Amber is likely lost."

"She's nay dear to him," muttered William. "She's *useful* to him. But he'd rather shuffle her off on Sarah than help her himself." He pointed to where Edward still stood, gazing wistfully out to sea. "My point proven. A fortnight and he wants to beg recourse to the crown already? Do you remember doing such when Gwenyth was missing? That's not what I remember. I remember begging her return the entire time she was married to that pig from Dwyre, and when she went missing, I do nay recall ever tossing in the flag and claiming defeat."

All the men stood still.

William looked down at his father's gauntlet gripping his upper arm, and shook his head. "Can you imagine if he did find her, and she returned home to learn that her fiancé'd abandoned her? You boast of wanting grandchildren, but might I add that none of us are prized stallions whose job it is to impregnate the mares with your line. I wait for Lady Amber, as she has waited for me, and won't apologize for it, even if it leaves you with wee Hershel as your sole grandchild. Honestly. Mother would be disgusted with you."

Lord Loddin actually smarted. Never had one of his sons insulted him so. William shrugged his arm free of his father's hand and hoisted himself into the saddle, turning the reins south toward Fort Michaelmas. The lord's eyes flashed angrily and he strode to his horse to follow him, when Hershel stepped in his path.

"Leave him be, Father," he suggested. "Let him blow off his steam. He has a broken heart. Do you still not recognize the affection he holds for Lady Amber? He cares nay about her eyes, but he did his own, for it was with a working body he would provide for a wife. You know he's felt less of a man for it, and I fear you continue to treat him as such."

Lord Loddin frowned, eyeing his three remaining sons. "Have I done so?"

They all looked at each other, grown men in their own right, and yet still afraid of offending their father, then nodded in unison.

"We all have, I fear," Hershel added.

Lord Loddin sighed and scoured his face with his gauntlets, the links holding the metal plates to the leather catching in his grey beard.

"Can you nay see how your suggestion to him, to break his betrothal, might have been ill-timed?" Hershel persisted.

Lord Loddin nodded with another resigning sigh. "All right. I'll give him breathing room. Gwenyth once told me he fancied Amber and I know since then he's admitted such, but I suppose I never realized how deeply he felt for her."

"He loves her," Hershel stated. "She wasn't just a pretty skirt to which he was betrothed."

"He's grappling with her loss, Father," Lod said. "He's not ready to accept that she might be dead. But as much as I wish I could stay with my family, I have duties to attend. Prince William is due to arrive in mere days to inspect the holding and deliver newly-crafted helmets. In spite of Amber's disappearance, I must work with my men."

Lord Loddin nodded at his namesake and mounted up, beginning the journey back to the fort. Gavin and Hershel did so too, trotting to catch up with Lod. When their father was well behind, Gavin finally conceded to Hershel.

"I suppose your words for Father were also for me," Gavin muttered. "'Twas poor timing to suggest Amber spoiled, wasn't it?"

Hershel shot him a sidelong glance, wind whipping rain and splattering their faces as they trotted. "Thinks you this just now?"

"I didn't mean spoiled as in, 'no good'," Gavin defended. "I just meant that if she's been raped, she might be put off to men now."

"My advice, Gav, is simply to keep your thoughts on women to yourself. Such comments, coming from a man who has *spoiled* his fair share of the fairer sex, aren't helpful," Hershel retorted.

The rains made the ride back to the fort slow and wretched, but finally, as dusk set in, Hershel and Gavin dismounted in the yard. They passed off their horses to a groom who had dashed out to collect them.

"Hey," they heard Lod call out, motioning them to a corner beneath the wall walk and behind a ladder.

They furrowed their brow, but followed their oldest brother's summons and disappeared into the shadows just as Lord Loddin trotted his mount into the bailey. Their sire dismounted and limped toward the tavern. Supper was underway.

"I'm ordering a knarr out to the dock for William, to leave after nightfall after Father has retired. Go with Will, both of you. His cause is noble, but no man can staff the boat alone on the strait, lame leg or nay. You'll need to steer the vessel over open waters in the dark of night, and though the moon is nearly a full one, the clouds will make going it treacherous. You'll need to go up the coast about two miles to hit the beaches beneath the cliffs. 'Tis up there that the nabbers likely made landfall. You'll have some basic supplies and dried foods. I'll inform Prince William upon his arrival and will offer for Ballymead to cover the cost of the knarr should he question it. My guess is he won't, however, for Gwenyth would never let him hear the end of it."

"A perk, I suppose, being married into royalty," Gavin jested. "Our sister has the future king of the realm wrapped around her finger."

"Father won't be pleased when he learns you helped Will," Hershel scolded. "Do you have a ready excuse?"

"What would you have me do, Hersh?" Lod complained.

Hershel shrugged. "What you're doing. All the same, he's going to think his sons conspired against him and will fear his lineage is about to be wiped out by the sea."

"I'll handle Father," Loddin replied. He looked them both in the eyes, his next words spoken with conviction. "Will needs to do this. He's never gotten to prove himself, what with his lame leg and his bad eyes. This isn't just about the Lady Amber. This is a test of his manhood and his honor for the woman he claims to love. A rite of passage all men of honor must endure, for I did with Mary, for certain, and you, Hersh, did so with your wife as well."

They both glanced at Gavin, but said nothing.

Gavin huffed and rolled his eyes. "I know you're thinking ill of me. So what, I like women," he dismissed. "And so, we'll meet where and at what time tonight?"

Lod shook his head. "The boat will be ready within the hour, down through the side gates to the port, outfitted with supplies. A guard will let you pass. You, Hersh, and Will can leave at your leisure after that." Lod put a hand on each of his younger brothers' shoulders and squeezed. "Safe travels and God speed. Try to be back within a fortnight, or else I fear I too will grow unnerved. Whether we're prized breeding stallions to Ballymead or nay," he jested, cracking a smile at Will's expense despite his absence. "I fear Father will die of a broken heart if three of his spares perish in the same instant. The waters in the strait churn angrily. I love you, my brothers."

Hershel and Gavin both leaned in to embrace their oldest brother and slap him on the back as he did them. Then all three slipped out from under the brattice, back into the yard, and went to eat their supper.

Chapter 13

"Wait here, my lady," the young man said to Amber. The morning air was crisp and the rains continued to lap at their faces and hair. "You've no cause to flee again, I promise."

The young man slowed his horse, halted, and swung his leg over the pommel to avoid kicking her.

"I'll trust that you help me," was all Amber said, her fingers clenching the cantle of the saddle.

Nearby, a dove cooed. Her ears perked and her brow furrowed. The weather was chilly, blustery, and wet. Not the weather for a dove to be out on what felt like a vast, upland plain whipping with wind as a river rushed nearby. Was she imagining it? Of course she was. The howling of the wind was so intense, it had to be her mind playing tricks.

"You kept them all."

William's voice snaked through her memory. He had been so awed that she had treasured each trinket. Her heart ached. But she was free of her captors. She smiled. She wasn't dead or raped or nabbed all the way to Lispagne. She would be marrying him, even if her longing for him right now was unbearable. If only the idea of being left in a remote monastery didn't give her such an uncomfortable feeling.

The wind continued to whip her curling hair into more disarray. She tossed her head to the side so that it blew free of her nose and forehead. She tried to hear the young man as he conversed with the priest.

***

Christophoro walked along the pavers embedded in the grasses and knocked upon the monastery door. Two unlit torches sat ensconced on either side within metal grates designed to block the wind at night. He waited, tossing glances back at Amber draped in her long cloak. At long last, the latch on the ancient wood clanked and the door was drawn back.

"Good day to you, lad," Father Crispen greeted, his brow knitted. He furrowed it further, looking past the young man to see the female perched pillion behind the saddle.

"And to you, Father," Christophoro dipped his head.

"To what do I owe this untimed visit?" Father Crispen asked, stepping outside and closing the door. "Are you expecting another missive? For none have come."

"No, Father. I bring a young woman from Dunstonwoodshire. She's blinded and lost her way in the forest."

"From the *fief* Dunstonwoodshire?" questioned the priest, a tall man as thin as a fence rail with kindly eyes, sunken cheeks, and closely cropped ginger hair. "Why, that is far southeast of here, nearly on the other fork of the Bainick continent."

Christophoro bowed his head respectfully to explain.

"'Tis indeed," he acknowledged. "She claims she was abducted by strangers. She's a long way from home and I believe her claims to be truthful, but I cannot take her on such a long voyage home myself. I had hoped to leave her here," he continued, beseeching the holy man's moral conscience. "I might be young, but I'm not incapable... I would hate for her reputation to be ruined." Of course he would never dishonor her. He contained more honor in one tiny part of his ring finger than Lispagne's whoreson of a king did. "Besides, I have little to offer her, in both food and shelter. Only one pallet for us to share—"

"Have you preserved her purity, my son?"

"Of course, Father. As far as I'm aware, she remains untouched."

"But you said she was kidnapped?" Crispen continued. "Surely her assailants have done something. Did she disclose any encounters with them to you?"

The young man shook his head. He knew Alonso and Sergio wouldn't have risked disembowelment and other tortures at the hands of King Fernando II simply to have a go at the woman.

"She seems most naïve and managed to escape them before anything of that nature could transpire." *Indeed, she was intended for a harem*, he thought. "She's also a betrothed woman. Perchance you can pen a missive to her father, Edward of Dunstonwoodshire, and one to her future husband, William of Ballymead, to be passed to the next messenger who comes to your door?"

Father Crispen gazed at the young lady atop the horse. "I have woefully little space, lad, and only one cell unoccupied. We use it to store extra grain given us by the crown in quarterly disbursements. A nunnery would be a much better alternative."

"Pity the Cambrian Forest seems to be fresh out of those, Father, as you well know," Christophoro argued. "Surely you cannot in good conscience allow the lass to stay in the custody of an unmarried man, however young I am. I fear one thing will lead to another, and we could both bear a massive sin on our immortal souls."

Father Crispen seemed to find his argument compelling. "I suppose we could make room for the fledgling. Go and fetch her. I'll have Brothers Daniel and Albert prepare a cot for her."

He thanked the priest and returned up the overgrown pavers.

"Good news, my lady. Father Crispen prepares a bed for you. He has agreed to house you and send word to your relations when the next messenger comes this way."

"That could be some time from now," Amber shivered. "I might not be able to see it, but I can feel the barrenness of these surroundings. We're far away from any villages, aren't we?"

There was the rushing of the River Fetch too, the stone foundation of the thatched, plastered monastery dropping off to the raging mountain rapids below.

"Yes, several days' ride," he replied, reaching to her waist to help her down.

***

Amber gripped his shoulders as he lowered her, and she felt confirmation of her suspicions. His shoulders, while padded with a gambeson and jerkin, were quite young. He was probably as young as he had claimed, which made his hiding in the woods even more peculiar.

"But it's safer for you here, and Father Crispen is a kindly man of the cloth. He'll see to your basic needs until someone can be sent to fetch you home."

She suddenly trusted the young man much more than she cared to admit and clenched his shoulders, yet released him quickly so as not to be construed as inappropriate.

"Are you well?" he asked.

"Aye...just, eh, weary. My thanks for all your help, sir."

"You're most welcome, my lady," he replied, taking her hand

and walking her to the door.

"Welcome, my lady," Father Crispen said, taking her hand from the young man. "I'm Father Crispen, the priest of this small and humble monastery. And what name might I call you?"

"Lady Amber of Dunstonwoodshire," she replied, curtseying.

"Do come inside, and I'll take you to a cell. It's small, and I fear it's somewhat of a storage chamber, but we're clearing some space for you as we speak."

"Fare thee well, my lady," the young man said, remaining outside the threshold.

She turned to his voice, but felt the shadow of the door closing upon her. The door latched shut. The hall smelled clean and echoed with the soft shuffling of sandals, what she could only assume were monks. *They're men of faith*, she told herself, trying to ease the discomfort in her stomach and slow her speeding pulse. But they were still men. And she was now alone with them. She panicked.

"I...I've changed my mind, Father," she whispered. "I should like to return with the man who brought me and await my father from his cottage."

"I'm afraid I cannot allow it," Crispen replied kindly. "He begs a safe haven for you, and did right to come to us. A messenger carries letters here frequently, news of court and changes to church rules, oh, I'd say every month. It's already been a fortnight since the last missive from the capital. I'm certain someone will ride this way soon enough. Come. You no doubt would like a bath and a comb."

He led her straight ahead, holding her hand to guide her. She trembled and fought back the urge to cry as the monastery swallowed her within. At the end of the corridor, the priest led her around a corner and walked her to a door. *Forty-two steps*, she counted. She sensed people passing her, breezing through a doorway, and heard water sloshing into a wooden tub.

"This is your chamber," he explained. "Straight ahead is a cot, a table, and a bible, should you wish to hold it whilst you pray. Mind the tub just in front of you lest you trip. A drying cloth has been placed upon your mat and no doubt you'll wish to wash your skirts as well. We haven't a comb for a lady, so you'll accept our apologies for the comb we keep in the byre for our nag. It's all we have to offer you."

She took a deep breath as more monks breezed by, as more water sloshed.

"You'll hear the bells toll the Vespers, and late tonight, the Compline hours. Otherwise, it should remain quiet, as the brothers maintain a vow of silence in recognition of St. Mithin's Day and will remain as such for a fortnight more. Supper is being prepared for you and after Compline, the cell doors remain locked until Matins, after which, someone will come to escort you to break your fast in our humble hall. Until Compline, I suggest you bar your door from the inside to secure your person further. Good eve, my lady."

She felt him leave, monks continuing to breeze in and out as the tub was slowly filled. She shivered and wrapped a hand around her stomach, when a monk brushed against her. She stepped back to move out of his way, feeling the open door at her back. A moment later, however, he brushed against her again, a hand grazing her arm as he went. A prickle of wariness stood her hair on end. Gooseflesh rose on her arms.

She pulled her cloak more tightly around her, dismissing it as an accident. She was stressed and exhausted. Her nerves were frayed. Certainly she was looking for mal intent where there was none.

At long last the sound of footsteps cleared from the room and receded down the hall. She pushed shut the door, finding the bar Father Crispen had spoken of beside it, and placed it across the wooden hooks embedded in both the door and the plastered wall. She let out a shaking sigh of relief at the privacy, wishing she could break free from the already stifling walls.

Turning, she took a careful step, then another, until her toes touched the tub. She bent down and felt the water. It was blessedly hot.

Maneuvering around the tub, she continued careful steps until she reached the cot. She patted up and down the sheet until she found the drying linen and comb. She exhaled and clutched the comb to her chest as if it were a golden treasure.

Her hair was so helpless now, so knotted, she feared she would need to shear the beautiful tresses, a humiliation for any lady. Who on God's green earth would care that the comb at her breast was used on a horse when they were so desperate?

She set it back down and began undressing, removing her cloak first before untying her bodice lacing. It was good indeed she had worn such a practical gown the day of her abduction, she thought wryly. Once her filthy bodice and skirts were stripped, she dumped them into the tub, doing the same to the chemise so that she was bare. She shivered in the dank cell, gooseflesh rising on her skin, and grabbed the soap before followed her clothing into the tub.

Dunking her hair beneath the surface, she rose out of the

water, her chest rolling up like a water nymph. It felt so good, so hot, despite her unease in her new surroundings. She rubbed the soap across her breasts, her arms, her pits, and stood to get her nether parts duly cleaned, then took the soap to the monumental task of cleansing and sorting through her tangled hair hanging water-logged and heavy past her buttocks.

She stilled. Listened to her surroundings. It was a strange place with its own foreign sounds, sounds she didn't yet know, but she was certain she had heard a rustling of fabric.

Nothing. No sound.

She eased herself back down and began scrubbing her hair, trying to relax her agitated mind, and secretly thought of her stolen moments with William. It was a sin, she knew, for they weren't married yet. But the times he had embraced her and offered her gentle strokes of his tongue against hers soothed her now. And that afternoon, in her work chamber, when she had felt his burgeoning arousal through his clothing as he wedged himself against her core... *"How am I supposed to wait three more bloody months?"*

Blush raged across her face as she remembered his words. She paused in her soaping. The heat, the need to squirm that had plagued her as William braced himself between her legs, had felt so wonderful and frustrating. And then a wave of sadness hit her.

"William," she stated aloud, as if saying his name would give voice to the hollowness inside her.

She knew he was sensitive about his missing foot, but how in the world could she care about something so unimportant when his arms could hold her so warmly? She shouldn't be so wanton for her wedding night, but she had every confidence it would be one of the best nights of her life.

Surely Will knew by now that she was missing. And now that she was delivered from Alonso and his fellow, it was only a matter of time until she was found. Her wedding, no doubt, would continue as planned. She smiled.

The sound of fabric shifting came again as she dawdled in the water.

She froze. The shifting had been ever so slight, and was that...breathing? She bolted to her feet, water sluicing off of her. The smell of candle smoke lingered in the air when the smell hadn't been there before. It was the smell of a tallow candle being blown out. She knew. She worked with beef tallow every day making soap.

"Who—who goes there?" she asked, her voice wavering as she

climbed out of the tub, feeling for the drying cloth.

She whipped the linen around her, huddling within it.

No answer came.

Wrapped within her cloth, she stepped to the door and felt the bar across it. Still locked. She turned about and walked to the opposite corner, a portion of the cell she hadn't explored yet, and it only took her a few steps to reach a stack of bags containing grains. Goodness, but her entire chamber couldn't be more than eight feet by eight feet. And then she heard more rustling and jumped as a mouse scurried across her hand and burrowed between the sacks.

She exhaled shakily. Her imagination was playing tricks on her, fueling her fear. She needed sound sleep and more food. *A mouse? Sakes, I'm acting like a babe, envisioning the worst sort of intruder.*

But her door was still locked and the culprit of the noise, a mouse for God's sake, had shaken her so badly she had lost all reason. She returned to the cot, dripping, and removed the linen, bending to towel off her feet and legs, then her stomach and breasts, then her arms and back, then her hair, tying the linen around her torso.

She proceeded to scrub her gown, ruined as it was, and found a cloak hook on the wall where she hung it to wring it out. She did the same to her chemise and undergarments. The floor was sopping, but there was nothing to be done about it. She took the horse comb to her hair and held the ends, working meticulously through the knots, until at long last, the tangles were combed free. "'Twill be a frizzed disaster after this," she sighed aloud, but at least it could be salvaged.

A knock came on her door.

"It's Father Crispen," came the voice. "I have a late supper for you, lady, and the brothers have returned to empty the tub and remove it."

She blushed brightly enough to light up what she sensed was a pitch black room. She was sitting upon her bed, stripped bare except for her drying cloth.

"One moment!" she called, scrambling for her cloak and wrapping it about her naked shoulders, clenching it closed at the throat.

She walked to the door, more confident in the room's placement now, and reached to the bar across it. Nothing was there. She patted her hand across it again, feeling alarm surge anew in her blood. She had barred the door. She had double checked. Grabbing the metal loop, she dragged open the door, her face ashen.

"The bar," she blurted out.

"Pardon?" asked the priest.

"The bar, where is the bar? I had the door barred."

"It's right here, lady," Father Crispen replied, leaning down and picking it up from its resting place. "Just where it was when I left you last."

He handed it to her. She sensed a fond smile with his words. She could feel the heat of the candle he held.

"No..." she shook her head.

She backed up, sensing a monk enter once again and smelling fresh broth in the air as he set down a tray upon the side table.

"Are you well, Lady?" asked Crispen.

"Nay," she snapped, her other hand now sliding up to cover her mouth. "I barred the door."

Crispen chuckled. "Clearly no, for the wood was by the door. Perhaps in your confusion you thought you did?"

"Nay," she insisted. "I thought I heard something and came back to the door to double check. Someone was in my chamber...I..." She lost her string of thought, took another step back, and fought dizziness. Then her mind went black.

She fainted, crumpling to the floor.

***

"Tie it down, Will!" hollered Gavin over the wind, feeling the knarr lurch as waves tossed it.

William dragged the sail rigging, his damned peg of a foot getting caught in the coil on deck and tripping him as the vessel popped off the thrust of another wave. They fought to retain control. There was no telling where they were in relation to the shore. Pray they weren't being ferried down the strait and out to sea.

The sail yanked violently on the wind. Will's sheet slackened as the spar swiveled on the mast and slammed into his midsection. He toppled backward, his head slamming on the planks while Gavin fought with all his might to control the sheets tethered to the other corner. Despite the moment's urgency, Will grabbed his head and blinked his eyes, ensuring he hadn't ruined his vision once again.

"To the left, Hersh!" Gavin grunted, ordering Hershel to adjust the rudder. Of the three of them, Gavin had the most experience sailing from his military training.

"'Tis pointless!" hollered Hershel. "Unless you control that damned sail, the rudder won't do shite!"

Both Will and Gavin stared at Hershel. It must indeed be pointless for their pious brother to curse *twice*. The boat tossed again, dipping sideways. All three brothers clung to the rail to keep from falling overboard. Proficient swimmers or not, they would die an agonizing death in these choppy waters.

And somehow, through the chaos, the boat ran aground. It took them a moment to realize that the knarr was beached, as if an almighty wave guided by a divine hand had given them a blessed boost. They tossed ropes over the bow, scrambled over the rail, and jumped into the shallows that lapped around their legs. They dragged the craft ashore as William struggled to keep his peg from sinking into the sand.

There would be time in the morning to stow the craft properly. Right now, fatigue threatened to make them collapse. They hiked up the shore to where the sheer cliffs blocked the gales and dropped in the sand, their chests heaving and their Ballymead surcoats drenched. William flopped backward. Their breathing slowed, and in spite of the rain, the three of them fell asleep where they lay.

***

Sunlight woke William first. Light blazed down on them and his skin was burning. His hair ruffled on a gentle breeze. He blinked open, staring at the first clear sky that they had seen in a fortnight. Gulls bleated out their calls as they floated upon the air, scouring the beach for food.

He looked down to see all his limbs were intact, his stump aching, then glanced to his left and saw his older brothers still asleep, Hershel upon his side, Gavin, with the obvious morning stiffness that plagued many a man upon waking pushing his clothing into a tent upon his lap. William groaned and sat up, shaking his head. If they weren't here on such a dire quest, Gavin's state would be of humor.

He rolled his shoulders, easing the stiffness in his joints, and looked around. Their knarr was lying tipped to one side in the sand, the square sail having come untethered and flapping freely on the breeze in all its wine and black splendor. They needed to hand in the blasted thing so as not to advertise their arrival to any spies observing them. They might already have been spotted.

The water had receded out with the tide, and – bless it! The Bainick shore was visible on the other side of the strait. Will shoved to his foot and peg, groaning again, and limping onto his good foot to ease the burden. Reaching down to rub the tender flesh where his nub met his peg, he sucked in air. It hurt, dammit, though he knew if he looked at it, he wouldn't like what he saw. Normally he relieved himself of the false appendage when he slept but since starting this expedition, he had been remiss.

You'll pay a price for this, his conscience whispered. He ignored it. There wasn't time for such a diversion.

Scanning the opposite shore, a brown speck on the top of the rocky banks sat well to the north of them. Fort Michaelmas. He smiled. They were likely a couple miles south of it, the opposite direction they needed to travel, but not nearly off course the way they'd thought after tacking through the wind in the dark of night.

"Wake, brothers," he said, bending down to nudge Hershel's shoulder. His cheek was burning in the stark midmorning sun.

Hershel rubbed his eyes and sat up.

"You too, Gavin," William added, poking his midsection with his wooden peg. God, but his stump ached. "We've only drifted a short ways off course. Look. The fort," he pointed as Gavin sat up and rubbed the sun from his eyes.

"Be damned," Gavin groaned, squinting. "I've a worse headache than any other morn following a night of merriment." He scoured his hands over his face. "What's worse, I didn't get to enjoy any drunkenness to make the headache worth it."

Hershel chuckled. "You just might get drunk, Gavin, as might I, when we return from this hellish voyage."

Both brothers looked at Hershel. He had actually jested. He had actually chuckled. Such humor was usually absent on Hershel's lips since the death of his wife. Even before then, he was the least likely of any of Lord Loddin's sons to laugh freely, for their puritanical sibling considered it a show of poor discipline for a pious man.

"Ah, Hershel, my churchman brother. 'Tis a laugh I thought I heard escape you," Gavin teased.

Hershel scowled and pushed to his feet. "Don't get used to it. I'm obviously feeling out of sorts."

Another jest. William's frustration over Amber kept him from laughing, but a fleeting smile graced his lips.

"So all we needed to do was give you a valiant cause to fight for and peel you away from the monks to get you to loosen those undergarments pinching the stick up your arse," Gavin teased, unaffected by the punch he received to his arm in reply. He grinned. "Ah, Hersh, I care not that you're a fair inch taller than me. You're still my younger brother and I can piss on your good mood if I choose."

"As much as your fraternal bonding charms me, the sails need to be furled," William interrupted. "I fear we're declaring Bainick intrusion on these very shores."

"Aye, and better that we stow the knarr out of public eye.

Come," Gavin motioned. "When I toured the island with the army, we came to study the coast line with Prince William's chief cartographer. If memory serves me, there is a cove down yonder. 'Twill increase our hike northward by a mile or so, but might be worth the peace of mind."

"Let's get going," William called over his shoulder, walking back down the beach to the stranded vessel. "Amber isn't going to save herself."

"Assuming she's even here," Hershel reminded him as he and Gavin jogged to catch up and step in line with their youngest brother. "Remember, you might also be on a fool's errand. We know nay if the smell the hounds' found yesterday was even hers or if it was just the same smell as someone else they sensed at the abandoned hut. She might be in Bain somewhere."

"She might also be dead somewhere," William stated the obvious, not looking at either brother but slowing his walk to look out at the gentle waves that belied the torrent of the night before. He rested his hands on his hips, feeling the crushing weight of her disappearance as he gazed at the sparkling waters. And then a horrifying thought entered his mind, causing his breathing to shake as he clenched his jaw.

"What if she fled on purpose?"

"What?" Hershel scoffed. "Why would she?"

William shook his head and closed his eyes. "What if she decided she couldn't marry me and her father refused to allow her to break our agreement?"

Even Gavin, not prone to sentiments of love, scoffed. "You worry yourself overmuch, man," he remarked, draping a firm arm over William's shoulders to shake him. "Are you daft? She adores you. We could see it clear as you can see the day. For my life, I cannot figure out what a fetching lass such as Amber sees in a cur like you," he jabbed, "but it's clear to me she wishes to submit to you as your woman. Your mind is playing tricks on you, man." He released William's shoulder and gave his head a shove so he lurched sideways. "Nay succumb to the desperation."

Hershel nodded. "Gavin's right...for a change." He shot a sidelong glance at Gavin walking on William's other side. "Stop thinking untrue things because your heart is heavy. If Lady Amber is alive, I've no doubt you'll find her and that she'll be all the more pleased for it."

If Lady Amber is alive. The words tolled in Will's mind. If she was alive. But what if she wasn't and he never found her body? He would never know if she was truly dead.

The three of them arrived at the vessel lounging on the sand. Hershel climbed inside and opened the hatch to the lower deck. Their belongings had been tossed about like a princess flinging gowns from her wardrobe.

"Ah, Gav, your prized broad sword has a scratch across the blade, man," Hershel announced.

"What?" Gavin exclaimed, hoisting himself up the rope and over the rail to inspect his equipment. "Christ," he muttered, running his thumb over a scrape that tarnished the blade all the way to the tang where the hand guard had deflected further damage. Hershel rummaged some more, handing up a crate and holding it aloft while Gavin turned the sword over to scrutinize the other side.

"Gavin," Hershel cleared his throat. "Cry tears for your metal phallus another day. We need to eat and move on."

Gavin set aside his sword, took the crate of food, and passed it over the rail to William. Taking the bar that was then handed down, William pried up the lid and tossed the slats of wood aside as his brothers jumped back down.

"I'm famished, man. Pray the food isn't a crumpled mess too," Gavin muttered, and Will handed out a loaf of bread, some bruised apples, and withdrew some salted meat.

William tore off a chunk of bread for each and they used their knives to slice off chunks of apples.

All three devoured the meager feast where they stood. Having deprived himself of a proper meal for over a fortnight, Will's stomach rumbled as the food hit it. Hershel passed around a jug of watered ale, all three consuming their fill. Nourished, they prepared for the daunting task of navigating the knarr into the shallows and sailing down the coast.

They shoved the vessel into the water again. Climbing up the ropes aboard, they took to hugging the coast to stow the knarr and begin their long hike.

***

The knarr was safely tethered within a towering cove. Will and his brothers ascended a tumble of rocks. It was dark within the consuming walls of the cliff, which loomed so high above them they almost appeared to touch overhead, leaving only a crevice of light. With packs laden with food stuffs strapped to their backs, daggers secured around their bodies, and swords sheathed upon their belts, the brothers began hiking around the base of the cliff, aiming for sunlight at the end of the cove that would deliver them into the open air.

"Father is no doubt furious right now," Gavin smirked.

"Father has a right to be angry," Hershel said.

"What's done is done, and God willing, we'll be bringing my betrothed back to Bain soon," Will reaffirmed. *And I'll be handfasting myself to the lass on sight,* he thought. He couldn't bear the thought of losing her again after waiting so long to have her. He couldn't bear the thought of losing out on all the memories that they had yet to make together.

His thoughts drifted to that very first reunion when their fathers had pushed them together. She was nervous, and he knew without being able to see it, that both their families watched their clumsy interaction from across the Ballymead great hall. He had been offered a betrothal. He had never thought such would happen to him.

"I hope it's not too bold of me to say that I'm pleased by it... if you are," he had told her.

"Oh, my lord, I'm pleased."

He had pressed her hand to his mouth at the eagerness of her response. Her hand had smelled so sweet despite the long voyage from Dunstonwoodshire to Ballymead. Like berries and cream. He had been unaware at the time that he was enjoying the scent of her handmade soap.

His head swam with the scent now as he reminisced.

"I have no eyes like I used to have, lady," he whispered. *"And my leg is gone. Why would you consider me?"* I'm more worthless than a lame horse, he had thought at the time.

Except Amber had squeezed his hand in reassurance. *"Is it true that you lost them fighting for your sister?"*

"Aye, 'tis true." He closed his eyes now, remembering the pain of his leg being sawed off, the agony, the thunder that had escaped his lungs... God, there had been no pain like it. Except the pain in his heart, knowing his wee sister and dear friend could be gone forever. That was the worst pain he had ever endured. Until now. *"There's not much left to like."*

"Oh, but sir, there is. You would lay down your life for a woman without a thought and that's noble, and, well..." She had faltered on her words. *"'Tis romantic. I should only wish that you—I mean, that a man would do that for me."*

She would wish him to come to the ends of the earth for her. The memories bolstered his faltering strength now. He couldn't fail her. He had to maintain his waning strength. There would be no stopping to reevaluate as Lord Edward was doing. Not for him.

He smiled now, remembering the newness of the emotions he had felt at that first meeting, man to woman, no longer a lass. He had wanted to touch her so much and had run his fingers over her features, learning the shape of her through his fingertips and sense of smell. It was the single most intimate experience of his life up to then. Until, of course, he had her to himself in the meadery, then alone in her work chamber where his reservation had finally snapped.

He had relived their betrothal visit over and over again in his mind since it happened. But with her lost, possibly dead, he had tried so hard not to think on it. Such a memory could ruin a man's resolve. But right now, with the sun beating down on him as he trudged up the sandy shore, it strengthened his fortitude. Even if she was dead, he hoped to never forget her. Eventually the pain would subside and remembering her in such a way would be a pleasure only he could enjoy.

***

They had walked for hours. The sun was dipping low on the horizon, illuminating the dark waters with silvery ripples. The occasional screech of a gull punctuated the rush of waves lapping the sand. The tide was rolling in, bringing fog with it that eventually blocked the sunlight and turned the sky grey.

"How are we to determine where the balinger came ashore when we cannot even see where we are in relation to the Bainick coast?" Hershel remarked.

The three men stopped and all began to look around. Soon they would need to make camp, and if more rain came with the fog, they risked losing every clue that their quarry had left behind.

"I'd say we're about a couple miles north of the fort," Will deduced, glancing to the cliffs at their left. "If they came ashore anywhere on this stretch, then they would need a way to climb to the top. Either they scaled this cliff—not likely," he added, "or there's a way up, a break in the cliff, stairs, something."

Gavin examined the cliff as well. "They had to hide their balinger somewhere. We ought to begin examining the shore for inlets or—"

"Or breaks in the cliff side," William interrupted, pointing ahead of them. "See that vertical line on the rock face up ahead?"

His older brothers squinted. "I hardly see it," said Hershel. "The fog thickens."

"It looks like a striation in the rocks, but in fact, I wonder if it's a break in the cliff," Will suggested.

Gavin shrugged, nodding. "It might be. Hard to tell from this angle. We need to get closer."

"If indeed it's an inlet, it might make a good place to camp for the night too," Hershel remarked.

They began hiking once again, hugging close to the wall where the sand gave way to rocky gravel, easier to walk upon. Will swallowed the winces that accompanied putting weight on his peg. He hadn't ever exerted so much continuous pressure on his stump. He gritted his teeth, forcing his face to remain impassive, knowing he was sweating more than usual. If his brothers noticed he struggled, they'd force him to stop and coddle the appendage.

The crevice William had spotted grew larger, but darkness was falling quickly. Finally, they began rounding the edge of the cliff. It opened into a finger-thin crevice filling with water as the tide rose. And deep within, beached, was a plain, beige balinger.

"Our quarry's boat, lads." Gavin grinned.

Weary and worn, William and Hershel smiled back. It was unmarked, abandoned, and tethered to a metal loop hammered into a boulder that had long ago tumbled down from above.

William dropped his pack, loosening the ties, and pulled out a candle. Jamming it into the ground, he withdrew a flint and an oil-soaked cord of wick. He cracked the flint until a spark took hold of the wick. Holding the burning rope to the candle, he lit it, and smudged out the cord in the sand. He carried the flame to the boat, looking up at the rails and at the seepage of water that was encroaching around the base.

"We need to find a path to higher ground," Hershel deduced, examining the collecting tidewater. "I think it's safe to say the entire cove fills with water. Not a good place to spend the night after all."

"And that's likely how they got the vessel in here to begin with," Gavin remarked, joining Will to walk around the water craft. "They sailed it in before the tide receded and hitched it to a well-placed ring."

"Which means they had no way to alight, considering they were surrounded by water," William considered, passing off the candle to Gavin while he climbed onto a pile of rocks to reach the rail.

"Here, let me help you," Gavin said, attempting to give William a boost off his maimed foot.

William ignored the offer and pulled himself up, thumped onto the deck. He took the candle back from Gavin who also climbed aboard. "And if that's the case," he continued, glancing around with his hand on his hip, "then it means they had a way to climb out of this inlet, unless they spent the entire night on the boat and waited for the tide to recede again. Also unlikely."

"You're right," Hershel remarked, climbing aboard after them. "Up there."

Hershel pointed into the darkness, the candle barely illuminating a series of rocks that appeared to be in a random pile, but upon further scrutiny, formed steps. William thumped to the bow and raised his candle outward, showing that the rocks gave way to a set of ancient steps carved into the crevice itself and smoothed from age, climbing up between the cliffs toward freedom high above.

"Christ," Gavin exhaled, ignoring the glare Hershel leveled at him for the profanity. "These have been here for ages. Likely this has been a useful dock for centuries. Or hideout."

"And someone's using it to their advantage and to Bain's disadvantage," Will commented.

"The steps are too high to reach right now," Hershel added.

Will nodded. "Not when the tide rises and lifts the boat."

"I'll get our packs before it rises any further," Gavin said, climbing back over the rail.

"Aye, and if we had hoped to camp in here tonight, we would do well to climb these steps instead while the water brings us up high enough to reach them," Will added.

He held out the candle, looking around the deck. There was nothing loose aboard. Only ropes and rigging, a furled sail tied around the mast, and a shroud. Extra coils of rope sat off to one side, but otherwise, the vessel was stripped of accoutrements. Sailors traveling along the shoreline would never see it if they weren't looking for it.

Hershel moved to the hatch in the floor where the oarsmen toiled. "Do I dare open it?" he said to himself, fearing what he might find below. He crossed himself, kissed his hand, and pulled it up. "Bring the flame, Will," he directed as Gavin tossed their packs one by one over the rail.

William did so, hoping they didn't find bodies. It was too silent to find living people, but bodies were another matter. The hull was empty. The oars were pulled in. Two saddle packs sat to one side, though they were empty. A crate sat afore beneath the bow. No bar was present to pry up the lid, but Hershel climbed down in, followed by William who winced as he landed on his peg.

"You're all right?" Hershel asked, noticing his pain.

"Aye, fine."

Seemingly not convinced, Hershel thankfully didn't press it.

"The crate's heavy with goods," Hershel said.

Having much experience prying off cask lids in the meadery, William passed off the candle again and looked around. He picked up a spare oar stowed beneath a bench, examined the flat paddle, and jammed it beneath the lid, prying and cranking until the nails fastening it gave way. Setting aside the oar, both he and Hershel pulled the lid completely off, yanking at some of the more stubborn nails.

Gavin also hopped down through the hatch and came to peer inside the crate.

An extra sail, a pouch of nails, and a map...

William picked up the map. "Hold the light closer."

Hershel obliged and they all three leaned their heads together to look. "It's a map of the oceans and landmasses."

"It's Lispagne," remarked Gavin, as he and Hershel exchanged an impassive glance with each other before turning their eyes on William.

William stood frozen. "Nay, it's the western part of Lispagne and the whole of Île de Neige. But it's only half a map. Bain is cut off to the east."

"The words are in old Lispagnioc, their ancient tongue," Hershel remarked. "I've studied much of it at the monastery, as well as under Father Kearney's tutelage at St. Andrew's in the capital."

"Why only half a map? Where's the rest?" Will questioned.

"The lines drawn upon it appear to be traveling routes," Gavin said.

"And they cut off where the map is cut," Will observed.

It made no sense, unless the men traveled with the other half of the map. His heart dropped to his stomach. What were men from Lispagne doing in Bain? A wash of dread rushed over his skin, giving him gooseflesh. "Do you think they act with the blessing of King Fernando II?" he finally said, unable to peel his eyes away from the Lispagnioc words.

The words gave life to a new fear he didn't have the strength to articulate. Were these men Lispagnioc smugglers selling goods on the black market? Were they mayhap not just selling goods, but selling...women?

Lispagne was hurting beneath the seven years of trading bans leveled against them by Bain and the other kingdoms. Just a handful of sennights previously his father and Lord Edward had been sitting in

Dunstonwoodshire's hall discussing the latest royal suggestion from the crown that they remain vigilant to ensure no peasants disappeared from their fiefs. The royal decree hadn't been urgent, but now that William thought about it, the prince had probably kept his tone neutral to prevent his lords from panicking.

But Amber's state of dress had been poor, he had remembered. She had been embarrassed that she looked disheveled in her worn gown. Was it possible there was more to the royal suggestion? Was it possible that Amber had been mistaken as a peasant and smuggled away in a burgeoning scheme against Bain?

"Don't think on the worst," Hershel cautioned, as if able to sense Will's thoughts treading on dark ideas.

"How can I not?" Will whispered.

At that point, they felt a lurch. The planks groaned and slowly, a floating sensation overtook the vessel. The tide lifted them off the ground. William shook himself from his thoughts and folded the map, tucking it inside his surcoat. He continued to rummage through the crate. Food stuffs. Hard bread no doubt for dunking in broth, a jar of small, brown, sticky fruits that smelled sweet, a jug of red wine.

"Take the foods. We drink the wine now to quench our thirst," ordered Gavin from above. "Such a jug is too heavy to pack about. A little higher and we'll rise to the stairs."

They packed up the food and Hershel stomped the lid down on the crate. Reaching through the hatch, they braced their hands on the deck to heave themselves up, joining Gavin, then strapped their packs to their back again. Hershel extinguished the candle and tucked it in his surcoat.

As soon as the bottom stair was within reach, Gavin stepped out, the gap between the rail and the stone wide. Hershel followed. Balancing upon the rail, William stepped out with his crippled leg first when the peg skid on the water-smoothed stone. He tipped backward.

"Ho there!" Gavin exclaimed, grabbing his youngest brother by the surcoat while he braced his weight against the wall of the cliff. "Easy, wee brother," he teased.

"Christ," Will swore, scowling.

"Curse not the Lord's name," Hershel muttered.

"Sod off," Will growled back as he steadied himself.

Faltering on his damned excuse of a leg never ceased to remind him how much less a man he was, but he was finished with his older brothers' teasing and coddling. And that he couldn't find Amber gouged more deeply, for his worth as a man from such a proud family was also at stake. His breathing increased until he exploded.

"'Tis nay your mouth saying the words, but mine! I'm sick of your holier than thou manners. I'm sick to death of my *foking* leg!" Rage more than two years in the brewing boiling over his lips. "I'm sick of hobbling like an old *foking* man when I'm not but five and twenty! I'm sick of dragging my arse around to do simple things that take a normal man less effort and I care not if my anger upsets your churchman sensibilities! *You* don't have to live like this but I do, my brothers always babying me, my father always telling me things are too hard for me to do because I'm blind and I'm crippled!"

Hershel stood quietly as William railed against him, his words echoing up the cavern, bouncing off the walls in a hollow ring. Finally he spoke.

"I meant nay to diminish you, Will," Hershel murmured. "I may not know how you suffer, but I know what it means to suffer. I find solace in faith, that is all."

"But I do nay," William stated. "I found solace in knowing I was going to marry Amber. It was the *one* thing I had left, seeing as I have no future as the fifth son."

He took a deep breath, paused, then moved onward, climbing the stairs. Gavin eyed William's back, then glanced at Hershel, and moved on as well. Finally Hershel followed too. By the time they reached the top, it was dark, save a faint glow upon the horizon making the edge of the sky orange and purple.

The cliffs were magnificent, a sweeping plain of scrubby bushes and grasses creeping to the sheer drop. In the distance, a dark shroud under the sky suggested a forest, though it was too difficult to see, and the rushing of the ocean sounded far away.

"There's no shelter for mayhap a mile inland," Gavin noted. "It might be best if we sleep here and look for a trail at first light."

"Aye," agreed Hershel. "There's no looking for Lady Amber in the dark when we can't even see any tracks."

Will couldn't speak, still tense with anger, but knew they were right and resigned himself to camping. Yet although his legs were tired and his body ached, he knew sleep would elude him. His mind raced along with his pulse. Was he on a fool's errand? Was Amber already gone forever and he simply prolonged the inevitable realization? That he would never get her back? Had she been raped, and then murdered to silence the evidence? Dumped in the strait?

He hadn't ceased feeling ill the entirety of their journey. God, but what he wouldn't give for a clue to simply fall out of the sky and lead him to her. He dropped his pack on a sigh, which was more mental exhaustion than physical. Plopping down to his rear, he rummaged through his packs for some dried bread and jerked meat while Gavin walked a few paces away and pulled free his cock to release his water.

He forced the food upon his stomach and jammed the pack under his head, lying back on it. Morning would come and his limbs would ache even more. His stump would pain him further, a warning that he was courting an injury he shouldn't ignore. But no. Deep down, he knew he couldn't delay the search further, let alone give it up. Amber might be lost, but he would feel it if she were lost *to him*, wouldn't he?

***

Amber waited with her hand upon the bar, making certain it was still in place, until Father Crispen arrived to escort her to her morning meal. It had been a fortnight since her arrival at the monastery. The regular messenger still hadn't arrived, and Amber had slept poorly once again.

"The chamber is secure," she said aloud as reassurance. "No one's in here with me."

Knocking on her door ensued. "It's Father Crispen," came the familiar voice.

She exhaled and lifted the bar, setting it aside. Upon opening it, Father Crispen greeted her and she took his offered arm. They walked down the plastered stone corridor when a line of monks breezed by her. Mentally she tallied the count. *One, two, three, four, five...* She felt a hand upon her rear. It was fleeting. She jumped. Then halted right in the middle of the corridor.

"Are you all right, lady?" Father Crispen asked at her side. "Are you still worried about—"

"Who was the last monk to pass me?"

"What's the matter, Lady Amber—"

"The name. The last man to pass me, up ahead. I counted five men. Who is he?"

Father Crispen hesitated, trying to figure out the source of her concern. "'Tis Brother Daniel. But why do you want to know—"

"He just touched me."

She could hear the smile in Father Crispen's voice. "The corridor is narrow. I'm certain it was an accident, 'tis all."

But she was shaking her head. "He just..." She let her voice trail away. How could she simply blurt out that the man had just fondled her rear as he passed them by? Talk of such body parts was vulgar, and she had never let any of those words pass her lips. Instead she changed the subject, feeling her knees quaking. "Is...is there word on your messenger, Father? I wish terribly to have a letter penned."

"No word, my lady. I'm sorry. Eh, come, child. I can see you're growing more unsettled each passing day. You should nourish yourself on what little victuals we have."

"Someone was in my chamber, Father."

She heard him exhale. He was probably rubbing the bridge of his nose, too, judging from the intensity of the sigh and the rustling of fabric.

"Your chamber was empty that first night, and you were indeed overly distraught when you were brought to us. I'm quite certain you made a mistake, mayhap thought you'd barred your door but hadn't. We mere mortals make such errors all the time."

He chuckled again, though his good-natured laugh was beginning to sound patronizing.

"Why, just yesterday, I was certain I had set my ring of keys on the bed stand beside me, when in fact they were hanging beside the door all along. 'Tis normally the spot in which I place them, and I must have hung them there without thinking about it."

"I double checked, Father. I went back to the door to feel it in place after I thought I'd heard a noise," she argued. She never argued. But then again, her father had normally been either fair in his expectations or dismissive of the blind daughter, as had her mother. There had been little need to argue. Most had equated it to her obedient demeanor, when in truth, now that she thought about it, it was because things had always seemed fine.

"My lady," Father Crispen sighed again. "The brothers are devoted followers of Christ. They've taken vows to live by *Iesus'* example. I trust them all to act with the utmost propriety. I must believe that because of your ordeal, you are becoming paranoid. Therefore, I must request that you cease to worry about this further. We sometimes become frightened when faced with uncertainty."

Of course he wouldn't listen to her. He hardly knew her, but had lived with the brothers of St. Matilda's for a long time and trusted them. Of course he would trust them over her, she fumed, shaking with anger. He must simply think her going mad. Apparently she had an argumentative streak that no one had ever known about.

"I've decided to return to my chamber, Father," she bit out, her voice trembling, "Before I say something regrettable. I know what I felt, and I know that I barred my door a fortnight ago."

And she also knew that Brother Daniel, as Father Crispen had just stated, was on his way to break his fast. She could bar her door safely and know that no one would be in her chamber with certainty, at least for a little while. Perhaps she could sleep in peace and awaken refreshed.

"You wish not to eat, my lady?"

"Please return me to my chamber, Father. I wish to be alone."

After a pause, he sighed wearily. "Very well," he conceded.

They turned back the way they had come. He deposited her in her cell. She shut and barred the door without so much as a good-bye. Tears pricked her eyes.

"I want to go home," she whispered. "I want to see William."

She threw her face in her hands. It was too much. She was fortunate she had escaped her captors, and she was indeed grateful to the strange young man in the woods. But something here didn't feel right. Blast it! If only she could see, she could walk away from this remote monastery and never look back.

She swiped the tears away and moved to her cot, pulling loose her laces and removing the pieces of her gown so she wore only her chemise. She flopped backward onto the cot and fought her way into deep sleep. For the first time since she had arrived, she knew without a doubt she was alone, and would do well to use the time to unknot her muscles and finally catch her breath.

***

The monk stood in the corner of Amber's chamber beside the stacks of grain sacks, having rounded up the back staircase from the commons after passing her in the corridor. His imagination ran wild, remembering his hand upon her rear for that brief moment, remembering her naked that first day as she washed herself. It had been since before entering the cloistered life years before that he had seen a woman. Lady Amber was certainly a maiden made for lust.

Her lips were soft and pink, her nose, small and pert, her eyes were the warmest and softest brown, and her hair was a tumbling fountain of brown curls kissed with auburn. He remembered well her small breasts, pink nipples, and nestle of hair at the joining of her thighs. He had watched her wash herself, had nearly spilled upon the sight of her as he reached beneath his cassock to pleasure himself. Indeed he had spilled after fleeing her chamber, realizing that her other senses worked over-well.

When she had circled the chamber, searching for the sound of his rustling clothing, he had thought he would have to flee right then, except that wonderful little mouse had saved him and allowed him more time to stare at the beauty. After fleeing her room, he had imagined her as he lay in his cell taking care of his needs, imagining his hands upon the young woman, his mouth upon her breasts, his hips between her thighs, fornicating with her...

Ah yes, she was a sweet young lady, and those thoughts had pushed him over the edge. He had made sure to do his own laundering too, to hide the soiled rags used to catch his seed each time he envisioned joining with the woman. It was clearly the devil's work. Satan had placed the woman in their midst to tempt them, to break their vows, to give them impure thoughts. Satan was tricky like that. It was the fallen angel's fault that he lusted.

And now the woman threatened to lure him off the path of godliness again. Right now, as he looked about her cell, smelling her pillow, running his hand along her bed linens, he knew he was inviting the devil into his heart by waiting for her return from the meal. He would watch her, enjoy the show she displayed, and slip out again. Lady Amber was upset, distressed, and had been through much. Father Crispen would once again blame her state of upset for why she hadn't paid attention to bar her door. She would insist she had secured it, and all would begin to think her mad.

He heard footsteps returning down the hall and dashed to the corner of the cell. Lady Amber strode back in, closed the door, barred it, whispered that she wished to go home, and then that...she wished to see William? She had mentioned a William that first night. The jezebel, wishing for male company.

He didn't feel so badly about lusting after her anymore. She obviously projected it upon men and clearly his defenses were more weakened than his brothers at St. Matilda's. Mayhap she had even lain with this "William." Mayhap she was fair game.

She strode to her bed and began stripping her gown with a confidence he hadn't seen before. It struck him. She thought she was alone. She thought everyone was at their meal, unaware that he had come back up the back stairway. And then her chemise slackened over her breasts, and it was all he could do to catch his breath before a groan escaped. He had already been pulsing to life beneath his cassock, but now...now he grew thick.

He needed to see more, needed to see her body again. He had been so starved of women since arriving here years before, and felt he couldn't contain himself. That first day a fortnight prior, she had awakened the sinful lust he had done well to tamp down long ago, and now he needed to see her again. The chemise was in the way. Her breasts were so close to showing.

As soon as he noticed she had fallen asleep, he moved a step closer, then another step, then another, until he stood close enough to see the detail of her breasts beneath the fabric. His hand beneath his robes stroked his cock to full attention, his grip making sweeps up and down. He imagined her laid bare before him, imagined his hands roving over her skin, her stomach, her thighs...

She was sleeping deeply. He reached out a finger, his other hand still busy gratifying himself, and felt the softness of the chemise. She didn't move but kept sleeping the sleep of the dead.

Incredible!

The fabric was soft, just as he imagined her skin would be. He fingered the fabric again, the loose neckline of her chemise, imagining her waking up and burying his forbidden lust betwixt her lips. He was going to spill right now upon her. He had to see her. He gave the neckline of her chemise a gentle pull to drag it down, slowly, slowly. If she woke, she might scream.

His hand pumped with more conviction. The soft rise of her breast grew larger as he pulled down the fabric, until the pink rim around her nipple peeked over the hem. He inhaled. She stirred and he stilled, but she remained asleep, shifting in such a way that the chemise loosened around her chest further.

Perfect, he thought, the rest of the fabric sliding down over her breast easily. There it was. A lovely little breast right beneath him. He placed a finger upon it, barely touching it, watching as it pointed, and she stirred again, this time opening her eyes.

And now she froze, a terrified sheen of white spreading over her face. He stood motionless, his cock in hand, looking directly down on her, his finger pressed lightly to her nipple. Her hand migrated up her stomach, over her chemise, over the lump of fabric now bunched beneath her breast, onto her exposed breast, and then to his finger...

"No!" she shrieked. "Help! Help!"

She clenched his finger and screamed, jerking it, snapping the knuckle, bolting upright, scrambling against the wall. She screamed still, blood-curdling shrieks. The jezebel had broken his finger! Running echoed down the hall, a pattering of footsteps that grew louder, and the monk knew he was in trouble.

"My lady!" Father Crispen called, knocking on the door.

***

Amber scrambled away from the wall, shoving past the monk in her chamber moaning in pain. He reached out to stop her but she screamed again as his hand clutched her.

"Let go of me!"

She shoved him hard. He toppled backward.

"Lady Amber!" Father Crispen called again, trying her latch, jiggling it. "Lady! Open this door!"

She fell against the door, shoving aside the bar and wrenching back the handle.

"I'm not lying!" she shouted in Father Crispen's face. "I'm not! I'm not—"

"Brother Daniel?" Father Crispen asked. The chamber fell silent. "What are you doing in here?" Still no answer.

Amber took a shaking breath, clutching her chemise at her throat. "Make him leave," she whispered. "He was…he was…" She threw her face in her hand, trembling as the tears came, relieved it was over, angered, frightened.

She swiped the water away that rolled down her cheeks, angered at being in such a helpless predicament. How on earth would she ever make a good wife to Will? Why did he like her so? Why was he willing to give up his chance at marriage on only half a woman? It was preposterous that she should think of him now when Brother Daniel had just been fondling her breasts, but her mind focused on William of Ballymead.

She put her hand over her mouth, holding back the wave of sobs that threatened to escape. Will had said sweet words to her, been kind to her, but the reality hit her like a load of boulders. He was blind, too, and she was his only prospect. And when married, they would be blind together. And when Sarah married Gavin, she would still be Sarah's problem to look after, as she had always been, and her father would finally be rid of the burden.

"Brother Daniel, come with me. We need to have a discussion," Father Crispen stated.

Amber felt him rustle past her silently.

"As if your vow of silence shows any piety at all," Amber bit out to him. "You're nothing but the devil in a monk's cassock!"

Father Crispen didn't say anything to her, but she knew the outburst irritated him. She had to leave. She simply couldn't stay. A fortnight had gone by and still there was no telling when a messenger would arrive. Tumbling blind over a cliff was a far better fate than remaining in these hellish walls. As soon as the men were gone and Father Crispen had ensured her cell was empty, she threw her bar across the door, fumbled for her gown now in a wad upon the floor, and fought her way into the garment's pieces.

One by one, she tied the laces, knowing her bodice was probably crooked and rumpled. And then she sat on the edge of her cot. And waited. She needed to slip out at the Compline bells when the brothers were all in the chapel offering prayers. Someone might still see her sneaking away, but there would be no better time to try. She had to try. As soon as the bells rang, she needed to leave, feel her way along the ground, and hope that no dips or ravines in the land were put in her path.

Because once the Compline prayers were recited, the cells would be locked for the night, and she would have no escape until the next day. And she couldn't stay another second.

Chapter 14

As soon as the Compline bell began to toll, Amber crept to her door. She pulled it open. Paused. It was silent. Retreating back inside, she felt for her cloak and yanked it from its hook, hearing it rip along the hem. It didn't matter. There was no time to worry about the deteriorating state of her garments. She twirled the wool around her neck and crept out into the corridor.

She recounted the steps to the main door. *Sixteen, seventeen, eighteen...* She continued to listen for signs of Father Crispen. *Twenty-three, twenty-four, twenty-five...* She felt the wall, following the course, placing each barefoot toe in front of the other, patting and feeling for anything obstructing her. Her breathing sounded loud in her ears with the silence engulfing her.

Forty, forty-one, forty-two.

She touched the main doors. The monastery had no guardsmen and the halls remained silent. Her pulse raced, faster, faster. She gave herself a shake. She wasn't a prisoner. If someone tried to subdue her, she would scream and flail like a mad woman until they were happy to be rid of her.

The door was closed, though not yet barred for the night. She opened it. A gust of wind breezed over her face. She pulled closed the door behind her, inhaling the nighttime air.

Exhilarated. Frightened. Nervous.

But the fresh air after languishing inside for a fortnight was refreshing. She was completely, utterly lost out here, and yet, she felt safer among the forest wolves and bears than she did in the monastery surrounded by men who had been starved of women.

She began walking, taking careful steps. The distant roar of a river was to her left. It might be far away, or there might be a drop-off nearby where water cut through the land. It was hard to tell. Wind swept her hair loose from her braid, tendrils flowing into her face. Her gown billowed around her ankles, fluttering upward. Thankfully her underskirts were heavier and kept her modest.

She laughed outright. "Modesty?" *That* was the thought to cross her mind at a time like this?

Mayhap she *was* going mad from her ordeal, but she stopped in her tracks and kept laughing. "As if the grass around my feet is scandalized by the sight of my ankles."

She could do this. She could feel her way and walk. Eventually she would have to run into someone, someplace, some*thing*.

The night wore on. More rain began to sprinkle, though the wind rolling down from the pine trees carpeting the mountains made it feel like mist engulfing her. She pulled the hood of her cloak over her head, cinching it around her ears, and continued to take delicate steps, feeling the ground with her toes. Nevertheless, she persisted. Pushed onward. Any place was better than St. Mathilda's.

***

Prince William led his contingent to St. Mathilda's to request some bread as they journeyed to Fort Michaelmas with their load of helmets. There had been no sight of Lord Edward or anyone from Ballymead despite sending out scouts each day to scour the countryside.

A scout reported back now, trotting over the plain to the group traveling alongside the ravine and swirling River Fetch. They were near the head waters of the river here, where it tumbled down the mountain and raged through the canyon bends.

"No sign, Your Highness," the man stated, guiding his mount beside Prince William and bowing his head.

"Nothing at all?" Prince William asked, though he knew his scouts were experts. They would spot a sign if there were any.

"I apologize, Prince William. The rains have ruined any hope for tracks," the man replied. "At this point, we simply hope to stumble upon them by hazard."

The prince nodded. "My thanks, man. Join ranks again."

The scout did as was bade and inserted himself into the procession draped in Bainick heraldry. They lumbered overland, the mountains framing the pitch of barren land. The wind flapped their banners and whipped the horses' manes into a frenzy. The sky was drab and a chill arrived on the summer air.

He looked back at Sir MacTierny, the man's feral beard hiding his mouth. MacTierny's eyes connected with his for a moment. It was all that was needed. MacTierny needed to continue to play the part of a secret messenger in case Prince William's informant had dropped off another missive. Lady Amber missing or no, he had to take advantage of his visit for his other pursuits, too.

But as they arrived over the crest of the horizon, the monastery appeared lively. Three monks were meandering over the plain, headed back toward the main door, where Father Crispen stood like a silhouette in his black robe against the weathered plaster of the monastery, holding his lamp in hand.

Father Crispen's attention diverted to the royal party dragging their wagons of helmets, the creaking and plodding of hooves noticeable long before the banners could be distinguished. At long last, they halted in front of the monastery. Father Crispen, visibly distressed, came to greet him.

"Good day, Father Crispen," Prince William addressed, eyeing the lone monks converging together on the path to the door. "What gives the brothers cause to be out of doors on such a blustery day?"

"Your Highness," said the priest, bowing his head. "Good day to you too. An honor to host your visitation. And in sooth, each day here is a blustery one."

Prince William nodded, but pressed him further. "Your brothers forage in the forest?"

"No sir. A lady was brought to us a fortnight ago. She had lost her way, said she was nabbed, and I agreed to take her in until it was convenient to send a missive."

"What lady?" the prince asked.

"Lady Amber of Dunstonwoodshire."

The words hung in the air. Prince William's jaw clenched. "What has passed? Who brought her here? Where is she? We seek her father and her betrothed who are sick with worry searching for her. We just departed Dunstonwoodshire and the lord has yet to return home from his searches."

"A mountain lad, young, brought her here," shrugged the priest, offering nothing more on that matter. "She was unsettled all fortnight, paranoid if I am honest, and now she's gone."

"And she is nowhere within? Father Crispen, King Bain and I have received a request to aid in finding her. Pray tell where the likeliest place to look would be. 'Tis a matter of great importance that I find her, speak to her, and inform not only her family but also my wife, for Lady Amber is betrothed to my wife's brother."

"We know not where else to look," the priest replied. "We've searched high and low. She must have left."

"When did she leave?"

Father Crispen's hands shook, making the lantern rattle. Prince William eyed it. An interesting behavior, something that afflicted those with something to hide. He had seen it well enough before. And he had thought Father Crispen an honest man.

"Sometime over the course of the night, Your Highness, which is unusual, for all the cell doors are locked and the lady claimed to be blind," Father Crispen offered. "Which makes me wonder if she actually had the power of sight and was simply pretending."

"The woman is blind. I know this personally," the prince replied sharply. "When last did you check on her?"

"I brought her a tray of supper," Father Crispen said. "She took it at the door and closed it upon me."

"At what point do you lock the doors?" Prince William pressed.

"After the Compline prayers, Your Highness. Once all the brothers return to their cells for the night."

"And you didn't look in on Lady Amber then?"

"Nay," Father Crispen replied. "She was concerned for her security. I didn't want to risk waking her or make her panic trying the door."

"Why would you have made her panic?" the prince continued, his eyes direct.

Father Crispen hesitated, then swallowed. "I fear I've made an error."

Prince William dismounted and the priest offered another bow. "Come speak with me, Father, for I can't place my finger upon it, but something feels amiss right now. Jonathan, come take the reins," he commanded his squire.

The lad, a young man a few years away from earning his spurs, trotted his horse forward and took over managing Titan, the prince's black warhorse.

Father Crispen nodded at the prince's demand, swallowing beneath the Bainick prince's scrutiny. Prince William ducked beneath the lintel and Father Crispen closed the door behind him. The corridor was lit by a single taper ensconced upon the wall and the priest's lantern, which he hung upon a hook. The smells of bread and broth filled the air as the two walked down the corridor to the priest's humble office: a roughly hewn desk, a candle stick, a window with shutters closed against the wind, and a plain, wooden chair. The walls were plastered, and aside from a crucifix of gold, there were no hangings decorating the space, only a shelf lined with manuscripts bound in leather.

"The fare today won't be as extravagant as it is in the capital, Your Highness, but your soldiers are sodden and the broth is hot," Father Crispen began, closing the door upon them. "All are welcome."

"My men will appreciate such fare, simple or otherwise," the prince replied. "And now. Level with me," he ordered, folding his broad arms still secured within his leather gauntlets across his chain-mailed chest. With his legendary height, he created an imposing shadow. "I know the woman you speak of, Lady Amber, and am vexed to learn that she was found and is now missing *again*. What has happened?"

Father Crispen sighed a shaky breath, the hollows of his cheeks gaunt in the shadows.

"The Lady Amber was distraught. She was brought here by a well-meaning lad, a young man who encountered her wandering lost. He deposited her in my care for safe-keeping. She said she was abducted from her home, and managed to escape her captors. She chanced upon the lad in the forest."

"Where in the forest?"

"I know nay where. The lad keeps to himself."

William watched the priest's eyes shift back and forth. "I sense dishonesty, Father, and I have to say such a trait is unbecoming of a servant to the cloth, especially the prized pupil of Father Kearney in the capital, who tutored you."

Father Crispen sighed and wiped his brow, already appearing to have penance moving silently on his lips.

"The lad... he sends missives... to someone in Bain, sir."

William pondered him, his arms still folded, and took a deep, contemplative breath. "Is he Bainick?"

"An odd question. Of course he is," the priest replied, then exhaled and shook his head, muttering to himself. "Who am I fooling here?"

"Certainly not me," Prince William retorted.

Father Crispen seemed to mutter to himself, summoning courage. "I believe he is from Lispagne, Your Highness, though I thought him to have the royal ear and was entrusted via a royal Bainick missive to continue to transfer his missives onward every fortnight."

"A Lispagnioc man?" Of course by now Prince William knew of whom the priest spoke. "He didn't have my ear, man."

"I have no proof. He speaks with a perfect Bainick accent. There is only something about his mannerisms, a pronunciation at times, that leads me to question his homeland. But a royal messenger from the House of Bain continues to arrive and receive his messages. I'm sorry, my prince, if this is news to you. Mayhap King Bain engages with the mountain lad."

It was as Prince William suspected all along. The secret missives he had pondered back in the capital were likely from Christophoro Maria de Fernando. The bastard Prince of Lispagne. A young man of seeming honor, and yet, so much more.

What the priest in front of him *didn't* know was that it was Prince William himself sanctioning the transaction of messages every fortnight, not King Bain. Without a change to his expression, he leveled a look square in Father Crispen's eyes.

"Carry on about Lady Amber." He continued scrutinizing the holy man, the deep scar down William's face from a previous battle cutting a menacing crease into his visage.

"It was on one of these exchanges of missives that I'd hoped to send word to the lord of Dunstonwoodshire about Lady Amber. But now she's gone and we cannot find her anywhere. I fear she has fled."

"Why would she flee? You promised a return to her family, a safe haven until she could be reunited with them," William reasoned. "If she was abducted as you say she was—and let me be clear that the maiden is too sweet to be considered a liar—wouldn't remaining with you be ideal?"

"One would think," Father Crispen muttered, his eyes darting away.

Neither spoke for a moment. William dipped his head to look into the priest's face, his arms still folded and his wide stance obstructing the exit behind him. "I'm neither daft nor dishonest, man. Spill what secrets you withhold."

Father Crispen took a deep breath. "I had hoped to keep the matter from blowing out of proportion. But I'm not a liar either. Upon her arrival a fortnight ago, Lady Amber was certain someone had been in her chamber whilst she bathed. No one was there when I came to inspect. She had insisted that the door was barred, though it was no longer, upon my inspection. I dismissed it as nerves from her ordeal, for the poor lass was distraught."

He paused. William offered no respite but deepened his scrutiny. "Why do you hesitate to proceed? What has happened to make the lady feel insecure?"

"She claimed a monk groped her person as she passed him in the corridor yesterday, and demanded of me the monk's name. I told her, 'twas Brother Daniel. He and four of the other brothers were headed to their nooning meal. She insisted on returning to her cell instead."

"What did you do about it, Father?" pressed William.

"I couldn't believe that one of the monks would do such a thing. The passageways are narrow and I assumed he had brushed against her."

"You assumed she was still distraught and not thinking clearly," the prince added, gesturing to hurry the priest to his point. "Clearly you were more interested in proving her wrong than listening to the validity of her claim. Keep going, and if you bear responsibility for this lady's disappearance, you had best fess up now before I accuse you of withholding information. I have a schedule to keep and now more than ever must continue to search for my vassal's missing daughter. Any less action from me would be unacceptable, for the lords that support the crown are deserving of Bainick benevolence and my wife, *your princess*, is dear friends with Lady Amber."

Father Crispen looked into the young prince's eyes, then solemnly nodded.

"After I deposited her back in her cell, all was well, until mayhap an hour later, when I heard her scream. I, and the other monks, came to investigate, and that's when we discovered Brother Daniel in her cell. Her chemise was mussed and he was clutching his finger. 'Twould seem he was untoward and she broke the appendage."

Prince William felt blood pulse at his temple. "Good for her," he growled. "It's unsavory behavior for any man, but a monk?" He laughed, though the sound was chilling, not humorous. "And so you protect him still? Such a man took vows. Such a man strove to be above the base impulses of our sex. And yet you would protect him?"

"No, Your Highness," Father Crispen hastened. "I have placed him in seclusion, until I can send word to Father Kearney and ask what advice he gives. I had hoped to handle this through religious correspondence and await instruction."

"Why don't I spare you the trouble?" Prince William fumed. "Take me to him. Now. I consider this not an attempt to handle the problem, but to keep such a scandal silent so as not to sully your reputation."

Father Crispen nodded, his face pale, and obliged. He led the prince back into the dark corridor. They proceeded around the corner all the way to the end where Amber's chamber had been, but stopped at the eighth door down. Crispen withdrew his ring of keys, unlocking the chamber, and pulled back the port. A small monk knelt beside his cot, his head dipped in prayer, his hands clasped together, and his finger wrapped in a splint.

He looked up, saw Prince William decked in full chainmail costume bearing the royal Black Lion. His face drained of color.

"Get up," William demanded.

The monk obeyed.

"You had better tell me what possessed you to attack Lady Amber of Dunstonwoodshire."

The monk didn't reply, though it was clear that fear coursed through him.

"He has taken a vow of silence, Your Highness," Father Crispen clarified.

Prince William strode into the cell and snagged the monk by his cassock. He shoved him to the wall causing the flimsy man to grunt, the prince's gauntlet clutching the fabric at the monk's throat.

"If you are schooled in the gossips about my wife, you will know that I harbor no sympathy for lecherous pieces of shite like you. If you are learned, you will know that your princess, *my wife*, has suffered because of men like you. If you know what is best for you, you had best break your vow of silence, man," William rumbled in his face, his nose practically touching the monk's, "and explain."

Though he trembled from top to toe, the monk remained tight-lipped.

"Order him to speak," Prince William demanded.

"Only the abbot can, and he doesn't reside here, only visits."

Prince William's attention returned to the monk in his grip. "Let me clarify," he proceeded. "If you do not answer my questions, this entire monastery will be cordoned off. I will place it and everyone in it under lock and key until all of you can be dragged before the king and Father Kearney. Make no mistake that if you choose not to cooperate, all of you will be sanctioned."

"Speak, Brother Daniel," pleaded Father Crispen. "What you did was wrong, and your brothers deserve to continue God's work unimpeded."

Still the monk remained silent.

"You are aware of the cliff overlooking the river, no?" Prince William pressed. "You are aware that a blind woman might very well have fallen to her death, fleeing the likes of you? If she has injured herself, or worse, I will consider you at fault. I urge you once more to speak."

Brother Daniel said nothing, casting his eyes at his feet.

William bit back a swear and hauled the diminutive monk out of his cell by his cassock, dragged him down the corridor so that his feet tripped over each other, and exited out the main doors. His score of men all turned to look.

"Your Highness!" Father Crispen cried, chasing him.

Prince William whirled around, pointing at him. "Do not act innocent, man." He fumed. "You hoped to cover this up. The very least you could have done was tell me up front what secret you hoped to harbor. The very least you could have done was have a missive already penned for the king to deposit into the hands of the next messenger to cross your doorstep, to tell of Brother Daniel's lapse in judgement. *This* man," he spun Brother Daniel around, "is a disgusting excuse for a man and is most certainly ill-equipped to serve God with such stains on his character."

"He is imperfect, true, as we all are," Father Crispen pleaded. "But he deserves forgiveness, as does anyone, for he has offered his penance."

"He can repent in a dungeon cell. And you, Father, are under investigation. Don't attempt to flee. If you have any good sense in your scholarly head, you'll cooperate to the fullest extent possible. Sir Cavanaugh!" he called to his first in command.

The blond knight dismounted and strode forward, questions on his brow as he looked from Brother Daniel withering in Prince William's grip to Father Crispen.

"Order five of our men to remain behind and secure the monastery," the prince continued. "There is a wolf in sheep's clothing here," he shook Brother Daniel to indicate the wolf. "Lady Amber of Dunstonwoodshire managed to find her way here. Father Crispen was supposed to offer her aid and instead, Brother Daniel took liberties with her."

Cavanaugh glanced down at Brother Daniel and frowned.

"She is now missing, likely fled," William continued, "for if she cannot feel safe in a House of God, where can she? And since our monk refuses to talk and Father Crispen is reluctant to condemn his behavior, he comes with us and the monastery is to remain secured. We question everyone before we leave today, and we will attempt to find a trail after Lady Amber. She has to be nearby still."

Sir Cavanaugh's eyes slid to the monk again. "If she fled, she'll lose her way," Cavanaugh remarked, angered. "She might have fallen over the cliff. Are we to launch a sweep of the area?"

"Yes," William replied. "Though the rains have ruined our chances of tracking anything. If we don't discover her whereabouts today, I'll leave a detail behind to continue scouring the terrain." His eyes drifted to the cliff again, knowing that if she had fallen, it was already too late. The drop was far and the rocks below, jagged. "See it done, Frances," the prince said.

Cavanaugh bowed. "Yes, Your Highness. I'll see to an assignment of men right away."

But a day of searching proved fruitless. William's weary men dismounted as their squires attended the horses and corralled them in a crumpled enclosure that had once formed an ancient ring of standing stones. They filed inside to eat supper. Frustrated, the prince approached Father Crispen standing at the monastery's threshold. He noted the worry eating Father Crispen's brow as the priest tallied the soldiers.

"Worry not about the food we deplete. Cordoned off or not, the royal stores will reimburse you. I'd hate for you to overly concern yourself with your stomach whilst the lady is in peril."

William entered the monastery, ducking beneath the crude lintel and back into the corridor. He loosened his coif, pulling off the chain mail hood and pushing back the fabric yoke encasing his head. His hair was matted and sweaty from travel since leaving the capital. Cavanaugh strode in behind him.

"Please see to it that foods are laid out for His Highness and his soldiers," Father Crispen said to a novitiate who bowed his head.

The narrow hall filled with soldiers and their jingling implements as they descended the stairs to the sparse dining hall with two long trestle tables parallel to one another. Pots of broth were delivered as well as loaves of fresh bread. The soldiers made quick work of it and filed back upstairs, returning outside to ready for departure.

Frustrated and behind schedule, Prince William stormed back down the corridor to Father Crispen's offices as the bell tolled the Vespers. Monks converged like ghosts in the corridor, headed to the monastery's small chapel room. Father Crispen was exiting his office when he looked up and saw the prince marching toward him.

Sir Cavanaugh strode right behind him, both men's boots sending vibrations through the flooring.

"You'll refrain from your prayers right now, Father, for Lady

Amber is still unaccounted for. Return inside," Prince William stated.

Father Crispen obliged.

"Sir Cavanaugh, collect the monks from their Vespers obligation. Each shall be questioned."

Cavanaugh gave a stout nod and continued down the corridor toward the stairs.

As Father Crispen arrived back behind his desk, William leaned over, bracing his hand upon the wooden surface. His eyes were angry and his brow tired.

"I know that lady personally. I am beyond vexed. I am distraught. There is no sign she went over the cliff, though the current might have swept her away. There are no tracks to follow. She could be dead. Make no mistake St. Matilda's is free of the woman, but also make no mistake that if your monks do not cooperate with Sir Cavanaugh, you will advise them to suspend their vows of silence and answer each question asked them as completely as possible. If they are loyal subjects of Bain, then they will oblige us. And if not, I have no problem seeing that each of you answer directly to Father Kearney *and* King Bain from behind dungeon bars. You are on thin ice, Father," William persisted.

"I truly thought her confused and upset, Your Highness," Crispen beseeched. "I have lived with these monks for many years and had complete trust in them. True, I had hoped to keep this managed through church channels, but make no mistake I was handling the matter."

"And have you ever taken in a female in need before?" William countered, standing back to his full height and refolding his arms.

"Indeed no," admitted Crispen.

"Then you would have had no idea how your men might behave with a woman in their midst. Monks or not, they're still men with base urges and neglected cocks." Father Crispen cringed at William's vulgarity. "Men who might try to satisfy an itch when a hapless woman is thrust into their midst. You, as the priest of this remote place, must do better to listen to the needs of those in your charge."

He strode away, leaving Father Crispen's potential censure from the capital hanging in the balance, and went to the chapel to see the progress Sir Cavanaugh was making.

"None will speak, still," Cavanaugh muttered, leaning close to Prince William's ear as they stood side by side surveying the chamber. "Though I don't think they do so to protect their brother, but indeed do so to maintain their vows. Still. There is little to gain from them."

"The monastery is already to be cordoned off. We'll send soldiers and carriages from the capital to collect them all," the prince replied matter-of-factly. "Brother Daniel comes with us now. I have no doubt he has sickness in his mind and might attempt to flee should we leave him here."

"Are you prepared to start a war with the religious clerics of Bain?" Cavanaugh persisted, smirking.

"Hell, if Lady Amber's abduction proves to be related to the secret missives I've received, I'm willing to start a war with Lispagne." William surveyed the monks again. "If these men have nothing to hide, they'll talk," William replied, shaking his head. "I care not that they are religious men. They had a wolf in their midst and are not above the law. Come. Our men have eaten. I've instructed a missive prepared and sent to Bain."

Cavanaugh nodded. "Lady Amber must be found but yes, we must move on. Pray we make good time."

Chapter 15

Will blinked his eyes, resting sideways, and watched the dove huddled down in the shrubs surrounding their camp. It ruffled its feathers and cooed. He didn't move, simply watched the bird turn its head to return his gaze with its beady eyes. And he thought of Amber as the bird flew away.

The brothers roused and began traveling southward, following the only route, a narrow and sparsely traversed deer path. A discarded piece of the same sticky fruit found in the balinger convinced him that whoever had been in the boat had also hiked this route. Considering it hadn't yet been eaten by a bird or critter meant it had only recently been discarded.

"The path seems to be leading in an arc down to the southern shore," William remarked.

"That would be the best location to launch another boat to Lispagne," Gavin concurred. "Though indeed they've troubled themselves greatly to avoid being seen by Bainick soldiers or citizens, coming so far out of their way."

"Then it must be that important of a pursuit for the thieves," Hershel deduced, "for them to create such a wide berth around the more populated parts of Bain instead of a more direct path."

"Did they force Amber to walk this length?" William asked, though his brothers knew that he wasn't fishing for an answer. "Look...over there."

His brothers looked to where he pointed. It was hard to spot, considering the scrubby grass hid most of it, but as they walked up to it, they noticed the burnt remains of a fire.

"There isn't firewood for miles around," William stated, looking to the trees in the distance.

"The forest looks close, but is indeed further inland," Hershel agreed.

Gavin examined the coals. "They're warm." He picked one up. "Not scalding, but not cold either. Whoever burned it did so this morning before moving on their way."

All three of them examined the surrounding area, but if the ones they pursued had sat anywhere, their indentations in the grasses had long since sprung back upright.

"But the fire was small," Gavin added. "Which means only a few people at most were here."

"A couple men and Lady Amber," William suggested. "They probably sent the oarsmen ahead to ready their next vessel.

Hershel nodded. "Seems probable. Especially after finding that piece of fruit along this pathway."

"If the coals are still warm, then they're not far ahead," William frowned. "We've also spied no horse tracks or manure, so they are definitely on foot. Let's get moving."

"We need to eat, Will," Hershel said. "You'll be no good to Amber if you're exhausted and hungry. You need to fight your best if required. We all do."

"I'll eat whilst I walk," William countered.

Gavin dug through his packs, pulled out a handful of sticks of dried meat and another piece of hard bread, then slung his pack over his shoulders again. "All right, I'm ready. Let's get your lady, Will, and geld some Lispagnioc bastards."

Hershel did the same, frowning at Gavin's lewdness—another thing that made Gavin a typical soldier—and Will, feeling his gut churning once again, withdrew a stick of dried meat and began walking. His stump was so sore, the rawness was almost unbearable. He dared not remove the peg to examine it. Pain jarred each footfall. But Amber was just outside of his reach and he intended to close that gap before the day's end. His worthless leg wouldn't be cause for any delay.

***

The upland plain gave way to sloping hills as they neared the southern beaches. They followed a burn meandering toward freedom into the sea.

"We could have avoided this whole damned trek had we simply waited upon the southern beaches whilst stowing our knarr," Gavin grumbled.

"Aye, we'd be there to catch the sods when they came off the hills," William concurred, but as they hiked further, a faint ringing of metal upon metal, as if someone worked at smithing, clanked in slow, steady hammers.

"We might not have done all of this work in vain after all," Hershel pointed out as they came to a series of rocks overlooking a drop in the ground.

"Aye, I hear it," William said.

They stilled, listened, crouched low, and crept up behind the rocks, remnants of old boulders. Two men, blond, *twins*, came into view, dressed in dark tunics, one black and one brown. William felt anger surge. Somehow, someway, he knew these were the ones who had nabbed Amber. They fit Lod's description exactly. But there was no sign of anyone else. Amber wasn't there. He could sense it. What had they done with her?

The men weren't talking. They fixed the links of a chain over an open fire, one holding the chain taut, the other hammering the red link. They had seen the smithy fire ring at the abandoned hut in Bain and it seemed that at least one of the men was an expert blacksmith. William shot a look at Gavin and Hershel as his brothers did the same to him and each other. Finally, William gestured that they should retreat.

Gavin acknowledged him and touched Hershel's arm to signal backing up. All three crept back through the grasses, away from the rocks, and down the path several paces.

"Amber isn't here, I can tell," William whispered.

"No one else is," Hershel replied.

"But it seems that there have been others here," William added. "The encampment seems worn, and the path we've followed stretches for so long with no off-shoots that it was likely worn down by these men traveling this route on more than one occasion."

William thought. Were these men Lispagnioc? Why were they on the Île de Neige? Why had they taken Amber?

The thoughts alone enraged him. He pulled free the half-map they had discovered in the balinger. A route traversed the Île de Neige. The route they were on, it seemed. And because the island was small, they had accomplished this path in a day.

"We need to catch them before they leave. Seems obvious to me that they're readying to set sail," Gavin said.

"Aye, and empty-handed, which makes me wonder if they plan to return," William added.

"We've three of us to two of them," Hershel deduced. "An

advantage."

"A narrow one," frowned William. "Let us nay pretend that my leg doesn't count against us. It does."

Gavin rounded on William. "The self-deprecation is too much, Will. I've trained with men who have missing hands from ill-placed swords, not to mention other problems. Your leg is only the hindrance that you allow it to be. You scold us for treating you as less, and yet, you pity yourself, too. If Amber is as important to you as you say, then your amputation matters not. Do you want our pity?"

William's chest filled with anger. "I'll be damned if these men get away. If I have to lose the other leg to force answers from their lips, I'll gladly give it up."

"As would we all for a woman we love," Hershel said, patting his shoulder. "I would have given all of myself if it meant my wife would have survived."

"You gave one leg for our sister, Gwen," Gavin added. "No doubt having done so will give you strength against these men now."

"We need a plan." Will stated, wishing to end the conversation, his words tight, and the sweat that hinted at a fever dampening his brow.

"Aye, but 'tis difficult to devise one. We know not the layout of their encampment and if any routes of escape exist," said Hershel.

"Nor have we accounted for anyone who might be nearby," Gavin added.

"No one else is here," Will countered. "But mayhap we should overlook onto the shore to make certain. Last thing we need is to engage these men only to find ourselves overwhelmed."

They trail blazed a wide berth around the encampment. A sloping hill led to the southern shore, ending in a drop off overlooking the sand. They sank down and shimmied forward upon their elbows. Overlooking the cliff, they saw another plain balinger, similar to the one they had discovered hidden within the cliffs, waiting to be pushed out to sea. Several oarsmen milled about, idly waiting.

"Something aboard the boat must have broken, hence the repairs being made now, but I see no one else," William whispered. "No prisoners."

"They could be within the vessel," Gavin offered. "But not likely, considering the balinger is beached and tipped."

"I have to know with certainty," muttered William. "If I could get down there, then mayhap you all could make a diversion up here, lure them to investigate and I'll sneak aboard."

"Way too risky, wee broth—Will," Gavin corrected. "And you've been quite the risk taker since regaining your eyes. What if only some of the men come running? What if more men rest within the vessel—as unlikely as that is—and you drop below deck only to land in their laps? Will, I don't agree to that."

"Then we have to take those twin men prisoner, and if the oarsmen come running to their aid, mayhap we can bluff that we have more men with us and they must answer our demands," Will suggested. "I *have* to know if Amber is aboard that balinger. I didn't come all this way not to investigate everything."

"There's no time to return to Bain to request Loddin's assistance from the fort, either," Gavin said, shaking his head. "They'll be long gone by the time we return. We need to act on these two men, for certain, but there's merit in Will's suggestion, too. If the twins act hostile, I suggest we knock them out and tether them. Which means we need to ensure there is rope among their personal effects. Otherwise, if they come to and we're in the midst of dealing with any oarsmen, we'll be in trouble. But," he continued, pointing. "If we could test the stability of these rocks and shove them over the cliff as the men come running, we could crush many of them."

"They've tossed ropes over the ledge to get up and down," Will noted, pointing. "Right there. What if we wait for most to be on the rope before rolling the stones off upon them? We could get most of them in a few goes."

Hershel was frowning, though he didn't disagree. They all knew he took his commandments seriously, including *Thou Shalt Not Kill*. The only time he had donned his battle gear and fought with divine ferocity was when the brothers had gone to find their sister.

"I pray it doesn't come to that. These men have the look of slaves to me. They might be pleased at the thought of liberation."

Gavin and William pondered it. In fact, they did look to be slaves. Their clothing was shabby, sleeveless, and though their muscles were pronounced from their tasks, they were thin.

"It didn't occur to me before, since Prince William had freed the slaves from Lispagne years ago, but aye. They do look to be slaves," William agreed. "And if they're kidnapping women for God knows what sort of sinful scheme, King Fernando II might very well have revived his father's slavery scheme."

Gavin looked pensive, then nodded. "I wonder... If their king has reinstituted slavery, then mayhap he doesn't have enough men...or *women*, to regrow the population. Lispagne took a blow from Bain back when Prince William was a fresh fighter and King Bain brought King Fernando I to his knees. It wasn't even ten years ago. If the new Lispagnioc king hopes to become powerful again, he needs men to fight, and women to breed, something he has much fewer of thanks to the prince freeing all the slaves and other countries willingly taking many in."

"And that might be why they wanted Amber," Will stated, his lips thin and his eyes narrowed as he watched the activity on the beach. "I wonder though. How many women have gone missing before her? Probably many, but if they weren't noblewomen, mayhap no one has alerted the crown. Amber wears her plain gowns often when she walks the hills. She might have been mistaken for a peasant lass."

"And Prince William sent missives to all his vassals asking the lords of Bain to keep track of their villagers..." Gavin remarked. Realization set in. "Prince William knows. Or he suspects."

"Those men who took her would then serve King Fernando II, but those men are probably in fear of the king's wrath, as are the slaves," Hershel considered.

"They probably fear their monarch just as much as they fear getting caught on foreign soil, or else why would they continue to serve their crown?" Will pondered.

"Aye, if they fear King Fernando II, then slaves or nay, the oarsmen will fight to defend their king to protect themselves from his wrath should they live."

Will and Hershel nodded.

The three of them retreated, gaining distance from the cliff's edge, then walked back to the encampment, from which the sound of metalwork still rang out.

"They still work," Will whispered. "Which means we still have time to catch them off their guard. See there? Rope," he pointed.

"So we surround them," Hershel said. "They don't need to see Will's leg right away."

Gavin nodded, thinking. "Indeed if we surround them, you, Hersh, on the far left side and me on the right—"

"And I remain above them among the rocks," Will interjected. "I can confront them. If they seem hostile, then both of you can flank them."

Hershel and Gavin nodded. "And quickly so that their exclamations aren't heard upon the shore."

"It's as sound of a plan as is possible. I want these bastards," Will growled.

They split in three directions, Gavin maneuvered deftly around to the right side and Hershel to the left, over the brush so as not to cause a stir and rouse the twins' suspicions. Will returned to where they had first spied the men, crouching low, waiting patiently to ensure his brothers had reached their spots. Hershel arrived behind a tumble of rocks and Gavin inched forward on his stomach in the tall grasses. God but his stump was hurting. He succumbed to rubbing it. More sweat collected on his brow, a spell of dizziness overcoming him, before he managed to right himself.

And if he untied the straps and pulled up his trouser leg, he knew he would see blood.

There simply wasn't time to waste upon it. Not yet. Not when he was so close to finding out what had happened to Amber. If he even dared mention it to his brothers, they would force him off his feet.

Finally, William stood to full height, his Ballymead surcoat filthy from their journey and his heavy coif removed so that his hair blew free. His broadsword hung ready at his hip. Behind his back, he placed his left hand on one of his daggers to ensure its placement. That weapon was getting drawn and flung first should the men turn hostile.

"I still don't think we should tell the king," remarked one of the twin men, his voice gravelly from a ragged line of scar tissue across his throat. "No one followed us. No one knows. As far as we know, the woman lost her way and is dead.

"Or she was found roadside and has since told all about us," replied the other, his voice normal.

Will bristled at their words. They didn't have Amber anymore. Be damned, but they had traveled all this way...

"Either way, I'm sure we've gotten away. The rains will have washed away our trail, and no one was following us. The king will never know," the gravelly-voiced man continued.

"You know King Fernando tolerates no lies. Yes, she's probably gone, but no, he won't be pleased that we return empty-handed. And don't forget, the king probably has spies spying on us, too. If he ever finds out we compromised his schemes, he'll torture us both without a thought. And if he sets that magus, Mateo, upon us, we may as well beg for death," the other reasoned, taking the chain and dunking it into a pot of water.

It hissed, steam billowing upward. He removed the link and laid it out, continuing. "You were a fool to fall for her lies. We cannot risk returning to Bain now, and we could face a royal storm upon returning to Lispagne. If the woman has told even one person of authority, our whole assignment will be compromised. King Bain will catch wind of it. Make no mistake, a noble will cry to his king about his daughter."

William's mind spun like a mill wheel under a heavy flow. Amber might be in peril elsewhere. He cursed himself. Hershel would throw the holy book at him for the vile words coursing through his mind. If Amber was lost to him, it was his own folly for following this trail.

He shook with anger. He might have wasted time coming all the way here. But these men weren't getting away.

"You there!" he called to the twins. "What purpose do Lispagnioc men have upon this remote isle, and pray, whilst you're explaining, what purpose do you have in Bain?"

The men's heads shot up, their eyes darting toward the upper ground. They spotted him and pulled knives, though both had removed their sword belts while working. They began backing toward their accoutrements.

"You're surrounded, men. You might wish to stop and answer a few questions!" William boomed.

They paused, as if trying to determine whether or not he bluffed.

"We've been tracking you!" Will continued, rattling them. "What we can't determine, is what you did with the lass you stole from her father's fief of Dunstonwoodshire!"

"What lass?" the twin with the normal voice asked.

William felt a grin, much too confident for the torrent swirling through him, creep onto his lips. "I think you know," he replied. "What did you do with her? If I find you used her, let alone discarded her body somewhere, I'll enjoy carving off each one of your bollocks, each one of your fingers, each and every part of you, slowly, so that your screams carry on for hours and vindicate her honor! You tampered with my betrothed, men! And I'll kill you if you do nay cooperate!"

A look of dread appeared upon the face of the one with the gravelly voice.

"He bluffs," muttered his twin, whipping around to dash for his sword.

"Does he?" said Gavin, emerging from the grasses, sword in hand.

The man with the gravelly voice threw his blade.

"Watch it, Gav!" called William and Hershel in unison.

They both broke through the rocks and grasses into the

encampment. William pulled loose his knife and flung it, catching the man in the arm.

"Ahhh!" the man cried.

The Lispagnioc men twirled around, noticing the other Ballymead men clad in dusty green. William hobbled forth, taking a retaliatory slash upon his own arm before throwing his weight upon his opponent. He tackled him. He grabbed the man's wrist, squeezing and jerking, attempting to dislodge the knife from his clasp, when the man's twin sent a left-handed punch to his side. William doubled over, pain shooting through his lower back as the twin man punched him again.

But he held fast to the one beneath him, twisting the man's wrist. The punching to his side continued. He was going to be pissing blood. He gritted his teeth, throwing all his effort into dislodging the man's knife. Bones finally snapped. The twin attacking him was suddenly gone, and the man beneath him roared in pain, his knife falling from his grip. William grabbed it, blood oozing through his tunic sleeve, and pushed back to his knees to straddle the man.

He stood. His opponent clutched his broken wrist, groaned, and made to stand, too. William, chest heaving, stabbed him back to the earth with the end of his peg. The man lay still, winded. William rolled him over, removing his daggers and dumping them into a pile. Glancing up, he noticed Gavin collecting the rope while Hershel threw a closed-fisted punch to the other man's jaw and sent him to the ground.

Lord, but William had been so focused on his own fight, he hadn't noticed that Gavin and Hershel had ripped the other twin off him.

"Toss me some rope!" Will called, wincing at the pain to his lower back.

Gavin removed a knife, sawing through the coil in his grip, and lobbed a wad over to him. Will tied the man's hands behind his back. His captive coughed for air and wailed in pain at the bondage to his broken wrist. Will knotted the rope tightly, hauling him to his feet.

"So I'm going to ask you again," he said, dragging the man across the encampment to a rock to sit upon, ignoring his cries of agony and his own dizzying vision as feverous sweat dripped down his temples. "Why were you sneaking through Bain, and what did you do with the woman?"

"I don't answer to you," the man rasped, spitting at him.

William struck him across the cheek. The man reeled sideways.

William wrenched him upright again.

"Was the woman blind?" William pressed. "And helpless, with curling brown hair and brown eyes?"

The other man said nothing, didn't even crinkle his brow.

"Was she young? Sweet? Did she mention me? 'William'?" he continued, his voice quieting and his words drudging up the pain in his chest. The man's eyes glinted at Will's pain and affection. "Her name was Lady Amber. I've known her all her life. She was my betrothed. What did you do with her? I must know."

"I don't have to say a thing to you," Will's prisoner finally said. The man glanced at his twin, shoved face down in bindings while Gavin jabbed a knee into his back as if bracing down livestock. Something passed between the twins. The man with the gravelly voice looked back up at William, a grin creeping upon his lips. "But she was indeed sweet."

William's fist swung. He couldn't tether it. He bludgeoned the man again. It connected with the man's jaw, who flew off the rock once more. William kicked him, jabbed him with his peg, cutting through his skin, bloodying his face, neck, chest.

"Soft, a tiny waist," the man continued, throwing his hands up to protect his face but not doing much else. "Sweet, round breasts..." he added, struggling to speak. "We...had our fill...dumped her blind and worthless arse in a wood..."

William's eyes burned with red haze. His leg punished the man, now nearly unconscious on the ground. He couldn't stop kicking. His lungs were collapsing as if a vice grip squeezed his throat. Hershel's hand came to rest upon his shoulder, gripping him.

He kept kicking. The pain in his leg was numb. He felt nothing, saw nothing but red. Hershel was saying something, though what, William was loath to listen.

"I'll kill you, you piece of shite, I'll kill you!"

"Will!" said Hershel again. His brother's presence cut through his anger, slowed his kicking. "Will, cease! He wants you to kill him..." Multiple hands were trying to pull him away now. He ripped his arms free of the grip. "Will, he hopes you'll deliver him from this life... He's trying to rattle you... they lost the woman, remember? They were talking together, lamenting that she'd gotten away? Stop, man." The hands were upon him again, clenching him, dragging him away. "You want him alive, you want him questioned...stop...."

Those words managed to finally stay his beating. His chest heaved up and down for air. He swallowed, his eyes burning with angry tears for what Amber might have endured. *Nay, Hershel's right,* he realized, swallowing. When it was just the two twin men talking, they had complained that the woman had gotten away and that they might be in trouble with their king.

"They lost her, remember?" Hershel added as William allowed himself to be coaxed backward. "He's using you as an opportunity. If you kill him, he'll never have to answer to his king for they know now they've been caught." Hershel succeeded in convincing him to recede a few paces as the blond man groaned on the ground, blood oozing from the gouges Will had inflicted.

His twin brother, sandwiched between Gavin and the ground, hadn't struggled or tried to intervene, but he spoke up now. "Aye, you need to kill us. If you don't, King Fernando will. And I'll take a death at your hands over his any day."

"Why?" William asked, turning to him. "In what have you embroiled yourselves?"

"Not embroiled. We have little choice but to serve King Fernando II. He saved my brother's life on the battlefield seven years ago and in return, he demanded servitude. He has spies all over Bain. We know if we're captured by Bain's authorities, then we're dead men, but we had a chance to stay alive if we continued to serve King Fernando II. But my brother made a mess of our mission. If we tell our king the truth about returning empty-handed, we risk his wrath. And if we lie to him and he finds out, we'll pay for it. I suspect he'll kill us. Slowly, and painfully."

Gavin pulled him to standing height.

"What did you do with the lass?" William asked him, now face to face. "I won't stop until I find her body. I care not if I kill you in the process. You took what belonged to her father. You took what was going to belong to me."

The man sighed, trying hard not to glance at his brother moaning in agony.

"She got away, just before the rains set in. Neither my brother nor I indulged. I swear this."

William sensed the man's sincerity. Maybe he was imagining it. Maybe he wanted so badly for it to be true, he was willing to believe anything. They were, after all, Lispagnioc henchmen, and he shouldn't trust a single word.

"She could be alive somewhere, or she could be dead. We couldn't find her after she eluded us," the man continued. "We thought her blind, but when we couldn't find her, we assumed she lied."

"She's blind. Which means she could have stumbled into any number of dangers," William replied. "Where did you lose her?"

"In a forest clearing a fortnight ago, at an old hut."

Amber's ripped stockings came to mind. Will suppressed a shudder.

"Why did you take her?"

The man looked at him, his twin still groaning.

"I cannot tell."

"Why not?"

The man refused to say more.

"Then you'll come with us and answer to Bain for your transgression," replied Gavin for them all, for William's frustration was about to erupt again.

The Lispagnioc man's face creased into a smile.

"Not if they can help it."

Gavin, William, and Hershel whipped their heads over their shoulder, seeing a few oarsmen standing upon the outskirts of the encampment, another hoisting himself over the edge of the cliff.

Gavin grabbed the man, his hands still tied behind his back, and thrust him with such force he tumbled off balance, knocking his head upon a rock. He lay unconscious. William wiped the sweat from his brow, clenching his eyes closed to stave off more dizziness. Hershel eyed him with concern, though there was no time to check on William's state.

They withdrew their swords, clustering together back to back, and watched as the oarsmen dispersed around them. Slaves or not, they clearly had the same fear as the twin men: dying at the hands of their king was a far worse fate. Four men...no five...no six, all gathered in a circle, gauging them, scrutinizing their movements, their weaknesses.

"Fight for Amber," Hershel muttered to William, rallying him, for they all knew Will was the greenest fighter.

"Fight for Ballymead," Gavin added, blowing puffs of air and rolling his shoulders.

If they went down, Will thought, he wanted his corpse to show he had fought to the bitter end. He bellowed a war cry and lunged forth, slicing his sword and slashing across the middle of two oarsmen, dispatching them. Gavin cursed, as did Hershel.

"Be damned, Will!" Gavin called, taking on two oarsmen charging forth to take Will out. "We weren't foking ready!"

They landed a sword into Will's side beneath his arm where he was bruised from his pummeling. He grunted, whipping out another dagger from his belt and jabbing across his chest, catching the man's thigh, then his stomach, then his arm, stabbing mercilessly. He spied Hershel out of the corner of his eye lifting his sword to finish another oarsman.

Another climbed over the cliff, saw the commotion, and came running forth. Gavin abandoned his fight, lunging forward to meet the new threat. William jumped up, staggering on his false leg, both his arm and now his side bleeding, and lifted his sword, blocking the blow that the adversary attempted to land upon him. His broadsword dropped heavily. William's wrists threatened to snap. He held the blow and with a grunt, shoved the man back. He swung his sword wide. The other man blocked it. The connection of metal rattled his arms, sending a tremor through his middle.

He withdrew and jabbed. His adversary managed to step aside. His opponent lifted his sword. William lifted his peg and jabbed the tip into his middle. The sword slipped from the oarsman's grip at the power of the jab. It fell, landing upon Will's outstretched knee, breaking the skin but otherwise bouncing away.

Will turned to see Gavin and Hershel bent at the cliff's edge, sawing at the rope. Two more oarsmen lay dead nearby. Blood seeped from Hershel's shoulder through his surcoat. Will hobbled toward them, the pain in his side deep where he had taken the blade and more delirium induced by fever swaying his step.

Be damned, but he hurt, as if his innards were spilling out. He placed his hand over his side, his other hand dragging his sword by the hilt, and tried to run. His stump was too raw, the ends of the bones in his calf having pushed through the flesh. He knew it was bad. He knew it would smell sour if he unstrapped the peg. Men died of infections. He wiped his sweat again, shivered with the chill of fever, and finally admitted the truth: he was festering.

He arrived beside them, looked over the edge, and saw the last three oarsmen climbing the heavy rope, thick like shipping shrouds. One of them neared the top. Sensing the sawing upon the rope, the man looked up. Will stabbed his sword downward, catching the man's shoulder and sending him tumbling, down, down, to the beach.

Hershel and Gavin continued sawing as the other two men reversed their ascent to hasten back to the beach. Will helped saw the rope. The final threads popped apart. The rope snapped and snaked over the edge of the cliff. The men upon it plummeted back to the sand. William dropped to his knees, his chest rising and falling, watching as they landed in a heap far below.

All three of them sat panting, each bearing fresh wounds that all needed tending, but Will could no longer resist doubling over.

"Will, what ails you?" Hershel finally spoke between breaths, wiping sweat from his brow.

William exhaled, felt his head swirling, felt chills rack his body, and fell back to his rear, then flopped backward into the grasses, casting his arms up beside his head. "Well that didn't go as planned," he muttered, feeling the blackness of sleep and fever swim before his eyes. Clouds were rolling in. *More rain,* he thought. "Apparently the oarsmen were loyal to Lispagne after all," he tried to jest. "More rain... We have to find Amber..."

***

Gavin and Hershel scrambled forward as their youngest brother's head lolled unconsciously to one side. His skin was pallid and sweaty.

"He's delirious," Hershel muttered, wrenching loose Will's sword belt and dragging it away.

Gavin began stripping Will's surcoat off. "Go tend to our captives," he ordered. "Ensure they remain bound and unthreatening. Will must have an ailment he didn't mention. He's burning up with fever. Dammit, but Father is going to kill us if his youngest son dies."

"Aye, he is that." Hershel jumped up, running back to the camp and noting that both prisoners remained knocked out. "They're secure!" he hollered, double checking their wrists.

"Good!" Gavin called back. "I need boiling water to tend him...*oh Lord God, Christ be damned...*"

Hershel furrowed his brow at the string of profanity and came back, looking down at William's stump of a leg. The peg was unstrapped, cast aside. His trouser leg was rolled up. His skin was discolored, the sour stench of infection strong. Gavin lifted his surcoat to his nose to obstruct the putrid smell.

"*Iesus,*" Hershel exhaled, crossing himself. "He never said a word. The bone is clean through the skin."

"He was so intent on finding Amber, he put aside his own pain," Gavin remarked.

"Damnation, Will..." Hershel remarked, knowing Will couldn't hear him. "He would have walked to oblivion without telling us. He could die."

"He's nay going to die. Not on my guard."

Gavin ripped the trouser up the side, splaying out the fabric. Gavin swallowed a gag while Hershel ran back to the encampment where the fire containing the balinger's chain still sat, the flame feeble. A small stack of underbrush and kindling sat nearby. He collected it and thrust it into the smithy fire. Neither Hershel nor Gavin spoke. Nothing needed to be said. As men, trained for this, they knew the drill.

A drum of water sat nearby, a supply that had been stashed in the encampment for return trips. Hershel filled the blacksmith pan and nestled it into the growing flame. He paced impatiently for the water to boil. When it finally did, he whipped it off the flame and brought it to Gavin sitting vigil, ripping his only clean tunic from his pack into rags. Face hard and jaw clenched, Gavin dropped the rags in the scalding liquid, removing them, placing the fabric directly upon Will's wounds.

An unconscious wail welled up from William's throat, his body arching. Hershel and Gavin braced him until he settled back to the ground. They flashed a look of fear between each other.

Neither of them wanted to say it. Hershel finally summoned the courage.

"It needs to come off," Hershel muttered, digesting the words he had just uttered. "At least to the knee. His stump festers badly. I fear we're too late with the water. *Iesus*, brother." He shook his head, his brow contorting as he looked into the distance at nothing. "I can run my sword through these bastards but I don't think I can bear to saw my brother's leg away."

Gavin too shook his head and swallowed hard. The first time Will's foot had been amputated, their father had done the honors. The only time their father had spoken of it, he had cried.

"It has to be done," croaked Gavin, looking at William's lifeless face. He took a shaking breath and nodded. "I'm the oldest one here. I'll do it. See what smithy tools they have, anything sharp."

Gavin looked away as well, swallowing, then forcing the words out.

"If there's nothing and we have to use a knife, then so be it, and we'll need a... Dammit!" He growled at his own weakness. "A mallet, man, to hammer the blade through as quickly as we can. Stick an iron in the fire too."

Gavin's face paled as Hershel sifted through the tools in the encampment.

"No mallets!" Hershel called out. "But indeed a saw!"

Hershel dunked it in the water barrel to clean it. Amputations were always risky. William had been through it once successfully, but he too had never spoken of the ordeal. He only screamed about it at night when he relived the experience in his nightmares. The first nightmare, over two years ago, they had raced to his chamber and found him sitting before the fire, wrapped in blankets, shaking. On a whisper, William told them never to come to him again on the matter. Repeating an amputation might be too much for any man.

"Will." Gavin shook him. "Will. Wake. We have news to impart to you."

Will groaned, his face groggy, and looked up into Gavin's ashen face.

"Will, brother…" Hershel began as he rejoined Gavin with the tool in hand. "Your leg festers. It's bad… We can't save it."

***

The statement roused Will, his eyes clearing.

"What…what are you saying?" Will whispered.

Hershel took a deep breath as if chewing on words he needed to spit out. "It needs to come off. Gavin needs to—to amputate to the knee."

William shook his head, side to side, trembling as the words sank in. He scooted backward, terror cutting through the haze induced by fever. "Nay…" he breathed. "Nay that."

Gavin captured Will's arm, alarm bright on his face. William yanked free and rolled onto his stomach, crawling, unable to walk without his attachment.

"Will, we don't want to. Trust this is the worst decision we have to make," Gavin beseeched, grabbing his arm again. "Stop and hear reason."

"Nay," William choked, his voice thick and tears threatening to roll down his face, ripping his arm away again. "Be damned, but I can't go through it again."

"Think of Amber," Hershel spoke, his voice also thick. "Think of the lass you love so, and get through it."

"You haven't any idea what you ask of me," William growled, turning to glare at Hershel.

Hershel threw his arms wide and erupted.

"You're right, Will! I know nay what this is like. I don't have a missing leg, and I don't intend to have one, either. But this is your problem, like it or nay. God has placed this burden on you. Unfair? Aye. It's damned unfair. But must it be done? Indeed. It must. Unless you give up so easily," he taunted. "Amber waits for you. You owe it to her to try to find her, since these sorry shites won't talk," he gestured over his shoulder. "Do we ask much of you? Aye. We ask you to suck it up, close your eyes, and get through it. Or else you're going to *die*." A tear rolled down Hershel's cheek. "'Tis that simple. And if you die, then part of Father will die. Part of me will die, part of Gavin, Loddin, George, and sweet Gwenyth and sweet Lady Amber, wherever she is. And dammit if I don't find that a wee bit selfish."

The wisdom of his words cut through Will's defenses, even if terror still lapped like flames within him, but Hershel continued, his voice shaking.

"To speak plainly, Gavin is going to saw off your leg, to the knee. And I'm going to burn it shut, and you're going to scream in such agony that both of us will fear we've killed our brother. But you had better bloody well pass out and sleep it off, and wake the hell up free of fever. And there's no two ways about it. Do you understand?"

Will's nightmares washed over him anew. He remembered the pain, the screaming, the writhing, only to awaken tangled in his bedclothes battling blindly against hands that weren't there. He took several deep breaths, gripping the ground.

"I fully intend to pass out again," he gasped, chest rising and falling quickly. His brothers were right. Roll over and die? Or do what needed to be done. "But aye, you're right," he swallowed. "Amber deserves more than a coward."

"That's not what I meant, Will," Hershel began, but William held up a hand.

"You were right. Waste not anymore time. Dammit, just..." He shut his eyes, lying down, holding out his wrists. "Bind my hands and legs. I cracked one of Father's ribs the first time," he admitted. "And pour some foking drink down my throat. Whiskeybae, dammit. God give me whiskey..."

He took more deep breaths, rallying for the fight he knew this would be. Tears leaked out of his eyes. Gavin rummaged through his packs for his flask of highland whiskeybae.

"Drink, wee Will," he whispered, placing the flask in an outstretched hand. "Drink heartily, and disparage me nay for calling you such a pet name. You're my youngest brother. Even when we're old and grey, you'll still be so."

Will obliged, taking the strong drink in gulps, groaning as the onslaught of inebriation made his head swim. Hershel rolled him on his side, sending pain through his body, and urged his hands behind his back to tie them. There was nothing to which to tie his legs, so Hershel straddled him instead to hold his thighs down.

***

Slowly, William settled and the aftershocks of pain seemed to recede.

Gavin took up the saw. He and Hershel bowed their heads together as Hershel administered a shaky prayer, and as they crossed themselves in the name of the Father, Gavin placed a hand upon Will's left knee. Tears fell over Gavin's eyelids and he looked to heaven for divine strength, shaking his head. Hershel sank his weight down upon William's chest, gripping each of his youngest brother's thighs.

Hershel seemed calm. But his lips moved as he recited the *Pater Noster*, staring at nothing as if the meditative words might protect his bleeding heart.

"Do it," slurred William, no longer trying to contain his fear. "I can't wait for you sorry sods to deliberate any longer."

Gavin took deep breaths again, scrunching his nose to stave off more tears, and looked to Hershel who still stared at nothingness, his lips moving, his strong arms and hands in a death grip upon William's thighs. He placed the saw to William's putrid skin.

"God, please protect me in his decision," Gavin begged on a whispered.

With a forceful thrust, he sawed through Will's skin.

William screamed. He flailed despite Hershel upon him, nearly bucking him off. His body torqued. No audible words. Only a long shriek, voice cracking. Words finally came.

"Ahhhhh, God! Ahhhhh!"

Gavin continued his task, bearing down in fast, hard jerks, unable to stave off his own tears at Will's shrieks of pain.

He tried to cut through the knots of bone and ligaments at the knee. "I'm sorry..." he whispered, the sound of the amputation causing his stomach to threatening an upsurge of bile.

At first, there was no blood, but then the seam of severed flesh began to pool rich red around the metal, rolling down his skin, onto Gavin's hand bracing his knee. William's legs twitched and jerked as he attempted to writhe free, wailing, curses flowing like waterfalls, and then his whole body slackened and went still.

Neither brother turned to look at him despite his silence. If they stopped, they wouldn't be able to finish. The bone finally broke through and the rest of the flesh cut quickly. Hershel jumped up, racing to the fire to grab the hot iron. He hastened back, his face streaked with water that highlighted the grime upon his skin.

Hershel shoved the iron against William's flesh. The skin sizzled, but the rotten chunk of leg was cut away, lying beside them in the grass, and pray to God no more festering was already setting in above the knee.

"He breathes," Gavin whispered, wiping his face on the end of his surcoat, waiting for Hershel to make sure the wound was good and truly sealed. "He bleeds from his side. Took a knife from that bastard with the shite voice."

"I'll reheat the iron," Hershel said solemnly, "and take care of it whilst he sleeps."

Gavin stared at his handiwork as if he could see right through it, holding his forehead. Hershel returned minutes later and thrust the iron with no preamble into their little brother's side. No reaction. William may as well be dead. Except for the rising and falling of his chest, his heart thumping beneath his ribs, he showed no sign of life.

Hershel cast aside the iron into a dirt patch and used a strip of clean tunic to wrap around William's new stump and tied his dangling trouser leg around it.

He rolled William upon his side to untie his wrists, pulling his arms free.

Then he sat beside Gavin, shoulder to shoulder, and crossed his ankles, resting his forearms upon his propped knees. A glance back at the camp showed that their prisoners had roused, but neither had attempted to flee. Neither spoke. Finally Hershel rose, leaving Gavin to remain at William's side.

"God watches over him right now," Hershel nodded to himself. "He will see him through...he has to. For all our sake."

Chapter 16

The sound of carts wheeling over the ground rose above the din of Fort Michaelmas' mills grinding, weapons clinking, and men training in an outer training field. Prince William, a couple days behind schedule, was finally arriving.

Lod strode from the outer wall where he had been watching each day for his brothers' return to the gatehouse, thankful for a diversion. He leaned through the opening. "Lift the portcullis for the prince," he ordered the men inside the stone barbican.

The guards noted the royal standards flapping from afar as a string of cavalry with Prince William at the helm grew closer. They cranked the chains, reeling up the gate. Lod spied one of Edward's son's striding across the outer yard and hollered down to him.

"Go tell our fathers the prince arrives! If he hasn't yet received your father's missive, he can make grievances directly!"

And so could Lord Loddin. His father hadn't forgiven him for aiding his younger brothers. Lord Loddin had raged against him, and when Lod refused to apologize, the man had refused to speak to him since. Each morn and each eve Lod had spied their father walking upon the ridge overlooking the shore, waiting and fretting, as if a widow hoping for the return of a husband.

Each passing day unsettled Lod more and more, too. If something had happened to his brothers, if Gavin, Hershel, and William had perished, their father would never forgive him.

Morgan jogged off to locate their fathers. Lod stood ready to greet his brother of marriage, righting his surcoat and adjusting his belts and swords to ensure he looked to rights.

"Loddin, man!" Prince William called up to the barbican,

raising his hand. "My wife will be pleased to know I've seen you and that you appear well!"

He entered the bustling yard as soldiers cleared to the periphery to make space for the royal contingent. Squires collected the prince's reins as well as those of the others. Lod nodded his head at their efficiency and jogged down the steps to the dirt. He strode to the prince and dropped into a bow at Titan's hooves.

"Your Highness. An immense pleasure to host you here. I hope everything appears well to you at Fort Michaelmas and that you're pleased with my leadership thus far."

Prince William dismounted and closed the gap between them with two strides.

"Rise up, Lod. Be damned, but I hate these flowery greetings." He pulled Lod into a slapping hug.

Lod returned the embrace and stood back, smiling. "All the same, Prince William. I cannot address you any other way and you know it. If my men question my lack of protocol, what's to keep them from thinking I have favoritism? What if some day you become a tyrant and I make the mistake of greeting you improperly? You could lop my mazard off."

"If I ever become a tyrant, then you have permission to knock the shite out of me and bring my lofty feet back to the ground," Prince William laughed, slapping him on his shoulder and turning to the yard where the other soldiers were bowing. "And I do exhibit favoritism. You're my brother now and they all know it. Gwenyth and I must plan an excursion to Ballymead for a visit one of these months, for it is only there that I can remove the shackles of this crown and simply be a man among my family."

"We would love to host a reunion at Ballymead," Lod replied, stepping back. "Do come in. Times have been something of a trial. My brothers, father, and the Lord of Dunstonwoodshire are here—"

Lod noticed Prince William's green eyes brighten.

"Has Lady Amber been found?" Prince William questioned as his men behind him dismounted.

"So Lord Edward's missive reached your ears?" Lod asked.

"Yes, I read his grievance, and promised Gwen I would search for Lady Amber and Lord Edward," Prince William replied, loosening his chainmail coif to allow it to sag around his neck. He shook out his mangy hair. "To no avail, it seems. I've grown disheartened by my lack of success."

"Amber's still missing," Lod conceded. "They've searched high and low, and Will is fairly devastated." Loddin escorted the prince across the bailey. "They arrived here six days ago and found a promising clue about the men who might have abducted Lady Amber. Lord Edward wished to reevaluate his search plan, but Will, well—"

"Your Highness!" greeted Lord Loddin, limping across the yard.

Lod turned over his shoulder to see his father coming toward them and felt the wrath of the old man's anger all over again. He looked beyond his father and noticed Lord Edward striding forward, perpetually grey-faced. His cheeks had grown gaunt and his ill-shaven face portrayed a despondent man.

"Lord Loddin, Lord Edward," Prince William nodded his head, extending a wrist to clasp with each.

They fell into bows instead.

"Rise up, men," the prince stated.

"Pray you received word of my missing daughter?" Lord Edward began.

"Indeed I did, and I searched for your party as well as the lady along the way. We had a close brush, almost found her, but—"

"How?" the men all exclaimed in unison.

They stepped back, allowing Lord Edward to proceed with the questioning. "How so, Your Highness? We arrived here and the hounds found a scent on the shore. Captain Loddin had seen an unmarked balinger crossing the waters not long before our arrival. We assumed the men who nabbed her had sailed away with her."

Lod cleared his throat and interjected. "They had the air of smugglers. You had ordered me to remain vigilant of the coastline, and I've already sent my report to the capital to inform you."

"And I would not have gotten it yet," Prince William nodded. "But I fear, your efforts might have been in vain, for I passed by the Abbey of St. Matilda's some days ago, and your daughter was brought there by a well-meaning woodsman, it seems, after she managed to escape and elude her captors."

"Pray... you speak the truth?" Lord Edward croaked. "She's been found?"

"Praise be..." Lord Loddin began, before his snarl rounded on his oldest son. "And you loaned your brothers a knarr so Will could rush off on a fool's errand. Had you just waited, fortune would have sent Prince William here with this news, and all would still be safe."

Lod stood his ground. "Will had every right to make the decision he did with the information he had, and I was right to support him. If he had waited and there wasn't any news, then he would have wasted valuable time," Lod retorted.

"Will can't handle such a mission," Lord Loddin pressed. "What, with his missing foot? And no sailing expertise? He's still green to the ways of the world."

"He's nearly five and twenty, Father, indeed, Prince William's age," he gestured at the prince. "And yet you regard our brother of marriage with the respect due an autonomous man, but you won't extend the same courtesy for your youngest son? This was his choice to make."

"He's probably gotten himself killed," Lord Loddin fumed.

"This was *his* choice," Lod repeated.

"What has passed?" Prince William interjected. "I've never seen this discord among my family of marriage."

"My lad, Will, was distraught, and schemed to borrow one of Fort Michaelmas' knarrs. He pursued the men who we presumed still had Lady Amber and took Hershel and Gavin with him. They did so behind my back, after I had instructed them not to," Lord Loddin said. "They disobeyed me deliberately."

Prince William, normally direct among his men, seemed to falter now, and proceeded cautiously. "I suppose I can understand Will's desperation."

"But if you say Amber has been found at St. Mathilda's, then he's done nothing but put his life in peril and waste time," Lord Edward stated. "We need to mount up to go to her. Does she remain there still?"

Prince William lifted his palms. "Calm yourselves, for it's not that simple."

At that moment, a Bainick knight marched by them, a monk in tow. The monk stumbled, his face having grown a stubble and his cassock dirty.

"Captain Loddin," the Bainick knight escorting him asked. "We've a prisoner needing confinement. Where are the dungeons?"

Lod looked at the monk, then at Prince William, then back at the knight again. "Indeed, what's his transgression?"

Prince William replied. "Might we go inside to discuss? Mayhap have a tankard or two?"

"I wish to saddle up," Lord Edward hastened.

"No, man. You must hear me out," Prince William replied, eyeing the monk. "Come. You might want to be seated for the news I am about to impart."

Lod answered the Bainick knight. "Across the bailey, through that portico beside the armory, and down the ensuing yard to the right. The prison door is in the curtain wall and descends below ground. A prison warden stands there."

The knight nodded and led the monk away.

"I sense the news isn't good," Lord Loddin finally remarked. He turned to Edward. "Mayhap we should go seek an ale and a seat."

"Nay," Edward ground out. "Tell me plainly, Your Highness, what has transpired."

Prince William took a measured inhale. All knew that appeasing lords was a more exhausting game than drilling soldiers. "She fled the monastery. We spent a day searching the area in hopes of finding her. A monk was caught in her chamber, making untoward advances on her, taking advantage of her blindness and intruding on her privacy. She was frightened and found a way to elude the monks to escape once again."

The men paused, thinking, then they all pivoted their heads back in the direction the monk had just been dragged. Realization dawned as their brows darkened. Lord Edward and his son's bolted after the monk.

"Lord Edward!" Prince William called. "Stop, man! We must discuss!"

Lord Edward didn't stop, as if the haze of anger shrouding him blocked out all good sense. Prince William shook his head, then turned to Sir Cavanaugh standing nearby listening. He motioned with a tip of his head. Cavanaugh nodded and jogged across the yard in pursuit of Edward.

"We couldn't find her," Prince William continued, resting his hands on his hips. "I've left men behind to continue the search. Tell me, have there been any signs of Will's return from across the strait?"

An angry scowl returned to Lord Loddin's brow. "Nay."

"Nay *yet*," Lod corrected. "But I have faith that my brothers' mission *won't* have been in vain. There was clear evidence that the men they tracked were also the smugglers I saw crossing the strait in their unmarked vessel. Lady Amber might no longer be with them, but the men are guilty and if Will and my other brothers find them, they could learn some valuable information."

"Who cares about such 'valuable information' when the primary goal is to find the lady?" Lord Loddin grumbled. "I didn't give you my blessing. I was clear, and you disobeyed me. 'Tis a dangerous endeavor my sons have embarked upon, and it would have been best to wait and devise a safer plan."

Lod scowled and made no effort to hide his anger now. "I answer to the crown first, Father. I'm nay a lad anymore. I understand that we are your sons, but with all due respect," Lod continued, taking a deep breath. "Will is a grown man. He's a grown man who loves a lass. And Hershel and Gavin are loyal brothers."

Lord Loddin's brow pinched with more anger, but his namesake pressed onward.

"He gave up a life when he lost his eyes and lost his leg. In fact, he gave up a life long before that, when he helped raise Gwenyth, when he spent hours in the meadery doing tasks we others were too busy to do routinely. But he found purpose again when he and Amber were betrothed. He's a grown man, a fifth son, with no hereditary claim to anything other than the good name of Ballymead. And it might be difficult for you to accept, but he doesn't answer to you either, nay anymore, or anyone else but his king and himself. What does he stand to lose by defying you? An inheritance? A title? We all already know he has neither accept a token purse from you.

"You've taken him for granted. If he wanted to search to the end of the earth for his betrothed, he should do so with our *full blessing*. He was distraught and would have attempted to cross the strait on his own. I chose to help my brother and minimize the risk of his perishing as best as I could, and see that he not only had safer means, but had two of his brothers with him to help him. You might have seeded us, but you don't own us. And before you censure me, ask what you would have done had it been Mother. Would you have listened to your father telling you not to take the risk? Or would you have sailed to the ends of the bloody earth yourself?"

Lord Loddin stood stunned to silence as the men of Dunstonwoodshire returned to the group, rage boiling unchecked on Edward's brow.

"I know you fear for him. I know he has a lame foot. I know you feel guilty about it," Lod said, softening. "But trying to protect him with your guilt is never going to help him. As a captain and a knight, if I coddled my men every time they earned an injury, instead of forcing them to pick up their arms again, they would never become soldiers."

Alarmed, Prince William frowned. "A knarr takes several hands to maneuver effectively. And you mean to say that *only* William, Gavin, and Hershel manned the vessel to the Île de Neige?"

Lod nodded. "It wasn't ideal, but like I said, Will was going to defy anyone. This was the safest bet. I decided that if anything happened to the vessel, I would gladly take the blow to my pay or risk demotion. The only reason I didn't also go with my brothers was because I hadn't royal permission and couldn't get it quickly enough. Otherwise, I, too, would have been aboard that knarr. I've watched for their return each day and expect them soon." Lod changed the subject. "What of the monk? Is that the man that molested wee Amber?"

Prince William nodded. "Mind you all, he didn't force her to bed, but he touched her inappropriately and aimed for more."

"Yes," Cavanaugh now added. "And he walked the whole way here tethered like a common ass. A sorry sod with an impure heart and the devil's cock."

"Remember your company, man," Prince William warned, sensing Lord Edward was about to snap.

Edward glared at Cavanaugh but allowed the prince to chasten his knight.

Cavanaugh rolled his eyes. "Oh *My Liege*," he exaggerated. "My tongue is tainted, but my honor is pure. Lord Edward, rest assured, that your daughter good and truly broke his finger. Snapped it clean backward. Only a bold woman would do such a thing."

"He got what he deserved," muttered Angus.

Prince William stifled a smile. He turned back to Edward. "Sir Frances might have an unchecked tongue, but his honor is indeed pure," he smirked. "And he made that bastard monk suffer on our walk. Rest assured Amber protected her chastity well. The monk will answer for what he's done."

Edward nodded to Cavanaugh. "I owe you both my gratitude and you indeed renew my hope that Amber will be found. We should begin trekking back from whence we came and diverge to St. Mathilda's."

Lord Loddin nodded in agreement, refusing to look at Lod, embarrassed by their public altercation. Morgan and Angus strode away to begin packing for their trek. Prince William turned back to his men when a guardsman on the parapet began running.

"Captain Loddin! Captain Loddin! Out there! On the water!"

Lod froze. "What is it, man?"

"The knarr! On the strait! It's a sunny day with good winds, and it's just visible upon the horizon—"

Lod, followed by his father and Prince William, ran across the yard to the steps, skipping up the stone pavers two at a time. Lod dashed in the direction his guard motioned to, running along the wooden planks. Grabbing the edge of a merlon to halt his speed, he braced himself within the embrasure and began scanning the waters.

Lord Loddin skidded to a halt behind them.

"There," his soldier pointed. "Off to the south."

Lod spotted it. It was tiny, but the Bainick colors were unmistakable. His face broke into a smile and he exhaled a lungful of relief.

"Don't assume all is well," grumbled his father. "Pray all three of your brothers are aboard that boat and alive."

Lod turned to his father. The old man had a point. Île de Neige was wild, uninhabited, with only scant settlements much farther inland. If one of them had become injured or fallen ill, there would be naught they could do about it, no resources, and no help.

He patted his guard's shoulder. "My thanks for the alert, man. I'm going down to the shore to see them arrive."

He strode down the wall and down the stairs to where he saw Edward and his sons returning to the bailey at the news of the knarr's home voyage.

"My brothers return!" Lod called in passing. "I need ten men to assist tethering the vessel when it reaches port!"

Several soldiers pushed away from the wall where they stood idle and jingled forward. Lod ducked beneath the lifting portcullis as Lord Loddin did his best to keep up with his namesake's punishing pace. The knarr was growing larger. The path down to the dock cut a meandering trail through the rocky ground. The three remaining knarrs sat tethered in the man-made inlet hidden by a cliff, bobbing along the ripples.

Wind swept sparse white clouds across the bright sky. The knarr grew closer, aiming for landfall. Watching the craft progress, Lod could finally make out Gavin and Hershel manning the sail, adjusting it to use the wind to the best advantage. William was nowhere to be seen.

"Where's Will?" remarked Angus.

Lod ignored his father's assessing gaze that begged the same question.

"I'm sure he's fine," stated Prince William who had joined them on the shore. He placed a hand on each Loddins' shoulder in solidarity. "Lord Loddin, Captain Loddin. I can sense anger betwixt you. This was Will's decision, please keep that in mind, and direct your distress accordingly."

Lod continued to ignore the waves of irritation his father directed at him and scrutinized two unknown men on deck whose heads had just come into view. They stood back to back, bound together around the mast.

"Wait a minute... Ho there!" Lod called to his brothers, waving his arm over his head, then turned to Prince William. "Those are the smugglers I spied crossing the strait! They've captured them!"

Hershel returned Lod's wave while Gavin wrestled with the shroud, their hair blowing wildly. Their faces were stoic, their surcoats torn, faded, filthy, and... bloody?

Lod's heart clenched. Be damned, but their father's premonitions about a terrible event befalling them was about to come true.

"Where's William?" Lord Loddin muttered under his breath, his anger giving way to worry.

"Where's Will?" Lod hollered, though his brothers didn't seem to understand.

The knarr was quickly approaching. Lod waded into the water with his soldiers and motioned for Gavin to toss him an anchoring rope.

"Ready a litter for Will!" Hershel called, cupping his hand around his mouth. "He needs a healer immediately! And prepare two prison cells! William returns without his woman, but we bring you the men who nabbed her!"

The panic churning in Lod's gut exploded. "Go back to the fort!" he pointed at two soldiers. "Gather a litter and make haste! Run!"

Their father hobbled into the water as well. They came close enough to throw the rope. It slapped the water. Lod snatched it up.

"If William is near death or dies soon, I do nay care what choice words you use to disrespect me," Lord Loddin fumed under his breath. "I'll hold you responsible and you'll be disinherited."

Lod rolled his eyes. As his father's first son, he was used to having the strictest treatment and smoothing the way for all his siblings to follow. Gwenyth, God bless her, had grown without rules at all.

"I work for the crown. Disinherit me if you will, but then Mary, rounding with my child and your grandchild, and young Hershel, come with me, your *only* grandson, I might remind. Last I checked, Hersh didn't select you to be his son's surrogate when he joins the cloth."

"I'm warning you, son—"

"Threaten me all you wish, Father. You're angry and scared for Will, and you're taking it out on me. I lead the men at this fort. I'm the oldest of six siblings, five of whom are my brothers. I'm about to be a father myself and have pledged to raise my wee nephew when Hershel takes his vows. I'm a leader in the king's army. Disinherit me. Make good on your threat. But if William lives, give Ballymead to *him*. I don't want to be a farmer. I don't want to run the apiary or the meadery. I want to be a leader in the Bainick Army. You'll hurt me none by taking the burden of Ballymead off my shoulders for believe me, as your first son, I've stressed about the responsibility my whole life. Now be of good use as a soldier or get the hell out of these waters and out of the way!"

He reached out toward the boat, turning his shoulder to any further argument. "I'm towing you in!" He leveled a silent request at his father to help. Lord Loddin cast aside his argument for the moment and the two, in a stalemate, pulled the boat onto the shore.

"How bad is he?" Lord Loddin inquired.

"He fights between life and death! So far, no more festering! But he rages with fever!" called Gavin, grey-faced.

"Be dammed," Prince William muttered, also wading into the water to gather the slack of rope already reeled in, dragging it to the docking hooks.

"What happened?" Lod called, glancing back at the shore to check on the progress of his men fetching the litter.

His men were jogging down the path with the platform suspended between them.

"Will..." Gavin said, nudging someone at his feet. "Will, look. The prince is here. You can make your grievance directly and see these two bastards into his custody."

Wind-beaten and sun-worn, the ill-shaven brothers bent down and hoisted up William under each shoulder so that he dangled between them. Will rose to the rail of the knarr, clinging to it to for support, his cheeks sunken, his face grey. Lod swallowed, staring at his brother, and didn't dare look at his father for fear of his angry glare.

"His fever looks to be raging," Prince William noted, waiting with the two Loddins to help Will down.

"He's been delirious or unconscious all the morn," Hershel said. "His leg festered. We had to amputate more of it—"

"You what?" exclaimed Lord Loddin. "*Good Christ* what befell the lad?"

Lod and Prince William regarded Lord Loddin, trembling at what must be horrible memories assaulting him. Hershel and Gavin didn't answer, but braced Will's arms around their necks, gripping him around the waist. His head drooped lifelessly at his neck.

"Bring the litter here!" hollered Lod to his soldiers who

continued down the rocky path. "Make haste! Make haste!"

The soldiers arrived with the stretcher as Gavin and Hershel hauled William over the rail. Lod and Prince William reached up to receive him, the sight of his leg missing all the way to the knee assailing them.

"My son..." Lord Loddin gasped, helping guide Will's waist down while the prince and his oldest son bore his weight, lowering him gently. They tipped him horizontally and placed him upon the platform.

"Take him to my quarters," Lod ordered, and his soldiers hastened back up the path, Will's arm flopping off the side to drag over the rocks.

"*Pater Noster*..." Lord Loddin whispered, abandoning the shore to chase the litter back up the rocky path.

Lod turned back to the knarr and readied to receive the first of two prisoners being dangled over the rail. Prince William turned to a burly, red-bearded knight, and Sir Cavanaugh, flicking his finger at them.

"Are you sure these are the men?" Lod asked.

Hershel nodded. "They admitted much. I suspect Prince William will wish to question them."

"Sir MacTierny. Take this prisoner," the prince said to the red-bearded knight.

The second man was then lifted over.

"Good Christ, look at his face," Lod remarked, shaking his head.

"He's a mangled one," Prince William remarked, whistling a decrescendo. "Took quite a beating."

"Will's handiwork," Gavin harrumphed. "The man boasted that he had swived Lady Amber."

"What?" came Lord Edward's angry growl from behind them.

"They didn't, sir, they simply tried to rile us," Gavin said.

"And got more than they bargained for," Hershel added. "As you can see, our youngest brother is quite capable with his false foot."

"Alonso is his name," Gavin continued. "He tried to bait Will into killing 'im. They're afraid of facing their king."

"From where do they hail?" the prince asked, passing off the beaten and bloodied man, skin split along his cheeks, mouth, eyes, and head, to Sir Cavanaugh, adding, "remove them both to the dungeons until I have time to interrogate them."

"Yes, Your Highness," Cavanaugh replied, prodding Alonso in the back with the hilt of his sword.

"They hail from Lispagne," Hershel replied, jumping over the rail to land in the shallows with a splash, followed by Gavin.

"Lispagne." Prince William remarked knowingly. "Gavin? Hershel?"

"Aye, brother-of-marriage?" Hershel replied.

"The clues, the missives...it is all making sense," the prince said cryptically, shaking his head. Then he leveled a stern gaze at them. "Bain has a crisis on its hands. And I think I am about to unearth its ugly face."

Chapter 17

"If you were ever in peril, I would protect you to the bitter end, eyes or nay. I would offer up my other leg if needs be to see you protected..." Oh, Will's sweet words.

Amber shivered, feeling her heavy braid sagging with rainwater. Why the memory entered her mind now, she had no idea. Her feet were freezing, cut and raw, her hands, icy, and her skirts offered no protection from the winds, for they were sodden, too.

"Where are you now?" she begged aloud, huddled against a boulder.

It had been days without food, and a steady water supply didn't exist as she wound further down the countryside. When she found a trickle from a natural spring, she decided to sit and remain beside it. Was this the end? It couldn't be, and yet, the future was bleak. She had encountered no one. No travelers, no villages. Nothing.

"William..." she whispered, wrapping her cloak around her and hunkering down more tightly.

She rubbed her sore feet, too hungry to continue, too tired, nay, too drained. She was physically and emotionally drained. *'Tis best to simply lay down and wait*, she thought. *I must be close to an edge of sorts.* The whistling wind told her so. One poorly-made roll, one step in any direction, might be perilous.

"I'm so turned around," she muttered, feeling a sob pinch her throat and threaten release.

She swallowed. There were no more tears. There was no more fear. There was only despair. She had lost track of time. Her focus waned. She should have waited at the monastery until a letter was penned. She shouldn't have reacted so impulsively. But it was too late for regrets.

She was unsure which way to turn. She patted the ground beside her, feeling that it was stable, and lay down, curling her feet beneath her ragged skirts. Wrapping her hands around her knees, her fingers met with her hem, devoid of the bits of trimming they had once displayed.

"If they were looking for me, they would have found me by now," she lamented on a whisper.

Her mind was fading. She was so tired. The folded edge of the parchment she had stolen from Alonso's saddle punctured her in the thigh, curled as she was. She had nearly forgotten about it after so long. She hardly noticed it now as her mind sank into sleep.

***

Lod jogged up the stairs from the dungeons. They were dank and despite efforts to keep them mucked out, they smelled sour. He nodded to his guard, standing vigilant at the portal to the inner yard. The guard turned the key so the door clanked open.

"Good eve, Captain," said the guard.

Lod walked into the night. Moonlight illuminated the cloudless sky and millions of stars twinkled serenely, as if the world was at peace. His jaw was set tightly, his pulse thumping as if he readied for battle. With Will barely clinging to life, his nerves were worn.

Striding across the yard, he detoured around the tavern and pushed open the door that led to his lodgings, climbed the steps, and marched down the corridor.

He entered the bedchamber.

"How is he?" he asked, noting Will laid out, bare-chested, pectorals rising and falling in shallow breaths. His brow and hair were soaked from the strips of water-soaked rags laid upon his forehead.

A linen was folded down to his waist, revealing that his trousers had also been stripped. The bedchamber, small but tidy, rested quiet. His brothers sat to one side, Hershel working his rosary beads through his fingers, his lips moving silently. Their father sat to the other side, dipping more rags in cold water to swap out the ones draped over Will's brow.

Gavin bounced his foot, causing the floorboard beneath him to steadily squeak. He leaned backward on his stool, arms folded across his chest. He stared at nothing, his eyes boring a hole in the opposite wall.

"He sleeps now," Hershel replied, standing, pacing to a window with the shutters drawn shut. "The priest of Fort Michaelmas has been alerted and awaits should Will require final rites."

He opened the window, leaned against the sill, and stared out at nothing. His rosary beads, frozen in his fingers as he broke his prayerful trance, resumed their mindful fingering.

"His fever rages... *Ad te suspiramus gementes et flentes in hac lacrimarum valle,*" Hershel mouthed, continuing his prayer to the Holy Queen, and watched a dove flutter to land on the roof beside the sill. It cooed.

"No good," Lod muttered. No good at all if the priest was now involved. "Will's fever has burned for hours without breaking."

"And days before we arrived back," Gavin added.

"His leg wasn't used to so much exertion," Lord Loddin said, his voice haggard.

"By the time we saw the damage, we knew he must have been in agony for much of this journey, but he was so intent on finding Amber, he spoke naught of it," Gavin mumbled. He didn't look at his brothers, didn't even blink. "Capturing those bastards... it bloody-well ought to mean something." Gavin paused, then swallowed, and though he didn't appear to be tearing up, his voice thickened and his foot continued bouncing. "Otherwise all of this was nothing but a waste of time, a waste of Will's health...I had to do it... Hershel, me... *my God,* brother." Gavin's eyes shot to Lod standing in the doorway, still having yet to close the door. Lod saw lines of stress on his second brother's brow that had never been there before. "God be damned, but it feels as if we've killed him in our efforts to save him. And I'll never forgive myself."

A tear managed to leak over his eye but he blinked it away and stubbornly swiped at the trail down the grime on his cheek.

"You did what you had to," Lord Loddin assured, nodding. "His leg was festering from his travel, nay from your excursion to the Île de Neige. It would have had to come off regardless." The lord looked to his namesake, nodded once, as if passing him an apology for all his accusations.

Lod gave a grim smile and a single nod in return. Apology accepted. Will's head lolled. It lolled again.

"Rest assured," Lod spoke. "It wasn't all in vain. Prince William interrogates the Lispagnioc men. I just left the dungeons." He shook his head. "Know that Will's decision to pursue them makes him a loyal servant to the crown, and he will be medaled soon. Prince William will be sending correspondence to his vassals in due course, with instructions. Bain might need to rally arms. I fear what you discovered has given us only a narrow advantage."

Lod closed the door and continued. "Prince William will transport the prisoners to the capital as you begin your journey home. He intends to ride with you. Gwen resides at Dunstonwoodshire, waiting to help Lady Amber when she's found. She learned of Lady Amber's distress and left at first light the next morn, without even seeking her husband's permission."

Lord Loddin shook his head, a fleeting smile shimmering over his otherwise grim face. "She always did determine her own course."

William's head continued to loll, shaking off the rag that his father had just placed across it. Lord Loddin looked back down at William, growing more and more restless, a groan escaping his throat. Will's fingers clenched the bedsheet beneath him. He shifted, creaking the bed ropes. His head rolled back and forth on the pillow as more sweat beaded his skin.

"Amber..." he croaked. "Amber, Love. I thought...I thought you would never come..." he swallowed, his parched throat bobbing. "Stop...stop moving...I'm coming to you..."

The men looked to Will, fear brimming their faces. Hershel crossed himself again, clenching the prayer beads, coming back to Will's side to drop onto his knee.

"He fantasizes. That's all. He's only fantasizing..." Gavin whispered, as if warding off the truth, shaking his head.

"Dear God, do we really lose him?" Lod whispered, clenching his jaw. "Has Amber died and he unites with her?"

"Nay," Lord Loddin cried, his voice deep and husky, his words clogged. He dropped his head to the bed, resting his forehead to the back of his son's hand. An angry sob wrenched from his throat. "Nay, son! Nay yet, I beg ye..."

He grabbed at his son's hot and sweaty body for something, anything, to cling to, to keep him in the mortal realm. All three sons crossed themselves again. Hershel remained stoic, his eyes clenched closed, prayers falling fervently from his lips like water spilling over a fall.

"*Spiritu Sancto cooperante, praeparasti, da, ut cuius commemoratione laetamur; eius pia intercessione, ab instantibus malis et a morte perpetua liberemur.*"

Lod came to Will's side, sitting on the straw-filled mattress beside his stump.

Will continued, his voice cracking. "What kind of husband do I make to you? Blind...maimed...worthless..."

"You're worth everything!" their father pleaded, looking up, grabbing his face and petting back his hair from his soaked brow. "I'm sorry I didn't see you as a man. I'm sorry… You deserve your Amber, you deserve a life, you deserve Ballymead—"

A groan worked its way out of Will's throat. He thrashed his head. "Let go!" he bellowed.

His body arched. He threw his head to the side so savagely his father's hands were thrust off. He trembled, shook, flailed, knocking both their father and Lod from the bed onto their arses.

"Don't cut me! Don't cut me!" he shrieked, thrashing, his bed linen flinging off, his undergarments twisting about his middle.

"Grab him!" Lod exclaimed. "Before he launches from the bed!"

Combative arms swung outward, catching Hershel, sending Gavin reeling as if leveled in a tavern brawl. Gavin stumbled against the wall, his jaw reddened, and jumped back into the fray.

"God in heaven make it stop!" Will wailed, his torso arching, twisting. "Ahh! God! Make it *stop!*"

His family wrangled him down. His stump, angry, red flesh, flew up.

"Get his leg, Gav!" Lod demanded.

"I'm foking trying, man!" Gavin shouted, a thumping noise and subsequent curse telling them that Hershel had been hit.

"*Iesus Christus*, when did he get so damned strong?" Lod ground out, finally tethering a leg.

"Easy! Don't make his wound worse!" their father thundered.

"It's his nightmare!" Hershel strained, bracing one of William's shoulders to the bed.

Boots scraped the floor for leverage, the men grunted, complained. Footfalls thundered up the outer stairs, down the corridor, rattling the floor planks. Prince William, Sir MacTierny, and Sir Cavanaugh barged through the door, trailed by a string of Bainick soldiers.

"Ahhhhh!" Will screamed until the exclamation fizzled out. His body sagged back to the bed.

"More cold rags!" Lord Loddin ordered.

Prince William hastened for the water basin and withdrew a rag, draping it over Will's stormy brow.

Will's delirium continued as his brothers finally let go and tried to catch their breath. Will's hand slid up his thigh, his stomach, over his ribs to press against his heart, balling into a fist so he could thump the left side of his chest as if trying to dislodge something.

"Why can't I find her?" he murmured, tears in his voice, his saturated face dripping with sweat, his head lolling again. "Her stockings... raped... sick, I'm going to be sick..."

They all watched him as he faded back to sleep, his energy spent.

Lod gulped for air, noticing his brothers doing the same. Gavin rested his hands on his hips, rotating his jaw to sooth the bruise Will had just put there. Hershel rubbed the corners of his eyes as if fatigued, though the truth lay in the redness of his eyelids. William's breathing continued to slow, evening out to a steady, soft cadence.

Lord Loddin tensed.

"His eyes are opening. Will, lad," Lord Loddin croaked. "Do you see me?"

At first, William didn't appear to see anything. "Aye, Father," William replied, his voice subdued. Then he paused, looking around at everyone with careworn eyes. "The pain...my *foking* leg..." He pinched shut his eyes and tried to breathe in and out. "I dreamed I found her."

His breathing sped up again. "'Twas a vision," he continued, fighting to sit upright. Their father and Lod forced him back down. "I know such a thing sounds preposterous, but I know it to be true. She was lying on the ground at the edge of a cliff and she couldn't find her way to safety. And when I tried to get to her, her... her foot slipped..."

"Hush, lad, just rest now," their father admonished gently. "'Twas only a dream. You've been through an ordeal—"

"Nay," Will defied. "How can anyone rest when she's gone? How can I rest when I know not of her fate?" His eyes were growing heavy again. "What sort of failure would I be to give up on her?"

"You're no failure," Lod said, dropping back to his rear on the mussed bedding. "What you did, finding those men who wronged Amber," he took his brother's limp hand and turned over his shoulder to eye the Bainick prince. "This means everything to Prince William."

"But I didn't find *her*."

"No, you didn't," Prince William replied, stepping forward. "But you and your brothers have given me an important piece to a puzzle. If it hadn't been for you following those men, such would have remained unknown. You are to be commended, brother-of-marriage."

"But I didn't find *her*," Will stated again, unaffected by the prince's words.

"No, you didn't," Prince William repeated. "Not yet, you haven't. But I have faith you'll keep trying, and try you must."

No one argued further. Will's eyes had closed again, listening to the prince's last words. "Aye, I'll keep trying...two days, that's all the time I'll rest...then I leave..." and he drifted back to sleep.

Lod stood, pulling up the blankets once again to cover Will's stump. But as the backs of his hands brushed against his brother's chest, he paused, then reached to Will's brow. He felt it, felt his cheeks, his neck, then his forehead again.

"The fever...it broke."

For a moment, no one spoke. No one moved, then Hershel crossed himself again and dropped back to his knee, holding the crucifix dangling from his beads to his lips as if suspended in time. Prince William moved to the wall and slouched against it to regard his wife's family as Lord Loddin also touched Will, noting that his skin no longer raged hot.

"And he hasn't died. He lives still. Pray, my sons," Lord Loddin said.

"Do you suspect Will's dream had any merit?" Gavin questioned.

"'Twas just a dream," remarked their father.

Hershel shook his head. "Mayhap, but mayhap not." His family all looked at him as the dove on the windowsill cooed, swaying their attention to its feathered form. Hershel turned back to his family and nodded at the omen the bird presented. "Pray that he can recover enough to travel, to assuage his need to find her."

"He's mad if he thinks I'll allow him to rise from bed in two days' time," Lord Loddin remarked, shaking his head. "That lad...stubborn, even on his death bed."

Hershel smiled and glanced at the dove as it flew away, wings beating out their tell-tale squeak. "Will has already been blessed with the return of his eyesight. There's room for another miracle yet."

***

And indeed, William was out of bed two days later, dressing, anxious to mount up and catch up to Lord Edward and his sons.

"You're completely daft, wee brother," Gavin shook his head, having just arrived with a morning meal from the tavern. He dropped the tray with a clatter onto the bedside table and grabbed Will's shoulders, attempting to push him back to sitting. "Look at you! You can't even stand without holding onto something."

"Impart something to me that I'm nay already aware of," Will retorted, shaking away Gavin's grip. "Will you bring me my peg?"

"It won't even fit you anymore. It's too short now."

"And I'll hobble like an old man until I can craft a new one. But

I won't stay. I need to catch up to Edward and his sons."

"You have nary a clue where they are," Gavin argued. "Your stump is raw. How on God's green earth can you propose putting any weight on it?"

"Are you going to bring me that peg?" Will stated.

Gavin folded his arms. "Nay. Get back abed."

Will shook his head and clenched his jaw, then braced the bed to achieve his balance. He began hopping to the chair opposite the bed upon which the peg rested.

"Christ, man," muttered Gavin, shaking his head and grabbing Will. "Sit the hell down. I'll go get it." He pushed him back to the bed, still shaking his head, and lumbered across the flooring to gather up the peg. "At least let me fashion some padding for it."

Gavin tore a piece of linen off the bedding and began bunching it up, fixing it on the support of the peg that would rest under Will's knee.

"Father is going to be pissing angry, Will," he said under his breath. "You're in no condition to travel. None."

"Do nay tell him, then. I'll leave on my own. Amber's alive somewhere, I know it. If, like you all said, she fled St. Mathilda's, then there's still a chance we'll find her alive. My fever already broke—"

"It's only been two bloody days. *Only two.* Your fever could very well return if you stress your leg any further. And alone in the wilderness? Nay. Someone has to come with you, you foolish, foolish man."

Gavin's admonishment ceased as he helped Will. Finally, the peg was reattached, the straps and leather fastened, and Will stood. He clenched his jaw and swallowed his groan of pain. He was lopsided. A good few inches lopsided. But he hobbled to the wardrobe and found his surcoat, belts, weaponry, gambeson and greaves, and began the task of donning his clothing.

The pain in his stump caused him to sweat. He grit his teeth, pushing through the haze of anguish. Soon enough, he would be in the saddle and his weight would be lifted off it. If God hadn't snuffed his life yet, he certainly wasn't going to keep wasting the precious moments he had left languishing in bed on the barren, northwestern coast overlooking a desolate expanse of water.

Dressed, belted, and strapped with his sword and daggers, Gavin accompanied Will to the stable.

"You do nay need to come, Gav, if you wish nay to invite Father's anger," Will stated.

Gavin scoffed. "You want to be regarded as a man, but you say such idiotic things. What kind of brother would I be if I abandoned our *wee Will* in his hour of need?" Gavin taunted, earning a scowl in return. He only laughed. "I'm coming. I'm marrying Sarah, as you're supposed to marry her sister. My honor is at stake, too."

He was still teasing, William knew, but it silenced him. Gavin might never be the serious one, and most often didn't speak of emotional matters. Jesting just now, as he had, meant something, even if Gavin was trying to hide it. *Mayhap,* Will thought, as he cinched his mount's girth strap and patted his neck, *there's a streak of honor beneath Gavin's philandering ways after all.*

The rains had ceased days before, but the earth was still mucky. They walked the horses for days to minimize Will's discomfort, camping each night in the Cambrian Forest. Will woke on the next morn. Not far to their right sat the abandoned hut where Amber's stockings had once been discarded.

The garments were now gone, and there was evidence of newer horse manure, suggesting that Lord Edward and his sons had passed though. He had been unable to sleep in the hut's protection from the elements, his imagination running wild with thoughts of Amber lying tackled beneath Alonso as he swived her.

The early light met his eyes, a dim, clouded glow through the pine boughs looming above. He rolled over beneath a bough. Groaning with discomfort, he listed against a tree trunk, further flattening the bed of pine needles he and Gavin had assembled the night before to cushion the hard earth and roots.

His eyes focused on a hollow in the tree trunk, what looked to be a knot in the wood. Was that a piece of fabric? Buried in a tree hollow in the middle of the uninhabited forest?

Nay. It was too small to be a piece of fabric. He dug his finger in and fished it out. He looked at it. It belonged on a dress or a woman's garment, a piece of trim that at one point had probably been beige. And it had, without a doubt, been jammed in the tree with purpose.

A feeling that he couldn't quite place prickled his skin. The sensation stemmed from his fingertips. He closed his eyes as if blind again and traced his fingers over the tidbit, hoping his anxious mind wasn't toying with his heart. The texture was familiar. The weave of the braiding made his pulse jump. His hand trembled and he swallowed, opening his eyes again. Hope cut through the bleakness of his thoughts. It couldn't be what he was thinking.

"Gav!" He bolted upright, his forehead connecting with the tree bough.

He dropped back, groaning.

"Wha? What is it?" Gavin jumped up, his back thwacking the branch, but he expertly maneuvered a dagger into an underhanded grip and scrambled to his feet.

"Shite," Will moaned, then eased himself up more carefully.

Face groggy, convinced of danger, Gavin prowled in a circle, assessing the woods, then turned back to William who was fighting his stump back into the fastenings of his peg. "Be damned, Will, why the rude awakening? I thought bandits had set upon us."

Grumbling, Gavin sheathed his dagger and scoured his face to wipe the sleep away. Will rose to his foot and peg, fighting to gain his balance.

"Look." He thrust the fabric into Gavin's hand, hobbling to another tree where he flipped aside his surcoat and dug through his layering of clothing to pull free his cock and drain his water.

Gavin looked perplexed at the fabric.

"'Tis odd... a piece of embroidered trimming... where did you find it?"

"Hidden in the tree. Down there," he pointed, nodding toward the knot hole as he shook himself off and tucked himself back into his clothing.

"Hidden?"

"Aye. Now you tell me why Amber's gown trimming would be stuffed inside a tree knot in the middle of the bloody Cambrian Forest of all places." Excitement resonated through Will's limbs. "She was here. If it was said she escaped her captors and stumbled upon a mountain man's cottage, then this might be the direction in which she wandered."

"It does look like that old trim on Amber's gown around her hemline. Her ankles were showing," Gavin remarked.

William scowled and squared his look at Gavin.

"What?" Gavin shrugged innocently. "Amber's a bonny maiden. I can't help but notice a fine woman's ankles, Will. Fault me naught for looking. They were showing. It's not as if I lifted her skirts."

"Gav," William fumed. "I'll thank you to respect the boundary and keep your eyes to yourself. I'm your god-damn brother, man. And you can't even avert your eyes for me?"

"I'm to marry Sarah," Gavin defended. "Amber's your woman. But indeed I looked," Gavin jabbed Will's chest, unaffected by his anger, "and you better get used to that as her husband, because when you find her," he amended, "you'll see why *all* men will be looking."

William's scowl didn't lessen. Gavin read the look, then placed a fraternal hand on his shoulder. "I would protect my betrothed's sister, and would never dream of injuring you in such a way as to disrespect Amber. But take note, man, that I, and every single man with a warm-blooded heart, won't be able to resist admiring."

Gavin's words softened. A rarity from him.

"You're a lucky man, Will. Her hair is lush, wild, curling, like a tumbling waterfall. Sarah always takes the time to perfect her coif and indeed I appreciate it. But Amber... she looks so free, so fresh. Her lips, ahh," he sighed like a young lad describing the first lass to catch his eye, "soft, kissable lips, man. And her eyes... gentle, brown, like a doe. Every time she notices your presence, man, she bites her lower lip and smiles a smile meant just for you. You're the apple of her eye and blind or nay, I can assure you many a man you encounter as her husband will be jealous of you."

The description was much too detailed for Will's liking and yet, he appreciated Gavin's admiration. He sensed nothing untoward. Men needed women, as women needed men, and if both were lucky, they would find one upon whom they could shower their affection for the remainder of their life.

"She's a beauty," Gavin said. "And eager for your company. Rest assured that no man stands a chance at diverting her affection from you. Sarah oft talks about Amber's eagerness to be your wife. Men will look at her, just as men look at Sarah, just like men look at our wee sister, but a man never has a chance at swaying Lady Amber's affections. This, I can tell you with positivity."

Gavin handed William back the trimming. "Like I said, it looks like hers. But how can you be certain?"

William gazed at it, rubbing his thumb over it. "I felt it."

Gavin paused, then grinned, folding his arms. "You sly cur," he drawled, waggling his eyebrows. "You had your hands upon her hems? *You?* You're too much of a prudish puritan."

William punched Gavin's shoulder as he hobbled to his horse, the animal's ears flitting at the sounds of the forest.

"Only you would think of such things, Gavin," Will rolled his eyes. "I have a touch more honor, man. But she did have trimming around her arms and waist, and of course I bloody-well acquainted myself to her in our moments alone. What man wouldn't when he has a stolen minute with his lass?"

Gavin chuckled, unaffected by the punch. Packing camp, they

walked their horses away from the abandoned hut, further into the trees. Brambles tangled around their feet and snagged at their surcoats. The silence of the trees engulfed them as they hiked. Aside from the horses crunching upon leaves and the occasional squirrels chasing each other around tree trunks, they didn't converse.

They sloshed through a stream, freezing waters seeping into their boots, and began a steep incline up the embankment.

"Will?" Gavin stated, pausing his mount.

"Aye?" William replied. He watched Gavin fish something out of the tangle of underbrush. "What have you there?"

Gavin held up a slipper, once beige though now brown and stained. "Your intuition was correct, man, to come this way."

Will dropped his reins and maneuvered to his brother, bracing himself on branches and trunks so as not to tumble down the incline. He wrenched the garment from Gavin's hand. "It's worn, but it isn't weathered."

"Aye, it hasn't been here that long. And indeed when I noticed her ankles," Gavin smirked, "I noticed her shoes too. This."

Over the toe was what appeared to have once been a triple spiral, embroidered in pink, though it was more like muddy mauve now.

"Let's continue," Will pressed, urgency renewed.

He couldn't think again on why her stockings, and now slippers, were discarded in the forest. But she had indeed left her trimming in the tree, and it seemed purposeful. *As if she's left a trail.*

He hardened his jaw and moved on. Amber might be quiet, but she was smart. Aye, smart. Industrious. And as Gavin had described her, beautiful. Perfect for him in every way. If she had left a trail for them to follow, then she had hoped to be found and rescued.

I can't fail her! He shouted to himself. *"I would go to the ends of the earth to see your honor vindicated..."*

They smelled smoke—a wood fire—and soon came upon a stone cottage. But as they walked their horses toward it, the door creaked open and a young man moved into the opening. His hair hung long around his shoulders, black, his eyes matching, and whiskers of a green lad, still sparse, had overgrowing his chin. His clothing was plain, a brown tunic, brown trousers, leather belts, leather boots, but even from their distance, one could see the clothing was finely tailored.

On his finger was a ring, in his hand was a dagger, and on his face was a blank stare, his assessing gaze fixed upon the trespassers.

"Who goes there?" he asked, a deep voice that still hadn't filled with maturity.

William and Gavin each held up a hand, hailing a greeting.

"'Tis William of Ballymead and my brother, Gavin."

"And what brings you to my doorstep?"

William took a crooked step forward, wincing at the pain in his stump, but the lad held up his dagger.

"That's far enough."

Will glanced at Gavin, then back at the lad, holding his face impassively. He held up the slipper. "I'm searching for a lass. This is her shoe. We found it back there in the forest," he pointed.

"What do you want with a woman out in this desolate part of Bain?"

"She was abducted. We try to find her, and clues lead us in this direction." Will held out the dress trimming. "This is a piece of her gown. Do you recognize it?"

The lad came outside, pulling shut his door, and revealing in his right hand that had been hiding a sword.

William nodded to him, eyeing his metal. "We come here peacefully. You've nary a reason to fear us."

"I'm not fearful," the lad replied flatly, scrutinizing the two of them. "I'm prepared. Was it Lady Amber?"

William's eyes brightened. "Aye. Of Dunstonwoodshire. Are you the lad who helped her and escorted her to St. Mathilda's?"

The lad lifted his chin. "How would you know that?"

"Prince William of Bain traveled past the monastery some days ago and discovered that they had harbored Lady Amber," Will clarified. "My brothers and I were on the coast when the prince arrived with news that she had been found. Though I'm distressed to learn once again that she has disappeared." He omitted further details.

"What happened?" the lad asked. "I took her there for safe keeping until her father could be summoned. Did the monks give your prince any details?"

There was something familiar about the lad, something in the strength of his posture, in his eyes. Will couldn't place it. He had certainly never met the young man before. And yet, he seemed to remind Will of someone...

"A monk attempted to molest her and it seems she fled," William ground out. "Pity I was sick abed when I learned that the monk is now imprisoned there."

The lad took a step back. "You don't bring a plague or some other sickness with you, do you?"

Will shook his head, patting his leg. "My amputated leg was festering when we captured her abductors. But the festering has passed, so I continue my search."

The lad seemed to think about Will's words and scrutinized his missing calf. "You captured the men who abducted her?" he asked.

"Aye," Will nodded. "They rest in the prince's custody now."

The lad said no more. His face remained impassive, but Will and Gavin glanced at one another again. For some reason, the capture of the abductors meant something to the lad, though what that was, there was no way to determine.

Will interrupted the silence. "I suppose we'll move onward, man, if you have nothing further you can tell us. Good day to you." He and Gavin began to leave.

"I can lead you on a quicker route to the monastery," the lad offered at their backs. "Two hours of normal riding, one if we ride hard. If you'll allow me a moment to prepare my mount."

They paused.

"We'd be most grateful," Will offered.

"Aye," Gavin interjected. "The sooner we can arrive, the better."

"Lady Amber only spoke briefly of her betrothal," the lad stated, finally resting his sword point against the ground. "But what she said was highly."

"And what was that?" William asked, wanting the reassurance of the lad's words.

"She was scared and stumbled upon me quite by hazard," he replied, sheathing his dagger, too. "In her desperation, she said she only wanted to be with you again."

William swallowed, nodded once, and turned to his horse to mount up and relieve the weight on his tender knee.

***

An hour of hard riding brought the trio to the front door of the Abbey of St. Mathilda's, and a tense greeting between William and Father Crispen only took a few moments. Will tamped down his anger at Amber's mistreatment in order to hear the information he needed. The remaining Bainick soldiers securing the monastery also described what they had learned, which wasn't much: The monk had been found in her chamber and Amber had broken the man's finger—*good,* thought William with satisfaction. The next morn, she was discovered missing. They assumed she disappeared sometime that night while the remaining brothers prayed.

There was nothing else.

The forest lad bid them farewell upon the threshold, departing back to his cottage without a backward glance.

"She's close, I know it," William told Gavin, looking around as if the very air might carry a clue.

Gavin glanced to the ravine beyond the monastery. "Brother," he began, resting a hand on his shoulder. "That ravine is dangerous and deep."

"She didn't fall over it," Will affirmed to himself. "Prince William's soldiers even said they found no evidence of her body."

"But even they said it was probably because she was swept up in the current," Gavin argued, softening. "It pains me to say this, but do nay rule out that she might have perished. Prepare your heart for the worst, man, and pray for the best."

"She *didn't* fall down the ravine," Will ground out, his voice cracking. He brought a fist to his mouth, clearing away the mounting thickness. "I...I have to have hope."

Gavin shook his head, squeezing his brother's shoulder with reassurance. "You always were the dreamer."

Will swallowed, averting his eyes down to his gauntlets. "I have to keep that faith, man. I *have* to."

Gavin nodded, then stepped back. "Do you remember when we found that map in the balinger, and you almost fell as we tried to climb those stairs?"

Will shook his head. "Do nay remind me of my lameness, in both body and words."

Gav didn't smile at the jest. "You yelled at Hershel. You laid into him that you found no solace in faith, as he did."

Will glanced at Gavin. If Gavin was about to say something profound, a blizzard was about to freeze Hell.

"Think on what you just said, Will. 'You have to keep that faith' that she isn't dead. And what is faith, but a fervent hope that God will reveal to you what you need to know?"

William pondered it.

"I'd say you're more like Hershel than you think," Gavin continued. "Or mayhap, Hershel is more like you than he thinks. Either way. Have your faith. But make sure, that you do nay misplace your faith by insisting God grant the wish you want, instead of having faith in what is meant to be."

William heard the words, words that belonged to Hershel more than anyone else, and nodded. He turned to mount back up.

He couldn't speak. He had vacillated back and forth between

feeling hopelessness and feeling hope so many times on this journey that he felt weary in spirit. He knew he bore the creases of wisdom now that normally didn't plague a man until he had aged. He knew he was ill-shaven, filthy, tired. But he was so close, that despondency now seemed only like a concession of defeat right before he was slated to cross the finish line. He wasn't searching for something he wanted. He was searching for some*one*. And he couldn't give up.

He began to ride, walking the horse, looking to the sodden ground that had been trampled so much now by Prince William's men that there was no hope of finding a trail there. He needed to widen his search area. He needed to think.

As Gavin began walking his mount northward from the monastery, Will took a deep breath and ordered all the clues in his mind:

The slipper, now safe within his surcoat, seemed to have been lost, not hidden. However, the trimming to her gown hadn't been lost. It would be nearly impossible for such a thing to become lodged where it was. She had put it there, which meant... *I need to search places where she would think to hide clues.*

He surveyed the landscape again for areas dense with options for hiding a bit of embroidery. Nothing close by. Trees yonder, across the tilted plain that stretched upward toward the forest, or much farther down the edge of the ravine where clusters of trees and tumbled rocks reached the cliff's precipice.

And then it hit him.

How quickly he had become accustomed to his eyesight again. It was when he had closed his eyes this morning and relied solely on his sense of touch that he placed the memory of Amber's gown. He needed to travel as if he were blind, too.

He dismounted again, a groan escaping him at the pressure upon his stump. He pulled the reins over his horse's head, closed his eyes, and began walking, leading his beast behind him. It didn't take long to revert back to the habit of tapping his foot and peg to sense the uneven terrain before placing his weight upon it. It didn't take long to adjust his course southward. Traveling up the landscape on foot was tiring and harder to do with no eyesight. Amber might have naturally veered south for sake of ease without thinking much about it.

For hours, he moved as such, reaching outward to feel for objects where a blind person might hide a clue. Wind swept more and more forcefully over him, lifting his hair up and throwing it around his face. His horse began to balk, grunting disapproval, dragging behind him, but he continued to coax the animal onward. Finally, he felt a ledge of rock, and at this point opened his eyes.

A gasp escaped his throat. He was on a ledge that had departed downward from the plain above them and his horse stood on only a few feet of width.

"Shite," William whispered, swallowing. No wonder the beast had protested.

The stallion began panicking more and jerked its neck. It flung its head, grunting, growing agitated.

"Easy. Easy, man." He pet its neck in slow, soothing strokes, and gripped the bridle to steady the animal's fear. "We're going to walk backward. You have to trust me."

He continued stroking the beast's neck, crooning softly. As the horse began to settle, he guided it backward. He clicked his tongue, pushing. Reluctantly, the horse's hind leg took one step back.

It tossed its head, ripping Will's arms upward.

"Nay, man. You're not allowed to panic. Easy..."

He steadied the beast again, making the mistake of peeking over the ravine. Dizziness assaulted him. He forced his gaze back to the horse's muzzle. "Come on. Come on." He clicked at the beast again, pushing. The horse's haunches flexed as, again, he took another step. "Come on..." The horse took another step. And then its hind hoof slipped. Breakage in the rock flaked off the edge.

Will closed his eyes, sweating, steadying himself as his horse began tossing its head more. He felt dizzy again, but not from imbalance. If he wasn't mistaken, he was starting to shiver. *No*, he argued with himself. He couldn't be feverous again. And if he didn't settle his horse, the animal could very well throw Will off his already-precarious balance and launch him over the cliff into the River Fetch.

Slowly, surely, he managed to maneuver the beast backward, up the ledge, until at long last they reached the plain above them. Except it was no longer a plain. While wandering with his eyes closed, the trees and the tumble of boulders he had seen from afar while standing at the monastery were right in front of him now.

He walked the horse up to the nearest tree, flipped the reins once over a low-hanging bough, and returned to the cliff's edge. He looked around. Where had the narrow path gone? It was nothing but a tumble of boulders and outcroppings of cliff side, the water roaring far below and cutting a twisting path into the canyon basin. Trees and plants grew out from crevices in the rock walls, taking root wherever they could find a bit of soil. He backtracked on foot, returning to the edge, looking deliberately up and down the canyon.

There it was, the entrance to the ledge camouflaged by scrubby plants.

"She's near," he thought, his heart jumping.

The soldiers had scoured the area, and one didn't earn rank in Prince William's army unless they were impeccably trained as scouts and trackers. The Bainick military was expert. But no one had told him that they had searched along a narrow ledge of rock overhanging the ravine itself. His blind-walking had naturally led him here.

He didn't hesitate further.

He descended the path, placing a palm along the cliff wall to keep his balance and prevent dizziness from threatening his senses. And as his hand brushed over a crack in the rock face, his fingers touched something soft sticking out from it.

"God be damned, Amber," he said, feeling tears prick the back of his eyes as he withdrew a piece of gown fabric. "Where are you, lass?"

He gripped it and looked down the natural pathway the ledge created. Above him, tree branches spilled over the cliff's upper edge. And then the cliff face began to turn blindly to the right, a vestige of the river's switch back when it had cut this ravine.

He continued onward, fighting the wind that threatened to throw him off balance, afraid of what he might encounter. A drop off? A wider ledge? The latter would be a blessing. Amber? And if he found her, would she be alive or mayhap...dead?

He shivered. It had been so long now since she was reported missing from the monastery. One couldn't survive more than a few days without water, a little longer without food. A sennight? Two at most?

"Where are you, Amber?" he asked the wind, hoping for a response. No response came, but a dove, of all creatures, cooed above him on a branch.

Chapter 18

Amber had lost track of time. She was exhausted. Her mind was frayed. She had lost hope. Her stomach no longer protested its emptiness. *Does this mean the end is near?*

Water, thankfully, was plentiful as it flowed down the rock from the natural spring that no doubt fed into the waterway below. She heard cooing. A bird?

"Nay, I'm delirious. I imagine things," she told herself, despite the bird cooing again. It was much too barren a landscape, too gusty with angry winds, for a gentle wee dove.

It cooed again. "I'm hearing things—"

"Amber!"

She froze, her skin tingling so suddenly as if shocked.

"It's nay real," she sighed, lifting her head from the pebbly ground she lay curled upon.

"Amber! *Iesus*, Amber! It's Will!"

Now she knew her mind taunted her. She lay back down, sniffling at despair clogging her throat. Will wouldn't know she was here. Will couldn't see her. Will was blind.

***

"Amber!" Will shouted again, watching Amber drop her head back to the earth, her toes a mere inch from the edge.

He hobbled forward, taking care to keep his balance.

"Amber, I see you! Amber. Do nay move!"

She lifted her head again as he drew nearer.

"W...Will?" she uttered, her voice barely audible.

"Aye! I'm coming, do nay move another inch! Hold still!"

"Will?" she asked. "Will! Will!" she erupted into a sob and tried to stand, her foot skidding on the ledge.

"Stop, Amber!" Will hollered. "You mustn't move another inch! Not one inch!"

But he watched her foot slip, tangled within her ragged skirts.

"Amber!"

Her foot disappeared, then her calf, and then a gust of wind whooshed upward between the rock face and her, sending her slipping, slipping...

"*Amber!*" he bellowed, hobbling, unable to get to her in time.

"William!' she screamed.

Her hands scrambled for a grip. She disappeared over the edge.

"No!" he roared, falling to his knees to peer over.

A sob tore from his throat. "Amber!" he wailed, gripping the cliff, hanging over the ravine.

"William!" she screamed again. "Help me! Help me!"

"Christ!" he swore, feeling air blast from his lungs as his face drained. "Be damned, woman! Hold still!"

She lay a mere two feet below upon the scraggly branches of a gnarled tree jutting from the side of the rocks. Below her, far in the distance, the frothy rapids cut a silver ribbon snaking through the ravine.

He threw himself flat and reached to her, feeling her bodice.

"Grab hold!" he shouted.

She groped out toward his voice. Their hands connected. He began to pull her up.

Her fingers slipped. "William!" she screamed again, flopping back. "I'm going to die!"

"You're nay going to foking die!" he boomed. "Grab my hand and hold it! Tight! Tighter than you've ever held anything! Do you understand me?"

She nodded. The tree branch supporting her crackled. Their hands reunited. He twisted and contorted onto his side, reaching out with his other hand to grip her wrist. The branch snapped, cracked.

"Will!" she shrieked.

He gritted his teeth as the branch gave way beneath her. It tumbled downward, growing smaller and smaller. He grasped her, his grip crushing. He hoisted her upward. Her feet scraped at the cliff face.

He grunted and pulling, contorting on the ground.

His bruising grip was sweaty.

It was slipping.

She flailed, twisted in the air. With a final burst of strength, he clenched his eyes shut, roared, and dragged her upward. She cried out as her breasts scraped upon the ledge. She landed beside him, shaking, her face pale and her cheeks streaked in dirty tears.

"William," she whimpered, curling against him.

His chest rose and fell. He closed his eyes and encircled her in his crushing arms, clenching her. Sweat had soaked his neck, making his hair stick in dirty clumps to his skin. He knew his embrace probably bruised her further, but he couldn't relent.

"I've got you," he exhaled shakily, gripping her hair, her shoulders, the feeling of her thin frame in his arms reassuring. "Amber, you're safe."

She fell to tears, burying her face in his armpit as he enveloped her. "William, praise God you found me," she exhaled.

He nodded, dragged her head back, planted his lips to hers and ravaged her mouth. He thrust his tongue against hers and brought his other hand up to grip her face. She returned the kiss, desperate thrusts of her tongue to match his.

"Christ, woman," he murmured, his lips still smashed to hers, devouring all there was to feast upon. "I was so bloody worried for you..." He kept kissing her. "So worried..."

His hand gripping her face slid down her neck, over her breasts to her waist, his tongue dragging across hers, his kiss sliding to the corner of her mouth in frantic pecks and bites, onto her jaw, her neck. His hand at her waist slid back up to grab her breast. There was no propriety, no gentleness. Just raw, unbridled fear flowing out of him, uncaring that they both sat with their feet hanging over a cliff.

He separated from her, his nose and forehead still pressed to hers, and cupped her cheeks.

"Amber, I've been so distressed. I've thought of nothing but you and what you might have suffered the whole of these sennights." She clung to him as he poured out what was in his heart. "Whatever has happened to you, whatever some bastard scoundrel has done to you," he swallowed, but Lord, if some bastard scoundrel had raped her, he would never forgive himself for not finding her sooner, "know that it changes nothing in my heart. It changes nothing betwixt us. You're still to be my wife and bear my children and be my partner and dammit, I—"

His voice cracked. He gazed down at her, her eyes damp with tears, and brushed back a lock of her curls.

"I love you so, woman."

"I love you too, Will," she cried against him, clenching him harder. "I prayed someone would come for me. Even in my final moments—"

"Hush there. Speak nay of final moments. I have you and we're going to get out of this." She nodded as he spoke, holding him so tightly he could feel pressure from her fingernails all the way through his gambeson. "We're nay safe here. I need you to be strong a little longer. We're on a ledge overlooking a ravine. We have two options."

He swallowed, exhaling again, trying to ease his tension.

"There's a long rock ledge. It's narrow. Somehow you managed to travel it without tumbling down to your death. Or, just above us is the surface of the ground, trees overhanging us. I can climb up it and gather rope from my saddle packs to tie it off to a branch. That way I can hoist you up—"

"Nay," she interrupted. It was only a whisper, but it was strong. Her grip on him turned deathly. "No trees. Not after what just happened...no."

"Shh," he crooned, rubbing a palm up and down her arm. "Then we'll walk it. No more trees." He pulled his legs from over the edge to begin the torturous endeavor of scaling along the wall.

"I'm frightened," she whimpered, gripping his arm.

"I know," he replied. "But if you managed to walk down this narrow path, you can walk up it."

"I can't," she replied, huddling into him.

"Amber," he tried to reason. "I know you're scared, but we cannot stay here. You need a campfire, warm blankets, and food."

"Food," she muttered, barely audible over the whistling of the wind.

"Aye, Love," he replied. "You look much too thin. You need nourishment and rest before we begin the voyage back to Dunstonwoodshire."

She paused. He sensed she was thinking.

"Amber," he prompted. "Come. You can do this. I'll guide you, just do as I say. You must."

She nodded. He dipped his head to hers, planting a firm kiss to her brow.

"Come. I know you're strong of mind and heart. Let's conquer this together," William murmured beside her, withdrawing his arm from around her and taking her hand in his.

He fought his way onto his foot and peg, turning to lean a shoulder on the rock face beside him. He refused to look down into the ravine as he helped Amber to her bare feet. Her toes and legs tangled in her skirts and she fell off balance.

"Will," she gasped, her knuckles whitening upon his hand.

"I've got you," he reassured.

He held her steady on her knees and reached to her skirts, taking bunches of fabric and wrenching it out from beneath her knees. She gasped. He ignored it and helped her stand.

She was unsteady and tears were pricking her eyes.

"William, honestly, I...I haven't stood in days. I haven't eaten...I'm so tired."

"There's no other way. I'd carry you if I could, but our balance would be too precarious. We either walk, or I climb up to one of the branches above and fetch a rope from my horse—"

She shook her head vigorously.

"Okay then," he softened, running a finger down her cheek.

With the situation so desperate, he hadn't yet taken a moment to absorb the sight of her. He had simply plunged his tongue in her mouth, his lips swiving hers in a desperate need to be connected. But here, perched on a ledge over a raging river with wind ruining all hope for their hair to be combed, he took a moment now. He remembered her from over three years before, the last time he had looked upon her with working eyes. She hadn't been fully a woman yet.

What time had done to her, he could only appreciate with every fiber that made him a man. Curling brown hair that wasn't just brown, but touched with auburn, eyes wide and shaped like almonds, a pert nose, high cheek bones, a heart-shaped mouth, full handfuls of beautifully balanced breasts, a narrow waist, and no doubt beneath her shabby gown, gently sloping hips. Gavin had been right. Men would look. How could they not?

He closed his eyes and caressed her facial features like he had done when he was still blind. He felt the hollows of her cheeks, knowing she needed good food and a lot of it. He trailed his fingers down over her lips, her chin, down her neck to her collarbone, also prominent in her need of nourishment.

His heart clenched to think of what all she had endured, what all he didn't know about yet that would unfold in the days to come. But right now, with his eyes closed, seeing her in the only way he had looked upon her since her coming of age, there was something distant about her. And a sensation, wariness, crept under his skin.

He opened his eyes. Now he could see it. Beautiful as she was, there was something about her expression that was cordoned off and distant from him.

He shook his head. He was seeing things. They stood on a cliff for God's sake. She was scared and traumatized by whatever else he had yet to learn. He had to get her to safety and then they could begin to sort through the complexities of her ordeal.

Slowly, inch by inch, he led her back the way he had come. One clumsy step on his uneven peg leg and he would topple off, dragging her with him. He peered down, a reflex, determining if there were any trees that might provide him with the good fortune of blocking a fall. None.

His head swirled at the immensity of the ravine. He righted himself, feeling himself sway. A ridge of rock jutting out of the wall thankfully gave him something to grab onto to steady himself. And finally, blessedly, they arrived on solid ground above. He hastened her away from the edge, toward the trees, where his horse stood lazily, swishing his tail.

Here, at the edge of the copse, he dragged Amber into his arms and collapsed, pulling her weight down on him. He had been so focused on reaching safety, he had failed to feel the pain screaming from his injury. Now, as the anxiety of the moment ebbed away, he realized he was lightheaded again. He shivered and sweat. He could feel that the bone was pushing through his unhealed skin again. He could feel the inflammation, what would appear to be angry flesh should he dare to remove his peg.

She sat against him and a flood of tears escaped her as her arms encircled his neck.

"Amber," he whispered, pushing aside his own pain, relief washing over him. "Hush, lass. Thank Christ you're safe."

He held her, feeling her convulse against him. He laid her out upon the ground and rolled on top of her. His lips crushed to hers and he nestled his hips between her legs.

"By God, woman, you're a sight for such sore, sore eyes," he muttered, cupping her head. His wild kissing resumed. He was unable to ignore the burgeoning of thickness in trousers as his smaller man rallied to arms in spite of his own fatigue.

He wanted nothing more than to cast off decency and take her, flip up her skirts, bury himself to the hilt, and bask in the feeling of being united. It would be beautiful. She would be beautiful, laid out beneath him, receiving his masculinity.

His tongue stroked across hers, feeling her desperate kisses in return, feeling her body supple for him. She wasn't guarded like a woman who wished to ward off a man's advances. She arched against him. He groaned, devouring her mouth and tongue. He couldn't resist a gentle nudge of his hips between her thighs. She mewed desperately and pushed against him, impulse guiding their frenzy.

"When the message arrived that you were missing, I couldn't sleep, couldn't eat. I've been so bloody sick worrying for you. I love you, Amber. I hope you can see how much I love you."

Rapid breathing seized his lungs. Tears pricked his eyes as reality sank in. He good and truly had her in his arms, her breasts flush with his chest, her thighs cradling his hips. He wasn't going to let go again. His kissing slowed. He peeled her hand away from his neck and laced his fingers with hers, studying the crisscrossed pattern, contemplating a ring of gold encircling her finger, denoting that she belonged to him.

"Handfast with me," he begged, his throat thick. "I can't bear to lose you again, I just can't. I want to see your bonny face always, every morn, every night abed beside me. The only way I can have that is if you're my wife. I do nay want to wait."

But his words were met with silence.

***

It was something about the way he was talking, Amber thought. *"The sight of you... see your bonny face..."* He had mentioned sight more than once. *"A sight for sore eyes..."*

No one else was with them, and yet, he had yelled to her as if he could see her. He had guided her off the cliff with the surefootedness and expertise of someone with...*working eyes.*

She tensed beneath him.

"Amber?" he asked, though she hardly heard him. "Amber, what's the matter?" Still, she couldn't push an answer over her lips. Her stomach tingled with nerves. He rolled aside, muttering a curse at himself for his beastliness. "Did I say something?"

She shook her head, struggling to sit up again. "How did you find me?"

He sat up too.

His hand, callused and grimy from travel, encircled one of hers and squeezed it. "I had a miracle," he admitted. "When Hershel came to tell me the news that you were missing, I fell from a ladder in the meadery and smashed my head through a cask. The blow restored my sight. And just in time to search for you. 'Twas disorienting at first, but as my vision cleared, I knew I wouldn't be able to enjoy one moment of it until I could lay my eyes on you."

She sat still and swallowed, knowing her face had paled. Her other hand kneaded her skirts. She forced a smile onto her lips.

"I see," she finally replied, trying to keep the wobble from her voice. But his admission punched her in the gut. *He could see?* "You must be so pleased."

"Now that I have you with me again, indeed I am. Amber," he said, running a hand down her cheek. "My God, but you're so beautiful to behold." His caressing continued and his words grew soft. "So beautiful. I do nay deserve you."

She tried to smile again, but this time, she failed completely. Her mouth trembled. She bit her lip to hold it steady, and then she threw her face in her hands. "But I can't behold you now. I'll never know what you look like ever again. 'Tis unfair now. The entire reason our fathers paired us was because we were both blind."

Will froze. His hand caressing her face dropped away, leaving emptiness on her skin. "Amber, I—" He cut himself off, but just as soon as he did, he began talking again. "I wanted to marry you, even if you were blind. I mattered naught to me."

"Why?" she begged.

"Because, you've always been sweet and kind. And you're industrious—"

"You didn't know that about me until our last meeting."

William scrambled for words. "Your craft added to my desire, aye, but I always sensed you were different. I sensed something about you, a strength. You were always more carefree than Sarah, less concerned with frivolities—"

"What man would want a woman like me who never concerns herself overmuch with her appearance?"

Will seemed to fumble for a better explanation.

"I thought we already discussed this. You never seemed to worry about your looks at the expense of your enjoyment in things... And I wouldn't care if you didn't coif your hair like a perfect lady. I care only that you look upon me with favor, as I look upon you." He took her hand again, imploring answers from her. "What has passed, Amber? I feel disconcerted."

Amber swallowed. She didn't know what to think or feel. She was tired. The burst of energy that had blessedly enabled her to escape her perilous prison was waning again. She was so cold, so tired. That had to be the reason she felt surly now. She should be delighted for William. She shouldn't wallow in self-pity over it. 'Twas a blessing that had been granted him so he could find her. So why did it hurt so?

"I'm sorry," she apologized. "My nerves are frayed. I'm so

hungry and cold."

He enfolded her in his arms once more and nuzzled her hair, but eased his grip when her stiffness didn't subside.

"Your eyes always twinkle with curiosity, and yet, right now, they're dull. What ails you, Amber?" His question was flat. Guarded.

"I'm weary," she whispered. "I truly am happy for your eyesight. What a gift."

She made a poor attempt at a smile, but his response was strained and told her it hadn't convinced him. "It came at such a time that my brother Hershel is convinced God granted me a miracle so I could find you. Why do you look fit to cry over it?"

She reached up to cup his face. She had dreamed of Will time and again on this journey through hell. Now that it was over and she sat in his arms, she should feel fulfilled, overjoyed. At first, she had. He had proven his devotion to her. She nestled into his neck and tried to regain that overjoyed feeling. He welcomed her into his protective hold.

And it was now that she realized his skin was hot. Nay just hot. Burning. Her hand patted his cheek, then his brow. She sat up straight again.

"Will, you burn with fever. What has passed to make you so ill?"

She felt him swallow, his throat bobbing against her forehead.

"When my brothers and I pursued your abductors, the journey injured my amputated leg." He paused as if thinking. "I developed a fever, 'tis all. Worry not for me. I'm fine."

He tightened his grip further and nuzzled his nose into her mangy hair, inhaling deeply as if smelling a fine posy, when she knew she had to smell worse than a mangy dog. Alarm gripped her. The effects of the fever were causing him to shiver. The thought made her stomach clench. A fever was nothing to dismiss lightly.

"Pray tell if they...if they forced you... God, Amber, please say they never touched you in such a way as to—" He seemed unable to push the words over his lips.

She shook her head. "I'm intact. Neither man did such, but..."

She shut her mouth. If she told him what the monk had tried to do, that he had touched her breast, would Will consider her unclean?

She felt his head shake.

"I heard about Brother Daniel," he remarked as if reading her mind. His voice deepened. His grip upon her tightened with possessiveness. "The shite bastard is aye lucky I didn't get to him before Prince William."

"I don't understand," she remarked, feeling her eyes begin to sag against all her efforts of control. But she was so tired.

"Prince William and a royal contingent arrived at St. Mathilda's to stop for a bite to eat. They discovered that just the night prior, you had been accosted and that Brother Daniel was confined to his cell until punishment could be devised." His words sounded distant. His hand was smoothing back her hair, the sensation so wonderful. "But Prince William wouldn't stand for it and dragged Brother Daniel with him all the way to Fort Michaelmas at the end of a towline...Amber?"

She felt a jostle and perked back up, realizing her folly. "I'm sorry, Will. I'm so tired..."

Somehow in her waning state of lucidity, she discovered herself in his saddle with a partial loaf of bread and some jerked meat in hand. She nibbled gingerly, the salt on her tongue from the meat so delicious and yet, the feeling of food landing in her stomach so heavy. And the thought of his eyesight lingered in the back of her mind.

Lord, she sighed, shaking her head. She needed to slap the self-pity right off her own face. It wasn't as if Will was gloating about his eyesight. It wasn't as if it changed anything about his affection for her. He had reinjured his amputation just to find her. He had used his restored eyesight for her benefit. He had kept true to his declaration to travel to the end of the world to see her vindicated, with his sword and life. But what if, now that he could see, his eyes should wander to someone new? After all, her looks had undoubtedly changed since she was younger and now he would be able to see all sorts of variety again.

She shook her head once more, focusing on the uneven cadence of his walking thudding the earth as he led the horse on foot. His shuffling seemed different than before, more pronounced, with more of a lull between each step. "Why did you injure yourself so? Why go to such trouble for me?"

The plodding of the horse stopped.

"I worried for you," he stated, almost with offense. "I made a commitment to marry you. Why on earth would I sit idle at Ballymead whist you suffer?"

"You shouldn't have. You burn with fever. And fevers are harbingers of death. Such a risk shouldn't have been undertaken, nay for just a woman. Your father needs his sons—"

"What is this about?" he asked, his voice guarded. And it carried with it an air of disappointment. In her? In what he saw? "I know you're weary and hungry, and I know those things make people vexed. But it's as if you push me away."

She sensed he, too, was tired. Likely he hadn't had much to eat, either. Likely the fever plaguing him now was exhausting him.

She dropped the bread to her lap, feeling too ill to eat further. "Imagine if I could see. The ways in which I could have gotten myself out of this conundrum much sooner if only I could have used my eyes. Instead, look what's happened."

Will took to hobbling again. The horse began to plod over what sounded like rocky ground, rocking her lazily with each bulge of its hindquarters.

"I get an uncomfortable feeling something about me is bothering you," he stated. "I wish I could wash away everything you've endured. All I can do is offer you assurance that I'm pleased to have found you and am glad my brothers and I brought in your attackers. I had thought such an act would affirm in your mind my devotion as a husband. So please, tell me what ails your spirit," William asked. "What else can I do to make you pleased? I had always envisioned our reunion to be a joyous one. If you need rest, I'll leave you be. But if something else is upsetting you, something I've done, I wish you would tell me so I might correct myself."

He sounded ashamed and blast it, but Amber had no ready response.

"No man likes to think he has offended, without knowing how to right his mistake," he added softly.

Tears collected in her eyes. She swallowed. Crying wouldn't help her any more than pitying herself would.

"This ordeal has made me aware of my shortcomings," she finally managed. "I realize that I cannot provide you with the care a wife should give." In spite of her best efforts, her voice trembled. "What if we have children? What kind of mother would I make? What if they injured themselves or wandered lost? It would be my fault."

The horse stopped moving again and Will's hand came to rest upon hers.

"These concerns matter not, lass," he managed, though his voice carried a hint of worry. "We would have household servants to assist in childrearing. And having children is still some time off in the future. We'll deal with babes in due course." He pressed into her hand a piece of gown trimming. "Do you remember this?"

She felt it, and brought it to her mouth where a sob rolled out with no control. "You found them. I didn't know that it would matter, but I tried to leave a trail, and it had been so long since I was nabbed that I feared no one came in search at all."

"Don't be daft, Amber," Will admonished. "Christ, but you thought no one would come in search? What did you take us for?"

Shame washed over her. Of course Will came. He was honorable in every way. Of course her father and brothers had come. Just because the Lord of Dunstonwoodshire usually dismissed her as the quiet one didn't mean he didn't worry for her. He was simply a busy man with a wool trade to manage, who had been burdened with her as his daughter and a wife who had died too early, she reasoned.

It was simply fortuitous that the man he had paired her with was the man who loved her and the man she loved too...wasn't it?

"Leaving a trail was brilliant. What you did was save yourself," Will pressed. "You looked out for yourself, you faced your fears, and you proved my suspicion long ago. That you're strong. I might never have found you had you not left a trail. And overlooking such an accomplishment is daft indeed."

She gasped at his insult.

Will's voice softened. "I'm sorry," he muttered. She felt the saddle shimmying, heard straps unbuckling, heard what sounded like a blanket being shaken out, and soon felt him hand up a bed roll. "Here. You shiver."

Did she? She hadn't noticed in her frazzled state. She wrapped the blanket around herself, resumed nibbling the bread, and rode in silence as he hobbled along on his poor leg that pained him. Sakes, he was in no condition to walk. He had just searched all of Bain for her, wearing himself down in the process.

"Will, you should ride, too," she said. "If your leg pains you so, you shouldn't walk on it."

He continued walking, not saying anything.

"Will, why do you nay ride?" she pressed.

He slowed, then stopped, and she regretted asking the moment he opened his mouth.

"My leg is paining me, and I fear I cannot mount up anymore," he muttered. "It's easier to walk," he said with finality, and began walking again.

But there was something in his voice. Despair? And she sensed she might have put it there.

***

"Will! Will!"

Gavin's voice was booming, and yet, it sounded muffled, distant.

"William?" Amber asked from atop the idle horse. "William, what's happening? Where are you?"

Will sweat. Shivered. He couldn't relate to the ground. Was he standing or lying in a heap? His vision was black and he realized his eyes were closed. He opened them, stars bursting on his eyes as if he had just taken someone's fist to his temple. Gavin's boots were running toward him, sideways, a blur of leather and Ballymead green. Bits of weeds and pebbles poked his cheek.

So I'm lying down, he thought. Had he collapsed?

"Christ in heaven!" cursed Gavin, arriving beside him and falling to his knees, sending a spray of dirt into William's face.

Gavin ripped off his gauntlets and grabbed Will's arms, heaving him up to sitting. He flopped in Gavin's grip like a rag doll, his muscles reluctantly flexing to hold himself steady.

"I'm freezing," Will chattered.

"You're raging with fever again," Gavin replied.

"I..." he croaked, feeling his hair pasted to his forehead in clumps. "I found her. I knew she was still alive."

"Aye, you did well, wee brother," Gavin murmured, brushing back his hair. "Christ's bones, but this doesn't look good."

William sat hunched, unable to move, as Gavin ripped off the straps of his peg, peeling it from his stump.

"Dammit, William!" Gavin growled, clenching his jaw as his eyes rimmed red. Will spied Gavin staring at the angry flesh. He snatched up a gauntlet and whipped it against the ground. "Dammit! Good Christ look at the mess you've made of your leg..." He shook his head, and Will's gaze connected with his brother's. "Will, you—" He fought his emotion until he had mastered his words, though nothing masked the panic in his voice. "You flirt with death. A second fever isn't likely to be recovered from. You bloody bastard, Father's never going to forgive me for not looking out for you—"

"I'm nay anyone's child to mind," Will retorted, his frame jolting with shivers. "I made my own choice. You merely followed me."

"William?" came Amber's feeble voice. "Lord Gavin, you're scaring me. What's happening?"

Gavin grabbed William on either side of the face. "Aye, you did, and you're a damn stubborn arse. And you're so bloody honorable. You impress me, man, me, a knight, and you, a farmer. You bloody impress me. Aye, you're your own man. But you're still our brother, still Father's son. And damnation but—" Gavin cut himself off. Instead, he heaved William up onto his good foot and whistled to his horse. The beast perked its ears and plodded forward at the summons. "I have to get you abed somewhere. You need a hot iron. It's the only way we have to kill the festering before it spreads."

"Lord Gavin," Amber fretted. "Pray tell what passes. What ails William?"

But Will couldn't answer, and Gavin didn't, as he grunted, heaved, and managed to get William aloft in his saddle.

"Lord Gavin I beg you for an answer," Amber beseeched.

William heard the trepidation in her voice turn to dread. "I'm fine, Amber," he offered, though his words sounded warbled, distant. He listed to the side and clenched the horse's mane to remain vertical.

"He's nay fine," ground out Gavin, collecting his reins and pulling them over the animal's head to lead it.

"You're leg...you said it bothered you," Amber continued. "Will, you said it had grown sore as you looked for me, that it had made you ill. Is it your leg still? Pray tell what happened to you?"

"It grew *sore*?" Gavin snorted indignantly. "Did you bother telling her how so?"

"Nay," argued William. "She needn't worry herself over the details. They sound worse than they are."

"What details?" Amber begged.

"Amber, worry nay," William tried again.

Gavin scoffed. "He bloody well wore it down so badly these past sennights, it festered to the point Hershel and I had to saw it off to the knee—"

"Gav," Will warned at Amber's gasp. "Spare her the grotesque details."

"Nay, Will. I'm surprised you didn't tell her."

"Pray, Lord Gavin, please continue," pleaded Amber.

Gavin began jogging, his pace much faster than William's.

"On the Île de Neige, having sailed over the strait, having chased down and battled the men who nabbed you with sword and might, his leg was so putrid he raged with fever. We thought we were going to lose him. By the time we arrived back to Fort Michaelmas, Hershel had already prepared for the fort's priest to deliver his last rights, when his fever mercifully broke, and it was only two measly days later when he climbed back in the saddle to search for you again."

"What?" whispered Amber. For a moment, it seemed she could say no more.

William glared at Gavin's back. But the truth was out, and Amber seemed dumbfounded into a silence. He couldn't turn to look at her without upsetting his fragile balance. Instead, he remained hunched, swallowing at the dryness in his throat as if he contained a mouthful of sawdust, shivering. Shivering. Shivering...

"There they are! Gavin! William...they have Amber! Praise God!" Hershel's voice sounded in the distance as they converged on St. Mathilda's.

Will shivered so intensely he could hardly look up, could hardly make sense that his father and brother had found them. His head ached. He couldn't keep his eyes open. His hair was wet and cold, sticking to his pasty skin.

"God in heaven! What has befallen him?" Lord Loddin thundered, horse hooves rumbling the ground.

But Will felt his eyes rolling back. His mind was going black. The confusion melted away. For some, strange reason, he felt himself look up to the sky, seeing in his mind's eye the dove that had perched itself on the branch above him as he edged closer and closer to Amber on the cliff. He felt himself falling, felt Gavin's horse beneath him grunting, stomping.

He was floating.

With a jarring thud, he landed on the ground, lifeless.

Chapter 19

Nay, nay, nay! It was happening again! Father was crying. Ballymead men were bracing him down, hidden in the woods near Dwyre. Gwenyth was gone. No one knew where his sister was. Her husband was dead, and in the confusion, she was missing. No one from Dwyre would tell them a whit about her whereabouts, only that she had been tossed out and good riddance to the undisciplined wife of William Feargach.

Will raged, he charged at the soldiers, as did his father, overcome with grief. But they pounced on him. They charged him, all of them against only him, the youngest and spryest man in the Ballymead party. He swung his sword, trying to defend himself. Enemy metal lacerated him, jabbed him, blades sheathing themselves in his flesh as if he were a giant's pincushion. The slice to his leg was so clean a cut, he didn't feel it. Only after the repeated blows did screams finally well in his throat.

Powder burned his face. A blow dislodged him from the saddle. He was falling, careening toward the ground off the back of his horse.

Thwack! His head smacked a rock, ridged with jagged edges. His scalp split. His skull rattled. His eyes went black. Hands were upon him, grabbing at him, snagging his surcoat, his chain mail, as if relentless beggars reaching through St. Andrew's gates for alms.

"Get off me!" he bellowed, flailing.

He couldn't rid himself of the hands dragging him away.

And there he was as his father cried, his muscles taut as the soldiers braced him down, as his father sawed off his mangled foot partway up his calf. Screams escaped him, like a banshee on a stormy night. His eyes saw only blackness, no matter how much he blinked them. They no longer worked. His world was black, and none of it mattered because Gwenyth was gone.

Nay, Gwenyth was happily married to the Prince of Bain...his head was lodged in a cask, mead rushing around him, a ladder trapping him to the rushes...

And it was Amber who was gone.

Hershel and Father were hauling him inside. His eyes burned, distorted shapes confused him. And none of it mattered, because Amber was missing. Gone, with no explanation. It was like reliving Gwenyth's disappearance all over again, but this time with the woman he loved.

And Gavin and Hershel were sawing off his leg. Torturing him. Murdering him. He was helpless, so helpless. Amber was gone, his leg was gone. His mind was gone. His skin singed. Smelled. Burned. Like meat frying on a griddle.

"Ahh!" he bellowed. "Stop! Stop! I pray you! *Foking stop!*"

"Hold him the hell down!" demanded Lord Loddin.

"Foking stop!" Will cursed, screamed, his deep voice cracking.

The cauterizing iron withdrew from his knee. His brothers relented their hold upon his appendages. He curled onto his side, writhing and clinging to his leg. He was naked again, save his undergarments. His lungs heaved, his wailing fizzled out. His world was still dark. He opened his eyes, tears having soaked his face, and shivered.

"No," he groaned, blinking. "No..." His world was black. He was blind again. He felt so bloody broken. He had to be dying. He couldn't endure the torture anymore. He kept shivering. Somewhere in the distance, he heard himself ask for a blanket. Of all the foolish things to worry about at such a moment.

Amber's gentle hand woke him from his nightmare, though he realized that the camp was quiet. The hour was late. A fire nearby crackled, heat radiating outward. It felt balmy to his bare skin. She was smoothing back his hair from his forehead. And his eyes... it was black when they opened. His heart sank. He was still blind... *Nay, I'm not.* He rolled his head and could make out her face and body, a silhouette against the orange flames.

He exhaled. Blessedly his eyes still worked. He reached up and encased the back of her hand in his palm.

"William?" she whimpered. "You wake?"

"Aye," he answered. His throat felt scratchy and the word sounded raspy.

"Your fever has broken," she offered. "God has seen fit to deliver you once again."

How was it possible? He had been a dead man. There was no

way that he could have recovered from a second fever induced from festering. He squeezed her hand, feeling gaunt and tired. But surely Amber's touch had delivered him. Surely, in his dire state, God had seen fit to let him live so that he could marry her.

"Shame on you for not telling me of your leg," she admonished, though her words were gentle.

The pain throbbing through his stump was unbearable. A flask of whiskeybae would do him well. He could still feel the bite of the hot iron frying his skin. The thought made him wince. Still, he smiled at her admonishment.

"Spirits?" he asked.

She moved her fingers over a spread of supplies and produced a waiting flask.

"Will, I was so scared," she finally admitted, releasing the words as if a dam giving way to a flood. "Your screaming... It's been two days."

"I'm sorry," he whispered, pulling her hand to his mouth to kiss it as he swallowed a gulp of the alcohol. "I'm embarrassed you had to witness it."

"Why?" she asked. "I cannot fathom such pain. Mercifully you passed out. How on earth can a man endure such torture three times in his life? You're so brave."

"I hadn't a choice." He dismissed the praise, still holding her hand. It would seem she had bathed. He could smell the clean scent of Hershel's soap. *Good.* He could rest assured that her modesty had been honored, for he would worry if it were Gavin's soap she had used. And now that his eyes had adjusted fully to the nighttime, he could see her auburn-brown curls were combed and tied back in a soft, loose braid.

"I'm so thankful you're recovering," Amber said. "So very thankful. You should never have harmed yourself so over me."

"Mayhap all I needed was to feel your hand upon my brow," he replied, basking in her touch.

He peered around her and noticed Hershel watching him, sitting with his knees propped up. He poked the fire with the branding iron to push unburned logs into the flame. In truth, he looked as if he pondered deep meanings of life.

"Where's Father and Gavin?" he queried.

Hershel looked back into the fire with a smile, and then sent a glance to the heavens with a 'thank you' on his lips. "Hunting. They've been gone all afternoon and I expect them back soon."

Will looked back up at Amber and dragged her down against

his chest. Her cheek was cool upon his pectoral. And she was stiff. "Relax upon me," he urged, but she remained tense.

He finally released his hold on her and she pushed back up to sitting. His brow furrowed. "What's wrong?"

Amber didn't answer at first and Hershel, watching the uncomfortable exchange, pushed to his feet. "Nature calls." He tossed down the iron and strode into the murky trees.

Amber still didn't answer, but tensed further.

"I thought mayhap I imagined your displeasure after I found you," Will muttered, no longer seeking her touch. He shifted, winced, and took a moment to let the aftershocks settle in his leg. "Now it's obvious to me I wasn't imagining anything. Something's wrong."

She remained frozen at the censure.

"Amber, I deserve an explanation."

He shivered from cold, his bare chest covered in gooseflesh. He withdrew the blanket rolled beneath his head and shook it out, gritting his teeth as his stump jostled.

"You put your very life in peril trying to find me... Oh William," Amber fell to tears. "Your leg, all because of me, and I can't even bloody-well see you. I couldn't come to you as you collapsed walking me to safety. I couldn't do a thing for you when your family burned shut your leg wound. I've been of no help caring for you aside from the damp rags Lord Hershel placed at my side with which to wipe your brow. What kind of wife will I make?"

He lay still. Blinked his eyes. What she was saying sounded an awful lot like a withdrawal of consent. He didn't want to believe it.

"What are you saying?" he croaked.

She took his hand and he allowed it, even if he didn't grip her in return.

"William, if you were to fall ill or injure yourself in the meadery, I would be of no use to you. I'm... I'm nay good material for a wife."

He pulled his hand free from her, knowing his face had paled. "This is about *my* eyes, nay yours. Isn't it?" he finally muttered. "Now that I can see, now that I'm nay like you, you don't want me."

"William, I'll never be able to care for you as a wife should," she hastened, as if further explanation would be helpful. "After everything I've been through, I see this now. I never saw it before. Before, all I saw was happiness. Me in your arms. Working side by side with you. But now I realize why blind women are undesirable. What use are we?"

His heart ached in a way he never knew possible, rendering

him breathless. He could hardly feel his leg. This was what it felt like
when one's heart was ripped clean out.

Rejection.

After everything he had been through. After all his years of
waiting. After thinking he would never be able to marry her with his
deficiencies, suffering silently until their fathers paired them. After
those sweet, private kisses, bodies pressed together... God, but life had
finally felt like it was improving. Life had finally stopped feeling like
the curse it used to be. How on earth could the happenings of the past
month change her heart? He might not be the most versed man with
women, but he knew rejection when he heard it, felt it... *saw* it.

Aye, his eyes strayed up to hers. She stared straight ahead at
the trees, eyes wet with water. The begging in her voice and the
stiffness in her embrace spoke of a woman who wanted to be
anywhere but where she was.

With him.

"William, give me time to think. I wish to go home. To rest. I
want to be the best wife I can be and right now," she took a deep
breath, "right now I'm having doubts."

He tried not to scoff, but the bitterness in his voice intensified.
"Time to think about what? About me?" The slap of those thoughts
rolling like vinegar over the tongue. His next words were quiet, but he
had to know. No sense in stringing something along that was already
dying. "Do you wish to break the betrothal?" he growled.

God no, please no. Sakes, but after everything he had gone
through for her? It was the wrong reason to feel angry, he knew. Help
ought to be given to others because they needed it, nay because the
helper wanted a reward. But dammit all, he had given her the rest of
his lower leg, nearly died of festering twice. Traveled across the ocean
strait for her. Captured her abductors. Used his wisdom as a blind man
to locate her. And this was his thanks?

"Nay break it...just postpone it," she replied, reaching to find
his hand. Her fingers patted down his chest, now concealed beneath
the itchy wool of his blanket. But when her fingers touched his, he
pulled away.

"Postpone it until when?"

She paused. "I do nay know."

He sighed. "I suppose, in sooth, we don't know much about one
another," he conceded, trying to deflect the pain. "All I know about you
is the way you feel, your scent, that you dislike your father's easy
dismissal of you, that you don't receive due credit for your

contributions to Dunstonwoodshire, that you kept those foolish birds I carved for you." He huffed. "I suppose I know that you're a good friend of my sister's. Young. Strong. And combined with your beauty, combined with the fact that I've known you your *whole* life, I thought that was better a foundation to begin a marriage than most betrothals."

He swallowed. "But if I knew you better, I would have also known that you rise to jealousy much too easily for my taste. And hell, but I never would have pegged you as so unkind."

She gasped. He rolled away from her, unable to swallow his groan of pain as he shifted. Sweat broke out on his brow.

"You're much too young for me, besides. Have your wish then. You don't have to marry me anymore."

"Pray, William," came a trembling reply, thick with despair. "I only wished to postpone it." She threw her face and arms down upon his side, bursting into a sob and clenching him. "I'm sorry!"

"Leave me be," he continued, resting his head on his bicep under his ear and warding her off with a nudge. He couldn't bear the touch. "I'm tired. And the journey home will be long."

Mayhap her blindness was in this moment more of a blessing than a curse, for what woman would love a man who...cried? *Damnation!* He cursed, but his eyes watered, and he rubbed them with his thumb and forefinger to clear away the burning.

His brothers had urged him to endure for Amber's sake, and so he had. *What a bloody jest.* He supposed he should thank her for that tiny bit. The thought of her safety had kept him from succumbing. Except what good was life now when he had to live it alone?

Postponement? Nay. Asking to postpone was the first step in submitting a severance to the contract. It would give Amber time to travel home, and then issue the dismissal from Dunstonwoodshire where she could hide behind her father's pen and not have to reject him to his face.

He faked sleeping until he truly did fall asleep. It didn't take long. He was exhausted, malnourished, and a glance at the streaks of bruising on his arms told him he had been bled profusely. It was a wonder he was even living still.

***

Amber finally rose as she sensed his breathing even out. She wiped her eyes, rubbing away the dampness. She regretted her feelings the moment they began to escape her lips. Nay. She regretted them the moment William tried to pull her down against his broad, bare chest.

Good Lord, but she had ruined such a pleasure. The moment could have been beautiful. A hiccup caught her throat. It was over. She had ruined it.

Jealousy.

"Oh God..." she whimpered, feeling sickness turn her stomach. Aye, it wasn't that she worried about being a good wife. She brought her hand to her mouth. It was that she was jealous of the gift God had bestowed upon William but not on her. Will had been granted such a gift, and she hadn't, and it hurt. Instead of rejoicing in the fact that Will had loved her enough to use his blessing for her, she had allowed it to hurt her. She was a horrible person, but she sensed attempting a hasty apology now wouldn't help matters. It would only make her look flighty, shallow, unable to make up her mind.

God above, but what had she done?

Chapter 20

Prince William dropped Alonso from his hold against the wall. The smuggler collapsed to the dungeon floor strewn in rushes.

"I expect more answers, man. If you wish me to show you mercy, you'll cooperate."

Alonso strained for air. "Where... where's my brother?" He tried to push himself to sitting, coughing. "I'll not answer anything until I know my brother is alive."

Prince William's eyes furrowed. He needed more information out of these bastards. Learning of Lispagne's operations in Bain wasn't enough. He needed details on Fernando. His informant had been right. Bain had lost many sons and daughters without knowledge of the crimes being committed. This man, Alonso, and his brother, had been smuggling away Bainick countrywomen and lads beneath his very nose. This wasn't just a tragedy for the victims and their families, it was an affront to the crown.

The prince looked up at a guardsman and nodded his head. The guardsman leaned out of the metal bars installed in the stone arches, old vaults in the foundation of Fort Michaelmas.

"Do it," the guard called to someone unseen.

Moments later, a heavy thud of an axe striking wood echoed. A shriek pierced their ears.

Alonso's face went white. "What did they do to him?" he begged, grabbing Prince William's boots. "What did they do to him? Sergio!" he called.

William thrust him off with a shake of his foot and looked down on the Lispagnioc spy.

"They chopped off his finger. Now listen carefully, for I don't want to repeat myself again. Every time you refuse to answer a question from this moment forward, your brother loses another finger. Then we shall start on his toes. And then each hand, and then each foot, and then each forearm... You understand, do you not?"

Alonso nodded, trying to clasp the prince's feet again in supplication. "I'll talk. Just don't hurt him further. This was my fault, all of it. Not his."

William folded his arms over the black lion upon his chest. "Good. Now, one last time: Who else operates in Bain?"

Alonso closed his eyes, clearly weighing which fate was worse. Dying at the hands of King Fernando? Dying at the hands of Prince William? Or living out his meager days in a Bainick dungeon?

"I'm listening," prompted the prince. When no answer immediately followed, he looked up at his guardsman again. "All right, I suppose another finger comes off. See it done—"

"Wait!" Alonso cried, doubling over again. The guardsman paused and both he and William watched. "There are two other pairs of men. One pair working to smuggle in the south, and one in the east, in Dwyre." He wiped his eyes, trying to clear away the blur. "That's all I know, I swear! We've never met each other, for reasons obvious. If we knew of each other, we might cave under pressure, like I do now! I know not their names, I swear this. I swear it on the Holy Bible, I swear it!"

Unimpressed, Prince William gazed down at him in the feeble torchlight. The dungeon cell was thick with smoke, a pungent smell that plugged the nostrils and made one careful to only inhale shallow breaths.

"You swear you don't know them?" the prince finally asked. Alonso wouldn't look up, simply nodded, doubling back over his knees.

The prince shook his head. No man caved so easily when they made their way in the world as a spy, as a smuggler, or a thief. "I'm sorry, but I don't believe you. Guard?"

"No...no..." Alonso shook his head, watching the guard push away from the wall and call down the stone corridor again.

Another axe chop. Another scream.

"Stop! Stop!" Alonso begged. "I pray you stop!"

"Then speak up," Prince William replied. "I harbor no sympathy for you, your brother, or your worthless king. It matters not to me if Sergio bleeds to death. I'll give Sergio his life and bandage his hands, but only in return for information."

Alonso wouldn't speak. William squatted down and grabbed a

fistful of the man's dingy blond hair, wrenching up his head. "Don't play games with me," he growled. "Or I swear your brother loses every last finger. Do you understand?"

Alonso nodded as best he could with his hair in such a grip. His nose ran, his eyes swollen from the crippled man's beating days ago, dripped tears.

"I beg you not injure my brother again. The men, I swear it I truly do, are anonymous to us in name. But the two that work in the south, in the region of the River Fey, are both brown-haired. One bears a scar upon his chin and is missing part of his left ear. Lost it in the Great War. His partner is tall, thin. His nose is bent from an old break. The other two, patrolling the Dwyre lands, I've only seen from afar. One was unremarkable, light brown hair. The other was draped in a cloak, propped in the shadows of King Fernando II's council chamber on the only occasion I saw him.

"King Fernando cannot secure an alliance through marriage, and so he hopes to breed offspring that bear the blood of powerful nations such as yours, to entice you into marriages with his children and thus, rebuild his trade. Lispagne ails. The peasants who aren't slaves die of starvation, disease, and pestilence."

"What other countries?"

"I know not," Alonso replied.

"Do it," William said to his guard.

"No!" Alonso cried. "No I beg you—"

Another shriek escaped the neighboring cell.

"I swear I don't know! I swear!"

"Another," William said, sparing no thought for his pleas.

"I beg you stop!" Alonso beseeched, crawling forth to tug on Prince William's surcoat as another chop dislodged another finger. Then the shrieking slowed, softened, and silence came from the other room.

"Sergio!" Alonso cried. "Sergio, answer me!"

Nothing. No sound. "Is he dead?" Alonso fretted. "I told you everything I knew! I told you..." He fell to husky sobs.

William nodded at the guardsman who left the room.

"Don't hurt him anymore!" wailed Alonso, trying to crawl toward the door, tethered at his ankles by chains shackling him to the floor. "Sergio..."

Moments later, two guardsmen hauled Sergio into the dungeon cell, releasing him with a shove. Sergio stumbled across the rushes to the opposite wall where the guardsmen proceeded to remove a gag from his mouth and lock his wrists in manacles.

"Serg..."

Sergio looked at him, though offered nothing in his gaze.

"I'm done with these two. For now," the prince said. "And Alonso," Prince William said, rising back to standing as the guards hoisted him up under the arms and clamped his wrists into manacles, too. "I don't torture my prisoners like your monarch has been doing to our Bainick sons and daughters. As you can see," he gestured, "your brother is well and retains every last finger."

Relief washed over Alonso's face. "But you would torture *me*," he countered. "Toy with my fears."

Prince William shrugged, unaffected. "I do what I must. But let this be a lesson. I may not torture, but I have been known to execute. And if you *piss* me off, you can feel my wrath. I thank thee for deciding to cooperate. Guard?" he turned to the dungeon warden. "See to it our guests receive a hearty meal. No scraps, no slop."

The guard nodded and left to see the meals ordered. Prince William quit the cell as his guards followed, leaving Alonso to see that all of Sergio's fingers, all his appendages, were indeed still attached. The iron bars clanked shut.

Sir Cavanaugh and Sir MacTierny dropped their axe on a stump of wood in the neighboring dungeon cell where they had playacted the amputations. They fell into step with Prince William, flanking him on either side.

Winding up the stairs toward the prison warden's offices, William waited until he was out of earshot before stopping. He looked at both his men in the wavering torchlight.

"Bain has failed one-hundred and forty-two young lads and young women."

He tried to mask the sadness in his voice, but he couldn't. Young Amber of Dunstonwoodshire had been dragged into the plot, but had she not been a noblewoman, if his Lispagnioc informant hadn't recently fled his homeland to pass information to him from Bain's Cambrian Forest, he and King Bain might never have been the wiser.

"The lads have been enslaved for labor, and the young women have been turned into King Fernando's broodmares. We owe it to them, peasants or nay, to learn of their fate and if possible, stage a rescue."

MacTierny's face had grown dark. His eyes furrowed. His jaw clenched.

"You have something to say, MacTierny?" William questioned.

When MacTierny eyed Cavanaugh and didn't answer, Cavanaugh took the queue and departed, leaving the two men alone. Once the door exiting onto the yard closed, William turned back to his man. "What's on your mind? Speak."

"Me wife was a slave to the late King Fernando, the current king's sire. Her older children are in sooth, the seed of none other than the dead king himself."

Prince William scrutinized him, absorbing the impact of his words. Fernando I had other bastards? Sebastien had other half-siblings besides Christophoro? He nodded for MacTierny to continue.

"Their mine now," the gruff highlander added. "But if you want an offensive led to rescue the Bainick subjects, I'd be proud to serve."

Prince William nodded, his mouth lifting in a weary smile. "I never knew that about her children."

"Make no mistake, my bairns will have naught to do with Lispagne," MacTierny warned. "They're shielded from such *bull*shite—" a humorless jest, for Lispagne's symbol was a bull "—with their claim to my proud name of MacTierny. They deserve a normal life, after the hell they've been through, and a normal life I'll give 'em."

Prince William nodded. But in spite of it all, MacTierny's step-children's parentage did indeed add to the intrigue. Eoin could shield them as best he could, but if his step-children learned the truth of their sire, they would have every right to vie for a Lispagnioc claim. Such worries were far off, considering they were young still. But someday...

***

Amber stood in the yard at Dunstonwoodshire, withstanding the joyful salutations from her brothers, her sister, Princess Gwenyth who remained in residence, and the servants of Dunstonwoodshire. She felt sick. The happiness that greeted her as she rode through her father's gates wasn't any comfort. She hardly felt the arms enveloping her, hardly heard a word spoken directly to her.

Not once had William spoken to her further, only general remarks to his father and brothers as they traveled.

That wasn't true. He had apologized for speaking to her unkindly a couple days later as they readied to begin traveling. That had been it. He hadn't sought forgiveness. Hadn't engaged her further. He hadn't once asked her to reconsider her decision. He hadn't touched her again except for just now when he had helped her dismount.

"You are a hero, William of Ballymead, as are your brothers and your father!" Lord Edward boomed. His declaration was met with enthusiastic cheers. "We shall feast tonight, and celebrate the return of my daughter and William's betrothed! You deserve every commemoration Prince William choses to bestow on you."

The cheering roared again, and then, as it died down, all realized that Lord Edward's voice had grown gruff.

"Such a quality in a son-of-marriage is the best gift a father could get, for I know that in William's care, Amber will always be cherished and protected. Come, son," he said. What was her father doing? Striding to Will? Embracing him? He was slapping his back, all could hear that. "Come have the first tankard of ale. You and your family are men of honor in my household and forevermore shall be."

Silence fell. Amber chewed her lip nervously. William cleared his throat as the sound of Gwenyth dashing to him to throw her arms around him rustled and the servants muttered about the humor. He remained quiet, and Amber could feel her face draining to grey.

"There—" Will's voice cracked. He cleared it. "There won't be a wedding."

Gasps and muttering ensued.

Lord Edward's shocked voice followed. "What?"

"I said, there won't be a wedding. Gavin will marry Sarah, of course, but Amber has requested—" He cleared his throat again. "She has requested postponement indefinitely."

After more silence, she could hear her sire round on her. She felt her sister and brothers part, felt her father's looming presence now before her. "Amber. What is the meaning of this? After all that William has suffered for you? You would deny him?"

"Father," she whispered, though couldn't say anything else. Her voice wouldn't work. She began to tremble.

"Lord Edward," William said.

Her father's belts creaked as he turned around.

"Aye, William."

"Do nay be hard on her. She's been through much. I bid you show compassion, for she's no longer the same lady you lost over a month ago. Give her the time she wants."

No one spoke. Finally, Gwenyth filled the void, and Amber heard her skirts rustling, then felt Gwenyth's gentle touch on her arm. "I shall remain here and tend to her, brother."

Will nodded. "No doubt you can offer her comfort none of us can."

Gwenyth retreated from her once again, and Amber could hear brother and sister embrace, then she heard Will murmur softly to

Gwenyth while her father moved away to talk to Lord Loddin. "Christ, sister, but I can no more remain here than I can walk on two good feet."

Amber's throat thickened at his distress, and she knew then that she'd made a horrible mistake.

***

Will had to leave before he succumbed to his heartache in front of every man here that he respected. He let go of his sister and turned back to his horse. Though pained, he managed to hoist himself into the saddle again, and cleared his throat once again.

"Lord Edward. Please don't take offense, but I'm unable to remain for the feasting. Please enjoy without me. I want to return to Ballymead. I bid Lady Amber well." He swallowed at the lump lodged in his throat, but didn't look at her as he spoke, for he could tell in his periphery that she cried. "I pray Lady Amber finds someone who will make her happy if it isn't me. But should she change her mind, I'll be in the meadery. It's where I always am."

He turned his reins, commanding the beast with his knees and thighs, and exited, leaving tears streaming down Amber's face.

***

"I'm going after him, lads," Lord Loddin began, when Gwenyth stayed her father, grabbing his arm.

"Leave him, Father," she said. "Give him the space he seeks. It's nay just his body that is broken. It's also his heart. And like any man, he has his pride."

"He's injured, Butterfly," Lord Loddin argued, his pet name for her rolling off his tongue. "If anything befalls him, he could die unattended in the wilderness."

"Nay," Hershel and Gavin interjected, staying their father further.

"Gwenyth is right, Father," Hershel said. "He's his own man. Has he nay proven this to you by now? Leave the man be to lick his wounds."

"He may be a man, but he's still my son," growled Lord Loddin, attempting to remount his horse.

"For as much as you like to boast about your paternity," Gwenyth began, "you certainly have little faith in how well you raised us."

A deadly hush fell upon everyone. Gwenyth swallowed for courage. She might be the Princess of Bain, but this was still her father she confronted.

"What did you say to me?" Lord Loddin uttered in disbelief. "Mine ears deceive me now."

"Will makes his own decisions. He knows what he is doing. He has traversed this countryside time and again and knows how to survive. Leave him be and have faith in the skills you have instilled in him since birth," Gwenyth argued, lifting her chin to stare into her father's angry eyes. "As his sister, and as his best friend, I implore you to stop thinking of your own fear and allow him to face his."

***

Stunned, Amber allowed herself to be led away by Sarah's arm around her as the bailey dispersed and the dinner was ordered, though much of the celebratory mood was lost. In spite of her state of hunger, she was unable to eat. Her heart ached. And the exchange between Ballymead's men and Gwenyth revealed one more thing she and Will had in common. They had both struggled against their fathers' control.

She felt like a mere wisp of her former self. Arriving in her bedchamber, she tore herself from Sarah and dashed to the bed, collapsing. She buried her face in her pillows. They smelled so comforting, and yet there was nothing that could offer comfort now.

Her sobs rolled forth and she convulsed. She gripped another pillow, wrapping her arms around it, squeezing. The bed ropes creaked as Sarah added her weight beside her, and then creaked again as Gwenyth sat on her other side. A hand took to rubbing her back while another hand pet back her curls.

"Amber, sister, please try to eat something. The kitchens are bringing you more food and you would do well to nourish yourself. You're much too thin," Sarah urged, still petting back her sister's tresses while Gwenyth caressed her jeweled fingers up and down Amber's back.

She remained in a heap of worn, dirty skirts, and allowed her heart to pour out of her chest. Slowly, the anguish subsided, and she lay lifelessly, thinking. How many times had she sat upon this very bed, fingering the fine wooden doves that William had carved for her over the years, imagining all manners of flirtations between them?

How many times had she, her sister, and Gwenyth sat piled together, while Sarah and Gwenyth gossiped about the frivolous diversions that captured the minds of young girls? And now, here they were, consoling her while she sobbed ridiculous tears.

"I made such a grand mistake. I was so upset and confused," Amber finally murmured. "Gwenyth, I never meant to hurt William. I just, I don't know what came over me. I was just...just so upset..."

"Of course you were," Sarah crooned, still petting her lifeless face and hair. "How could you not be? What happened to you was horrific, and if William can't see that, he's a fool."

"Nay," Amber replied as her nose clogging with unladylike mucous. Dear God, but her nose probably looked like a fat, red turnip. 'Twas good indeed she couldn't see her reflection. "He was ever grateful I was safe, so pleased, so giving with his affection, and I...I..." A sob racked her frame again and she buried her face into her pillow. "I felt so sorry for myself! I couldn't see William's eyesight as the blessing it was or what it would mean for us, for his ability to provide for me...I was *jealous!* Of all the things to be. And I took it out on him."

"There, there, bonny Amber," Gwenyth fretted. "You've always been so quiet and gentle, your sobbing now is worrisome. Try nay to cry so."

"How can I not?" Amber argued. She had never been argumentative. "My marriage to William is ruined. I ruined it. My future is ruined, for he'll never have faith in me ever again. Ever—"

"William is a kind brother to me," Gwenyth continued, still rubbing up and down her back as Sarah gripped one of her hands. "He has always been understanding and patient. His heart no doubt hurts as much as yours, even if he won't admit it. I can tell he is confused. But he'll understand your feelings with time—"

"I fear I made him think I no longer wanted him," Amber interrupted. "After all he went through to find me. After beating the smuggler who captured me. Gwenyth, he defended my honor and I was so hurt, so confused, by the monk, by that horrid Lispagnioc man with his, his *hated* voice. I was so lost and desperate." She shuddered at the memories, knowing that she would likely have the nightmares again tonight, hands grabbing her breasts, slipping off a cliff and falling, falling...

Gwenyth lay down beside her. Amber could sense that the princess was face to face with her tear-streaked visage.

"Dear Amber. In time, I hope you can talk of what you've gone through. When that time comes, I will listen. I promise. I will travel from the capital to hold your hand and let you describe your ordeal. Just know that I understand, and the only way I could overcome what I endured was to allow my heart to love the prince in spite of my misgivings, and not push him away because of my insecurities. My brother Will is a wonderful man, and it was his advice I followed when it was I that was too confused and hurt to accept the prince's offer."

"He dismissed me," Amber murmured, blinking to pinch

another round of tears from her eyes. "I was so jealous of his eyesight that he turned away from me. Lord! I was so foolish! Of all the trivial things to be worried about. After all the things that happened, I chose bitterness." Her voice fizzled away.

"Nay, you weren't foolish," Sarah defended her, giving her hand a stout shake. "You had been kidnapped, wandered lost through the woods, placed your trust in a stranger who could have..." Rape was too difficult a word to say aloud as a lady of breeding, but they all knew what Sarah was implying.

"I almost was," Amber whispered, unable to say anything more, curling into her pillows more tightly.

Gwenyth embraced her, still lying face to face with her. "Then have faith that William knows you suffer. Just know that he suffers, too. He gave up his leg for you. And do you know, he has nightmares that plague him? He wakes up screaming from the pain of his amputation on occasion. That pain will always be with him, but he was willing to endure it again. For you. But in spite of his hurt, he told you in front of us all that he'll wait for you, and Will is a man of his word."

She felt Sarah petting back her hair again. "And if he was so hurt, it only means he loves you so."

"What kind of a wife would I make?" Amber interrupted, as if Sarah hadn't already been talking, another behavior unlike her. She bolted up, her hair in disarray and her eyes puffy, as if having an epiphany. "*Good Lord.* Isn't it good I discovered what a wretched woman I am now rather than after William was shackled to me?" She sighed the words. "No doubt I would become a shrew, one of those horrible women who nags constantly."

Sarah and Gwenyth laughed outright. "Good gracious, Amber! You're a hopeless mess." Sarah pulled her younger sister into a maternal embrace. "This isn't as dire as it seems. I will miss you standing at the altar with William as Gavin and I say our vows, but I have faith all will work out as it should."

"William has fancied you for a long time, Amber," Gwenyth added. "Remember, he wasn't always blind, and he still liked you. I feel confident he will wait for you."

Amber took a deep breath. There was nothing left to do. No amount of hugs from her sister or gentle pats from Gwenyth would change the fact that she had dismissed William and shied away from him. It hadn't just been her hour of need that had mattered, but his too, and she had withheld her affection from him. And it had nothing to do with not being attracted to him. Lord no. She had wanted to feel him in all his naked glory as he lay before her, recovering, dragging her down to lie against him. All she had needed to do was overcome her own bitterness and quit thinking of his eyesight as an unfair advantage.

It hit her. She would have made a fine wife in such a moment, not a poor one. All she had needed to do was offer a gentle hand, hold him as he had held her in her time of need, and be there for him, help him in the ways she could, and it would have been enough.

"When William comes with Gavin's wedding party, I'll begin to make amends," she nodded to herself, despair in her heart. "I might never repair things betwixt us, but I'll try. I'll try my very best."

"Some sennights to recover and consider what you'll say to him might not be so bad," Sarah replied, as Gwenyth pulled her back down to lying so the three of them could cuddle and gossip together like they had done so many times before.

Chapter 21

The days turned into sennights and the festivities for Sarah's wedding heightened. Excitement had overtaken Dunstonwoodshire. Amber cloistered herself away from the merriment in her work chamber to make what soap she could since her father had forbidden her to venture to the glen alone for more material.

There was little other space to occupy where she could be by herself.

Her father had spared little time for her since her homecoming. Princess Gwenyth had bid he withhold his anger from her, and so he had left her alone. But it soon became clear that if she wasn't going to be marrying William, then her needs were secondary to everything else. She still had yet to speak to her father about her ordeal. He knew the basics of what happened from Ballymead's men and Prince William's accounts and for now, she had chosen to leave it at that. He was preoccupied anyway.

She sat at the board, scooping a spoonful of stew, letting it drip back into her bowl. Only a few bites and she had lost her appetite.

"A missive was sent ahead from Ballymead's wedding party today," Lord Edward said from the head of the board. "They will arrive in three days. And they bring a small household of their own servants and guardsmen, too. 'Twill be an added burden to feed and house, but we must do our duty to accommodate them."

The old man sighed. The rustling sound of parchment landing upon the board followed. Amber could hear him rubbing his face, his palms scraping across his stubble.

"William will be with them, of course?" Amber piped up among the dinner clinking.

Her father took a swallow of wine and plunked his goblet down. "Nay. He has elected to remain at Ballymead."

Amber's melancholy overtook her face. She had hoped, no *prayed*, for his return to Dunstonwoodshire, so she could fall at his feet and beg forgiveness.

"Do nay look so saddened, daughter," Edward added. "A man knows when he's been rejected, and I should think the reason for his absence is obvious."

Both she, Sarah to her right, and Gwenyth across from her, gasped.

"Father," Angus muttered. "Have sensitivity."

Amber couldn't find any words. She stood and pushed back her chair, hastening from the hall. She stumbled upon a basket laid out on the floor with linens and napery for the wedding feast, tripping to her knees with an outcry.

Several servants rushed to help her, but she pushed off their hands and scrambled to her feet again.

"What a horrible thing to say!" Sarah exclaimed behind her as Amber quit the hall, dashing down the corridor to her work chamber.

"Indeed, sir, that was unkind. Have you any idea what she has gone through?" Gwenyth added.

Amber catapulted herself through her workroom door, jamming it shut, and tried to make her way to the chair that sat beside the hearth. She collapsed to the floor instead, feeling loose tendrils of hair fall into her face.

She cried.

What she would have given for her father to wrap his burly arms around her, to hold her, to tell her she would be all right. What she would have given to go back in time and change her behavior so William would know that he could always count on her affection. Their reunion should have been the beautiful moment he had hoped it would be. She missed William. She was so foolish.

She ceased crying and thought about what Will had said. *He was right. Look at what you've overcome, in spite of your eyes? You really are strong. But right now, you're acting weak. This isn't who you are, woman.* If she wanted the love and respect of a man, she needed to act like a woman, nay a child. She was blind, and there would be no changing that. What needed changing was her heart. She needed to smile, to rejoice that she was alive, healthy, and had attracted the devotion of a good man she loved.

She sighed at the revelation, the weight of such a burden lifting from her shoulders.

She heard a fluttering of wings as a bird came to perch on her windowsill. She knew the window shutters were open—she had opened them that morn as she boiled her beef tallow and ash water so the odiferous scent had a means of escape. If it flew into the chamber, it might begin to pillage her stores of dried herbs and berries.

"Away, bird," she shooed.

The bird cooed.

It's nay just any bird, it's a dove, she realized, and ceased waving her hands at it.

She managed to push herself to her feet and ignored the sting upon her shin where she had hit it tripping in the hall. She reached to the mantle over the hearth. Her fingers found the first little figurine Will had carved her. She traced over its shape, the curves, the scoring lines of the detailed feather work. *William's trinket for me from that Christmastide so long ago,* the first one he had ever made her, that year of her twelfth birthday after she had been blinded, as her breasts had begun to bud, as her body had begun to flux with a woman's courses, when she realized she was transforming.

She held in her hand what she had never realized in her youth:

She was becoming a woman and William of Ballymead, in his own, quiet way, was noticing.

Each dove he had made her since had been a special gift, separately given during their family gatherings, so that no one would notice his favoritism. He never spoke to her during those exchanges, for he had seemed shy when he wasn't teasing her in the company of her sister and Gwenyth. When his eyesight had been taken and their families hadn't congregated for the Yuletide, he had sent a trinket along with the Ballymead messenger who delivered Lord Loddin's holiday missives of goodwill.

The dove on the windowsill cooed again. *Soft, gentle...* She heard his words as he partook of her affection and tangled his body with hers mere feet from where she stood now. She shuffled over the clean rushes to the window, sensing from the soft clicking of the bird's claws that it was moving down the sill to make room for her.

She arrived beside it, sharing its presence. It cooed again. *Odd,* she thought. Doves startled easily. The creature shouldn't be so calm with her nearby. It cooed again as her door pushed gently open.

"It calls to its mate," Gwenyth voice came, and Amber could sense both Gwenyth and Sarah slip into the chamber.

"Why would it search here?" Amber remarked, the hair on her arms prickling at the ridiculous thought of William vying for his mate as this bird searched for its.

No answer came. She could sense Sarah's disgust at being in the workroom by her sister's muttering. Someone was walking, from the sound of a gown swishing. Then the clinking of woodwork being picked up ensued.

"I always wondered at these wee trinkets," Gwenyth said as if remarking to herself. "Every year, William would sit in the meadery and whittle down a piece of wood. I spied him doing so each year before my first marriage, for William and I spent much time together. I simply thought he enjoyed making them. But look here." The soft clatter of wood indicated Gwenyth had picked one up. "He was making them for a special lady and none of us at Ballymead, not even I, knew."

Gwenyth's hand now came to rest upon Amber's arm and the dove, startled, took to flight with the squeaking beat of its wings. Amber threw her dampened cheeks into Gwenyth's waiting arms.

"I did know he fancied you, for he told me so."

Amber blushed. Gwenyth had mentioned to her that William had thought her pretty.

"He admires your strength, for you're always so humble, so hopeful and bright," Gwenyth said, clenching her. "And after his accident, he came to understand you, knowing what it took every day to live without light in his eyes. It might sound preposterous, but I believe that dove on your windowsill was a messenger. I believe, in all of my lovesick naivety as a girl who used to daydream relentlessly, that it means my brother still vies for you, even if he's too afraid to come to you again and risk further heartache."

"I know how you looked forward to William coming to the wedding," Sarah finally spoke, also coming across the rushes to take her sister's arm. "But it makes me certain that William loves you even more. If he was as much a mess as you over perceiving your rejection, it only means he had his heart set upon you. And if he loves you still, he won't reject you. His dismissal, sister, was to protect his own heart."

"I know. I was foolish to make him doubt himself," Amber said.

"Will isn't a fighter, Amber," Gwenyth remarked. "He's a peaceful man. If he fought so hard to see you vindicated, that means something special. I think you realize that now. He's ever-conscious of his leg. The loss of it has made him feel incomplete. But I saw the two of you at my wedding, chatting with your heads put together. You complete him. His smile never leaves his face when he's with you."

Amber pulled her kerchief from within her bodice to rub her eyes and nose, no doubt making the redness worse. "The thing is, none of the horrible things that happened to me make me feel half as horrible as the idea that I might have lost Will. He wasn't bothered for a single moment that I might have been..." Oh God, but the words hadn't yet left her lips this entire time.

"Violated?" Gwenyth finally said for her.

Amber nodded.

"Oh, bonny Amber," Sarah cried, and threw her arms around her sister. "Why have you nay spoken of this to me?"

"The monk didn't succeed," Amber muttered, cocooned in the clenching circle of her sister and dear friend. "He tried but..." the words left her mouth on a whisper. The women clenched her harder and she inhaled a shaking breath. "I broke his offending finger."

"What?" exclaimed Sarah.

Unexpectedly, Gwenyth giggled. "Goodness, as you should have, dear Amber! He deserves much worse."

"I believe he gets that, for Prince William incarcerated the guilty monk and dragged him behind his contingent on the end of a rope to a dungeon cell, so he might answer to Father Kearney for his transgression."

Gwenyth took her hands and squeezed them.

"I am glad to hear of my husband's valiance. It makes me proud of him for being your champion and I shall speak to him on the matter, to determine what sort of punishment will befall such a disgusting animal parading as a man of faith."

Sarah wiped Amber's eyes again.

"Will never once questioned my purity, or thought to turn me away. He only held me. I behaved so childishly, so ignorantly."

Sarah shook her. "Nay say such a wicked thing again! You're nay anything of the sort. You're simply inexperienced concerning your heart. You know you must make it right with him, you *must*," Sarah chastened gently. "But you did need time to come to this conclusion. William will understand. He wants *you*, sister. If he says your blindness matters not to him, then you must honor it as the truth. Imagine!" Sarah admonished. "He cared nay that you're blind. He was willing to lay down his life." She stroked a soothing hand up and down Amber's back, tangling her hair further.

"I was so fearful at the time that he might see another, now that his eyes work, and he would be inspired to stray," Amber admitted.

"You must trust him. You must take his fidelity at his word," Gwenyth spoke, and in her words was a warmth for the brother that had helped raise her. Amber listened. "If ever there was a solid man, my brother William is the one. He would be hurt to think you've thought him capable of such unfounded infidelity."

Amber swallowed, mortified at such a chastening. "Goodness, Gwenyth," she breathed. "I meant not to insult your family."

"You have much to offer him," Gwenyth continued, ignoring Amber's remark. "When I look around your work chamber, I see industrious hands, ambition to craft something others will enjoy. My, but this is exactly what Will does every day in the meadery. What a fine pair you would make together."

"And you escaped your captors," Sarah added. "Had you chosen nay to risk it, William might never have found you. Such a feat for any woman is nothing short of incredible."

"You protected yourself, never losing hope. Don't you see, Amber? For you nay need working eyes to see the feat you have accomplished." Gwenyth remarked. "You're a strong lady, meek or nay. Such fine qualities. Amber, allow yourself to build up your dream with Will again."

Sarah pet Amber's cheek. "Do you remember what William looks like?"

Amber stilled, remembering all too clearly the last time she had seen William with her own eyes. She was young, a girl still, and he, newly a man. My, but how fresh and untainted by life they all were back then.

At the time, her infatuation with William had been the innocent musings of a young girl. But Amber had fallen ill with fever the following winter, and the fever had stolen her eyesight. One day she could see, and the next, her world had gone dark. And in that moment of losing her innocence, she lost her dream of marrying William, even marrying anyone, until the day her father had brought her to Ballymead as a young woman only months ago to see if she and William would suit. It had been such a surprise, such cause for joy. Her heart had surged to life anew the moment Will whispered to her that he was pleased with the pairing.

"I remember what he looked like when he was barely a man," she replied, her voice wavering as she attempted to gain control of her emotions.

"He looks much the same," Sarah remarked, "though his muscle has filled out more. He's a man in every regard now, knighted, experienced in making a livelihood. His face has a few more lines in it, creases where his cheeks once dimpled," Sarah continued. "But he is still just as handsome. More brooding in his expressions than he used to be."

"No doubt losing his leg, his eyes, and then losing you, has made him quieter still," Gwenyth murmured.

"But he hasn't lost me," Amber argued.

"Then make him know that," Gwenyth replied.

Amber shook her head. "How? When he won't even come for Gavin's wedding?"

"You could have Father pen a letter to him on your behalf, expressing your regret, and invite him to visit you," Sarah suggested. "When I move to Ballymead with Gavin, Gwen and I could deliver it to him."

Amber nodded, yet wasn't satisfied. Somehow a missive written in her father's penmanship didn't seem genuine. As Sarah left on Gwenyth's arm to attend her final wedding gown fitting, Amber imagined William's arms. She drifted out of her work room hours later, clutching the dove, and meandered down the corridor, to the stairs, and up to her chamber. Closing the door, she loosened her bodice, stripped off her kirtle and overgown, and lay down on top of her blankets. It was still early, but the evening was winding down and her heart hurt. She imagined William whispering to her on that night so long ago when their fathers first revealed that they wished to match them together.

"I hope it's not too bold of me to say that I'm pleased by it... if you are."

Aye, she had been pleased, a girlish fancy turning into an adult marriage. It was a dream not many lasses could ever claim.

And then she imagined the taste of the youngest son of Ballymead's lips upon hers, hidden in the depths of the meadery. Her first kiss. The meadery. Where she had felt for the first time what happened to a man when he wanted a woman as Will pressed his body to hers. The meadery, where he had placed a sweet taste of the drink to her lips, informing her that she would forever be welcome to sample it. The meadery, where William had expressed that he wished to build a life with *her*, run the meadery together with *her*, bind himself to *her*.

She bolted upright again. He had said he would be in the meadery if she ever changed her mind, and she would find him there. She had been pitying herself, crying like a babe since her arrival home. And now because of her ridiculous uncertainty, she was missing her wedding day. Enough. She knew what needed to be done.

She threw on a robe haphazardly over her shift, her kerchief and her dove still in hand, and pattered across her chamber to the door. Entering the corridor, she dashed down the spiraling stairs to the great hall. The hall was still clamoring with wedding preparations. Trestle tables for guests had been set up in advance. Their finest linens were laid across the wooden boards. Amber could hear the clunking of pewter ware, heard the clinking of the family's fine silver among the din of servants' conversations and directives.

"Amber, daughter," Lord Edward called, striding across the room. "I eh... I apologize for my harsh remark at supper."

She threw herself into his arms, and though he embraced her, she sensed he might still be perturbed with her. She let go, and he didn't fight it.

"I had hoped you might be able to talk," she finally said. "We've hardly shared a word since my return, and I wish you—"

"Not now, Amber. Your sister and Princess Gwenyth bid me leave you be, and so I have."

"Father," she dipped into a curtsey. "I'm sorry I postponed my marriage. I've—"

He huffed. She sensed that he was put out. Always, she had seemed to put him out. He had never been comfortable with her since her blindness. He had always pushed her off on her sister. It was as if her deficiency...oh Lord, but after all these years, why was she just now figuring it out?

Her blindness frustrated him. He hadn't sought a betrothal with William so that she might have a good future with a good man, rather, he had sought the betrothal so she could continue to be Sarah's problem, so he wouldn't have to cope with the blind daughter for the remainder of his days.

"You look, eh, a fright," Edward stated, patting her on the head like a pup. "'Tis no way to present yourself around the castle. What with no gown, messy hair—"

"I know I look dreadful," she began. "But I must beg you to allow me to travel to Ballymead when the wedding party departs for home with Sarah."

"Why?" Edward asked.

"I need to speak with William. I must apologize to him—"

"Amber, this is poor timing. I'm inundated with demands for the wedding and the celebration afterward. I have less than a day to build a scaffold, the wood shop needs to build five more benches, I—"

"Father, I must speak to him. I must know that I've put to rights my errors, and since he isn't coming here, I wish to go to him."

"Let us talk about this in a fortnight, when the revelry has died down. I don't have time to listen just now, lass."

He began to walk away. Amber felt anger well inside of her. A fortnight would be too late. He wasn't even hearing her. She wanted to depart with Sarah for Ballymead in a sennight after the nuptials and she needed his blessing. She hadn't consumed a single second of his time since her return. Why couldn't he spare a moment for her now?

"Father!" she called after him, feeling her hands ball into fists.

The hall hushed a degree. She knew her face burned. Aye, she most assuredly looked as frightening as she felt.

"Father, I *must* speak to you! I need only a moment, but I'll nay let the matter die and postpone it until later."

She heard her father begin walking back to her, knew the rhythm and vibration of his step.

"Since your kidnapping, you've developed an unbecoming personality and a bold tongue," he began. "And now you bring embarrassment upon us in front of the staff, running about in your night shift with your hair a disaster and face tear-worn, shouting at your lord and father. Return to your chamber, and do not speak to me again until you are properly presented."

She wanted to scream, especially when she knew he walked away again. She gritted her teeth and marched back to her chamber. If her father wanted her presentable, so be it. One way or another, she would talk to him about traveling to Ballymead.

She stormed through her door, went to her wardrobe, and found a gown with delicate seed pearls embroidered upon the stomacher. She dragged it out, took a comb to her tresses, and when they were tangle-free, tied the masses back into a simple braid, securing the end with a ribbon. Heaven only knew if the ribbon matched. She slipped into the gown, pulled the laces at the sleeves tight, and exited the chamber again. Her back wasn't fastened completely, but she wasn't about to demand Gretchen take time away from her sister's fitting just to secure it.

She could hear Sarah and Gwenyth in the chamber next door, the maids tittering, the seamstress laughing, her sister gossiping about Gavin of Ballymead's fine physique. Gwenyth threatening to taunt her brother with Sarah's descriptions. Gretchen teased Sarah about her wedding night. Right now, Sarah was happy, and Amber had been like a stormy roll of thunder for sennights.

Instead, she reentered the great hall, teeming with servants hanging decorations and erecting more trestle tables. A guardsman greeted her as she made her way toward the bailey.

"My lady Amber," he said. She knew he bowed by the creaking of his leathers.

"Good eve, sir. Can you tell me where I might find my father?"

"He's in the chapel, my lady, conversing with the visiting priest. Something about the banns."

She thanked him and moved through the door he opened, relishing the blast of fresh evening air. Just the breeze was enough to lift her spirits. She hurried down the steps.

"Make way!" called one of the smiths, running a cart of supplies in front of her. She halted, then proceeded, careful to avoid other household workers as they zipped around her.

Arriving at the chapel, she climbed the steps to the arched door and drew it open.

"...I know, I know, but did we actually expect him to be pure? He's a man over thirty years of age," Lord Edward was arguing. "Of course he's lain with women. That in no way should disqualify him from marrying Sarah."

"All I'm suggesting, is that you counsel the man," the priest replied. "The objection has been raised as to his, shall we say, seed sowing, and the woman in question doubts his fidelity."

"Why on earth should her word matter over Gavin's?" Edward complained. "He has never declared fidelity to a woman before now. He's never been married or had to prove this quality."

"I know this," the priest sighed. "But she claims to have born his child, even though her child is unrecognized, and so I suggest you counsel him, determine for yourself whether or not he speaks the truth to you. Certainly seeding a bastard is no cause to disqualify marriage, but when an objection to the banns is raised, I *must* ensure that I've followed up on it," the priest emphasized. "And then there is the matter of your other daughter's marriage to Gavin's brother. The banns were posted for *two* presumptive couples, not just one."

Amber reeled from what she had just heard. Of course most men had slept with women. And when a man sought a women abed, all knew the possibility of a babe resulting from it was far too common. But if Gavin chose to recognize a bastard child, how would it hurt Sarah? He had always flirted mercilessly with Sarah and clearly adored her, but the rumors had followed him, whispers of gossip that were never spoken outright, that he enjoyed the womenfolk.

Lord, but her worry about William had been misplaced, that he might be unfaithful with his new eyesight. She had never doubted Will's commitment, but she had now experienced his honor. Of course he, too, had probably lain with others, but he had been devoted to her. Lord Loddin had done his absolute best to raise proper children and five out of six successes wasn't a poor outcome. His other sons had always been deemed good, kind, and loyal. Even Gavin was kind to all and loyal to family. Look at what Gavin, too, had endured to ensure that she, his youngest brother's betrothed, was returned home safely.

But if Gavin had a bastard child, how would Sarah cope? How would it affect his legitimate succession with Sarah's future children?

"What is the problem with that? Amber has chosen to wait, mayhap nay even marry William of Ballymead at all. She's just returned after a terrible ordeal, having been kidnapped, and has been addled since. One wedding will proceed as planned. The other is canceled indefinitely."

"Many of your guests don't know that yet," the priest countered. "They arrive with gifts for two weddings, not just one."

"And they can return home with one of their gifts," Edward waved his hand. "Unless you're telling me that this changes your ability to wed Gavin to Sarah, then I see no further point to this argument."

"No argument, sir," the priest replied, undeterred. No doubt he was used to irate fathers the sennight of a wedding. "Simply inconsistencies that need explanations. Talk with Sir Gavin about his *former* behavior. As I said, when someone objects to the banns, I must investigate. I'm satisfied that if you wish to move forward with the wedding, that Gavin is eligible. But if he has a bastard out in the world, you need to know if he is aware of it and how it could affect his own succession created in his marriage bed with your older daughter."

"I see no point in mentioning this to Sarah," Edward grumbled. "And so I won't. She's excited and this would only serve to hurt her and make her doubt her betrothed at a time when she needs to trust him."

Amber must have made a noise, for Edward's next words were for her and filled with alarm that she had overheard him.

"What do you need, daughter? You're supposed to be in your chamber."

She cleared her throat, wondering what to do or say. She couldn't mention such a thing to Sarah either, for it would indeed hurt her. "I stated before that I needed to speak with you most expediently, and you requested I be dressed decently first. And so I am."

"Amber," he sighed, and she imagined how she had seen him countless times rub his forehead with his thumb and finger to stave off a headache. "Not now."

"Then when?"

"In a fortnight you may bring whatever is so pressing to my table. Unless someone is dying. Is that the case here?"

She furrowed her brow.

"No, but—"

"Has there been a grave accident?"

"Of course not, but—"

"Then I haven't time to be bothered. Away, lass. I hate to be so stern, but I have more important things to which to attend."

"Father, a fortnight will be too long to wait," she rattled out when she sensed he was leaving.

He sighed again, annoyed. "Fine, what is it."

"I wish to travel to Ballymead with Sarah and Gavin's wedding party," she replied. "I need to speak to William and apologize."

He stood quietly for a moment, and his next words were incredulous. "You mean to tell me you interrupt my busy schedule over your lovesick heart? This couldn't have waited until the morrow? The day after?"

Her face burned. She was growing to hate her father's dismissiveness. She knew she was always the quiet one, always well-behaved. But after her kidnapping, she had realized that life required boldness not just to survive, but to thrive, and she knew now, without a doubt, she wanted to thrive.

"Father, I never bother you with concerns. I never come to you to demand a moment of your time. But I'm asking you now and only need your answer."

"Nay," Edward stated sharply. "There's your answer. I'll write William in a fortnight requesting an audience, but only after you divulge what you hope to discuss with him. I do nay need you to do more damage by rushing away with your emotions."

She cringed, biting her lips to withhold the tears his words provoked. But Gwenyth had said she knew Will waited for her, that the dove meant he loved her. She couldn't let her father's anger at her cause doubt to fester in the depths of her mind again.

"Whatever you endured, you owed it to William to be gracious of his sacrifices. For all we know, he wishes nay to see you again. If I don't approve of your message to him," Edward continued, "no missive will be drafted. And no further discussion of this matter will occur until *after* a fortnight. Busy yourself with your sister or in your chamber for the remainder of the day. Have I been quite clear?"

Amber's lips had disappeared into a thin, furious line. She balled her fists into the fabric of her gown to keep a rude retort from rolling off the tongue. "*Quite.*"

"Good. Now bother me not again unless the fief is on fire. I love you, daughter, but clearly you need more time to recuperate from your ordeal, to temper your harping tongue. Good eve."

He walked out of the chapel. She felt a waft from the door opening and closing. She was so angry at him she forgot about the priest several paces away at the altar and stomped her foot. Such frustration had never overcome her before. Her father left her no choice. She was going to have to defy him and make a hard decision, one in which she might completely regret. But if it meant she might win back Will's confidence in her, then so be it. And if all went well, she would never have to answer to the discipline her father was certain to administer for the audacity she was about to display.

That was that.

Chapter 22

The meadery was exactly the same as William remembered it. The racks were the same olden wood. The knots he had traced with his fingers over the years as he had grown up were still dark and smooth. Not seeing them for so long felt like a lifetime. Lean from his travels and ill-shaven, Will stood in the doorway of the meadery on his crutches, staring at nothing, staring at visions of a future he wasn't going to have as the wind made his beard tickle.

He hadn't combed his hair since the day before, and it was now unruly. Since Amber had been abducted, he hadn't asked for it to be shorn. He pulled up the flask at his hip, balancing on his good foot with the crutches pinched under his shoulders, and removed the cork with his teeth. He spit it into his hand and took a long draw off the whiskeybae. It had stopped burning a path to his stomach the first night he was home as he sat by his hearth, wrapped in blankets, with his stump propped upon a stool. He had imbibed well into the early hours every night thereafter.

Now everyone was gone. Gavin was marrying Sarah at Dunstonwoodshire, a voyage he should have been on, too. When his family and their retainers had ridden out of the yard, leaving him alone at Ballymead, he'd dismissed the regular servants to their crofts and cottages in the village. He only needed a few household servants within the castle proper for himself.

But he woke mid-morn this day, ready to go mad. He needed to busy himself or else his depression was going to get the better of him. No word had come from Amber, and if he sat idle by his fire one more night, he was going to scream.

He looked to a crate containing his woodworking tools and remembered carving Amber her latest dove. *God be damned, but I cannot think on it.* He had been so pleased to present her with a new one each year. Mayhap he should whittle a new design now, something for the meadery, or the Ballymead fief... for there was no reason to carve doves for Lady Amber anymore.

Nay, you'll have to go to great lengths just to get the wood, he told himself.

With his new peg fashioned but his stump still too tender to wear it for any length of time, he would have a hell of a time harvesting wood from outside of their fief's wall and hauling it all the way home.

He hobbled to the bin, taking another swill, and looked within. There were enough scraps to fashion a few more doves, but that was it. He closed his eyes, then turned away. *What the hell is my problem?* What man became so heartsick for a woman? It couldn't be healthy.

No. Making mead was really all he was good for at this point. Not rides across the hills in which he used to indulge. Not woodworking. Just carrying on the Ballymead tradition in hopes that someday his brothers seeded children and that one of his nephews wished to apprentice with him to learn the craft.

He remembered Gavin's anger when he told him he wasn't coming to the wedding.

"We all attended Loddin's wedding, and Hershel's wedding, and both of Gwenyth's weddings. We were all standing in support of them. If I were marrying anyone other than a daughter of Dunstonwoodshire, you'd be there to get drunk with me on my final night of freedom. Hell, even Loddin is riding from Fort Michaelmas to celebrate. Good God, even Gwenyth remains at Dunstonwoodshire to be there in support. The Princess of bloody Bain, our sister, is attending my nuptials. But you won't put aside your heartache long enough to wish me well and stand with me in support?"

No. He couldn't. William couldn't expect Gavin to understand. Gavin had never been in love. Hell, Gav was probably spending today, the actual eve before his wedding, betwixt a tavern whore's legs, nay drinking with his brothers.

Gavin didn't know that the pain of a man's heart being ripped out of his chest hurt far worse than his leg being hacked off with a filthy saw. A man's heart being ripped away was a slow, agonizing process with seemingly no end.

"I'm sorry to disappoint you," William had muttered, *crutching across his bedchamber to his hearth, and dropping another log onto the*

waning fire with a spray of sparks. "Give Lady Sarah my best wishes and congratulations."

"And what of Lady Amber. Any salutation for her?" Gavin had pressed.

He hadn't answered Gavin. He'd simply put his flask to his lips, pretending he hadn't heard the question, and closed his eyes, imbibing heavily.

He shook his head now, trying hard to toss off the melancholy, and crutched back to the meadery doors, closing them. Taking his false leg out from his belts where he had jammed it, he moved to the work table, the crutches thumping, his foot thumping, the crutches thumping, his foot thumping... The progress was slower than walking, a reality that he hated. He hadn't truly run in over two years, hadn't jumped, and apparently could no longer climb ladders either, thanks to his accident that sent him crashing into a cask of select mead.

Except then it hit him. It hit him harder than his head had hit that cask. It hit him so hard, he almost toppled off balance: *I'm being the self-pitying arse I accused Amber of being.*

She felt rotten about her eyes. When he thought about it, it made sense. Even he remembered thinking about the injustice of being able to see her now when she would never be able to return his looks. But he was being a pathetic daftie about his foot. He'd felt sorry for himself for more than two years, almost three at this point.

"Where is my resolve?" he muttered, hardening his scowl.

He bent to strap the peg to his knee and thigh. Once the straps and clasps were secure, he discarded the crutches and thumped to a row of empty casks. The middle shelf needed to be re-racked. It was overdue thanks to his recent expedition.

He set to work. He wasn't going to pity himself again. His leg be damned, he was lucky to have his life. One by one, his brothers would marry off. Or in Hershel's case, enter the cloistered life of St. Augustine's. Pretty soon it would just be him and Father until Father passed away and Ballymead transferred ownership to Lod.

And when Lod took over, he supposed he'd just live on his brother's generosity and keep the meadery afloat while training a nephew to continue the tradition when he died.

He pried up the lid of a cask with a metal bar, then inserted the siphoning tube made of a cured cow intestine. Sucking on the end to get the liquid flowing, he aimed it into another cask for re-racking, propped it within the barrel, and began prying up another lid to have the barrel ready. He worked like that for the remainder of the day, hammering down the lids, heaving up the barrels onto his shoulders, carrying them like labor oxen in a yoke, and settling them on a rack in the back.

His brow sweat. He had long since discarded his tunic. The labor felt satisfying. Thankfully it had kept his mind too busy for thoughts of Amber. The hour late and the sun long gone, William dropped onto a stool, grateful for his exhaustion. It meant he might sleep well without having to induce it with the liquid fire at his hip. Which meant mayhap he would rise in the morn without an aching head.

The castle was dark except for a guardsman at the door beneath the torchlight. William entered the great hall and sat down at the family board to the meal that had been laid out hours before, rinsing his fingers in the nearby bowl for washing. He picked at the trencher, staring at the empty board where his family usually sat. Lord Loddin at the head, Gavin to one side of their father, Hershel to his other, George next to Gavin, he, William next to Hershel, an empty chair where Gwenyth had sat beside him, Mary next to George, and their brother Loddin at the other end closest to Mary when he was home.

Everything felt sparse. Only Beatrice scurried through the hall, banking a torch.

"Is there anything else you require, sir?" she asked him from across the room. Her hair, he noted, had been let down and braided for sleep, and he soon realized the remaining serving staff awaited his retirement for the night so they, too, could seek their pallets.

He shook his head at himself for being rude. "My thanks. No. I'm finished. Wasn't hungry anyway."

"You haven't eaten well since your return, sir," Beatrice countered. "You're so thin, so tired-looking."

William frowned. "I feel like shite, lass. My leg kills me still. Hard to eat when one is in pain. Good eve and sleep well. I'll clean up my setting."

Beatrice bobbed a curtsey and departed, leaving a single torch lit for him.

He held out his trencher for their old dog to lick clean. The shaggy animal rose from its slumber near the waning hearth fire, stretched, and obliged the offer for the late meal, cleaning the dish. He pushed to his foot, took up his crutches, and thumped to the kitchens where he discarded the wooden trencher in the wash basin. The loneliness was suffocating and dammit, he wasn't going to pity himself any longer. Instead, he thumped to the buttery, refilled his flask with whiskeybae, turned the flask over and over again in his palm as he thought. He removed himself above stairs to his bedchamber to knock himself out again. He indeed might have that headache in the morn after all.

***

Gwenyth draped a cloak over Amber's head, fastening the buckle at her neck. Sarah handed Amber a basket of sewing supplies to carry.

"Now follow directly behind me. We walk straight down the main stairs and out the main doors. My covered cart awaits there with my maid and my trunks," Sarah said in a low whisper. "Father is below stairs, but busies himself with Lord Loddin and Gavin, ensuring their animals are harnessed properly. I'll help you into the cart, and you must go and sit beside my maid and make nary a sound."

They were acting foolishly, but Gwenyth, and Sarah now a sennight married, had both adored Amber's plan. *A quest of love*, Sarah had called it. *Bold and valiant*, Gwenyth had smiled.

"Father is going to be livid," Amber muttered, nerves bouncing around her stomach like a swarm of bees.

"He'll get passed it," Sarah remarked. "But if you make a misstep now, he'll discover you and thwart our plan, and then we'll receive the chastening of a lifetime and I fear such a transgression might get you punished, wee sister, for I answer to Gavin now, nay Father."

Gwenyth placed a hand upon her shoulder. "Should he raise a heavy hand, I shall intervene. I promise."

The three put their heads together and gave each other a final conspiratorial embrace. Sarah pulled open the door. Gwenyth exited first, then Sarah.

"Come, sister," Sarah hissed.

Amber followed behind them.

They descended the stairs, walked across the rushes, and exited out the main doors. The canopied cart sat waiting. The Ballymead men, Edward, and his sons, were visiting together as Lod's squire, Michael, busied himself with final preparations for their return to Fort Michaelmas. The serving staff also stood outside, the sky threatening a rain shower, and waited to send off Dunstonwoodshire's older daughter.

"Ah, there's my Luna," Gwenyth exclaimed, moving to her prized mare.

From the remarks uttered, Amber knew that Gwenyth had

mounted without any assistance and sat astride. Such was vulgar for a woman to do, and downright scandalous for a princess. She knew Gwenyth had purposefully diverted the entire yard's attention to herself to allow her to slip onto the cart unnoticed.

It worked.

"What?" Gwenyth asked, challenging the friendly murmur. Amber smiled to herself as she found footing with Sarah's assistance and climbed into the back of the cart. "I've been a horsewoman all my life and certainly won't ride aside like a contorted doll simply to make all of you comfortable."

Her brothers chuckled, as did Morgan and Angus who had known Gwenyth all her years, and the men congregated to clasp wrists in farewell.

"Come, Ballymead. We depart!" Lord Loddin announced.

The journey northward began.

The cart lurched and creaked, bouncing Amber so much so that relaxing was impossible. Sarah took her hand and squeezed it. Pray the Ballymead party gave them enough of a head start before Lord Edward came in hot pursuit, for Amber's family was weary of travel after searching for her, and indeed, he might be angered enough to deliver punishment.

***

William had run out of casks to rack days earlier, so he had taken to repairing the hair strainers, necessary for the next round of racking. Aye, his brothers had been right. He was winning no awards for the beauty of his stitch. He kept himself so focused as the days passed to avoid thoughts of Dunstonwoodshire. But the thoughts invaded his mind now as he tried to work the needle upon another strainer, this one sewn from scratch. He had helped Amber repair her withy strainers three months earlier, when their courtship was still so innocent. It was all he could think about now.

His family should be arriving back any day. Lady Sarah would be with them, his new sister of marriage. Sarah would talk of home, talk of her sister, and William didn't have the strength to hear it.

No self-pity, he reminded himself, pushing and pulling his needle, clenching his teeth to stave off the emotion.

He finally dropped the needle back into a bin upon his worktable and collected all of the empty casks that were piling along the far wall. The sludge lining their bottoms needed scrubbing. He worked well into the afternoon when he heard the thudding of guardsmen upon the wall and dropped his rag on the work table with a soggy splat. He moved to the door, opening it. The late summer breeze upon his bare chest cooled his sweat and caused a shiver to skitter over his skin.

The guards were conferring with a rider on the outside of the portcullis.

"What passes?" William called up to him.

"The wedding party returns, sir!" the guard called down. "They've just passed through the village and come over the hills!"

William nodded once, took a deep breath, and hobbled back into the meadery, closing the door. Barring it would expose his insecurity. It would be too cowardly. So he left it unbarred and returned to his job. Pray that everyone was too excited and preoccupied to look for him.

He needed to hit something, so he began hammering down lids on empty casks, a foolish endeavor, the mallet slamming the fasteners in one swift thwack a piece. He would just have to pry them up later, but he didn't care. The grinding of chains vibrated through the walls. The wagons hauling chests, goods, and the wedding party, rolled into the yard. He could hear weapons jingling and happy salutations among the guardsmen. Horses grunted, carts creaked to a halt, his brothers' voices and women's giggling filled the silence.

"Where's William?" called Lord Loddin to the guard upon the gatehouse.

"Working in the meadery, sir," replied the guard.

William rolled his eyes. His father was probably perturbed he hadn't come out to greet them. *Well bollocks to them all*, he thought, carrying a cask to the back rack.

He would continue working and take supper in the kitchen when the hour was late. Sarah would take up the empty seat beside his, which would never do, so she would probably be placed beside Gavin, displacing George who would probably take Gwen's old seat. Or Will would get pushed down one more space. That was more likely. The fifth son. The youngest son. The least important son. Shift him down one more.

"Shut the hell up," he muttered to himself. It wasn't his or anyone else's fault he had been the last-born son. It was just a fact.

The door to the meadery cracked open. He didn't bother to look, but snatched up another cask and hauled it into the racks so he could hide. "I've a lot of work to do still, so..." He heaved the cask onto the shelf with a grunt. "I'll see you after board this eve, Father."

There was no answer, but the door remained ajar. The evening sunlight from outside was thrown in a streak across the rushes. Hell, what was he supposed to do now? He didn't want to come out until he knew his father was gone and he wouldn't have to see the old man's disappointment in him.

"I was hoping you might look upon me now, William, with those beautiful eyes of yours."

His heart sputtered to a halt and raced like a galloping horse at the same time. So suddenly, he felt like he needed to sit down. That voice most assuredly didn't belong to his father. He didn't know what to do. He stood lamely among the racks, unable to budge.

The door pushed shut. Then he saw the flashes of skirts through the gaps in the racks as the visitor stepped carefully, feeling with each toe before adding her weight.

"Amber?" he finally said, his voice soft.

He needed to see her so intensely, he hobbled with all his speed out from behind the rack he had been such a coward to use as a shield. There she was.

"Hello, William," she replied.

His eyes were jarred by the image of her. She was breathtaking, more mature. Her hair was so clean that it shown in the torchlight. Her curls hung unbound, flowing down beyond her rear with the exception of a braided cord of hair arching over her head like a band, woven with sparkling beads.

Her cheeks were so rosy, mayhap flushed, her lips were full and shining from the berry paste that had been applied to them, and her eyes... her gentle, doe eyes... They twinkled again with... anticipation? Did she hope to run to his arms and have him accept her back after how she had hurt him?

He hoped the hell so with every fiber of his being.

His breathing sped up. And here he was, bare-chested and a waif of his former self. He looked like shite, like the scum from the bottom of a cask and she looked so pure, so stunning in her burgundy gown. Dunstonwoodshire was a proud fief, but he knew Lord Edward, like many other lords, had much of his coin tied up in his lands and trade. Her gown had cost a pretty coin, no matter one's station in life, and he got the inkling she had requested it sewn for his benefit. It hugged her waist, lifting and accentuating her virgin assets at her chest, and draped upon her hips with a seamless flow to the ground around her feet. Not an ounce of wool had been used in its creation, only velvets and satins.

"Do—" His voice cracked. He cleared it. "Do you accompany

your sister to help her?" he managed, rather than make assumptions that she had come for him.

"No," she replied. He waited. "I stowed away on my sister's cart. She helped me do it, for Father refused to let me come. No doubt he'll be raging here soon, trying to track me down again."

His heart kept hammering. "Why?"

"I came for you...to tell you what a fool I was. I came for my would-be husband, to let him know I love him so very much and miss knowing his affection is mine." The words came out so softly, with a rising lilt that spoke of coming tears, words that were no doubt hard for her to say. "If he'll still have me."

He was already moving, hobbling across the rushes and slamming weight he shouldn't down upon his peg. He crushed her against his chest and gripped her, lifting her from her feet. She gasped with surprise, but threw her arms around him, too. His lips sought hers, needing to taste the berries on her lips, her mouth, her tongue.

He devoured her, thrusting his tongue with such force, it was a wonder that she kissed him back as ferociously as she did when she should have shoved him away and admonished him to behave.

God she tasted sweet, like sugary desserts on his tongue. And her hair, *Lord*, her beautiful, rich, full hair. It smelled of floral water, perfumed with rose petals, and felt so silky to the touch he needed to dig his fingers into it. He wrapped it around and around his hand to hold her tightly to him. He must taste disgusting, he realized, as he walked her backward to the stack of hay in the front corner and laid her down. He certainly hadn't been the shining example of personal hygiene since returning, but she didn't seem to mind.

Her hands gripped him so hard, her nails dug into his skin. He tried not to groan, failed, and continued feasting on her lips, nudging his hips against her as the need for thrusting consumed his groin.

He dragged his hand up and down her waist and side, over a breast, down her side again, back up, back over the same breast, listening to her suck in air with each scandalous pass of his hand. Still, she encouraged him with innocent mews so sweet he wanted to deflower her right then. She sighed against his lips with such unabashed excitement, he wanted only to hoist her skirts up and claim her to the fullest hilt, leaving no doubt in her mind as to where and to whom she now belonged. He had never been so bold with a woman. He ought to be ashamed, but he wasn't. He was desperate for her and he cared not how obvious it was. He didn't even look up when the door to the meadery opened again.

"Will, Father requests your audience in the great hall..." Gavin's voice trailed away at the image of his half-naked brother lying atop Amber, wedged between her thighs, with hay clinging to her hair. Their clothing was the only barrier preventing William from slamming his manhood into her to race the stallion home. "I'll be *God-damned...*" Gavin exhaled, the sound of smile in his words. "'Tis about time."

William never once parted his lips from Amber's as he raised his hand behind him with a vulgar gesture that promised Gavin he would indeed be God-damned if he didn't get the hell out. Gavin laughed at the threat but retreated.

The door closed, but Gavin had exposed a problem.

"Wait here, Love," William murmured, drawing his lips away from hers to see the dreamy smile on her face.

He jumped back to his foot and peg, marched to the door, and barred it. Arriving back beside her, he bent and took her hand.

"Come. Let's move to the back for privacy. That is," he hesitated, watching her as he helped her rise. Her hands were shaking. She bit her lower lip, softened from his kissing. "That is, if you consent to further..."

He couldn't finish the sentiment.

She reached up with her other hand and found his fingers raking through his unruly locks. She took them, bringing them down to her waist. He felt her gown, the slender dip inward over her hips as his palm slid around her. His heart clenched. She was so bonny.

He wanted to drag her against him, but nerves bouncing around his gut preventing it. He had just propositioned her to pre-marital relations. She had every right to tell him off for it.

His hand secure on her waist, she slid hers up his bare arm, over his muscle, feeling every dip, every swell. Her fingers finally reached his face, brushing over his beard, exploring him. She finally cupped his face, her other hand still in his grip, and stroked his cheek with her thumb.

"I consent, Will. I want no one else, if you'll have me."

His heart, clenching just moments before, swelled. He drew her against him, dropping his lips back to hers to seal the decision and scooped her into a cradle, carrying her farther into the depths of the meadery.

Their sounds were muted, dampened by the rushes and racks. He set her down upon another haystack, used for insulating the mead. He sat up on his knees and straddled her waist. He touched her lips with his finger, trailed to her hair, and brushed back the luscious curls he couldn't wait to be tangled within each morn as he woke to greet the day.

He trailed his nail down the side of her cheek, over her jaw, and down her neck, farther, reaching the neck of her gown. He pulled a lace on her bodice, letting the string slide through the bow, until the knot popped loose. Her bodice slackened, she inhaled, her breasts relaxed. He had long since grown heavy, his manhood thickened to the point of pain, and he began to pull down the fabric from her chest.

Inch by inch, her flesh was revealed, until finally, two round, perfect handfuls were exposed, the tips light pink and pointing with anticipation. His manhood was straining for room. His trousers were too damn tight. He bent, encasing one of the two most perfect breasts he had ever beheld in his palm, and placed his lips upon her.

She inhaled again, squirming beneath him in the way that spoke of unquenched need. Her hands gripped his shoulders.

He suckled her. He couldn't stop nourishing himself on her body. He glanced up at her face. Her eyes were closed, her lips parted, and her fingernails were biting into his skin. He laved his tongue across her and again she squirmed, sighed, feeling every sensation.

He switched to the other to dish out his affection fairly, doing the same, pulling her into his mouth, letting his fingers linger on her other breast to draw circles upon it. She kept squirming, her grip on his shoulders so forceful he expected the skin to break. She broke her grip and clasped his head to hold him to her.

He smiled.

He settled his groin between her legs, releasing her breast and trailing his lips up to hers to kiss her again. His tongue pushing into her mouth. She opened for him. He smiled again, nudging his hips against the inside of her thighs. His bare chest pressed to her breasts. She was so warm.

"Untie my trousers," he whispered in between kisses and lifted himself up to hover over her, guiding her hand down his chest, over the muscles of his stomach, over the dusting of blond hair upon his navel.

"I...I've never..." she began, unable to speak as he pecked the corners of her lips, her chin.

"Take your time, Love," he encouraged, continuing to peck her. "I've got nothing better to do than keep seducing you."

She giggled nervously, and he allowed her fumbling fingers the time they needed to grow familiar with a man's garments. But God be damned, he thought, her fingers were tickling his shaft as she tried to make sense of his laces. He nudged into her hand, unable to remain still, his eyes fluttering closed. Finally he felt the flaps holding his trousers shut slacken.

"God, but I have to have you," he muttered, barely retaining his self-control, his kissing intensifying as he felt his column rubbing against her thigh. "I've missed you, Amber. Missed knowing you were to be mine."

***

"I missed you too. William, I was just distraught. I was so confused about what had happened and in my distress, I pushed you away. I acted jealous, a mistake I will forever regret. I'm so sorry," she rambled, when she was cut off by his palm cupping her cheek and his lips settling against hers.

"It's all right," he whispered, but she shook her head.

"Nay, it's not. I owed you so much more than my gratitude, but instead I gave you my insecurity, and it was wrong, and I've been so miserable this past month. And when you didn't come to Gavin's wedding...I had been so set on seeing you then, to beg amends."

"You're with me now and that's all that matters. So let's make amends," he replied, half-teasing.

She nodded. He was still cupping her cheek, resting his elbow beside her, kissing her, sending butterflies skidding across her skin and through her stomach. Sakes, but his unbridled affection was almost too much to bear, so warm, so gentle, yet in command. And she so defenseless to it.

Nay, she was in much control, she sensed. Each time her hips squirmed, he sucked in. Every caress her fingers now made upon his arms, he moaned and pushed himself between her legs, barely in control at all.

His other hand brushed over her thigh, up and down, in slow drags of the palm. Then his fingers took hold of her skirts and began pulling them upward to expose her legs. Her chest was heaving for air. Anticipation rendered her motionless. His touch, now caressing her legs covered in nothing but her stockings, was, oh... would it feel like this every time they made love? She hoped so, grabbing his shoulders again to steady herself. Some ladies had mentioned that the first time with a man was uncomfortable, sometimes painful, but how could that be so with a man as careful as William?

He pulled back, both hands coming to the waist of her stockings, and rolled down the fabric, peeling the garment along with her undergarments down her legs until her skin, her center, sat exposed to the air and to him. She tried to hide, pulling her legs together, but he stayed her reaction, taking her knees in each of his hands.

"Let me see you," he whispered, a gruffness in his voice so thick, she wasn't sure he could speak any louder if he wanted to. A callused finger grazed along her tender seam, shielding her core. She sucked in, quivering. "Ah, love, every inch of you is so beautiful."

He took her hand in his and guided it to his front, placing it over the bulge of his shaft in his undergarments.

"Look upon me too," he croaked.

"What...what do I do, Will?" she begged, her words soft.

He helped her with pleasure, pulling himself free from his undergarments, and placed her hand upon him. He encased her hand within his, folding her fingers around him, and guided her.

"Ah, God," he moaned, as if his head had tipped back. His hips began to pulse back and forth with each stroke she made, and soon, he released his hold upon her to allow her to proceed alone. "Like, ah, that..."

She remembered to finally to breathe. His skin was so thick, so warm, so smooth and yet, rock hard. It was such a mystery of a body part. He settled back down against her, resumed kissing her, and groaned as she continued to massage the length of him.

"Amber, I...I have to join with you. I have to know you in that way," he whispered, his voice so coarse.

She nodded. Her pulse raced, her cheeks were flushing. She had only ever imagined this with him and it was truly happening. She wiggled beneath him. She was on fire, her stomach raged with heat. She needed him and knew not how to achieve the satisfaction.

"I need you too, Will."

He was nodding, kissing her, his lips moving in a frenzy across her skin. "Hold onto me," he encouraged. "I'll be as easy as I can."

"But what do we do about *proof*?" she asked, suddenly worried.

"Proof of your purity?" he clarified, unaffected, and continued to kiss her.

"We usurp our families' right to see this done properly," she sighed as his kissing roved back down to her breasts.

She couldn't think straight with his lips on her breast.

"Do you wish to wait?" he asked lazily, as if he knew she didn't.

"Of course not," she sighed, smiling and gripping his head, her breaths rising and falling.

He smiled against her. "Then worry nay. They'll have no

recourse except to force us to marry after this."

She nodded, releasing the girth of him, and wrapped her arms around his torso, snaking her arms underneath his shoulders. He reached down between them, his fingers caressing over her inner thighs, upward, until they brushed against her center. She shook, inhaled, clenched him, sucked in, and held her breath.

"Breathe," he whispered in her ear as his finger coaxed her to relax with gentle caresses that made her body weep in a way it never had. "Have trust in me. You truly want this? 'Twill be no returning from this decision, love."

She nodded, her grip upon him deadly.

"Breathe," he encouraged again, sliding a finger between her folds, exploring the warmth that awaited him.

She sighed, wiggled, arched naturally against him.

"That's it," he kissed her ear, pecking alongside her face.

His finger now pushed within.

"William." Her voice fluttered. She clenching him. His touch had been unexpected, and yet, his invading hands felt so good. She couldn't stop herself from arching into him, couldn't stop her body from undulating with the gentle thrusts his finger delivered so that he was pushed deeper. Heat raged through her. "What's happening?"

He offered no answer to her plea, withdrawing his finger, and leaving her wanting. But then she felt the tip of his shaft at her entrance. She held on for dear life as he guided himself to her center, feeling him push into her.

Slowly, he inched in. His kissing grew wild again. He clenched her nape and cheek, though there was nothing forceful in his grip. No, she sensed he too held on for dear life.

"Breathe as well, my love," she whispered to him and she felt his lips grin upon her face.

"'Tis impossible, sweeting, when my woman is so bloody beautiful."

And in one final push, he slide to completion, resting against her skin to skin. His mouth descended on hers to swallow her moan of pain and pleasure that accompanied breaking her maidenhead. The pain eased as her body clenched his generous size. His hold on her tightened. He began to undulate his hips, rocking back and forth against her, turning the discomfort into a feeling unlike any other. Friction, badly needed, warmed her, soothed her.

"You're mine now. Truly mine," he whispered, working slowly and gently.

She released her hold around his torso, took his cheeks in her hands, and pulled his lips back down to hers. "There's no place I'd rather be than here. With you."

***

"Where's your brother?" Lord Loddin inquired as Gavin retreated from the meadery to the well to wash the traveling grime from his hands.

"He and Amber are having a heartfelt and private discussion," Gavin lied. "I would give them some solitary time to work things out. He'll be in for supper with Lady Amber."

"He isn't being untoward, is he?" Lord Loddin pressed as George helped to haul a chest inside and Hershel carried his young son on his back. Gwenyth looked around with anticipation to see William while her traveling maids alighted the cart and their guardsmen unloading their trunks. "The lad's been a walking ghost this past month. Seeing her could cause him to behave irrationally. I expect Lord Edward will have received my messenger sent from the roadside and will no doubt be here to reclaim her, and he better be reclaiming an unspoiled maiden."

Gavin scoffed, taking up Sarah's hand, and gave her a wink. "William? Untoward? You know William. He's more of a monk than Hersh. He'll be within in due course for supper."

Lord Loddin conceded and walked onward. "You're probably right about that."

Gavin entered the great hall. The staff boisterously prepared for the evening meal and the return of the Ballymead family. He walked to a sideboard where a cask of great mead had been tapped and poured himself a tankard.

"The door to the meadery is closed. 'Tis improper," Hershel muttered under his breath. "William might be a puritan, but he's still a desperate man."

Gavin turned and saw Hershel and George's curious expressions as they hovered nearby, then glanced down at his new wife to whom he handed the tankard, filling another for himself.

"You're certain they have a heartfelt discussion and nothing more?" Hershel pressed, coming up beside him.

"Hell no," Gavin chuckled, taking a long, refreshing swallow of his drink. "He's stripped to the waist with his tongue jammed down her throat. Laid her out in the haystack. But I'll be damned to tell that to Father, and curse upon any one of you who divulges the secret."

Sarah gasped, though Gavin clenched her hand harder, shooting her a wink. His brothers laughed, including Hershel in spite of his terse brow, at Gavin's vulgar language.

"Best to let the lovebird have their moment before Lord Edward barrels through the gates and all hell breaks loose," Gavin added, passing Sarah a fond smile at her look of distress. He tempered his humor. "Worry nay, bonny wife. Will is a fine man who holds your sister in high esteem. I banter with your new brothers, 'tis all."

Something softened in his eyes as he flashed his flirty smiles at his new bride. He had always been playful with the fairer sex, but what he felt now was calm, pleased, and proud. She had been so pretty, so pure. He remembered on their wedding night, standing naked before her, looking at her skin, her breasts. He remembered her smile at the altar with tears brimming her eyes. He had never felt such completeness before, but now realized it had been sorely missing. Some thought men were too serious to feel such fullness, but they were wrong. A man in love was a wonderful thing.

Aye. He was in love. For the first time. What a revelation.

He looked up, noticing Hershel watching him. His younger brother's eyes were wistful. Was Hershel, destined for the monastery, lost in thought? Aye, but not just lost in thought. He wore unabashed longing on his face, though Gavin didn't sense that Hershel was thinking on Sarah. He was thinking on his wife, mayhap reliving the joy of his own marriage and still begging for answers now as to why she was taken from him.

Hershel turned away, withdrawing a chess board from a bin and taking it to his son to engage him in a contest. But Gavin watched him still. Childbirth had killed Hershel's wife. The idea of seeding Sarah beside him and possibly killing her was an unfathomable thought. No doubt Hershel carried guilt with him that Gavin had been unable to see before, and mayhap that was why their monkish brother refused to marry again. Mayhap he was afraid of killing another woman. Mayhap that was why he wanted to become a man of the cloth. Mayhap he sought such atonement for his wife's death even now.

***

"What news of court, sister?" Gavin ask Gwenyth as the family gathered for refreshments in the great hall of Ballymead. "No doubt Prince William has missed you, for the rumors say he's shameless in his want of you," he added with a teasing wink.

Gwenyth laughed.

"Indeed no matter how long the journey, the first thing he always does upon returning home is ascend the steps to the castle and swoop me into a cradle." She rolled her eyes. "It has become a point of gossip in the capital, that the prince will reserve his first attentions for me instead of his king, and you can imagine the lewd direction *that* gossip takes. But of more newsworthiness, Lady Caris Feargach, one of King Bain's wards, is coming of age. King Bain seeks a suit for her, though she shows no interest in the men who come to call."

"Have there been many offers?" Gavin asked.

"Indeed," Gwenyth replied, filling her tankard of mead and retiring to a chair beside the hearth, "for now that she is in the king's protection, she thrives, and is quite fair. But she would prefer to while away her days in the royal library pouring over books of botanicals rather than entertain suitors. I taught her to read, and she has been interested in botanicals ever since."

Hershel looked up from his chess game with his son, listening, then returned his gaze to take wee Hershel's pawn.

"I have no doubt the woman could become quite a scholar if she were able to pursue such studies with a tutor, for I can read, but am not overly knowledgeable on botanicals," Gwenyth continued. "And of course, there's growing concern over King Fernando II, though most details are kept private betwixt King Bain and my husband."

"King Bain has shared a few concerns with his lords," Lord Loddin stated, propping a foot upon the hearth and leaning onto his knee to take a swig from his drink. "There are more details now to be certain, considering that your husband has interrogated the smugglers who abducted Lady Amber. I wish he'd told us more, but alas, Will was intent to continue his search for the lass and we were intent to find Will."

"Mayhap George should consider asking Lady Caris to suit," Gavin called across the hall at George who was now settling into a high-backed chair to enjoy a tankard of mead himself.

Gwenyth shook her head as George scoffed. As the only son without a marriage prospect, there would now be immense pressure put upon George to tie the proverbial knot. "We already considered and asked George privately," Gwenyth stated, implying "we' to mean her, the prince, and the king, her new family. "But he refuses to consider anyone bearing the name 'Feargach,' after what the Feargachs of Dwyre have done to us."

The words sobered the hall. Gwenyth changed the subject. "However, I do have glad tidings to share, though I cannot speak of it until William and Lady Amber join us."

She flashed a look at Gavin, indicating that she wasn't daft to what was transpiring between Will and his woman in the meadery.

"Will can find out in due course," Gavin dismissed, grinning back at her. "What's your news?"

"You have to be good and wait, Gav."

"Do tell, Gwenyth," Sarah began. "Am I already privy to it?"

Gwenyth shook her head with a satisfied smile. "I haven't told a soul."

"Come now," George interjected. "Tell us!"

"Oh please!" Mary begged, joining Sarah's side.

The room exploded with similar pleas. Gwenyth folded her arms resolutely and shook her head. But as she stood again, moving to the cask of mead to top off her drink while the chamber reverted to chatter, her hand slide over her belly. Hershel abandoned his son to play with the rooks and knights upon the checkered game board and came up behind her, bending beside her ear.

"You're carrying a babe," he whispered.

Gwenyth's head shot up and her brow furrowed. "How do you know?"

A smile lifted the corner of Hershel's mouth, softening the typically hard lines of his face. "I watched my wife hold wee Hershel in the same way as you do now...before he was born. I memorized it, what she looked like doing so, and oft think of her sitting among the wildflowers as we frequently did, holding her womb as such."

Hershel's face dropped as Gwenyth, suddenly overwrought, set aside the tankard and wrapped him in her embrace. She hadn't known his bride well, for the woman was quiet, studious, much like Hershel, and the two had departed for Hershel's small holding shortly after their marriage. Apart from a few sisterly visits, Gwenyth and Mary's final visit to Hershel's home was when wee Hershel was born, and his wife had bled so profusely, she had passed only hours after their nephew took his first breaths. Hershel had never spoken of it, and that he did so now, meant something.

"I'll pray to God each day that you safely deliver, Gwen, for if what happened to my wife happens to you, it isn't only Prince William's heart that will be destroyed by it."

He returned Gwenyth's hug with firmness, being so much taller that he dwarfed her in his hold, and as far as all could remember, it was the first time Hershel had held anyone with such affection other than his wife.

"I'll be ever grateful for such a prayer from you," she replied.

But just as Lord Loddin opened his mouth to ask of Hershel and Gwenyth's odd coupling, the main doors pushed open. Mathew

Whitcroft, Ballymead's loyal guardsmen, ushered in a breathless and disheveled Lord Edward of Dunstonwoodshire.

"Lord Edward!" Lord Loddin chuckled at his friend as the hall erupted into celebratory salutations. "An *expected* surprise! You made good time! Do come in and take your weight off your weary feet."

"Where is she?" Edward breathed. He took out a kerchief from within his surcoat and mopped his brow. "I was given your missive roadside, Loddin, as I headed this way. Amber wasn't in her chamber or anywhere to be found the day after your party departed. For a moment, I feared she was nabbed again and wasted a day searching the countryside for her until I remembered she wanted to come see William. She's here, aye? Is she well and safe?"

Edward's eyes sought Sarah as they traveled over the hall, landing on her holding Gavin's arm. Her chattering with Mary ceased. Sarah glanced at her father, then released Gavin and came forward, though Gavin made sure to depart his own discussions and stand vigilant at her side.

"Father, she did indeed come."

"How, I might ask?" Edward demanded.

Sarah bowed her head as if she were still a child. "She stowed away on my caravan."

Edward took a long, shaking breath. "And who gave her permission?"

"I, eh, told her she could," Sarah nearly whispered.

Edward's brow furrowed with anger. "I told her *nay*. Why on earth did you nay insist she alight? Why on earth did you nay tell me?"

Sarah bit her lip, her frown unleashing a waterfall of words as she grabbed her father's arm. "She wanted to see William. She was so lovesick, she missed him so. After everything she's been through, how could I refuse?"

"You refuse by reminding her that she is still in her father's charge and remains so until the day she marries, *if* she marries at this rate," Edward retorted. "For if she isn't careful, she'll be sent to a nunnery for her foolishness. 'Twas a fool's errand, dashing up here like some desperate pup to beg the man's forgiveness. 'Tis most unladylike for her to throw herself at William's feet and brings embarrassment to the good name of Dunstonwoodshire."

"She'll nay be going to a nunnery," Gavin smirked. "'Twas no hardship for William to receive her."

Edward's eyes narrowed and he took a slow step closer to Gavin, a silent challenge to come toe to toe. "I don't know that I should be consoled by that remark, coming from a man with, shall we say, quite an understanding in the matters your statement regards. Tell me, does William have ways like yours? Should I be concerned?"

***

Gavin's jaw hardened at the insult. Sarah went stiff. Edward was distraught. But Edward's strike affected Gavin's new wife, judging by her reddening cheeks. Gavin didn't like the way that made him feel. He had a bad reputation and he knew it. He'd slept with countless women and loved every minute of it. But when Edward had confronted him the eve before his wedding to explain the objection to the marriage banns, that he might have a bastard daughter, the reality of his actions finally hit him.

The lessons his father and his family had tried to beat into his head, that he'd refused to hear, finally sank in all at once, as if they had piled up into a heavy weight to be dropped onto him in one plunge.

Eventually he would have to call for the bastard child and learn the truth of her parentage, and even the possibility of it might be enough to drive a wedge between him and his rosy-cheeked woman, so pure, so excited to start a life with him. In his ignorance, he had assumed he was invincible, untouchable. But in that moment of Edward's marriage counseling, the reality of his actions struck him as immoral.

There was no question in his mind that when the time came for him to determine if the peasant child was his, Sarah would be devastated. Because just his uncertainty alone would be proof of his former habits. One mention of a bastard, the day before their ceremony, would have dashed the beautiful smile from her pretty lips. And Edward, in his anger now, was close to divulging that secret.

Gavin made a decision as Edward counseled him that he should have made long ago: he would damn well be faithful, even if it killed him, from that moment forth. The village whore at Dunstonwoodshire who had intended to entertain him the eve of his wedding, he had turned away, because the idea of hurting Sarah hurt far more than the idea of going without feminine variety for the rest of his days. It would take his family a long time to grow confidence in his faithfulness to one woman, but he would prove he could do it to his father and siblings and most importantly, to Sarah.

Thankfully Lord Loddin intervened, noticing the defensive posturing of his second son.

"Edward, man. Amber and William are in the midst of discussions at this moment. They're in the meadery. William has missed her tremendously. I promise you, William is most respectful, as are all of my children. What Gavin intended with his remark was that William has no intention of allowing her to slip away from their betrothal again."

Edward turned on his heel to march to the meadery.

Gavin flashed his father a desperate glance. "Stop him," he mouthed.

Lord Loddin furrowed his brow.

"William's indisposed!" Gavin mouthed more forcefully.

Loddin's curious brow transitioned into a frown as he realized his youngest son did indeed have it in him to be disrespectful with a lady, but he intervened anyway. "Eh, Edward man," he said, grabbing his peer's arm. "Give them a moment, eh? Come sit. They discuss important things, and it's long overdue. Neither of us ought interrupt."

Edward stopped, looked at Loddin's hand upon him, and narrowed his eyes.

"I insist," Loddin persisted, flashing Gavin a furious glare. "You've traveled far and wide these past months with hardly a moment's breath. She's in good hands with William."

"'Tis my very concern, friend, that she's in any man's hands at all until she's married."

Loddin steered his friend away from the door. Gwenyth was already pouring Edward a tankard as Gavin took a calming breath. She came forth, placing the hospitality in his hand. "Sit and enjoy," she smiled. "I have it on account that William has been in love with Amber since she was old enough to be fallen in love with."

Lord Edward, stunned, felt the sudden need to bow. "I apologize, Princess, for not seeing you. I was so intent to find Amber that—"

"Rise up, sir," Gwenyth smiled. "You needn't apologize. You worry for your daughter." She took a seat beside him, back straight in a diplomatic way, folding her hands in her lap as she set aside her own drink. "Might I suggest, however, that you relax your rule upon Lady Amber? Her emotions are fragile. It would be wise to consider all that she has gone through, and try to see why her reasons for coming here were so important."

Edward looked as though he wished to argue, but held his tongue. Gwenyth might be Loddin's young daughter. But she was also now the future queen of Bain.

"I see my words have created distaste in your mouth, my lord," Gwenyth conceded, "but Sarah and I sat with Amber in her bedchamber as she poured her heart out. She came to you in hopes you would listen. Did you allow her to pour her heart out to you as well?"

"With all due respect, Princess Gwenyth," Edward began, his words more controlled than they'd been before. "I was over my head with wedding requirements, not to mention my regular business. Do you think she ought defy her father when the whim suits her, simply because her father hasn't a moment to listen to her just then?"

"Honestly, my lord?" Gwenyth asked. Edward nodded that honesty was what he sought. "I cannot recall a single moment when my father didn't listen to me when I needed his ear. I cannot relate to a household where a father hasn't the time for his children, for the lives of men will always be busy. When I returned from my horrible ordeal with the Feargachs of Dwyre—and make no mistake the magnitude of what fighting to escape will do to a fledgling soul—I know not a single moment when my father wasn't visiting my door, begging me to talk to him and tell him what demons festered in my heart.

"And so, my original remark. I feel you ought see Amber for the young woman that she is and allow her to feel what she feels in her heart. As her father, you owe it to her to be a stout shoulder for her to cry upon and a strong arm to embrace her when her tears weaken her, and most importantly, you owe it to her to listen, to demonstrate to her that you—"

William's ill-shaven face and unkempt hair came into view from the servants' entrance through the kitchens. He wore a wrinkled and untucked tunic that looked as if it had sat in a wad on his worktable all day. It probably had. Amber followed behind him with her hand encased in his grip, stray pieces of hay clinging to her curls and redness having turned her cheeks a pleasant pink.

Gwenyth averted her eyes and smiled at the pair's lack of discretion. Lord Loddin turning to see them, along with Edward and his sons who had also now come inside, as well as the rest of the hall. William thumped out into the middle of the room, Amber behind him. It was then that they noticed a strip of tartan wool in William's loose hand.

***

William eyed Lord Edward. Edward eyed him in return, making sense of their appearance.

"Do mine eyes suggest what I think they do?" Lord Loddin asked before Edward had a chance to explode.

"Daughter," Lord Edward began, balling his fists to temper the rage trembling his jaw. "Pray, tell me, you haven't done anything regrettable."

Amber swallowed. "Father—"

"Nothing regrettable," William interrupted. He turned to Hershel. "Hersh." He held out the strip of fabric. "You're the priestliest of us all. Will you do the honors?"

Hershel straightened, glanced at the anger boiling on Edward's face, and took a few hesitant steps forward to William.

"What do you wish of me, Will?" he asked.

"Handfast us. We wish to be married."

"What?" bellowed Edward, striding forward to drag his daughter away. "First you reject William, and now this? 'Tis improper, all of this!"

Will pulled Amber behind him to protect her.

"Easy, friend." Lord Loddin intervened, reaching out to catch Edward's arm.

"Enough, Loddin!" Edward shouted, throwing his arm off. "You're nay the one in my position!"

"Oh Father, you must let her," Sarah begged, gripping his arm. Edward dragged himself free. "They love each other! They missed their wedding day—"

"And why is that?" retorted Edward.

"The reason is behind us both," William said, still clenching Amber's hand in his while feeling her tremble. "We look to the future now, not the reasons that sullied the past."

"Nay! She defies me, debauches herself, and then wishes my blessing?" Edward fumed.

"Please, Father, I beg you," Amber offered, her words full of conviction despite the quiver to her voice. "You said yourself Ballymead was a good family to marry into, and I want this, and..." Her next words leaked out of her, knowing such words might earn her a smite. "And we must marry now... if we are to sit in good judgement with God."

"I'll handfast you." Hershel smiled, stepping in front of Lord Edward just as the man began to land his stride.

"Nay, she's coming home with me," came Edward's dark words.

"Edward," Lord Loddin said, his words also dark. "One more step, and we might not be considered friends anymore. 'Twould seem," he eyed his youngest son who scowled at Edward and clenched Amber's hand, "that they must marry now, to right the sin they have just committed. I don't know about you, but I'll nay have such a sin staining my family honor. Handfasting is the quickest solution until we can plan another church wedding."

"It breaks convention," frowned Lord Edward as his hand came to rest on the hilt of his sheathed sword. "And not only did my daughter defy me, but William has done this to usurp me."

"I'll take fine care of her, sir," William pressed, not arguing the accusation. "I won't lose her again. We were supposed to have been married a sennight ago. What has changed now? Haven't I proven myself worthy? Haven't I already demonstrated my honor? She's nay leaving here today." Edward calculated William with stern eyes, but he continued. "I won't allow it."

Glancing at William and Amber's hands clenching one another, Edward seemed to finally resign himself. Exhaling, he glanced at his younger daughter in the grip of the youngest son of Ballymead usurping his authority now. He shook his head, and in that moment, William grinned, sensing the lord capitulating.

"The dowry hasn't been delivered," fumed Edward.

"The dowry can be dealt with later," Lord Loddin dismissed, gazing at Will's eager conviction. "I'd be pleased to see my household swell with another fair face, and you know, Edward, I will look after Amber as another daughter of mine until my sons are allotted their inheritances."

"Lord Edward," William began. "I'm fine dismissing the dowry, if Amber's industry may be fully transferred to Ballymead."

Edward furrowed his brow. "You would pass up all the silver set aside in her chests?"

William nodded. "If it means Amber's soaps may be made exclusively from Ballymead, aye. She has a gift. She has much to offer. And together, with me running my father's meadery and Amber assisting, we will grow Ballymead even more prosperous."

Loddin chuckled. "Ask your lady, son, if that proposition is agreeable to her as well."

"It is," Amber replied, her other hand coming to grip William's fingers clenching hers. "He already asked."

Finally, after Edward thought on it, Lord Loddin offered his wrist, willing Edward to take it. Edward exhaled, dropped his hand from his sword, and relented. His words grew gruff as he accepted Lord Loddin's clasp.

"Aye, William of Ballymead, I see the entire hall is against me. We'll scratch the contract already drawn up. Fine," he waved his hand, exhausted. "You may handfast her."

Will's face split into a grateful smile. Amber threw herself against him. He wrapped her in his arm, pressing her cheek to his heart and gave Hershel the fabric.

He lowered his lips to hers. She accepted, sliding her hands alongside his beard into his locks to hold him to her. His other arm came around her, weaving through her tumble of hair.

Gwenyth, Mary, and Sarah inhaled at the boldness, the brothers grinned, and Edward shook his head miserably. Loddin limped to the sideboard and this time, brought a decanter of whiskeybae with him to shove into Edward's grip. "You may as well give up control, man. Nature has a way of getting its way when it wants it, eh?"

William squeezed Amber, his tongue pushing into her mouth, his hand tangling in her curls.

"Eh-hum," came a priestly clearing of the throat carrying with it a reprimand that only Hershel could produce. "You're not handfasted *yet.*"

William chuckled. Amber giggled. They rested their foreheads together. William kept an arm circled about her and clasped her hand in his other, holding it out to Hershel.

Hershel draped the woolen tartan around their joined fists, tying it into a symbolic knot, then held it up for the room to see.

The hall erupted in whoops and congratulatory exclamations. William gazed at his bride. Amber's whole face smiled, her lips so full that William wanted nothing more than to devour them again. Sarah and Gwenyth dashed forth and threw their arms around them. William could feel his back lurching as his brothers slapped him. He pulled his hand free of the knot and scooped Amber into a cradle again, ignoring the room, when a point in her skirts poked his arm.

"What is that? In your pocket?"

"Oh, a parchment," she replied.

"What sort of parchment?"

She released his neck, digging down between their stomachs, and fished for the pocket lips. Withdrawing a folded parchment, she handed it to William as he set her down.

"I hadn't a chance to tell my father about it. So I brought it with me."

"Tell him about what?" Will asked.

"I took it when I escaped my captors. It was in their saddle packs. They traveled lightly, and so I figured it might be important."

William unfolded it. Silence fell. He studied it, his eyes falling wide.

"Christ," he muttered, gazing to Gavin and Hershel. "Beatrice," he called to the household maid.

"Aye, sir?" she curtsied.

"Go to my chambers and fetch from my saddle packs a fold of parchment, a map. Immediately."

"Certainly," she curtsied again, scurrying away.

Gavin and Hershel peered over his shoulder, casting their eyes to the parchment from Amber's skirts.

"What is it, Will?" Amber asked.

He squeezed her hand. "You did well to take this, Love."

Beatrice scurried back down the stairs into the main hall. "Is this what you requested, sir?"

She produced a folded parchment. William took it, hobbling to the main board. He laid out both sheets and slid them together.

"It's the other half of the Lispagnioc map," exclaimed Gavin.

"Aye, the part consisting of the Bainick landmass," Hershel deduced, sliding his finger along a route marked by a broken line. "This line here looks an awful lot like the route we traveled to Fort Michaelmas."

"Indeed," thought William. "And it extends onto the map we found onto the Île de Neige. And these lines here," he added, "are prescribed routes through Dwyre to the east, through the bloody capital itself down through Soughgate… wait a moment." He scrutinized the parchment. "It's nay just another half. It's another *third*. Look at this edge. 'Tis also cut."

Murmurs rippled through the hall.

"What would you wish to bet that the missing portion depicts routes through the Hadstadt and the Land of Spices? Be damned, but there've got routes throughout the world," Gavin exclaimed.

Will pulled Amber to him.

"Smuggler routes," Hershel added, rubbing his chin. "An entire warren throughout Lispagne's enemy kingdoms, to smuggle victims out unseen. Prince William is going to be pleased indeed to have this in his possession."

"Amber. You found an important map," Will praised.

"What map?" she asked.

"We found a partial map whilst searching for you. You found another section that shows smuggling routes to Lispagne." He smiled, lifting her and spinning her around. "Praise to you, woman, but your intuition served you well!"

She beamed down at him. He let her slide down his front to the floor again, sinking into a celebratory kiss.

"You'd best get this into your husband's hands, Gwen," Gavin insisted, taking both halves and folding them upon each other.

Gwenyth came forth, taking them. "I'll deliver it first thing upon my arrival home. He will be most pleased with any information, big or small."

"William," Lord Loddin said as Gwenyth tucked the discovery into her pockets. Will pulled apart from Amber and looked up at his sire, his hand sliding down to hold her fingers still clasping the bit of plaid wool.

"Aye, Father?"

Loddin stepped forth and gripped William's shoulder.

"I had intended to discuss this matter in private with you, but seeing as we celebrate your union now to Amber, I think this is a fitting time to share what I have to say."

William furrowed his brow as he watched Gavin, Hershel, George, and Gwenyth huddle together, smiles on their faces.

"What is this?" Will asked warily.

Lord Loddin grinned.

"You might have been my fifth-born son, but you have always been just as important to me, and mayhap I haven't always seen you as the man you are, but feared for you as a father might his lad. I apologize for that." He swallowed, the grin on his face dropping into a serious look of consideration. "The rules of succession imply that the first-born son be heir, but that is just it. They're rules, nay laws. And I've never been known to be a man of unwavering tradition. You and my newest daughter of marriage," he reached out to clasp Amber's hand as well, "will have a good life here as Lord and Lady someday."

He withdrew his grip upon Will and produced a parchment from his tunic, rolled into a cylinder and tied with a green ribbon the color of Ballymead's banners. Will furrowed his brow.

"What is this you speak of, Father?"

William noted the confusion crinkling Amber and Edward's brow, too. Loddin smiled fondly.

"At Gavin's wedding, I met with your oldest brother. With his blessing, I drafted changes to my inheritance. You'll see that all of your siblings have also signed this document to demonstrate it was a unanimous decision. Lod's decision to abdicate for you was given fully with his best wishes. He sees, as do I see, that you belong at the helm of this land when I pass."

The air left William's lungs, but Lord Loddin continued.

"Ballymead will no longer pass to Loddin when I die. This home, our ancestral lands, the apiary, the meadery... all will be yours, and then to your oldest child. You have the passion for the family craft, the motivation to perfect your art, and now the woman you want at your side to help it prosper further. You sacrificed a future to help raise your sister when Lady Amaranth—" The sound of his wife's name still ached to say, and mention of her now caused his throat to choke. "When your mother fell ill. You've always been dutiful, even though you knew you stood to inherit nothing. But you have a big future now."

William stood speechless, staring at the roll in his hand. He felt his chest clench, his breathing grow heavy, and sensed tears threaten to moisten his eyes. Sarah inhaled. The Dunstonwoodshire men all furrowed their brows, having been unaware of Loddin's decision. William's siblings all beamed at him.

"Go on, open it and look for yourself," Loddin prodded.

No words came to Will's mouth. His throat thickened. He didn't trust his voice, so he drew his lips into a thin line to keep them from wavering. He nodded once, feeling Amber's hand squeeze his in reassurance, and withdrew from her to pull the green ribbon open. He let it slip to the rushes, unrolled the parchment, and read his father's script. Over and over again, his eyes traveled across the ink.

He finally looked up, his eyes rimming red despite his best efforts. "But this was Lod's inheritance. As your namesake."

Lord Loddin smiled. "Aye, it *was*."

"Lod's a soldier, and now one of Prince William's captains. He wants a military life," Hershel stated. "'Twas his idea to give Ballymead to you, for he wants it to prosper and knows it will do so under your lordship.

"He hopes to secure a landholding from the crown and eventually be instated there," Gavin said. "We all want this for you, Will."

"You deserve it," George added.

Will fought for words, dropping his gaze back to his hands. Then he closed the gap between his father and himself and embraced him. Lord Loddin pulled his youngest son tightly to him. "I know nay what to say," he muttered against his father's shoulder. "'Tis one hell of a wedding gift."

"Say that you'll be a fine steward of these lands and all their riches when I'm called to your mother's side, and then take that bonny bride of yours up to your chamber and do the deed properly," Loddin jested in his ear. "A hay stack? Indeed, are you a lad or a man?"

William chuckled and drew back, wiping the back of his hand across his eyes. He looked to his siblings who stood together grinning. Then he turned back to Amber and wrapped her in his embrace.

"I'm proud of you, husband," Amber whispered to him.

William gazed down at his woman. He had nearly lost her for good. It would never happen again. She was now his and would make Ballymead proud with her strength and skill. His missing foot mattered not. He could offer her a fine life now. He scooped her up. Thumping across the flooring on his peg, he disappeared above stairs with Amber in his arms.

Sarah, Gavin, Mary, Gwenyth and George all hastened after them, accompanied by Amber's brothers, cheering and whooping to properly embarrass them. Will slammed the door upon them and they burst out laughing at being shut out of the marriage bedding, continuing to heckle them as a bar slid across the door.

***

Edward fell heavily into a chair in the hall, and Loddin, chuckling at his expense, dropped down beside him, sliding the decanter of whiskeybae toward his long-time friend. The greying man obliged straight from the spout while the cheers and laughter persisted above stairs, echoing out of the gallery.

Hershel resumed his game of chess with his son. The serving staff continued supper preparations. There might indeed be trouble brewing with Lispagne, but right now, in this moment, life at Ballymead was as it should be. Good.

Epilogue

Prince William, decked in a plain surcoat denoting no crest, drew his cloak around him to stave off the autumn chill. The mountain air of the Cambrian Forest was crisp and his breath escaped in puffs. Titan plodded nimbly over the pine needles. Fog settled above the trees, giving the forest the feel of mist and nymphs.

He maneuvered the horse through the towering tree trunks until he arrived before a tiny stone cottage well off any beaten path. Eoin MacTierny had done well to scout out the cottage based on William and Gavin of Ballymead's descriptions. He knew he risked startling the young man he was certain he would find within.

A shutter cracked open. Prince William knew he was being watched.

He took off a gauntlet studded with metal about the wrist guards and wiped his hair from his eyes. He dismounted with a jingle and made no effort now to be silent.

Pushing back his hood, he approached the door.

It opened before he neared it. Christophoro, the bastard half-brother to King Fernando II, stepped into view. In his grip was a silver dagger encrusted with blue stones denoting the royal Lispagne house from which he descended. Clad in a simple tunic, his fingers were ringed and he wore a jerkin studded in round metal plates across his chest.

He was tall for his age and no doubt had more inches to gain before his growth to manhood was complete. But peaking physically was only one sign of manhood. The lad was worldlier than many a man, and more experienced as well. William could relate to him.

Neither of them had been graced with an easy childhood. Both would forever bear the stigma of being born a royal bastard. And here Christophoro was, helping him by passing information to him.

William studied King Fernando's half-brother. He'd never seen him in person, but he saw the resemblance he had anticipated after his months of secretive research. Christophoro's dark eyes evoked memories. They were like his mother's eyes.

"Are you my informant?" Prince William questioned.

The lad scrutinized him, clearly taking in William's dark hair, like his own. "Who wants to know?"

William cracked a smile. "I assume that's a 'yes'." The lad's weapon didn't relax. William persisted. "You helped save Amber of Dunstonwoodshire's life, did you not? She is now my sister of marriage, recently married to my wife's brother. I wished to reward you. So I've tracked you down."

"We agreed on anonymity," Christophoro replied, shooting glances into the trees as if sensing an ambush. "Whoever you are, you agreed to honor that request in exchange for information."

William tossed a purse, the strings tied about a sealed missive. Christophoro snagged it out of the air. He continued scrutinizing William, his blade still on guard. William lifted both hands in peace, revealing two dagger sheaths under his wrists as he did so. Christophoro's dark eyes roved over his opponent, and William couldn't help but see a resemblance between the two of them in the set of their jaw, the nuances of their cheek bones, similar contours of their noses.

Christophoro wasn't nearly as built with muscle yet. He was young still. But William knew that would change if his knightly training were resumed.

"How did you find me?" the lad asked, still glancing about for others.

"I've known you were in the Cambrian Forest," Prince William replied, his eyes still piercing the bastard prince with scrutiny, his ears ever perked to the surrounding noises. Titan was always good at alerting him to dangers he couldn't sense and so far, the horse stood lazily. "You're here, in Bain, because I've allowed it. I'm a good friend to have, I dare say."

"Who are you really?" asked the lad. "I have an inkling."

"What's your inkling? Who do you think I am?" William returned the question.

"I think that when I wrote for a royal ear months ago, I gained yours," Christophoro replied. "Prince William's."

William pulled aside his surcoat across his chest, twisting his belts in the process, to reveal beneath it the wine and black divided crest showcasing a gold-fringed black lion rampant. "I am, as you guessed, Prince William Murron of Bain, King Bain's commander and heir to the throne, and..."

He let the statement hang.

Christophoro waited. "And what?"

"And you, Christophoro Maria de Fernando, are the son of my mother's sister. My cousin."

Enjoyed **Son of Ballymead?**
Start the saga from the beginning with **Prince of Lions.**